MICHELLE VERNAL LOVES a happy ending. She lives with her husband and their two boys in the beautiful and resilient city of Christchurch, New Zealand. She's partial to a glass of wine, loves a cheese scone, and has recently taken up yoga—a sight to behold indeed. Michelle's written eight novels to date as well as the popular Guesthouse on the Green series—all her books are all written with humour and warmth and she hopes you enjoy reading them. If you enjoy The Cooking School on the Bay then taking the time to say so by leaving a review would be wonderful. A book review is the best present you can give an author. If you'd like to hear about new releases and take part in fun giveaways you can subscribe to Michelle's VIP newsletter via her website www.michellevernalbooks.com[1]. To say thank you, you'll receive the first ten chapters of her novel, Sweet Home Summer FREE!

---

1. http://www.michellevernalbooks.com

The Cooking School on the Bay
By
Michelle Vernal

For my lovely boys, Paul, Josh, and Dan

Chapter One

DUBLIN 2002

"My name is Rebecca, and I am a binge drinker," said the image staring back at Rebecca Loughton from the bathroom mirror that Saturday morning.

Last night's make-up had indeed lived up to its promise of longevity, but sometime during the last twelve hours, there'd been a landslide south. In its wake, it had left behind a berry stain smear that made her mouth look like she'd done ten rounds with a Botox injection. Mascara had settled into the horrible lines that, since she'd turned thirty-four, seemed to be breeding like mice under her eyes. These, in turn, had puffed up nicely for the occasion, and there was a network of red squiggles around her irises, turning her normally hazel eyes a very unnatural shade of green. That wasn't the worst of it, though—oh no. While she had slumbered, her hair had somehow mussed itself into a beehive beyond belief. It made the expensive flaxen highlights that her hairdresser Tarquin had assured her 'will 'ide ze leetle mature ones' resemble pieces of washed-up seaweed.

"Sushi head," she muttered in disgust as the mirror slowly fogged over.

Standing under the hot spray of the shower, Rebecca squeezed her eyes shut as images of the night before flashed up in front of her. Oh no! She hadn't tried to lead the dance floor in *Saturday Night Fever* again, had she? An action replay sprang to mind of her marching through the middle of the parted crowd of revellers. She had one hand on her hip, and the other pointing heavenward. She was such a saddo. Why, oh why, did she always think she was John Travolta after a few too many wines? Her head hurt too much to answer that.

Wincing as another needle-like pain shot over her left eyebrow, she wondered why it was that her hangovers always manifested themselves there.

Surely that wasn't normal? Mind you, it had been said (by her mum and dad mostly) that carrying on like she was in her twenties when she was in her mid-thirties wasn't normal either.

Her mother's voice had ricocheted down the line the last time Rebecca bothered to phone her. "What are you doing cavorting around Dublin at your age?" When no reply was forthcoming, her mother had huffed, "What's Ireland got that New Zealand hasn't?"

Ah-ha! Gotcha, Mum, she'd thought smugly. "Irish people."

Pamela Loughton had not been amused. "You should be settling down at your age and making a proper life for yourself, like Jennifer has."

Ah yes—*like Jennifer has*: that was one broken record that had been playing for most of her adult life. Why had she been blessed with a sister who was one of life's little super-achievers and a mother who was not only an ageist but a sexist too?

Rebecca had once heard her sister's tumbling mane of curls being described as 'the colour of sunshine'. With her classic English rose features, Jennifer did not look a day over thirty, even though she had long since gone over to the dark side of thirty-five. You'd never see 'a leetle mature one' daring to poke its way out of Jennifer's scalp. Clean living and regular hair appointments did that, Rebecca reflected, feeling guilty as she scrubbed at her face with a flannel. Jennifer never went to bed with her make-up on either. That is, if she ever went to bed. Her sister must be a secret insomniac, which would explain how she managed juggling her own business while looking after two kids, her husband, and running a home. No normal person requiring eight hours' sleep a night could be expected to do all of that.

Without a doubt, though, Jennifer's best achievements were Hannah and Jack. Hannah, a robust three-and-a-half-year-old with pigtails, and seven-year-old Jack with his missing front teeth. When had they gotten so big? Hannah had been a snuggly baby in a Stretch-n-Grow the last time Rebecca saw her. Thinking of her niece and nephew made her smile through the pain, but as the strains of *Greased Lightning* struck up, their impish faces were replaced by yet more dazzling Travolta moves.

Rubbing her towel furiously over her hair to banish any further dance floor flashbacks, she pondered just how she'd come to be in such a state. It had started out innocently enough with a Friday night drinks session in the boardroom to see her pal, Emma, off.

There had been a good turnout. Mind you, she mused, there wasn't one red-blooded male at Fitzpatrick & Co, the law firm they both worked at, who would say no thank you to free drinks. Or miss the chance to say cheerio to Emma, for that matter. With her endless tanned legs, a tawny mane of hair, and perfect white-toothed grin, she was the quintessential Aussie babe. Who, after a year and a half of wearing thermals, had had enough of the cold weather and was returning home to work on her tan.

Rebecca cringed, recalling how she had practiced her sexy Natalie Imbruglia smile on some pleb from the Property Department. That was bad enough but upon taking herself off to the ladies to see why, instead of being smitten, he had looked disturbed, she had discovered a big chunk of marinated chicken wing stuck between her front teeth. Emma, who thought it was hilarious, hadn't bothered to tell her.

"Cow," she muttered aloud to the empty bathroom.

It was after her fourth—or was it the fifth?—wine that things got a bit hazy, though. She vaguely recalled linking arms with Emma and their fellow law firm skivvy, Derbhilla. James, the pimply-faced summer intern, had invited himself to join in on the night on the town too.

Stumbling along the banks of the canal in search of another drink, they'd wound up in Maddens. It was the sort of bar you might go to on a first date for a quiet drink. Contemporary, with plush leather couches, its dim lights added a moody quality to the soft jazz music filtering out from hidden speakers. However, its understated style had been wasted on the four drunken larrikins huddled at the bar, each holding a tiny glass of some concoction the barman had whipped up for them. Derbhilla had insisted on standing a round of shooters in commiseration for the bombshell Rebecca's nemesis, Pariah, had dropped earlier in the evening.

The four of them had raised their glasses and, as a team of synchronised swimmers, knocked them back, gasping in shock at the alcohol burn. They later staggered over to the couches and sank into the soft leather.

"What's she got that I haven't then?" Rebecca had slurred to her comrades.

James had leered down her top and said that it was pretty obvious while Derbhilla squeezed her arm in consoling reassurance. "Ciaran doesn't fancy her. He told me that she more or less invited herself along when she heard there was a spare room going."

"Whatever," Rebecca had mumbled despondently. She had conjured up the moment Fitzpatrick & Co's receptionist had sashayed the length of the boardroom to where she and Ciaran had been in the midst of a deep and meaningful. They had been discussing the pros and, in her case, cons of drinking Guinness. Ciaran, her born and bred Dubliner boss, liked to refer to it as downing the black, and he swore it contained magical healing properties.

"Hi, Ciaran," Tania, aka Pariah, had simpered. Rebecca had christened her Pariah due to her unpleasant personality and uncanny resemblance to Mariah Carey. She also possessed the superstar's purported diva attitude and love affair with skin-tight dresses.

"Thanks for the invite; I'd love to come."

Seeing Rebecca's quizzical glance up at her boss, she added, "It's going to be fun, isn't it? All of us bunking down together."

"You're coming to the races?" The penny dropped. Rebecca couldn't suppress the note of horror that had crept into her tone. The thought of the Queen of Lycra tagging along on what Ciaran liked to call their team-building trip to the Galway Summer Race Festival was too much. They all knew, though, that this was just his fancy talk for debauched booze fest.

"Oh yes! I wouldn't miss it, and I can't wait for Ladies Day. I'm entering Best Dressed, of course. Were you planning on going in for it as well, Rebecca?" Then, sizing up her competition, she aimed her dart and hit the bullseye. "Personally, I'd have thought the Mad Hatter competition would have been more your style."

Rebecca winced; the barb still stung. Sitting there in Maddens an hour later, she could think of at least half a dozen comebacks. *Oh, I didn't know formal wear came in Lycra these days* sprang to mind, followed by *But how will you possibly get a hat over all that hair?* At the time, though, her mind had gone annoyingly blank. Feeling a tickling sensation on her décolletage, she realised it was James. He was in danger of nosediving straight down into the depths of her top if he leered in any farther and she swatted him away like the annoying little fly he was.

The evening's events did a bit of a hop, skip, and a jump from there because, the next thing she knew, she'd gotten her second wind as the effects of the alcohol kicked in. It was all downhill after that. No longer content with sitting sedately on a couch, she'd bounced around like a cheerleader until the rest of the squad had put on their dancing shoes in readiness for Temple Bar. It was here in some nameless, faceless bar that she'd gone all *Saturday Night Fever*-ish, but what had happened after that?

She racked her brain and then wished that she hadn't because the picture that popped into her head should have come with a warning: 'graphic images may disturb some viewers.'. If only it were like a tele programme; she'd switch it off or change the channel, but the image before her was firmly planted, and it had taken root.

There she was, illuminated by a flickering neon light down a cobbled alley, the back exit of a bar presumably. The scene she was setting was decidedly seedy, with her shirt hanging forlornly out the back of her skirt, the hemline of which had risen several inches up her thigh. Surely the clothing manufacturers made size twelves smaller every year? It was probably a cost-saving exercise, along with getting everything made in China. While she was on the subject of China, her feet had felt as though they were tightly bound, unused as they were to her strappy Versace heels.

Oh no; it was all coming back to her now. She'd kicked the bloody things clean off on the dance floor. They were the only pair of designer shoes she'd ever owned, and she'd be gutted if she'd lost them. So what if they'd fallen off the back of a lorry and wound up in the Moore Street Market; they were still Versace, right? As Rebecca drummed up more of last night's memories, she envisioned the shoes dangling loosely from the fingers of her left hand. Her right arm lay draped over the shoulder of someone she appeared to be snogging the face off. When they came up for air, she emitted a low moan as she saw who she'd been mauling. *Nooo!!!*

It couldn't be! He was just a child, for goodness' sake. She could be had up for molestation! Jolting back to the present, Rebecca wrenched the shower handle round and nearly stumbled out of the narrow white box in her haste to wrap her robe around her. Leaving a billowing cloud of steam in her wake, she reached her bedroom door in three giant strides and then froze as icy terror raced through her veins.

She'd been in such a state when she woke up that a sumo wrestler could have taken up residence in her bed and she wouldn't have noticed. What if he was in there now? What would she do? Go to AA and commit herself to a bloody convent, that's what! Taking a deep breath, she forced herself to push the door open. The room was in its usual state of disarray with the bonus of a stale, boozy smell. Her bed was pushed up against the far wall and was rumpled. *Oh hallelujah! Thank you, Lord.* It was empty! The relief was overwhelming, and she slumped against the doorframe, trying to regulate her breathing.

"What are you doing?" Melissa's voice startled her, and she swung around guiltily. "Pooh, it stinks in there." Rebecca's flatmate waved a hand in front of her nose, which wrinkled with the self-righteous disgust of someone who had not stopped out half the night.

Registering Melissa's matching tracksuit ensemble, Rebecca guessed she was off to the gym. It wasn't fair; she always managed to look groomed, even when she was going for a workout. Rebecca, on the other hand, hungover or not, was more a baggy, T-shirt sort of lass. She liked to hide in the back of the class. Mind you, the only physical activity she actually did these days was done undercover in her bedroom and no, it wasn't sex—thank goodness for that! It was the ballet exercises of her youth: pliés, dégagé, tendus, and her old nemesis, the grand battements. How many times had Miss Haines banged her stick and shrieked, "Rebecca, the toes! Point the toes—you are a ballet dancer, not a builder."

Ballet was a foreign language to the uninitiated. She'd close her eyes as she raised her arm in a sweeping arc over her head. Her leg would be lifted high and straight, and her toes bent at a cramp-inducing angle as she saw the words in her mind's eye. The quote emblazoned on a plaque that sat in pride of place on the walls of the studio in which she had spent so many hours practising read:

To dance is to be out of yourself. Larger, more beautiful, more powerful. This is power, it is glory on earth and it is yours for the taking.
Agnes de Mille

Those words had been inspiring, but there was nothing whatsoever glorious about the Travolta moves she'd pulled last night. Miss Haines would be horrified by them, she thought, shuddering. Sporty Spice (well, with her pretty, delicate dark features, matching tan and sulky expression, she was more Posh than Sporty) inquired, "So what time did you crawl in then?"

"Late, and I need some painkillers."

Sensing there was gossip, Melissa hurried after her into the kitchen like a beagle sniffing blood. "What on earth were you up to last night? Just look at the state of you!" Her top lip curled with distaste.

Rebecca sighed while her fingers searched inside the cabinet for the paracetamol. She'd been in this position many, many times before. Ever since high school, Melissa's favourite game had been Truth, Dare, or Promise, and she never gave in until she got the truth. Pouring herself a glass of water, she forced herself to knock the paracetamol back, trying hard not to gag as she swallowed them down.

At that moment, a muffled ring sounded from somewhere in the apartment. "My mobile!" Rebecca was grateful for the reprieve. "That will be Emma ringing to say goodbye; she's flying out at lunchtime." Ringing to rub my nose in it, more likely, she thought while stomping off to identify the location of her phone. Emma might have the body of Elle MacPherson, but she had the memory of an elephant, and last night's debacle was one she wouldn't be letting her friend forget in a hurry.

She found her mobile where she'd left it: in her handbag stuffed down the side of her bed.

Melissa flounced past the door. "Take your call, but you're not off the hook. I'll be back."

"Right-ho; look forward to it," Rebecca tossed back sarcastically as the apartment door banged shut. Bloody Melissa had a memory like an elephant too, she grouched, flopping down onto her bed and punching the green button. She sighed. "Hi, Rebecca speaking."

"Rebecca?" a voice echoed down the line. "It's me, Jennifer, your sister."

She felt a frisson of annoyance; it wasn't as if she didn't keep in touch. Anyone would think she'd been away ten years instead of two the way Jennifer was talking. If anyone were a stranger to picking up the phone, it was her.

"Rebecca, are you there?"

There was a definite quiver in her sister's voice, and Rebecca sat upright, beginning to chew on her thumbnail as she wondered whether this was the phone call everybody dreaded. "Yeah, yeah, I'm here. What is it? What's happened?"

She heard her sister take a deep breath—slow and measured—but her voice, when she spoke, was shaking. "Look, I don't know how to tell you this..."

"Just tell me!" Rebecca screeched. In her mind's eye, she was already visualising car pileups and ambulances.

"I, uh, I hate having to do this over the phone."

"What! What, for goodness' sake?" She felt herself break out in a cold sweat as panic began sweeping through her.

"It's Mark. He's, ah... it's just that... oh, fuck it, Rebecca! The bastard's been having an affair."

Rebecca's whole body sagged. No one was hurt—well, not physically at least. She raised her eyes heavenward and mouthed a thank you before allowing her sister's words to sink in properly. She was pretty sure she'd just heard Jen, who never swore, use the *F* word. Come to that, she was also pretty sure she had used the words 'affair' and 'bastard' in the same sentence, too. She placed the phone down on the bed and rubbed frantically at her ear. A build-up of wax, maybe? Yes, that was it; she must have misheard. After all, the likelihood of her poker-faced brother-in-law having a fling was in the same stratosphere as her sister selling her beloved cooking school to become a lap dancer.

She squeezed her eyes shut and felt ill as she tried to conjure up an image of Mark in the throes of illicit passion with a floozy. No way! It just didn't fit the profile of her brother-in-law, the man who had been married to her sister for the last eight years. Picking the phone back up, she asked hesitantly, "Um, Jen, I didn't quite catch what you said. Could you run it by me again?"

Her big sister, the one with the perfect life, slowly and unmistakably stated, "Mark has been having an affair."

Chapter Two

JENNIFER'S UNBELIEVABLE revelation sat like Indian take-out in Rebecca's stomach: heavy and indigestible. Only, an antacid wouldn't cure this stomach ache. The sensation built up inside her until, like a belch, her repertoire of colourful phrases erupted. "The fucking wanker!" she shrieked, surprised at how good it felt, and she was only warming up. "I can't believe he would do that to you! What a total fucking shit for brains! The prick, the wanker—"

"Stop it, Rebecca! Just stop it!"

Rebecca nearly dropped the phone as her normally cool and calm sister shouted back at her.

"Enough already! Don't you get it? You're wasting your breath. There's nothing you can call him that I haven't called him myself." Jennifer's voice dropped a notch as she added, "Please try to remember that he's still Jack and Hannah's dad no matter what he's done to me."

Rebecca felt her surging loyalty dissipate; she couldn't believe what she was hearing. Surely her sister wasn't defending him? This thought quickly became overshadowed by more urgent questions vying for attention, and in one foul breath she exhaled them all: "How long? Who with, for pity's sake? Is he still seeing her or is it over?"

When she found out that Mark had been sleeping with his secretary for the last three months, she almost wished she hadn't asked.

"I know, I know, it's the ultimate cliché." Jennifer's voice was weary, and Rebecca could visualise her rubbing her temple the way she always did when she got stressed.

"I mean, *she* was there, willing and able, whereas I, trying to run the business and looking after Jack and Hannah, wasn't."

Jen was right. Though, even if it was all true, it did sound banal.

"Mark's sworn to me that it's over."

Something about the way her sister delivered this last comment irked Rebecca. Where had her super staunch big sister disappeared to? The sister who would let no one walk all over her or, for that matter, her little sister. How many times when they were kids had Jen stood up for her in the playground? So why the hell wasn't she sticking up for herself now? If it were up to her, she would have kicked Mark's no good arse all the way up to Auckland. She spat, "Well, bully for him, Jennifer. Did you smack his bottom and tell him not to do it again?"

The static of the international phone connection lingered in the lull between the sisters. Then, using that irritatingly placating tone usually reserved for her children, Jennifer broke the silence. "Please don't be like that, Rebecca. I don't expect you to understand, but couldn't you at least try to see things from my point of view for once? It's not just about me, or her, or him. There's Hannah and Jack to consider in all of this as well." Her voice quavered as she mentioned her children's names.

"So, what was her name?" Rebecca refused to soften her stance.

Jennifer inhaled sharply. "It doesn't matter."

Rebecca squeezed her free hand shut, feeling her nails dig into her palms. "Tell me," she insisted.

"Why? What difference does it make?"

"Because I want to be able to put a name to the harlot's face, that's why."

Resigning herself to the fact that she wasn't going to let this one go, Jennifer reluctantly mumbled, "Natalie. Her name's Natalie Freeman. She began work for Mark at the beginning of the year, and she's only twenty-nine. Needless to say, she is now seeking other employment, no longer employed by him." Fumbling over the words, Jennifer continued, ranting. "She's ten years younger than me. I got traded in for a younger model. Oh, and she's a blonde too. Is that a big enough joke for you now?" Her voice broke into sobs.

Unable to remember the last time she'd heard her big sister cry, Rebecca began backpedalling. "I'm sorry, Jen. I had no right asking."

The sniffling didn't abate, and her pleading intensified. "Please stop, please stop crying. Tell me what I can do to make it better."

Jennifer hiccupped and sniffed. "There is something you can do..."

Stunned by the requests that followed, Rebecca flung the duvet to one side and perched on the edge of her bed, opening and shutting her mouth like a goldfish on speed. Two whole weeks—Jennifer wanted her to come home and look after Jack and Hannah for two whole weeks!

"B-but why? Where are you going?"

"Away with Mark, of course," Jennifer answered matter-of-factly, as though it should have been obvious. "We need some time out. Just the two of us, to see if we can put what he did behind us and move forward." A heartfelt sigh filtered down the line. "Oh, Becs, we've gotten so bogged down with everything else in our lives that we've lost sight of ourselves as a couple." Jennifer's mental rummaging produced a trump card with a flourish as she shamelessly played it. "Please give us a chance to make our marriage work. If not for me and Mark, do it for Jack and Hannah."

Talk about laying on a guilt trip. "Where were you thinking of going?" Rebecca asked grudgingly.

Jennifer's upbeat response implied that she took this as a positive sign. "Australia. I've booked an apartment in Mooloolaba near where we camped that time when Jack was a toddler, remember?"

How could she forget? She'd always hated bloody camping, but Mark, with all the enthusiasm of a first-time dad, had gotten it into his stupid head that Jack needed to experience the great outdoors. A cabin in the Big Four chain of camping grounds on the Sunshine Coast didn't qualify as the great outdoors, in Rebecca's opinion. Then again, so long as she wasn't sleeping in a tent she wasn't going to argue the point. Besides, she was tagging along for free as Jack's unofficial nanny. In hindsight, she should have known there was no such thing as a free ride because Jack had been a wee demon. She'd been run ragged with trips to the playground and pool, not to mention hauling him out of the communal toilet block on numerous occasions due to his obsession with the urinal. All the while, Jennifer had lounged on the deck of her and Mark's self-contained cabin with a book while Mark fetched and carried. It had struck Rebecca then that life was easy when you were beautiful like Jennifer. People gravitated towards you and ran around after you just like *she* was doing. It didn't sound as though she was being offered a free ride this time round either.

"Please, Rebecca." Jennifer's wheedling brought her back to the present. "Mark and I have discussed it and agreed that we'll pay your airfare and match your wages."

"That's very generous of you both," Rebecca replied with more than a hint of sarcasm as she slid her bare feet into her slippers and padded back out to the kitchen. She was in desperate need of coffee. "What about Mum and Dad? Why can't they do it?"

Thousands of miles away, Jennifer rolled her eyes. "Because," she replied as though she were talking to a simpleton, "they won't be around. They're off on their cruise. You didn't forget, did you?" She snippily carried on, "Besides, I haven't told them what's happened, and I don't want you to either. They'd only cancel their trip, and you know how long they've been planning it. You don't want them to cancel, do you?"

Why did Jen always have to imply she was selfish? If anyone was selfish, it was her laying it on that thick but then she'd always been Queen Manipulator when it came to getting her way. "No, of course, I didn't forget the cruise." She'd been so caught up in her plans for the Galway Races that she *had* clean forgotten about it, but she wasn't about to admit it and give her sister more ammunition. "And you know full well I wouldn't want them to miss it."

So that was that, and there it was: the moment when they both knew her coming home was a foregone conclusion.

"I DON'T BELIEVE IT! I just don't believe it! Not Mark with his secretary? That's, that's—well, that's just sad!" spluttered Melissa. Despite having just done a Body Burn class, she was spread out on their lime-green two-seater, looking as pristine as a sportswear model. Mark's affair had temporarily overridden any interest in her best friend's nocturnal activities.

A very small consolation prize, Rebecca reflected as she reached for one of the salted peanuts she'd poured into a bowl with hopes of an energy boost.

Melissa stormed on. "Poor old Jennifer. Mind you, I always did think your sister and her hubby's life was just a bit too Barbie and Kenish." Studying her long painted fingernails for any signs of chipping, she added thoughtfully, "Still, I wouldn't wish this on her."

Rebecca threw a peanut at her. "That's very magnanimous of you, but I'd hardly go so far as to call Mark a Ken."

"Rebecca, Rebecca, Rebecca." Melissa flicked the peanut off her track pants onto the floor. "The phrase 'tall, dark, and handsome' was invented for your brother-in-law. Any red-blooded secretary with twenty-twenty vision and no morals would leap at the chance to get into his underdaks."

"Melissa!" Rebecca nearly choked on her peanut. "That's disgusting!"

"Maybe, but it's also true. You've just never been able to see it. As far as you're concerned, there isn't a man in the universe who would be good enough to fit into your sister's perfect life."

Rebecca childishly rebutted, "Well, I was right where he's concerned."

"Maybe so, but you'd do well to remember your sister isn't perfect. Nobody is."

Melissa brushed her fashionably long fringe out of her eyes and looked hard at her friend. Rebecca's heart-shaped face and perfectly respectable nose accented a wide and sensual mouth, which totally belied her best feature—large and expressive hazel eyes. She was very pretty, she thought; maybe not in the classically sculpted way that Jennifer was but in her own uniquely quirky way that, in her opinion, was far more attractive. For as long as she'd known her, Rebecca had been drawing unfavourable comparisons between herself and her sister, and she'd had enough of it.

"Don't take this the wrong way, Becs..."

Uh-oh, Rebecca thought, not liking the sound of where this was heading but nodding her head and finding herself saying "okay" nonetheless.

"It's just that ever since I've known you, you've had this enormous chip on your shoulder where Jennifer is concerned, and I don't get it."

"No, I haven't!"

Melissa's raised hand stopped Rebecca from going off.

"Calm down. I am not having a go at you; I'm simply trying to tell you a few home truths. Will you let me finish?"

Rebecca refused eye contact but managed a sulky nod.

"Like I was saying, you've always had this thing where Jennifer's concerned that she's the prettier sister, the more successful one, and I have never been able to understand why. You've got loads going for you, but you need to step out from her shadow, Becs, and stop holding her up as this impossible role model."

Shoving a handful of peanuts in her mouth, Rebecca was silent as she chewed agitatedly, mulling over what Melissa had just said. Maybe she was a tiny bit in awe of Jennifer.

When they were little, she'd always been the podgy kid who got picked on at school and Jen had always been there to stick up for her. Nobody was allowed to upset her Becka-boo, as the family used to call her. She had idolised her older, beautiful sister back then, even when she found her niche with dance. It had been a surprise to everyone but most of all to herself when the baby fat dropped off, and she had blossomed into a ballerina. She was a talented one at that, too. As they'd grown, though, and Jennifer had begun to shine on her chosen path, the realisation had dawned on her that she was never quite going to make the grade when it came to dancing. That's when they'd kind of just drifted apart. If she were honest with herself, a seed of resentment had begun to sprout as she had sat back and watched as Jennifer's life panned out exactly how she wanted it to, unlike her own.

The only blip in Jennifer's life plan had been that brief tussle with the baby blues when Jack was born. Apart from that, her older sister had led a pretty charmed existence to date. Jennifer *was* the prettier, more successful sister, and that was all there was to it. It was a fact she had learned to accept and live with because nobody had ever said her name with the reverence in which they breathed Jennifer's name:

"*The* Jennifer Carlton of Cuisine with Carlton's—of course I've heard of her. Wasn't she on the cover of *Woman's Weekly* not long ago?" Instead, with Rebecca it was: "Who? Rebecca Loughton? Oh, do you mean *the* Jennifer Carlton's sister?"

Jennifer's love affair with cooking had begun early, and she could always be found standing at the kitchen bench. With her sleeves rolled up, and her arms sunk into a bowl of dough, their mother would hover back and forth overseeing as she set about making scones for morning tea.

As a young girl, her idea of heaven had been helping their mother plan one of her many dinner parties. Pamela Loughton lived to entertain, and mother and eldest daughter would perch themselves at her pride and joy—a polished mahogany table that seated six—for hours, plotting. Sitting cross-legged on the floor beside them, Rebecca's task was to turn the paper napkins into swans for the table arrangement. From under her lashes, she'd watch the way their two heads were bent companionably together, discussing the merits of brandy snaps over éclairs. In a bid for attention, she'd make the swans look more like ugly ducklings, spoiling the afternoon for them all.

By the time she was at intermediate school, Jennifer was a whizz at home economics. Mrs Manly never got over the disappointment when Rebecca didn't follow in her golden-haired sister's footsteps. She never even got past the basics of making fudge, having been far too busy practising her pliés and dreaming of herself pirouetting centre stage instead of stirring. Hers had been the only batch in Room 4 that wouldn't set. It had still tasted pretty good, though.

While Jennifer sailed through high school without so much as a sneaky cigarette in the toilets or a day's truancy, her little sister had regularly participated in both activities after failing her all-important Grade 9 ballet exam. That little setback had knocked her off course and instead of taking it on the chin and trying again, she'd thrown in the towel and admitted defeat. Besides, at sixteen there was much more fun to be had at parties than practising to be something she knew she just didn't have the raw talent to be.

The difference between them was something Rebecca had often pondered, coming to the conclusion that Jennifer had been focused from the minute she graduated school and accepted an apprenticeship at Sophia's Brasserie in the central city. On the other hand, Rebecca had strolled out of the school gates and boarded a raft that would sail her down life's unstable river. Instead of taking the oars and steering it confidently through the rapids, she'd let it drift in no particular direction, never mooring up at any one thing for very long.

Jennifer completed her apprenticeship and set about making a name for herself in Christchurch before jumping the ditch to begin working as a head chef in one of Sydney's five-star hotels. That's how she'd met Mark. Over from Christchurch on business, he'd been staying in the hotel and, having finished the best meal he had ever eaten, asked to pay his compliments to the chef.

It was just the sort of thing the pompous git would do, Rebecca had decided as she examined his over-the-top good looks upon their first meeting.

Proposing on a gondola in Venice was also just the sort of thing the cheesy git would do, she thought one year later when her sister announced their engagement. Jennifer had bleated on and on about how romantic the proposal had been while Mark stood with his arm wrapped proprietarily around her, grinning like one of those idiot clowns at a funfair. If she'd had a ball handy, Rebecca would have stuffed it in his mouth.

The wedding—well, that was as close to hell as Rebecca wanted to get. Jennifer had glowed in a stylish champagne gown that set off her lithe frame to perfection. Joanne and Angela, waitresses at the hotel she was working at, had been picked as bridesmaids for their photogenic qualities and indeed they were ethereal in smoked pink. Rebecca, who had been going through a particularly curvaceous period in her life, had felt like an overfed salmon. One who'd forgotten to run the rapids as she'd trooped dutifully up the aisle behind her sister.

The newlyweds had worked and travelled before settling down to the serious business of being married and starting a family. Rebecca remembered when Jennifer had arrived on her doorstep one sunny Saturday morning, jiggling baby Jack on her hip, to announce that she was going to realise her dream and open a cooking school. "I'm going to call it 'Cuisine with Carlton's—*Living, Learning, and Loving Food*.' What do you think—catchy?"

Perhaps a good sister would have gushed over the idea despite her concerns. It was fairly obvious this was the response Jennifer was seeking as she stood there looking in need of bolstering, but instead of answering her with enthusiasm, Rebecca's face creased with genuine worry. "But what about Jack? He's not even a year old yet. Won't it be too much?"

Jennifer hadn't been right since Jack was born. Tired and tearful, motherhood was the only role she hadn't seemed to adjust to with ease. How on earth did she think she was going to manage Jack and a major project? Rebecca had chewed at her bottom lip anxiously as Jennifer replied curtly, "We'll manage, thanks."

Not one to be put off, Rebecca demanded, "Well, what does Mark think about it all?" Surely he would have noticed the changes in his wife's behaviour since Jack's arrival and would be all for her taking things easy and concentrating on her son for a while, but apparently not.

"He thinks it's a fantastic idea," had been the firm reply that said the subject was now closed to discussion.

Indeed, Mark had backed Jennifer's new venture all the way, never uttering a word of protest about them moving from Christchurch where his architectural firm based itself to Akaroa. Jennifer had fallen in love with the small seaside village's breathtaking harbour views, café lifestyle, and mix of French colonial architecture. It was Jennifer's ideal location. Mark had smiled indulgently, telling everyone that it would be great for Jack, growing up in the country, and that the commute wasn't *that* bad—only an hour and a half drive each way.

Rebecca's trip down memory lane hit a stop sign just then as Melissa's voice took on the nasal twang she adopted when feeling under stress.

"Oh my gosh, I just remembered—what about the races? We've had that planned for ages!"

Chapter Three

REBECCA WAS STILL A tad peeved with her so-called buddy and her home truths, and so she spat, "There's nothing stopping you going."

Melissa's whingeing twang grew more pronounced. "But I don't know any of the others well enough to go without you."

"Oh, for goodness' sakes! You're a big girl, aren't you?"

"You're just annoyed because of what I said."

"No I'm not, because what you said was a load of old codswallop."

"Truth hurts, Becs."

"Get stuffed."

They sat in frosty silence as Melissa picked up the remote and began channel surfing, an act she knew her friend found irritating.

Rebecca screwed her eyes up tight and rubbed her temples; she didn't need this. Falling out with Melissa was the last thing she was in the mood for tonight and having been down this road before, she knew she'd have to be the one to hold out the olive branch.

"Maybe Tamara would like to go to the races with you in my place?" Rebecca thought she'd hit the jackpot with that one until Melissa, placing the remote back down on the coffee table, shot her a scathing look.

"Hardly. She'd be mobbed. You seem to forget that Tamara is a superstar."

That was a bit over-the-top, but Rebecca opted not to voice this thought. She remained quiet until, as befitted her current churlish mood, Melissa stuck out her bottom lip and said, "Well, she is."

Too knackered for an argument, Rebecca left it at that. Tamara's fame did stretch across Ireland, after all.

"So, you tell me what exactly it is I am supposed to do while you're away?" Melissa demanded, her tantrum now wearing Rebecca's nerves thin.

Bloody typical Melissa, Rebecca fumed, wondering—as she often found herself doing—at their rather one-sided friendship. They'd met on the very first day of high school when their form mistress, Miss Duncan, hauled them both aside for wearing eyeliner. If Rebecca closed her eyes, she could still conjure up the teacher's high-pitched whine as she shrilled, "Eyeliner! I see eyeliner! Go and wash it off, girls, and I don't want to see either of you wearing it again."

There was nothing like a little bit of teenage rebellion to forge a friendship on and the girls had made it their daily challenge to get past their form mistress with their blue eyeliner intact.

That was then, and this was now, though Rebecca had to admit to finding a comforting solidarity in their both being manless and childless.

It was this same single status plus their friend Nicola's effusive emails on the merits of life in the Emerald Isle that had sent them winging their way over to Dublin. Where, as the new millennium rolled in, the Celtic Tiger had begun to roar.

Girls, Nicola had emailed, *you should come over and check it out for yourselves; the craic's great.*

The what? they'd typed back.

It means the fun—the enjoyment, Nicola had translated, and the seed was planted.

What would they be leaving behind, after all? Okay, so they shared a smart Christchurch townhouse close to the mall and Hagley Park. They were spoilt for choice with the local restaurants and cafés, but they were also stuck in the cycle of renting. House prices had gone through the roof of late and here was a chance to double their money by saving some Irish puint for a deposit while having a bit of fun. Job-wise, they were both in a rut. Rebecca had had enough of feeling like the oldest legal secretary in town. Melissa's position as PA to a smooth-talking property developer had also lost its gloss once she realised her boss's only son and heir was spoken for.

"I feel old," Rebecca had moaned the last time they'd bravely ventured into the city for a night out. Seeing a line of youngsters all chomping at the bit to get into the latest night spot, she'd had to fight the urge not to tap one of the girls on the shoulder. She wanted to tell her to get herself off home and put a thermal on before she caught her death. Yes, they'd agreed, it was time to accept the fact that their knights in shining armour might take a bit longer than originally planned to rock up on their white chargers. It was time to take some responsibility for their lives. Besides, weren't women of independent means extremely attractive to the opposite sex? That argument had won the debate and so, they'd packed in their jobs and their non-existent boyfriends to wing their way over to the birthplace of both U2 and Ronan Keating.

Nicola had been right. The city had enveloped them into its exciting, overcrowded atmosphere, and Rebecca realised she'd felt at home in Dublin from the moment her feet had stepped onto Irish soil. There was a sense of freedom in being so far from home and a perception that here, anything was possible because here she had an identity.

Upon obtaining work permits for the thriving city at the ripe old age of thirty-two, they'd made themselves at home in the living room of Nicola and her fiancé Andy's one-bedroom apartment. Then they had begun their assault on the Irish job market.

"With your legal background, you'll be in high demand," the coiffed woman seated in the Dame Street office of the employment agency had assured her. She had finished scrutinising Rebecca's CV and her words proved prophetic. She'd nabbed her position of PA to Ciaran Cahill, who was one of the ten partners at Fitzpatrick & Co, in a single interview. It had surprised her considering she hadn't got off to the most auspicious of starts.

Rebecca clutched the slip of paper the agency had given her, along with the hand-drawn map and instructions to meet with a Miss Grainne Mangan at two pm. She made her way to Fitzpatrick & Co's imposing concrete offices. With confidence, she strode out of the lift and up to the receptionist, who bore an uncanny resemblance to Mariah Carey. The woman looked like she'd be more at home wearing a spangled minidress and writhing around to *All I Want for Christmas* than at the front desk of a law firm. Nonetheless, when Rebecca had asked to see "Miss *Grain* Mangan, please," the receptionist had eyed her up and down with disdain. Her voice had sounded like a snippy little girl's as she replied, "*Ms Groinya* Mangan will see you shortly. Take a seat please."

Despite her little faux pas, Rebecca got the job. She then had to do a crash course in the correct pronunciation of Irish names. She did not wish to offend Derbhilla, Padraig, Mairead, and Piaras, the latter of which she had nearly called Pie arse—*correct pronunciation: Pierce* and who she'd be working alongside in the commercial division.

After her first day of work, Rebecca rushed home to share the dirt on her new co-workers with her best friend. Even after one day, the cliques easily stood out, and of course Melissa wanted to know all about the boss man, Ciaran. When Rebecca left it at his age—a young thirty-eight and seemingly nice enough—Melissa wasn't satisfied. As with any male she had yet to see in person, she had come back with her usual, "Yeah, yeah, but what does he *look* like?"

The question had made Rebecca giggle. She flopped down on the two-seater; then, seeing that her friend considered this to be no laughing matter, paused for a moment. Hugging a cushion to her chest, she conjured up an image of him.

Average height, lean build, closely cropped dark-brown hair and those brown, almost black eyes that were uniquely Irish. No, you wouldn't call him classically good-looking but he had something about him. Maybe *rugged* was the best word to capture her new employer, Ciaran Cahill.

Melissa nodded wisely when Rebecca announced the description. She was acquainted with rugged. "Rugged's workable and he is a partner. You need to get yourself a copy of *The Rules,* Rebecca," she urged, referring to her latest Bible and bestselling dating book that under no circumstances whatsoever did she loan out.

"Melissa, you know how I feel about that book," Rebecca had rebutted.

"The only reason it hasn't worked as yet is because I haven't met Mr Right," she huffed. "I'm only trying to be helpful you know."

"I know you are and thank you, but there's no need because Ciaran fancies himself enough for the both of us." She gave a sardonic little laugh. "Honestly, you want to see him in action. He's like the lawyer equivalent of a rock star in that firm, and it's a PA he needs, not another groupie." She frowned, thinking about the way Pariah—as she had come to think of the receptionist (it was only one step away from Mariah, after all)—fawned all over him.

Rebecca had been working for just over a week when the novelty of their cramped living conditions started to wear very thin. Nicola had been great about their extended stay with her cheery, "No rush, girls; it's great having you around." Andy, however, was a different story. He wasn't coping with the 'all girls together' setup. He'd been dropping some pretty heavy hints Melissa's way, like, "Did you not see the ad on the board at Tesco's for an office cleaner?" More often than not followed by, "Beggars can't be choosers."

To that, Melissa would hold out her dainty, well-manicured hands and say, "Do these look like dishpan hands to you, Andy?" As an added condolence, she would pat him on the shoulder and assure him that she had plenty of things in the pipeline. Then she would turn her attention to Rebecca to casually ask, "Can you lend me a tenner?"

At long last, one balmy evening, Melissa had bounced onto her end of the couch with the news that she had scored a job. Clapping her hands together excitedly, she screeched, "I'm going to be Tamara Lewis's personal assistant!"

"What?" Rebecca's eyes widened with disbelief as she sat hugging her knees to her chest. "As in *the* Tamara Lewis?"

"Ireland's answer to Miss Minogue. Yep, the one and same," Melissa affirmed. "Me and Tamara are like this," she added, crossing her fingers.

Rebecca could hardly believe what she was hearing. Melissa, her best friend, was going to be working for Tamara Lewis. One couldn't turn the music channel on in Ireland without being assailed with images of the cutesy blonde.

"How?" she managed to utter.

"The agency sent me for an interview and we hit it off straight away. Tamara just loves Kiwis, which is why the agency put me forward. She's into all that Peter Jackson *Lord of the Rings* crap, you know. Plus she kind of digged the fact that I am just a teensy bit older than she is. She thinks that me being a woman of the world means that I'll be able to share the benefit of my wisdom with her."

Rebecca leaned over and smacked her friend over the head with her pillow. "You're such a tosser, and what do you mean a *teensy* bit older? Tamara's barely out of her teens, isn't she?"

"She's twenty-one, and I used a spot of creative licence when it came to my age. So what?" she challenged.

"You mean you lied?"

"If you must put it like that, then yes, I told a porky pie."

Sceptically perusing her friend, Rebecca's eyes narrowed and Melissa threw her pillow back at her. "Don't look at me like that! The girl thought twenty-eight was ancient; no way would she have given me the job if she'd known I was in my thirties."

One of Rebecca's mother's little pearls of wisdom sprang to mind: *No good ever came of telling a lie.* Well, bollocks to that, Mum, she thought while looking across at her friend with admiration.

The spin-off from Melissa's amazing new job was that it scored them their Quayside apartment. Finally, both employed and armed with the hefty deposit needed to get themselves into a flat, they had begun the depressing search for accommodation. With both of them working full time, the only chance they had to view anything was after work. They'd joined the hundreds of other foreign desperados looking to get out of their overpriced hostels and into an overpriced apartment.

Too many wasted evenings had been spent queuing up to view apartments too small to swing a cat in, let alone expect two grown women to share—with or without sex lives—and Melissa's face told all. Tamara had asked her what the problem was, and no sooner had she finished telling her than Tamara picked up the phone. One brief phone call from *the* Tamara Lewis got them into their very own fully furnished, two-bedroom apartment for a song. Or rather, a signed photo of Tamara in hot pants that would give Kylie a run for her money, for the landlord's hormonal son. Nicola had waved them off with a tear in her eye while Andy did a little jig reminiscent of a Morris dance.

From the armchair where she was sitting with her legs curled up under her, Rebecca surveyed her surroundings. When they'd moved in, the apartment had been bland. It looked like a plain cardboard box with a view. They'd put their mark on the place now as various knickknacks gave apartment 2A, Ha'penny House, its homely feel. Rebecca's eyes alighted on the Egyptian papyrus print they'd bought on a week's break in Luxor. She felt a smile twitch at the corners of her mouth as she remembered how they'd wound their way around the dirty streets of the souk before being lured over by Haji and his toothless grin. The three of them had stood by his stall haggling like they were in a bigamist marriage—Haji over the price, Rebecca and Melissa over which print to choose. As it happened, the Golden Eye of Horus didn't exactly go with the lime-green furniture their landlord supplied them with, but it was a talking point.

The living room afforded them a great view over the river. On the mornings when she didn't oversleep, Rebecca liked to curl up on the sofa to sip her coffee and munch on marmalade toast. Her morning wake-up routine gave her enough time to watch the mist waft like tendrils of hair across the Liffey's dark waters. She loved Dublin. For her, it was magical, always buzzing with the unspoken promise that something exciting was about to happen. There was nothing like a stroll down Grafton Street with its colourful streetlife and up-market shops, or O'Connell Street—a hub for both vehicle and foot traffic with the battle-scarred GPO standing sentry over the proceedings. It always rejuvenated her with the knowledge that here she had a second chance. In this hustling city, she wasn't Rebecca Loughton, the girl who didn't follow her dream, the younger sister of Jennifer Carlton of Cuisine with Carlton's fame, and spinster-daughter/constant worry of Dick and Pamela Loughton. In Dublin, Rebecca had an identity of her own and, being a thirty-four-year-old single woman, employed by a rather attractive partner in one of Ireland's largest legal firms didn't seem too bad at all.

Now, though, she sighed as she came back to the present with an unpleasant jolt, she was going to have to go home.

Chapter Four

ON MONDAY MORNING, Rebecca woke to find that the pain over her eyebrow had disappeared, but the cocktail of self-loathing and alcohol had not. Feeling more than a bit sorry for herself, she clutched her stomach and debated whether or not to pull a sickie. That always appeared so suss on a Monday morning, though, she thought while staring up at the ceiling as though the answer lay in the crack spidering across the drywall. She did feel sick, but she supposed she'd better stay in Ciaran's good graces if she wanted time off.

Get up and face the music, Rebecca! she admonished herself before gingerly pulling her dead weight up into a sitting position, hoping the nausea would soon pass.

An hour and a half later, as the ten storeys of concrete that housed Fitzpatrick & Co loomed up at her, she felt her stomach lurch. Swallowing the bile that threatened to rise into her throat, Rebecca forced herself to pull open the heavy glass doors. It was a small bonus to find that instead of a firing squad waiting for the lifts, there was only Mary from the Word Processing department.

"Morning, Rebecca," the older woman grunted, pushing the little arrow that pointed upwards. "I don't like Mondays, me."

For once, Rebecca was in agreement with her. "You and me both, Mary. You and me both."

"Sir Bob got it right with tat song of his, didn't he?" Seeing Rebecca's nod, Mary carried on in her broad, working-class twang. "He was a fine ting in his day, tat one. I'd have let him park his shoes under me bed and administer a bit of Bob Aid, so I would!"

Ugh, what a thought! Rebecca managed to scrape up a watery smile as she held her hand up in protest. "Too much information for me, too early in the day. Thanks, Mary."

"So how was ya Friday night then?" The lift doors picked that moment to ping open, and the two women stepped inside it. "You were well on your way when I left, so you were. Did you go on from here then?"

Mary had a horrible habit of living her life vicariously through the younger staff members of Fitzpatrick & Co, Rebecca thought grimly, nodding by way of reply as she punched the button for the ninth floor.

She crossed her fingers in the hope that the lift would jam after Mary waltzed out on the third floor. No such luck, though, and Rebecca watched the numbers light up with breakneck speed—*4, 5, 6, 7, 8, oh bugger it, 9.* Hastily checking to the left and right to make sure the coast was clear, she stepped out into the corridor and headed for the kitchen. The pressure was getting to her. A caffeine fix was her only hope for getting through the morning.

Her stress levels went through the roof a moment later when she pushed open the kitchen door because there, sitting at one of the Formica tables in the otherwise empty kitchen, was James. Despite her face feeling like she'd just bitten into a hot chili, she managed to choke out a relatively civil, "Good morning," noticing as she did so, James pale at the sight of her, which in turn made his spots look even redder than they usually did.

He stammered out a modest "hi" before—like the little Dutch boy pulling his finger out of the dyke—his words spilled out in a great big torrent: "Look, Becs..."

Aagh! She hated it when he called her that!

"Friday night was great and everything and I think you're a nice person..." He paused, twirling the straw nervously around in his can of Coke.

Hang on a minute, Rebecca thought, frowning. It sounded vaguely familiar, and she didn't have to wait long to find out where James was going with the conversation.

"The thing is, Becs—you're a bit old for me, don't you reckon?"

Rebecca was gobsmacked. He was calling her a cougar, and if he weren't right, she'd smack him one, she silently seethed, staring at his smugly apologetic grin.

However, instead of resorting to fisticuffs, she behaved in a manner befitting of her age and took a deep breath before bowing her head. "You're right, James. Let's just put Friday night behind us, shall we? Pretend it never happened."

Naturally, over the course of the weekend, James had texted all of his fellow summer placement pals about their dalliance. They, in turn, were now busy lounging on various PA's desks, spreading the hot goss. It had (judging by Pariah's contemptuous announcement of a courier parcel at reception for Mr Cahill) also spread as far down the ranks as reception. By lunchtime, the pointing, stares, and loud, growly cat noises for Rebecca's part were beginning to die down. As were the "way hey heys!" followed by a thump on the back for James's part.

"Oh, Rebecca, how could you?" Derbhilla's eyes were like china-blue saucers as she quickly deleted the winpop up message her friend had just sent her.

"Don't!" Rebecca hissed, poking her head around the divider separating their two workstations. "I already feel like I've been branded with the letter S." Shuddering, she added, "I just feel sick every time I think about it."

"You and me both."

"Thanks for that, Derbhilla. It's alright for you to sit there like Mrs Morality. You've got the sanctity of marriage to stop you from doing stupid things."

"That and an ability to curb my alcohol intake."

"Yes, and if you hadn't bought those shooters—"

Rebecca didn't get a chance to finish because Derbhilla's eyes nearly popped out of her head as a truly heinous thought occurred to her. "Did you, you know, do the deed?"

Rebecca's face flamed as she spluttered, "I most certainly did not!"

Derbhilla's eyes slowly returned to their normal size and, sinking back into her seat with relief, she crossed herself, murmuring a Hail Mary before asking, "Does Ciaran know?" She was convinced there was sexual tension between the two of them despite Rebecca's continual protestations to the contrary.

"How should I know?" I hoped not, she thought, trying to shrug nonchalantly because not even Derbhilla was privy to the information that at last year's Christmas party they'd shared an inebriated snog hidden from view in the cloakroom. It was a snog from which they had reluctantly prised themselves apart upon hearing footsteps approaching. It was not seemly for a senior partner to be caught carrying on with his secretary. Rebecca had smoothed her dress down and tottered back into the hall—shaking her groove thing for the rest of the night as though nothing had happened. Until they happened to share a taxi home together, that was—his home. Neither of them had mentioned that night. She sometimes wondered what was running through Ciaran's mind, though, when she caught him looking at her unawares.

Rebecca shook those thoughts away and filled her friend in on what had transpired in the kitchen earlier that morning, promptly sending Derbhilla into a fit of the giggles.

"Serves you bloody right for being a cradle snatcher!" Derbhilla snorted.

Rebecca managed a small smile in return, still not quite able to see the humorous side of it all. Okay, I like a joke as much as the next person. Enough is enough, though, she thought moments later while watching Derbhilla reach for a tissue from the box she kept handy. The woman was crying with laughter, for goodness' sake; it was time to change the subject. Her eyes roamed down the corridor to Derbhilla's Gestapo-like boss Eileen's office. Good, the door was shut; that meant she'd be frantically dictating. Ciaran was down in the boardroom with the Miller Group's president, signing off documents. With the coast clear, Rebecca had some more news to impart. Like a demented frog, she scooted her chair around to Derbhilla's side of their desk and gave her the edited version.

"My sister phoned me yesterday. Turns out her hubby Mark's been having an affair, and she wants me to come home to look after the children while they go to Aussie for a fortnight to try to work through things."

Derbhilla immediately sobered up, her eyes beginning to widen again.

"Would you stop doing that?" Rebecca glared at her.

"What?"

"That thing you do with your eyes. It's freakish."

"Alright already! Calm down. My mammy always did say I had a theatrical streak. I get it from Granny McGuire, apparently. But bloody hell, Rebecca, your life could never be described as dull!"

"I wish it were dull," she answered flatly, scuffing at the carpet with her boots.

Derbhilla ignored Rebecca's attempt at sympathy; there was gossip. "An affair, you say. Tell me now, who with?"

With an air of sufferance, Rebecca looked up. "Are you ready? It will make your eyes pop out."

Once Derbhilla's eyes returned to their rightful size, the girls spent the next half hour gainfully employed in trashing Rebecca's brother-in-law. Then, having exhausted that topic for the time being, Derbhilla asked, "So when are you going?"

"Just as soon as I can get the flights sorted. To be honest, it will be a relief to get away from here for a couple of weeks."

Her friend smiled sympathetically, knowing what Rebecca was inferring. "I can see where you're coming from, but you have to admit that you and Spotty James is a pretty darn juicy piece of gossip. If it weren't to do with you, we'd be lapping it up."

"I know," she acknowledged mournfully.

"Still," Derbhilla said brightly, "you're away for a whole fortnight. Someone's bound to get up to something disgusting with someone else in that time and then you'll be old news."

"That's of great comfort to me, thank you."

Though Derbhilla was probably speaking the truth, it didn't diminish the fact that right now felt like the longest day of Rebecca's life. And if she had to listen to one more catty giggle from where she sat with her head lowered behind her desk, Derbhilla would have to hold her back from thumping somebody.

Both girls jumped as they heard a door open but carried on yakking as the easy-going Piaras meandered by them, oblivious of the fact that neither secretary was doing any work.

"Do you think I should wait until after lunch to ask Ciaran for the time off?" Rebecca asked, while gnawing down her thumbnail.

"Definitely. Men are always more receptive to things on a full stomach," Derbhilla answered with a knowing flick of her long, dark hair. "Besides, he's going to be in that meeting with your Miller Group man for most of the morning, isn't he?"

"Uh-huh."

"Right, so why not get on his good side by being Wonder PA?"

Rebecca stared at her friend blankly. Surely she wasn't suggesting Rebecca wear a tiara and a red, white, and blue leotard to take dictation?

Derbhilla rolled her eyes. "Do I have to spell it out to you, woman?"

"Um, yes please."

"Offer to go and get him one of those spicy lamb wraps he likes from O'Connell's. And while you're at it, make mine a chicken Caesar."

Much later that morning, after they'd tackled their respective typing piles for at least ten minutes, Derbhilla suddenly threw her headset aside as yet another distressing thought occurred to her. "You won't be here for the races!"

From behind her computer screen, Rebecca sighed. It was bloody hopeless; she'd just rewound and played the same sentence at least five times. Pushing her headset down round her neck, she was just in time to hear a panicked screech, "So who am I going to pick apart all the other women's outfits with?"

"How about Pariah?" Rebecca shrugged as a dark head popped round the desk partition.

"Oh piss off, Rebecca!"

"Look, Derbhilla, you'll still have a good time. Shane will be with you, won't he?" She was referring to her friend's husband of two years.

"Yes, and don't get me wrong, I love him dearly, but the reason he's going to the races is to watch the horses, not the women." She paused as she realised what she'd just said before adding darkly, "At least he had better be going to watch the horses."

Rebecca laughed at her friend's frown of consternation. Shane Murphy, with his unruly shock of red hair and cheeky, green eyes, only had eyes for his wife. "Of course he'll be watching the horses. Liz Hurley could walk past in the nude and Shane would be too busy gazing at you to notice."

Derbhilla smiled, semi-mollified. "It's not going to be the same without you, though. Shane might be my partner in life, but you, my friend, are my partner in crime."

Rebecca felt a twinge of guilt at letting her friend down at the last minute, but there was nothing she could do about it because when push came to shove, family came first.

Chapter Five

"COME IN." CIARAN ANSWERED the knock on his door later that afternoon. By the gruffness of his invitation, it was apparent that he was in a foul temper. That prat from the Miller Group had kept him hard at it all morning. He'd just heard via the Fitzpatrick & Co bush telegraph, Tania on reception, that his PA had been up to no good on the weekend. The worst thing was that it was with that little git James, of all people. For chrissakes, he growled to himself. The boy was nearly half her age. What was she thinking? Not that it was any of his business what she chose to do in her spare time; she was his PA, not his girlfriend. She had made that very clear, taking off the next morning the way she had after their little dalliance last year. *Oh, speak of the devil.* His frown deepened as Rebecca peered tentatively round his door; here she was now and with lunch. *Well, well, well—would wonders never cease?*

Fifteen minutes later, he was feeling marginally better as he tossed the sauce-sodden paper bag into the wastepaper basket under his desk. He was just wiping his mouth with a napkin when Rebecca poked her head round his door once again, clutching a mug of coffee.

"Everything alright?" She was referring to the spicy lamb wrap that he'd just polished off.

"Yeah, ta for that. I didn't think I'd get time for lunch today. Not after that wanker from Miller's decided to take up my whole morning." He put the napkin down and fished, "So how was your head on Saturday morning?"

She refused to take the bait and smiled sweetly. "Fine, thanks—how was the rest of your weekend?"

Butter wouldn't melt, thought Ciaran. If that was the way she wanted to play it, then so be it because two could play at that game. "Great apart from losing a tenner to Jordy because he thrashed me at tenpin bowling again."

Jordy was a ten-year-old boy who had been dealt a crappy hand in life thanks to his dad buggering off when he was barely out of nappies. He'd left Jordy and his mother, along with her four other children, to struggle on alone. Ciaran, who could relate to coming from a large family but a large family with pots of money, had felt that being a 'big brother' was the least he could do to help kids like Jordy.

Rebecca had found it hard to picture her gigolo boss in the role of caring mentor when he'd told her about Jordy. She'd seen a different side to him, though, when he'd brought the young boy up to the office to say hi for the first time. His natural rapport with him was obvious, and it was a side to Ciaran she liked. "Bowling sounds like fun and you're welcome for lunch. I can't have my boss working on an empty stomach all afternoon, now can I? Oh, I almost forgot—here's your coffee, just the way you like it, with plenty of milk." She placed the mug on his desk and then took a seat across from him.

Ciaran eyed her speculatively. His PA she might be, but lunch and coffee weren't usually on the cards unless International Secretaries Day was looming, and she was pumping for something really big. Still, he might as well enjoy it while it lasted because, knowing her, it wouldn't last long.

"Um, Ciaran?" Rebecca hedged, "Well, you see, the thing is, I need some time off. I wouldn't ask except that it's a family emergency. I've already spoken to HR, and they have a temp who can step in for me. Her name's Kate and she's a Kiwi too, so if you close your eyes you won't even know I'm gone. Oh, and I'm sorry about stuffing up the arrangements for Galway." Rebecca finished her sentence in one big gulp as her boss drained the mug of instant coffee she'd made him.

He plonked it down on his desk with a sigh. He was right; it was too good to be true.

Rebecca crossed her legs and began twiddling her hair nervously. It *was* short notice; what if he said she couldn't have the time off? Ciaran was easygoing, but he hadn't earned the title of senior partner in one of Ireland's largest law firms by being a pushover either. Nor by being neat, she thought as her eyes swept over the room. It was less than a week since she'd last tidied up in here, and there were already stacks of overflowing files lying on the floor in no particular order of urgency.

Ciaran had obviously attempted to sling his jacket onto the little lemon-coloured sofa over by the window—the view from which denoted his position of power within the firm—but missed. No wonder he always looked crumpled, she thought ruefully. Mind you, that 'just rolled out of bed' look was part of what made him so appealing. With his dark head bent forward as he checked the dates she'd requested on her holiday form against those in his diary, she noticed how tousled his hair was. It must have been a stressful morning, she gathered, reflecting on his unconscious habit of raking his fingers through his hair when he felt under pressure. While working for him, she had picked up on his mannerisms and learned how to read him—which came in handy at times like this. She looked fondly at his little boy's cowlick and nearly had to sit on her hands to stop herself from reaching over to smooth it down.

She averted her eyes to the bomb site that was his desk, littered with everything from scrawled handwritten notes to a copy of today's *Irish Times*—opened to the financial pages, of course. He slid open his top drawer to retrieve one of at least a dozen ballpoint pens. She couldn't help but notice the two bottles of supersized White-Out, three boxes of paper clips, and an abundance of yellow Post-it pads he'd also squirrelled away in there. No wonder she and Derbhilla could never find a bloody pen when they needed one!

Ciaran had a well-known penchant for raiding the stationery cupboard. He claimed that getting away from his desk for a few minutes to fossick in it helped him clear his head. Gives him an excuse to relive his sexual conquests, more like, she thought contemptuously. The whole office had heard the rumour about him and that overenthusiastic temp who'd done more than get a box of paperclips out of the cupboard for him. It had been before her time and was the stuff of office legends. It made her feel justified in not having hung on the morning after their short-lived tryst, too. She'd have only been giving him a chance to put another notch on his belt—or should that be a bottle of White-Out in his drawer?

"Penny for your thoughts." Ciaran snapped his fingers and, as he leaned towards her, Rebecca heard the soft creaking of genuine leather from his standard issue partner's chair. Seeing his quizzical expression, she stopped twiddling her hair and straightened in her standard issue visitor's chair, feeling the fabric of it snag her tights as she did so. *Buggeration!* Thoroughly annoyed—they were brand-new on that morning—she squirmed around in her seat to investigate the damage. Spying Ciaran's bemused expression, she forced herself to stop fixating on her pantyhose and answer her boss.

"Uh sorry, run in my, er... I was miles away then. It's the shock of the news from home, you see." A little white lie, sure, but more palatable than talking about her hosiery or bringing up the whole office supply room debacle again and she'd die before she ever mentioned their one-night stand.

She spared Ciaran none of the gory details, however, regarding the state of the Carltons' marriage, and as her explanation came to a close, he splayed his hands out flat on the form in front of him. Rebecca looked down at them admiringly. They were strong, manly hands with no sign of that limp-wrist-ed look with which men in suits are often afflicted. Glancing up, she fell in-to a pair of sooty brown eyes until, catching a twinkle in them, she felt her face flush. *Don't say he'd heard about Spotty James too?* Then, as he continued his nonverbal glimmer, she felt a surge of annoyance. *So what if he had?* He was in no position to judge her one measly misdemeanour. Not when he was Fitzpatrick & Co's reigning king of drunken office liaisons.

As it happened, Ciaran's twinkling did have something to do with James but not in the way she was thinking. If Rebecca were to go home for two weeks, it would more likely than not put the kibosh on any budding relation-ship between the two of them. He would be doing her, not to mention him-self, a favour by signing the form off. With his ballpoint pen hovering tan-talizingly over the form, he asked, "So, this Kiwi Kate, is she good-looking then?"

"Ciaran!"

He held both his hands up in front of him and, for the first time that day, grinned. His smirk revealed his utmost pleasure in winding Rebecca up as his eyes grazed over her puckered mouth. "I was only joking!"

"You're hilarious." Rebecca applauded flatly. "Now can I have the time off or not?"

"Ah, go on then. I don't suppose it will matter too much seeing as I'll be away for half the time you'll be gone."

"Oh, I'm sure you'll all have a great time regardless." Looking down at her tightly clasped hands resting on her lap, the unwelcome thought whirled around in her head that he'd hardly have time to think about her—especially with Pariah drooling all over him. She'd do her utmost to make her partner's wife fantasy a reality.

The sudden intensity in his voice surprised her as he said, "No, Rebecca, it won't be the same without you."

Unsure of how to react, she instinctively flicked a non-existent piece of lint off her skirt. He must have sensed her unease, for Ciaran swiftly signed the form and held it out to her. "Admirable quality—putting family first over fun."

"Yes, well, my sister might not agree that it's one of my strongest points," she muttered.

When she didn't elaborate further, he asked, "So, you'll be looking after your niece and nephew?"

She eyed him suspiciously and, yes, just as she'd suspected, he was smirking. "Don't look at me like that. I am perfectly capable of handling a three-year-old and a seven-year-old, you know." She offered a mischievous smile. "It will be a doddle after looking after you."

He threw back his head and laughed. "Fair play to you. Don't get me wrong, Rebecca. I have total faith in your abilities. One thing, though?" She eyed him expectantly. "Promise you'll email me while you're away?" Then, seeing the surprise register on her face, he hastily added, "To fill me in on the craic like."

She felt vaguely disappointed, though what she had expected him to say she didn't know. "Huh? What craic? I'll be far too busy being a responsible auntie to have fun."

Snatching up the form with a mumbled thanks, she got to her feet. She stalked out of the room, not breaking her stride as he called after her, "Hey, Rebecca, did you know you've a run in your stockings?"

Just what was he doing, looking at her legs?

TWO DAYS LATER, REBECCA flung her handbag down on her desk. Flopping back into her chair, she kicked off the black stilettos that added at least another two inches to her legs. Not the ideal choice of footwear for legging it halfway across the city, she thought, wriggling her toes. Jennifer had kept her side of the bargain and transferred the money through as they'd agreed over the phone. Fiona, her favourite travel agent at the Henry Street branch of Thomas Cook, from where she'd just picked her tickets up, had been brilliant arranging the flights at such short notice too. After that, she'd whizzed in to see Tarquin, grateful that he had been able to squeeze her in for a trim and blow wave, thanks to a last-minute cancellation.

He had, as usual, been resplendent in skin-tight black from head-to-toe. When he'd finished working his magic, he held up a mirror so Rebecca could admire his artistry from all angles. Looking pleased with himself, he declared her hair to be, "Perfectionnement!"

"Wow, it looks so much better!" she enthused, twisting and turning as he preened. It did, too. Her dark blonde hair grazed her shoulders, shiny and full of bounce.

Placing the mirror on the spotless countertop, Tarquin held a finger up to his lips as if he was about to share a great secret with her. Rebecca sat up straight, her ears cocked for either juicy gossip or an invaluable hairdressing tip.

"Now, watch closely, *chérie*, because I will show you zis only once." He flung his arm in the direction of the salon's glass frontage and declared, "The weather out zere, it is not good, right?"

Huh? What was he going on about? It had been blue skies, and the sun had been shining when she first left the office. In fact, she remembered donning her sunglasses to shield her eyes from the numerous hairy, white male chests on display in St Stephen's Green. What was it with Irish men? A teensy weensy bit of sunshine and they whipped their shirts off as though they were in the middle of an African drought. It didn't concern them in the least if the goods they were displaying were seriously faulty.

Shuddering at the memory, she followed the direction of Tarquin's eyes to where an assortment of shoes danced through freshly formed puddles on the worn cobbled paving. It was totally peeing down. Why was she so surprised? Ireland, after all, was home to the handbag with the inbuilt umbrella, or so she wished. Once again, she vowed to get that idea patented. Swivelling back to face the mirror, she returned his gaze steadily until he was satisfied that he had her full attention.

"Zis means all my 'ard work could be wiped out." He made the same swishing motion as before, "like zis! So, if you get back to work with flat 'air, you will need to do zis." With the flourish of a magician, he pulled, seemingly from thin air, a tiny white bottle. His voice dropped to a conspiratorial whisper. "Zis is *ze* serum."

Unexpectedly, he swung his head down towards his knees. Straining to hear the next bit, she leaned over the side of her chair. "Spray ze roots of ze air like zis," he mumbled, demonstrating a spraying motion by making a sort of shushing noise as he pretended to squirt the serum onto his roots. The charade over, he reared upright once more and, looking for all the world like a peroxide blonde porcupine, clapped his hands together. "Voila! Your oomph is restored. *Chérie* wishes to purchase, *oui*?"

The smaller the bottle, the dearer the price it would seem, but Rebecca had already decided she was not leaving without her gravity-defying serum. Tarquin dropped the tiny canister into a cute white paper bag with the word 'Vertigo' stamped in black ink on it, and then took her proffered credit card.

"You will not regret zis, *chérie*," he gushed, as though she were buying the elixir of life itself. Indeed, from his perspective, she supposed that life with flat 'air' was simply not worth living. Signing the receipt, she averted her eyes from all the zeroes along the bottom.

"Thanks for that, Tarquin," she said, adding automatically, "you're the best."

Not unlike the practice of tipping, it was important to praise his efforts liberally if she wanted a decent haircut the next time she came. Something she'd learned the hard way, or rather, the too-short way. Pulling open the heavy glass door, she stepped out onto the wet pavement and wondered, not for the first time, why it was that Tarquin, whom she knew for a fact was from Cork city, had a French accent. It was one of life's little mysteries, she decided, popping her umbrella open.

Glancing down at the gold oval of her watch face, she swore softly to herself. The ridiculously long hour and half's break she had for lunch had flown by today, leaving her with ten minutes in which to get her feet parked back under her desk! Taking a preparatory breath for her trot back up Grafton Street, she passed by the familiar green logo of Marks and Sparks when she felt someone brush past her, exclaiming fiercely, "Watch it! You nearly took my eye out with that brolly!"

Rebecca didn't bother to look up as she muttered darkly, "Far better your eye than my hair, mate."

Making it back to the office with two minutes to spare, she had headed straight to the ladies' to unleash her secret weapon and restore the oomph the damp day had all but destroyed. Hanging her head down over her knees, Rebecca aimed the serum at her roots as Tarquin had demonstrated. She'd just swung her head back up when the door creaked open.

"Good look, Rebecca!" Pariah sniggered.

Why did the silly cow always have to use the loos on their level? she griped, mentally cursing Tarquin as she frantically turned to the mirror, trying to smooth down the frizz that had just taken oomph to the next level.

"What's that? Can I have a squirt?" Pariah tossed her make-up bag onto the counter and snatching up the precious bottle, she squinted at the label.

Not at forty bloody euros a pop, you can't! Rebecca thought, lunging forward to reclaim it, but Pariah had already whipped the top off and begun squirting and fluffing with a vengeance.

"I'd rather you didn't use it, Tania. It's hellishly expensive stuff."

"Oh sorry, you should have said so." Admiring her considerably fuller hair in the mirror, Pariah handed the serum back.

Putting the significantly emptier bottle back in her handbag, Rebecca made one last-ditch attempt to smooth hers down. Then, mentally cursing the younger woman, she left her to finish her primping in private. She knew exactly for whose benefits Pariah was trowelling all that slap on.

Now ensconced behind her desk, she was contemplating doing a spot of work when a broad Kiwi accent startled her. Hastily shoving her feet back into her shoes, she looked up.

"G'day, I'm Kate. Grainne from HR sent me up."

Chapter Six

KATE, REBECCA NOTED, had an open and attractive face sitting atop a solid build that matched her voice. Her much-too-pretty temporary replacement held her hand out in greeting and finishing her once-over, Rebecca replied, "Hi, Kate. I'm Rebecca."

Indicating a spare chair over by the filing cabinets, she suggested the younger girl grab it and pull up a pew. Derbhilla, who for once had a spare afternoon—Eileen would be tied up in a meeting for the rest of the day—was trying to catch up on her filing backlog. She threw a smile over at the younger girl as she approached.

"Hi, I'm Derbhilla. I sit on the other side of Rebecca's desk."

"Kate," the girl exchanged politely. "Nice to meet you. That means you must work for Eileen Donnell?"

"Uh-huh."

Kate grimaced. "Poor you. I've heard she's a bit of a slavedriver."

"Can be," Derbhilla agreed, tucking a stray strand of hair back behind her ear. "I like to be busy though. It makes the day go fast."

Wheeling the chair back towards Rebecca's desk, Kate tossed back cheerily, "Well, I doubt my days are going to drag either, working for Ciaran. He's gorgeous! All the temps rate him a ten on the babe-a-scale." She grinned, revealing slightly crooked front teeth that only served to make her face more interesting. "Either way, he'll be a vast improvement on crusty old Fitzpatrick. I just finished a two-week stint covering for Orla Brennan, and I tell you what, girls, I don't know how she puts up with that awful wind problem of his."

Derbhilla's jaw dropped. Kate obviously didn't believe in mincing her words then, and she hadn't finished yet.

"Now Ciaran, he's got that whole broody Colin Farrell thing going on." She shivered exaggeratedly.

The snort that erupted from Rebecca could have rivalled Vesuvius and Derbhilla glanced her way, her filing temporarily forgotten as she waited to hear what her friend would say.

"Okay, so let me get this right—you think Ciaran looks like Colin Farrell?"

"Yeah, don't you, with those brown eyes of his and all that stubble?" Kate didn't wait for a reply. "Are long, lingering, liquid lunches part of the job description then?"

Rebecca's flat "no" fell on deaf ears as Kate hugged herself gleefully. "I am so going to enjoy the next two weeks."

"So where are you from?" Rebecca inquired shortly, determined to change the subject. "I'm from Christchurch."

Kate looked sheepish. "Promise me no wisecracks because I've heard them all."

"Okay," Rebecca answered hesitantly, now bemused.

"Hamilton originally." Kate glared as Rebecca guffawed. No wonder she'd looked sheepish. Blink and you'd miss it; Hamilton was hardly the Mecca of New Zealand.

"You promised," Kate said accusingly.

"I didn't say a word," Rebecca replied honestly.

"You didn't have to." Kate then offered a peace-treaty grin. "I've been living in London for the last five years, but Immigration finally cottoned onto the fact that my permit was well and truly up and booted me out."

"Bummer," Rebecca replied sympathetically.

"Yeah, it was. I didn't want to go home, for obvious reasons." The two women exchanged a smile. "But I was due to catch up with everybody and while I was home, I applied for a work permit here. It's the next-best thing; all the ex-pats are doing it when their UK visas are up." She finished with a shrug as Ciaran popped his head round his door.

"Hey, Becs, could you..." Spying Kate, his voice trailed off as he sidled over to check her out.

Rebecca noticed his shirttails were hanging out of the back of his pants, and she had to resist the urge to tidy up his act and tuck him back in.

"And who might you be?" he inquired with a raised eyebrow and impish grin. Perching himself familiarly on the edge of Rebecca's desk, he eyed the newcomer with unabashed curiosity.

His suit pants could do with a jolly good iron too. Rebecca frowned, thinking that on anyone else, an opening line like that would have sounded sleazy but flirting was in Ciaran's DNA. His boyish looks would let him get away with murder and, if the dozy expression on her face was anything to go by, then Kate was lapping up his charm offensive.

"I'm Kate and you are?" she replied with a coquettish bat of her eyelashes—already knowing full well who he was.

Oh, for goodness' sake. Rebecca rolled her eyes, and Derbhilla pretended to gag behind the filing cabinets. "Ciaran, this is Kate; Kate, this is Ciaran." Her tone was businesslike because one of them had to act like a professional. "Kate is filling in for me while I'm away." When Ciaran didn't remove his butt from her desk and go back to his office, she added, "I was just about to show her the ropes, so if you don't mind..." She made a shooing motion with her hand.

Ciaran twiddled his tie, that remained stubbornly askew, and deliberately didn't take the hint for the simple reason that he thoroughly enjoyed winding his PA up. Childish, he knew, but hey, weren't women always on about men needing to grow up? Getting Rebecca to bite was worth it every time because he got to see those big hazel eyes of hers grow even more enormous with indignation. Turning his attention back to Kate, he decided to wind a little tighter. "Ah, so you'll be the one looking after me while Rebecca here goes swanning off around the other side of the world." It had the desired reaction.

"Hardly swanning around, Ciaran! I told you I will have sole charge of my niece and nephew while I'm away." Taking in his hangdog expression, she added, "And stop doing that puppy dog face thing. It won't wash. You are more than capable of looking after yourself." She wagged a finger in Kate's direction. "Don't let him con you into making him endless cups of coffee. Oh, and if he asks you to go to the bakery, make sure you tell him that he has two perfectly good legs of his own. Take my word for it, Kate—you give him an inch, he'll take a mile."

Ciaran winked at Kate. "Don't listen to Rebecca. She's a firm believer in the tough love motif." Then, catching a glimpse of the time on the clock behind Kate's head, he shot off his perch as though something had just bitten him on the backside. "Shite and shit!" He disappeared into his office, reappearing with a stack of papers and his briefcase. As he sailed past them, shirt-tails flapping, he called, "Rebecca, I'm going to be late for my three o'clock in bloody Wicklow. Can you ring that old fart White and tell him I've been unavoidably delayed? I'll think of an excuse on my way over there." Waiting for the lift, he grinned over at her, simultaneously tucking his shirt into his pants—saving her a job. "Thanks, babe. You're the best." Then, seeing Kate slide into Rebecca's seat, realisation dawned. He slapped a hand to his forehead. *Double shite and shit!* It was Rebecca's last day.

The lift doors opened, and he stepped in, holding them open with his free hand. "I was going to take you for a drink after work, but bloody White and his cronies have buggered that plan up. They've insisted on booking us into Malones for a celebration meal after we've signed the documents. I can't get out of it. I'm sorry. You take care of yourself and email me, alright?" He blew her a kiss. "Bon voyage. See you Monday," he added, directing the last bit at Kate, who was all but drooling over him.

Not much of a goodbye, Rebecca thought dejectedly as the lift doors slid shut. Her mood didn't improve with Kate's next comments either.

"Wow, he is something." Her eyes were still glued to the lift in hopes that he'd reappear. "No wonder all the girls think your job's primo."

Rebecca chose to ignore Kate's obvious crush and the rest of the afternoon whizzed by as she showed her temporary replacement the ropes, and before she knew it, the wall clock's hands had crept around to five thirty.

"I'll drop this down to reception on my way out. Have a great trip home, Rebecca." Snatching up the A4 envelope for the courier that evening, Kate stampeded over to the lift. "Say hi to the sheep for me and thanks for showing me the ropes," she called over her shoulder.

Humph. Kate obviously didn't believe in staying a minute longer than she had to, Rebecca thought, conveniently forgetting that she was a firm believer in clocking out on time. Smiling as sweetly as she could through gritted teeth, she offered a cordial wave goodbye. "No worries, Kate." Then, ducking her head because she just couldn't bring herself to wish the girl good luck, she began busying herself by tidying all her personal bits and pieces away. Baa yourself and don't make yourself too at home, she snarled silently, shoving her hand cream into her bag.

She spied Derbhilla ogling her from over by the filing cabinets. "What are you looking at me like that for?"

"I was wondering why it is that you've a face on you like a cat's arse when you've just officially finished work for the next two weeks?"

"I don't."

"You do, actually. Are we feeling a little bit threatened perhaps?"

"No!" she snapped, a little too quickly. Now *that* was ludicrous. Kate was no threat to her job unless Derbhilla was referring to something else.

"Ha, I knew it!" Derbhilla pounced. She gave the metal cabinet drawer a triumphant shove shut. "You're jealous!"

"I am not," Rebecca shot back indignantly.

"You needn't worry, you know. She's not his type—far too wholesome."

Rebecca picked up the tiny silver frame housing Jack and Hannah's photo. With a heavy sigh, she accepted the fact that Derbhilla was probably talking such nonsense because, being somewhat of a newlywed, office romance was always on the woman's mind. And so, she resigned herself to playing along, just to appease her friend. "And how would you know what Ciaran's type is? From what I've seen, he doesn't discriminate."

"Ah." Derbhilla swatted the comment away with her hand. "He's just sowing his seeds while he waits for the right woman to realise she's been right under his nose all along." Striding back to her desk to switch her computer off, she asked, "Now, do you want me to come and help you choose some tacky Irish trinkets to take home with you? Or are you going to sit there sulking all night?"

Turning her computer off, Rebecca rose slowly from her desk. It felt strange knowing she wouldn't be back tomorrow. If she were honest, though, what was odd was that she was feeling weird in the first place. Normally, the thought of being on holiday would have sent her linking arms with Derbhilla and running down the road, punching her fist up in the air, shouting, "YEEESSS!!!"

As she picked up her handbag, she supposed she'd better leave a note for Ciaran with her contact details and remind him that she was planning on coming back.

"I won't be a sec."

Upon entering his room, she saw he'd left his computer on as usual, even though the IT gang had sent a memo around recently insisting everybody turn their PCs off at night. Typical Ciaran move—rules don't apply to *him*. On the screen, brightly coloured fish swam lazily around, and she hit a random key.

The bold black heading *'80s Lyrics Quiz* blinked back at her. It took a moment to register what she was looking at, and when she did, she laughed loudly. How typical of Ciaran! He'd been industriously working his way through a *very* important music quiz when he'd popped his head round his door that afternoon. She scrolled down to find that he'd only gotten as far as number 20: *What is the only song by Australian band Men at Work to break the UK Top 20?* Or maybe he'd gotten stuck on that question? Perhaps that was what he had been going to ask her when he'd been sidetracked by Kate's arrival. She grabbed a pen and scribbled her note, unable to resist adding a PS at the bottom: *The answer's 'Land Down Under' (an Australian classic).* Then, switching his computer off, she flicked the light switch and left the room.

"WHAT A GORGEOUS NIGHT." Rebecca stepped out into the warm evening air and paused to let it wash over her. The moment came to a screeching halt when Derbhilla tugged at her arm.

"Come on; the sooner we get the shopping done, the sooner we can go for a pint. I am gasping."

The streets were alive with people, all enjoying the balmy weather and the good humour it brought with it. Linking arms, the two women pushed their way out into the throng.

Within a half hour, Derbhilla had found an ideal gaudy addition to Rebecca's shopping basket. "You have to buy this!" she exclaimed. They were standing in a garishly lit souvenir shop on O'Connell Street, and Derbhilla was holding up an apron emblazoned with a great big green, glittery shamrock. "It's so awful that it's perfect. What with the cooking school and every-thing." Not wasting a moment waiting for Rebecca's response, she tossed it into the basket and moved on to tasteless souvenir number two. "Look at this!" She grabbed a glass dome off the crammed shelf in front of her and, blowing the dust off it, gave it a shake. Snow began to fall all around the wee leprechaun trapped inside. Rebecca wasn't paying attention to her friend's antics, though. Seeing the apron had taken her right back in time to the day Jennifer and Mark had made the offer for their new home.

The flashy apron in Rebecca's shopping basket was not only the reminder of Jennifer's big news about the house purchase, but it attached a slightly traumatic relevance to it as well. It was several years ago now, and Rebecca had been waiting, not so patiently, for her sister and entourage to arrive at their parents' house so she could begin hoeing into her lunch. It was a Loughton family tradition—the Sunday roast followed by a healthy dollop of Pamela's pavlova. As the two girls had gotten older, the meal had gone from being a weekly occurrence to a fortnightly get-together until it got rel-egated to its current position of the second Sunday in every month. Seeing how it was the most nutritious meal she ate all month, Rebecca looked for-ward to it. This particular Sunday, with each and every hunger pang, she was getting more and more annoyed with her sister.

Just as the spuds were beginning to stick to the roasting pan, Hurricane Jennifer whirled in through the front door, Mark and baby Jack the calm after the storm. "We've made an offer!" she'd shrieked. Their mother had clapped her hands in excitement, causing her freshly tinted ash-blonde curls to bob up and down. Pamela had been in the process of giving in to old age ungracefully when an episode of *What Not To Wear* aimed at the mature woman had spurred her into action. Having dyed—sorry, *tinted*—her hair, she'd gone on a rampage around their local shopping mall. Dick had been worried his wife was having an affair. She was forever saying she felt like a new woman, but she assured him it was all down to *What Not To Wear*'s Gestapo-like hosts, Trinny and Susannah.

Dick's eyes had lit up as he urged, "Come on then! Don't keep us all in suspense; where is the house located?" He abruptly changed the subject to shout, "Stop fussing, woman," at his wife, who was attempting to cool her daughter's flushed face by doing a Mexican wave with her new apron. Depicting a pair of juicy red lips and bearing the slogan 'Hot Lips', the apron had been a present for his wife, in keeping with her new image. It nearly put Rebecca off her dinner every time her mum pranced out of the kitchen wearing it, because it reminded her of the fact that her parents still had sex.

This unhealthy insight into her parents' private life had come to her while rummaging under their bed a few years prior when she'd still been living under their roof. She'd been looking for her missing left knee-high boot thanks to her visiting cousin, Jacqui's, three-year-old daughter. She'd had a ribald game of Puss in Boots with Rebecca's $280.00 boots. As she lifted up the bed skirt, there it was—all the evidence she needed to convict her parents of sexual relations: a tube of KY Jelly! All she had to say on the matter, thank you very much, was thank goodness she hadn't touched it!

"You know how we've been looking in Akaroa?" Jennifer began her story of how they stumbled across their dream house—yet another perfect move in Jennifer's fantasy life. There was a collective nod of heads round the table. "Well, the house is in the most fantastic spot. There in the hills behind the harbour." Her voice became cautionary. "It was built in 1882 and, to be honest, it looks like it, but the views are just to die for."

"How many bedrooms?" their dad interrupted his daughter.

"Well, the house is two storeys. There's one bedroom downstairs, along with a study and a separate kitchen with a dining area and sunroom attached. The living room runs off from the kitchen, and it still has the original fireplace. You'd pay a fortune for it now. There're three bedrooms upstairs," she finished breathlessly. Then Dick asked the million-dollar question:

"How many toilets?"

"Two."

He visibly relaxed. His fear of one-toilet homes stemmed from years of living in such a house alongside three women. If you asked him what his proudest moment was, he'd tell you that it wasn't the birth of his children. Oh no, it was the ribbon-cutting ceremony for the new bathroom with the *additional* toilet he had put in.

"Like I said, Dad, it's old. It's going to need a lot of TLC to bring it back to its former glory, but we can do it, can't we?" She sought her husband's reassurance from across the table, and Mark nodded, his eyes sparkling with his wife's childlike enthusiasm. It was so good to see her excited about something again. Ever since Jack had arrived, it was like her inner light was slowly dimming. Her vitality and sparkle were what had first attracted him to her—that and the fact she was drop-dead gorgeous and a fantastic cook to boot.

"Jen's right about the views, too. You can see right out over the harbour," he added; her enthusiasm was catching.

"That's not the best bit, though," she interjected, and then paused for maximum impact.

Rebecca wished she'd just bloody well get on with it so she could chomp into her lamb chops before they got cold. Didn't her sister realise that enthusiasm was much easier to muster up on a full tummy?

"As well as the original homestead, there are three cabins and a dormitory building on the grounds, which was once run as a youth hostel! They'll be perfect for Cuisine with Carlton's."

Everyone ooh-ed and aah-ed as Jennifer articulated every detail of her renovation plans. And sure enough, Rebecca had to suffer through it until the microwave-reheated lamb chops were at last served.

"Well, what do you think?" Derbhilla brought her out of her reverie by flapping a tea towel accented with a grinning Molly Malone selling her cockles and whatnots.

"It's great," Rebecca answered with a grin. "I could just about open an Irish gift shop when I get home." Then, feeling her eyes begin to fill up, she surprised her friend by enveloping her in a big bear hug. "Thanks heaps, Derbhilla. I'll miss you."

With her own eyes beginning to prickle, Derbhilla stepped back from the embrace. "You'll be back in two weeks, you big eejit." She was saying it for her benefit as much as Rebecca's. "Besides, with today's modern technology, sure I can text you from Galway and I've had a word with Niall from IT. He said he'll let my emails through to your Hotmail address while you're away."

"Ha!" Rebecca exclaimed. "I told you he fancies you. Have you told Shane there's an IT man who is just itching to get his hands on your hard drive?"

Derbhilla laughed, and then held up a pair of shorts with a leprechaun saying, *Help yourself to me pot o' gold.*

"If you don't watch it," Derbhilla threatened, "I'm going to buy these shorts for Ciaran and tell him they are a gift from you! Who knows—it might just give the pair of you the push you need to sort that chemistry over-load you've got going on once and for all."

Chapter Seven

"SURPRISE!" MELISSA shouted as Rebecca ventured out of her bedroom, mug in hand, en route to the kitchen. Her eyes swung from the oversized suitcase, standing to attention by the front door, back to her friend, who had a pair of Jackie O style sunglasses perched on top of her head despite the horrendously early hour.

Melissa was wearing a white hoodie over her favourite blue lounge pants, the ones that she always wore for flying. "Are you going on holiday too, then?" Rebecca rubbed her eyes, still half-asleep despite having stood under their so-called power shower for ten minutes. Bugger bloody terrorists; thanks to them, she had to be at the airport at six in the morning, two whole hours before her flight. At this ungodly hour, she wondered why Melissa was still standing in the hallway, grinning like a nutter.

Forcing herself to pay attention to what her friend was saying, she caught the words, "I'm coming to New Zealand too!"

What? Her befuddled thought processes went into overdrive. *Had Melissa just said something about coming home too?* Wide awake now, she held her hand up, ordering Melissa to shut up before demanding, "What on earth are you on about?"

"I just told you." She sighed exasperatedly. "I'm coming home too."

"Yeah, yeah, I heard that bit."

"I couldn't let you go on your own. It wouldn't have been fair."

"How very noble of you," Rebecca muttered, but Melissa—oblivious of the sarcastic undertones—just swatted her comment away.

"Don't sweat it, Becs. That's what being friends is all about. Besides, I am more than due for some time off." Being the martyr that she was, Melissa continued, "Tamara was reluctant to let me go. Then she realised that it was a sacrifice for me, too, what with missing the Galway Races and for what?"

Giving a shrug of surrender, she looked wide-eyed at her friend. "Two weeks in the heart of the South Island's winter, but I couldn't let you look after the rug rats all on your lonesome, now could I?"

Rebecca gazed back at her friend in disbelief. Melissa truly believed what she was saying—and she wasn't finished yet either!

"Oh, and Tamara pulled some strings and got my seat upgraded to first class." Bending down to pick up her case, Melissa opened the door. "Gotta dash. Tamara organised a car to take me to the airport, and I'd offer you a ride but seeing as you're not quite ready…" Her voice trailed off, and she blew a kiss over her shoulder as she called out, "Bye! See you at home."

AT ELEVEN FIFTEEN THAT morning, Rebecca was trying to catch her breath as she stowed her hand luggage away in the overhead compartment. She'd barely made it. Heathrow Airport was such a navigational nightmare. Standing guard over her now, like an underfed watchdog, was the flight attendant. Bitch, Rebecca thought, stealing a glance at her out of the corner of her eye. There'd been no need for her to be so horrible. It was Fiona, her travel agent's, fault. She shouldn't have allowed her precious little time to catch her connecting flight.

The flight attendant's long and narrow face was buried in at least a centimetre of tangerine foundation, and with her hair pulled back into a severe ponytail, she was reminiscent of an orange felt-tip pen. When Rebecca had first thundered down the corridor, she'd breathed into her walkie-talkie, "Our missing passenger has arrived, Captain." Like she'd just apprehended England's Most Wanted. She then followed it up with, "You're holding the entire plane up," before marching down the jet's narrow aisle with Rebecca trailing apologetically behind, feeling like a naughty child being led out of the assembly.

With her eyes steadfastly fixed on the little lights on the floor in front of her, Rebecca had managed to avoid the angry stares of her restless fellow passengers. They'd been buckled in and ready for take-off since ten forty-five that morning. She now knew what it felt like to walk the green mile, she'd thought ruefully as Felt-tip at last came to a halt somewhere near the wings.

Opening the overhead locker, the flight attendant held her hand out and snapped, "Give me your bags."

No way, José, Rebecca thought, glaring back at her. She wasn't letting that harridan anywhere near her bags. Inevitably, a tug-o-war had ensued which, through sheer bloody-minded determination, Rebecca won.

Felt-tip wasn't a gracious loser, judging by the snorting sounds emitted through her nostrils. Nor by the looks of things was she going to go away until Rebecca's rear was in its rightful window seat. Rebecca snapped the luggage compartment shut before flicking her eyes over her seated flight-mates. *Great—Fatty and Skinny*, she thought as she slipped nimbly past Skinny, who had the aisle seat. Pausing, she eyed the rotund female passenger ensconced in the middle seat. Getting past her was going to be a tad more challenging. She cleared her throat. "Er, excuse me?"

The woman looked up at her with the panicked expression of an overweight deer caught in headlights. If she hadn't been in such a bad temper, she'd have felt sorry for her. "Could I just squeeze past you, please?"

Tiny beads of sweat popped up on the woman's forehead as, licking her lips and breathing in heavily, she attempted to manoeuvre her legs over to the left. It made no difference whatsoever to the miniscule space, and there was no way Rebecca's size twelve frame would squeeze through. With a great deal of huffing and puffing, the woman tried angling her legs over to the right. It was a marginal improvement and Rebecca decided to seize the moment before she got lynched by an angry mob. A split second later, her nose was buried in a strange man's scalp while her chest was jammed up against the folded dinner tray. Her bottom was blocking off the large woman's airspace and Felt-tip was beginning to lose what little was left of her composure as she shouted, "Would you just sit down!"

"I'm stuck," Rebecca mumbled as her breath sent wisps of sparse black hair wafting in the air. The man whose personal space she had just invaded was in a frenzy, trying to twist around to see what had just landed on his head. She grimaced, momentarily distracted from her dilemma, and made a mental note to remember to tell him she knew a good shampoo for flaky scalp when this nightmare was over.

"Pardon me?" snapped Felt-tip, tapping her nails ominously on the headrest in front of her.

"I'm stuck," she repeated. Then, seeing Felt-tip's disbelieving look out of the corner of her eye, she decided to spell it out for her. "S-T-U-C-K—STUCK! I can't bloody well move—got it!"

Panic set in as Rebecca sensed the drama unfolding, and hundreds of pairs of eyes swivelled towards her. Felt-tip was quiet for a moment as she assessed the situation. There was nothing in the manual on how to deal with a situation like this and screaming, "Move both your fat arses now!" most likely wouldn't earn her any brownie points with Captain James. Perhaps giving the not-so-fat one a good shove would shift her.

"Ouch!" squealed Rebecca a moment later, still firmly wedged in place.

Okay, that didn't work. Time for Plan B. Felt-tip grabbed Rebecca's arm and yanked it violently towards her.

"YEOW! I think you've dislocated my arm!"

Damn. The attendant bit her lip nervously, deciding to ease up before she found herself being sued. Dislocating a passenger's arm wouldn't look good on her unblemished service record, even if it were due to extenuating circumstances. She swiped angrily at a stray hair that was making a bid for freedom and looked frantically around the plane for help.

Ah—there was Megan, a useless lump of a girl, but better than nothing. The younger flight attendant was standing over by the toilets with a lifejacket on in readiness for the safety spiel. Waving her over, she quickly explained the situation and instructed her to put her arms around her waist for support. "Take the life jacket off first!" Felt-tip screeched. "The sodding thing will probably inflate otherwise."

"Oh, right," mumbled Megan. She was the last person you'd want in a crisis for her head became a muddled mess when asked to think. If it hadn't been for Captain James putting in a kind word for her with the 'powers that be' she'd never have gotten out of the training centre and onto an actual plane. Smiling to herself as she pulled the vest up over her head and tossed it aside, she recalled how Captain James had told her that her in-flight service was the best he'd ever had.

"Right—on the count of three!" Felt-tip yelled. "One, two, three—PULL!" With her face buried in dandruff man's scalp, Rebecca wondered if the crowd that had now gathered in the aisle would notice if she burst into tears. Probably not, she surmised. They were all far too busy joining in the circus by shouting out their instructions to the ringmaster: "Try lifting her up and then out." "No! That won't work. Keep pulling her towards you." "I think her rear end is too wide to squeeze through that way. She has to back out then climb over. It's the only way." And on they went, discussing various parts of her anatomy until a booming voice diffused the comments.

"Good morning, this is your captain speaking. We seem to be experiencing a slight seating problem, which we hope to have rectified shortly. In the meantime, I would request that all passengers return to their seats in preparation for take-off."

Like scolded children, the crowd dispersed.

"I can't breathe," gasped the size-challenged woman.

"Move your bottom to the right a bit," directed Felt-tip.

"I can't," hissed Rebecca. "Besides, I'm only a size twelve; she'll survive."

Raising one thinly drawn eyebrow, Felt-tip shook her head. *Size twelve? The poor girl was delusional.* Five minutes later, as the British Airways jumbo jet rocked on the runway to thunderous applause, Rebecca slumped down into her seat. She felt bruised and battered both physically and emotionally, but she was alive.

Six, seven, or possibly even eight hours later, she was fervently wishing she wasn't. She sat with her nose glued to the porthole window, anxiously keeping watch for any sign of their first stop on the way to New Zealand: Los Angeles. Every time they hit the slightest bit of turbulence, the woman trumpeted like a baby elephant and grabbed hold of her arm. She had introduced herself as Una and after their shared near-death experience, had decided she was Rebecca's new best friend.

Amidst Una's assaults, an annoying toddler kept popping his snot-nosed face over the seat in front of Rebecca and blowing raspberries. It had been cute at first, but when he dribbled into her choice of 'fish in white sauce' lunch and with her temper already frayed, she snapped for him to sit down. The toddler's mum had peered through the gap in the seats and given her the evil eye. She'd elbowed her husband, who had poked his uncomfortably familiar head over his seat and said, "If I were you, love, I'd be keeping a low profile." His rounded face bore an uncanny resemblance to Tony Soprano; perhaps she'd be best to keep her bit of anti-dandruff shampoo advice to herself then.

Bugger bloody Melissa. Her eyes were glued to the inky sky. She could just picture her friend stretched out on a reclining chair in her comfortable but elegant lounging pants. She was probably sipping on a cold glass of champagne and eating big fat strawberries, or whatever it was people did in first class, right this very minute. It wasn't bloody fair, she thought, wiping away the mist her breath had left behind on the small window. Not to mention that she hadn't decided how she felt about Melissa having invited herself along for the ride. The extra help with the kids on Melissa's part would be good, but then, doing anything selfless wasn't exactly Melissa's style.

She'd probably lie around for the next two weeks, enjoying the view and cadging free food from Carlton's if she could be bothered to get off her bum to get it. *Yep, that would be right.* Rebecca frowned as a picture of herself scurrying back and forth to wait on Her Highness sprang to mind. A whiff of something eggy and unpleasant drifted past her, and she waved her hand in front of her nose; she was pretty sure Una had just passed wind. Violent and, unlike the woman herself, silent.

Stumbling into Los Angeles International Airport's transit lounge, Rebecca breathed in great big lungsful of the closest thing to fresh air she'd smelt in what felt like days. With only an hour to spare, she found a row of spare seats and buried her nose in the bestseller she'd bought specifically for the long flight home. Thanks to Una's constant trumpeting, though, she had not yet had a chance to lose herself in it. Enjoying the sensation of stretching out, she felt comforted by the knowledge that the last leg of her journey could in no way be as nightmarish as the previous one.

Nor was it. Everything had gone just swimmingly until the Boeing 747 touched down at Christchurch International Airport.

"Get off! Go away. Shoo—go on, get!" Rebecca hissed at the beagle who was having way too much fun sticking his randy little nose up her nether regions to take the hint. His handler, a stern New Zealand customs officer, had taken note of the exchange and through narrowed eyes sized her up. Behind her, the bags on the carousel kept whirring around and around because none of her fellow passengers were the slightest bit interested in collecting the rest of their belongings. Why would they be when the airport was providing free in-house entertainment?

The officer made his way over with one hand resting on his walkie-talkie in case he needed reinforcements. Aware of his attentive audience, he put on a big show of clearing his throat.

"A-hem, could you step this way please, miss?" It was more of an order than a request.

Jeez, give a man a little authority and it goes straight to his head, Rebecca fumed, eyeballing him back. He was on the stout side of fifty, and she recognised his type. A frustrated wannabe cop for sure. Unfortunately, batting her eyelashes wasn't going to hold much sway here, she concluded.

"You can bring your bags with you, miss." He gripped her firmly by her elbow.

"But why? I haven't done anything wrong!" She so wasn't in the mood for this.

"That's what they all say, miss. Now, we can do this quietly, or you can create even more of a scene than you have done already. It's up to you."

Rebecca's eyes swept round the crowded arrivals hall and were met by a sea of accusing faces all glaring right back at her. "I'm not a drug smuggler, if that's what you're all thinking," she shrilled. Feeling the panic beginning to rise, she began waffling, "It's this bloody dog here that's got issues. For goodness' sake, the last time I smoked a joint was in 1991 and I ate a whole Madeira cake afterwards. Do I look like I eat whole cakes on a regular basis?"

The jury was apparently out on that one, and the dog handler was now looking seriously unimpressed. Unlike his dog, still engaged in the act of nose diving and snuffling before coming up for air sporadically.

"For goodness' sake, get your bloody dog off of me!"

"Down, Rollo!" Rollo reluctantly obeyed, and the officer led Rebecca away, announcing to the curious onlookers, "Show's over, folks."

One hour and one bag search—and thankfully no other kind of search—later, Customs Officer George conceded that perhaps Rollo had been feeling a tad repressed. Next time she might think twice about hoarding her complimentary cheese and crackers in her bum bag.

Chapter Eight

"THERE SHE IS—LOOK! Oh, thank goodness she's alright." Pamela Loughton began jumping up and down, waving madly from the arrival area. "Rebecca, sweetheart! Yoo-hoo, over here!" Giving her husband a violent nudge forward, she ordered him to "Grab her, Dick." Having spent the last forty years doing as he was told, Dick Loughton stumbled forward to meet his youngest daughter.

The hordes of people who had been milling around in anticipation of the flight from Los Angeles had long since dispersed, making Dick easy to spot. Decked out in his customary beige slacks, whiter than white sneakers, and black windbreaker, he was a sight for Rebecca's very sore eyes. Upon falling into his open arms, she felt a surge of love and then a sense of gratitude that Trinny and Susannah hadn't gotten to him too. Over his shoulder, she spied her mum smiling and waving.

Ah yes, the style gurus would be proud of her mother's ensemble of a peasant skirt with colour-coordinated top and this winter's must-have, knee-high caramel-coloured boots.

"Come on then, love," Rebecca's dad said, plucking her off him and taking hold of her trolley. "Mum can't wait to see you."

"We thought you'd missed your flight. What happened, love? Are you alright?" Pamela cupped her daughter's face in her hands, her familiar blue eyes creased with concern. Thirty hours of sleep deprivation suddenly caught up with Rebecca and, bursting into tears, she slumped down onto her mother's ample bosom just like she had done when she was little. Safely snuggled in, she sputtered all the details.

"It was horrible, Mum, just horrible."

Dick patted her back reassuringly. "There, there, love. You're with your mummy and daddy now. Let's go home."

Sandwiched between her parents, she allowed herself to be led out to the car park.

"What do you reckon to a nice cup of tea and a slice of Mum's cake when we get home, love?" her dad asked as he heaved one of her cases into the boot.

"Chocolate cake?" she managed to snuffle out hopefully.

TWENTY MINUTES LATER, they were pulling into Noel Place, and Rebecca smiled fondly at its familiar sweep of front lawns and letterboxes. She'd grown up here, playing out on the street in the days when you still could, along with all the other neighbourhood kids. There'd been a gang of them back then who would gather at the Ryans' house for morning tea before working their way round the little cul-de-sac until they'd stuffed themselves full of treats. Nothing much appeared to have changed in the two years she'd been away, but as the little Honda hatchback crawled towards their house, there was a loud sniff from the passenger's seat.

"They just had to go one better than everybody else." Pamela inclined her head towards the large conservatory protruding from the side of the Ellis family's house at number seven. That certainly hadn't been there before she went away, Rebecca thought, amused at her mother's petty neighbourhood rivalry. Some things never change.

"Ever since their Timothy made it big with that KY2 bug—"

"Y2K bug, Mum."

"If you say so, dear—they've had grand notions. I mean, look at them." Mr and Mrs Ellis were reclining in matching cane armchairs, sharing a pot of tea. They raised their teacups in a salute as the Loughtons drove past, and Pamela graced them with a queen-like wave of her hand.

Once they were safely past, Pamela carried on with her monologue. "The Smyths have gone. They moved out to Rangiora to be closer to their eldest. Do you remember Roanne?"

Rebecca nodded, remembering a big lioness of a girl who was far better to have as a friend rather than foe.

"She's expecting. The baby's due in April. It's her first, and her husband's a bit of a dead loss, you know."

Letting the comforting sounds of her mum's voice wash over her as her dad indicated left and pulled up the drive of number thirteen, Rebecca sighed contentedly. *Home sweet home.*

It wasn't much to look at, the Loughton family home. A house plonked in the middle of its quarter acre of well-tended lawn, it was built in the 1960s. Clad in tired red brick and shaped like a shoebox, it had three bedrooms and a tiled roof. Its selling point was the second bathroom. Dick often congratulated his forward thinking as he tended his dahlias. The best thing they ever did, getting that put in. One wouldn't call it a pretty house, but it had all the qualities that mattered in a home. It oozed a welcoming warmth, and it was solid and dependable, just like its mainstays, her mum and dad.

"Come on in, Rebecca, love," her mother urged after unlocking the door and stepping over the threshold into the dark L-shaped hall. Following her in, Rebecca suddenly found herself enveloped in a bear hug. "Welcome home, sweetheart. We've missed you." Pamela blinked back tears.

"Out the way," Dick ordered as he staggered in behind them with Rebecca's cases. "Good grief, my girl. What have you got in these? A man?" He chortled to himself, clearly pleased with his witty joke, but Rebecca wasn't listening. Something had caught her eye.

There, still hanging in pride of place right where one couldn't miss it, was what she'd fondly nicknamed 'The Adams Family Portrait'. It depicted the Loughton family as they had been some time in the late '80s. They were modelling matching high-waisted, stonewashed denim jeans. Their jackets (also stonewashed denim) were slung casually over their shoulders. Pamela had insisted they all wear white crew-necked T-shirts—tucked in, of course. The four of them were immortalised forever by the photographer's soft tones. Even Dad's hair was big back then. Rebecca grinned, remembering how they'd gone for the sitting, just before Jennifer left home, at their mother's insistence.

An awkward teenager at the time, it had been bad enough being seen out in public with her parents and big sister, let alone being made to pose under an autumnal tree in Hagley Park with them. As cringeworthy as the picture was, it was also comforting to see it again. Spying her daughter smiling up at it, Pamela puffed up with pride. "It's a real talking point, our family portrait. I get loads of comments about it, you know."

"I'll just bet you do, Mum." Rebecca's tongue was in her cheek.

True to their word, in no time at all Rebecca was sitting at the informal pine table situated in the corner of what, two decades previous, had been a state-of-the-art kitchen. The mahogany six-seater, not so fondly remembered from her childhood, now sat gathering dust in the dining room cum living room. Shovelling a piece of cake into her mouth and spraying crumbs everywhere, Rebecca filled her parents in on her flight from hell.

"Put it behind you, dear. Another piece of cake?"

She nodded and her mother looked pleased with herself as she sliced off another good-sized wedge. "You always were a good eater."

Rebecca rolled her eyes. *Here we go.*

"Of course, these days, Plunket and the like would probably say you were one of those obese children they're always talking about. But you know, Rebecca, in my day we liked to see a bit of cushioning on a child. What was it we used to call her, Dick?"

"The Michelin Man," Rebecca supplied helpfully, hoping to end the conversation. "Thanks for the memories, Mum. Now can we talk about something else, please?"

"You were always overly sensitive, too. Look at the way you gave up on your dancing at the first little setback." Pamela huffed, snatching up her daughter's plate. Her tetchiness, however, was short-lived. "Oh, before I forget, something exciting happened out at the airport while we were waiting for you."

Rebecca stopped chewing and looked over at her mother expectantly.

"We saw a celeb arrive, didn't we, Dick?" Pamela elbowed her husband sharply, who promptly raised his head from the sports section and nodded his confirmation.

"Really—who?" Rebecca's interest was piqued, but her mum needed to ease up on her *Woman's Day* consumption, she thought while snatching her plate back.

"I don't know who exactly, but she was a celeb because she was wearing a pair of those big black glasses. You know, the ones the stars wear to look incognito?" Seeing her daughter's sceptical look, Pamela backed this up with, "*And* she was striding along, looking straight ahead—you know, the way famous people do. Wasn't she, Dick?"

He offered a cursory nod.

"Of course, I was all for going up to her to get an autograph, but Dad wouldn't let me in case we missed you." She pulled a face in her husband's direction.

"Wise move, Dad," Rebecca said, and a smile of complicity passed between them as he glanced over the top of his newspaper.

"She was tall and willowy." Pamela wasn't letting this go.

"Anorexic you mean, Mum?"

"Borderline, like that Beckham lass. Do you know they superimpose a bottom on her in some photos? Imagine that. In fact, I'd have sworn it was her if I hadn't been reading about her Mediterranean escape in the supermarket queue the other day. Whoever she was, she had on these lovely blue pants. Ideal for travelling because they didn't have a crease in them." While her eyes moved pointedly over her own daughter's rumpled cargoes, Rebecca put two and two together and came up with Melissa.

"Oh. I didn't recognise her with the glasses on." Pamela looked like a balloon that had just gone pop as she listened to this revelation. "Well, I'll be telling Melissa she needs to be putting a bit of weight on—she's getting too long in the tooth to be that thin."

IT'S LIKE BEING TRANSPORTED straight back to my youth, Rebecca thought while peeling back fresh flannelette sheets from her childhood bed. She'd gone straight from the cot as a toddler into the bed pushed against one wall of her former bedroom. Of course, back then the bed had seemed simply enormous, and she'd refused to go to sleep until she had her menagerie of soft toys stuffed down either side of it to keep her company. Tonight, she reflected ruefully, she'd be doing well if she managed to squeeze the hottie in next to her.

The walls of her bedroom were covered in the lilac wallpaper she'd been allowed to choose for herself all those years ago. Dangling from the ceiling was the lightshade oh so carefully picked for the way its lilac fringing matched the wallpaper. The inbuilt wardrobe at the end of her bed had, in its time, acted as a busy A&E for her dolls by day and home to the bogeyman by night. Hence, the little pink nightlight plugged into its socket by the door. Pushed up against the wall over by the window on her left was her duchess. The middle drawer with its lock and key had been privy to all her teenage angst. She'd poured it all out onto the pages of a diary and then safely locked it away.

Rebecca remembered how her dad had scoured the garage sales for that duchess, telling her it would look brand new by the time he'd finished with it. She felt ashamed now, remembering the strop she'd thrown as she shouted that she didn't want stinky old second-hand furniture. True to his word, though, Dick had put a coat of glossy white enamel on it for her and the chest of drawers with its oval mirror ended up looking pristine.

It was there that Kelly was sitting, perched right where she'd left her with strict instructions to keep a watchful eye over her room. Kelly, named after Jaclyn Smith's character in *Charlie's Angels*, was her buxom Barbie. Seeing her clad in the same red bathing suit she'd been wearing since Christmas '79, Rebecca felt a tremor of guilt; it was winter, after all.

Down the hall, she could hear *Coronation Street*'s muted theme and her mum stampeding in from the kitchen. She pictured her clutching two teas with a biscuit clenched firmly between her teeth. "Where's mine?" Dad would ask, eyeing up the biscuit as she plonked his tea down on the mahogany side table (bought to complement the dining room table) next to his La-Z-Boy.

"I've only two hands and one mouth, Dick. Go and get your own," Mum would undoubtedly reply, her eyes riveted to the old-fashioned box television.

Rebecca yanked the duvet up, trying to cover the sudden surge of loneliness she felt at knowing how comfortable her parents were in each other's company. She spied the small dark outline keeping a lonely vigil atop her duchess and whispered, "You're lucky, Kel. You don't have to worry about getting old and being all on your own." Kelly didn't respond, so Rebecca assumed she was still in a snit about the haircut she had last given her—who could blame her? It couldn't have been easy looking like Dyke Barbie for the past twenty years.

"AUNTIE BECCA... AUNTIE Becca—WAKE UP!" Jack shouted in her ear as Hannah gleefully climbed onto the bed and began using it as a trampoline. Rebecca pulled herself up into a sitting position and, despite still being half-asleep, made a successful grab for her niece, who squealed delightedly.

"Come here, you little monster. When did you get to be such a big girl? You were just a baby when I last saw you." Planting a big kiss on the top of her head, she inhaled the scent of Johnson's No More Tears shampoo and cuddled her tightly. "Ooh, I've missed you."

Hannah giggled and wriggled away, and Rebecca turned to Jack, who was standing reticently by the side of the bed. Shyly peeping out from under his fringe, he said, "Dad bought me my bike. It's a fifty cc four stroke."

Jennifer, who'd plonked herself down at the foot of the bed, mouthed, "Motocross."

Rebecca nodded. So her nephew was still mad keen on dirt bikes. Good, that meant he should like the Honda Race Rig she'd picked up for him. "Jack, open that big suitcase over there and you'll find two little surprises in it." He didn't need her to ask twice, and a moment later, there were shrieks of excitement as the new truck was revealed. Next came the Village Sweet Shop she'd bought for Hannah to add to her Sylvanian Families collection.

Smiling at the children's excitement, Rebecca took a moment to study them. At seven years old, Jack had lively brown eyes and an unruly shock of brown hair so dark that it bordered on being black. He was turning into a mini-me of his dad, only much cuter of course. She turned her attention to Hannah; while she might be Jack's sister, they were like chalk and cheese in the looks department. Even at the tender age of three, it was obvious she was going to be a beauty in the blue-eyed blonde category belonging to her mum.

"Hanny goes to school," Rebecca's niece announced proudly, trying to tear the cardboard packaging of her new toy open.

"You do not!" Jack glanced up from where he was ramming his new truck into the side of his auntie's suitcase.

"You go to a preschool, don't you, Hannah?" Rebecca mediated as a voice floated down the hallway.

"Jack, Hannah—come and see what Nana's got for you."

Picking up their new toys, they both clattered out of the room.

"Good flight, sis?" Jennifer got up and pulled the curtains open, letting the winter sun stream into the room. The rays bathed Jennifer in its weak light, making her look like an angel. As usual, she was immaculate in a military-style jacket with three-quarter length culottes and soft leather boots. Her sister didn't do casual nor cheap, Rebecca noted, taking in her chic ponytail and carefully made-up face that belied her years. She did look pale, though, despite the war paint.

"That sun's way too bright." Rebecca squinted away the light. "And no, since you're asking, it was not a good flight but I can't face talking about it until I've had a coffee."

Jennifer's grin didn't quite reach her eyes as she perched back down on the end of the bed. "Just as well Mum's made a pot of plunger especially for you then." Since this didn't have the desired effect of seeing her toss the duvet aside and leap out of bed, Jennifer further tempted, "And she's talking fry-ups." That did the trick.

Moments later as she shrugged into her dressing gown, a thought suddenly occurred to Rebecca, and she called out to Jennifer, who was already halfway down the hall. "Hey, is Mucky Mark here with you?"

The comment brought her sister scurrying back into the room, hissing. "Keep your voice down, for goodness' sake, Rebecca! And no, he's not. *Mucky Mark*, who is still my husband, thank you very much, opted to work this morning."

Rebecca snorted. "He's probably scared of what I'd do to him if I got my hands on him, as he bloody well should be." Tying her dressing gown and glancing round for her slippers she added, "I still can't get my head round it." Jennifer wouldn't meet her gaze, so she ploughed on, determined to get a reaction. "I mean, the guy's got it all. Why jeopardise everything like that and for what? A fling with his bloody secretary?" Shuddering, she slid her feet into her slippers. "Ugh. It's just too much of a midlife crisis for words."

At that, her sister's eyes went flinty. "I don't want to burst that little bubble you seem to live in, Rebecca, but life isn't always as black and white as you paint it. In the real world, grown-up people make mistakes—you'd do well to remember that from time to time." Turning on her heel, Jennifer stalked out of the room.

"You keep on defending him, and he doesn't bloody well deserve it," Rebecca threw back, stung by her sister's comments, but Jennifer didn't reply.

Chapter Nine

"MUM'S JUST TOLD ME your shadow Melissa tagged along for the ride."

"Yeah. I didn't exactly invite her but she's here now, so is it okay if she stays to give me a hand looking after the kids?"

Jennifer raised an eyebrow at this. "Sure, she can stay but good luck with getting her to pitch in." There wasn't much Rebecca could say to this because she knew her sister was right. Jennifer knew she wasn't going to get a bite, so she changed tack. "I thought you could drive yourself and the kids over in my car whenever you're ready." She pushed her empty plate away from her. "And that was great. Thanks, Mum."

"You're welcome. I'm enjoying having both my girls under the same roof for once." She beamed at her daughters. She was sporting her new shamrock apron that, in Rebecca's opinion, was a vast improvement over the hot lips one her father had chosen. Pamela rose from the table and began scraping and stacking the plates. Outside, the three women could hear the delighted shrieks of Jack and Hannah as they chased a soccer ball around the frost-covered garden with their granddad.

"Mark said goodbye to the children this morning," Jennifer explained, obviously for Rebecca's benefit. The two sisters exchanged a look behind their mother's back as she carried the empty plates over to the sink. "He's meeting me back here at lunchtime and Dad's going to drop us off at the airport."

So, in other words, bog off before lunchtime, Rebecca thought as she helped herself to another coffee.

Jennifer carried on brusquely, "I've left a detailed list of the children's routines for you at the house. Though, I think you'll find they are pretty good at telling you what's what these days."

Her half-hearted smile promptly vanished as Rebecca, unable to stop herself, remarked, "I see you're still Superwoman in the organisation stakes, then."

"And I see you're still pretty quick off the mark with the snide remarks. I think a fortnight of having to think about two little people instead of just yourself for a change will do you the world of good."

Rebecca couldn't believe what she was hearing. "Um, excuse me... who exactly is doing who the favour here?"

Jennifer was unrepentant, though. "Oh, I'm sorry I forgot what a big ask it was to expect you to take some time out of your jet-set lifestyle and be part of this family for a couple of weeks."

Scowling at her older sister, who suddenly looked every bit her age, Rebecca fumbled for a suitable rejoinder when a loud bang coming from the sink snapped her attention away from the dispute.

"Enough!" Pamela emphasised her scolding with another thump of the breadboard against the counter. "Honestly, you haven't seen each other for two years and you're at it already! Will you two ever get along?" Leaving the breadboard to recover, she began frantically scrubbing at the frying pan, sending a quiver of shame throughout the room.

Their mum was right—it had been forever since they'd seen each other, and it wasn't as if they were going to be seeing a great deal of each other on this visit home either. Surely they could make the effort for the sake of an hour or two? Eyeing Jennifer, whose own eyes were downcast as her fingers toyed with her placemat, Rebecca realised that once again she would have to be the first to surrender.

"Sorry, Mum," she apologised before asking sulkily, "So what's happening in the cooking school while you're away, Jennifer?"

Recognising a white flag when she saw one, Jennifer looked up and attempted a smile. "Betty's got that side of things under control, so you don't need to worry about it."

A picture of Jennifer's trusty sidekick sprang to mind. A warm and bustling woman, Rebecca liked her immensely. Betty's inherently good nature made her the ideal candidate to take over the tuition side of Cuisine with Carlton's. The idea of this had been that Jennifer would have more time for the marketing side of the business and, of course, more quality time with her family. Didn't work too well where Mark was concerned, Rebecca sniped silently.

Jennifer's voice began to defrost as she warmed to her theme. "There's a group coming up from Timaru to learn Thai—"

At the muffled sound of ringing, Rebecca pushed her chair back and stood up, looking around her. "That's my phone. Where's my bag, Mum?" she asked, cutting her sister short. Jennifer frowned and then got up and went outside as Pamela pointed at the sideboard where she'd slung her bag down in her rush to get at the chocolate cake the previous afternoon. "Right where you left it."

"Oh right, ta." Rebecca rummaged around until, holding her phone aloft, she squinted at the display panel, unable to make out the name. "Oh, please don't tell me I'm old enough to need bifocals," she muttered to herself.

"Hello?" she addressed the receiver.

"Hiya, babes!" Melissa sang back at her. "Did you have a good flight?"

"No, I didn't, since you're asking." Rebecca opted to leave it at that. There was no point ruining the day by reliving the embarrassment for Melissa's entertainment.

"Oh, that's a shame. First class was brill. I was born to it," Melissa raved.

"Good for you."

"You sound a bit snarky; everything okay?"

"Fine, fine." Rebecca stifled a yawn. "It's just the jet lag setting in."

"Oh, you don't get jet lag flying first class," her best friend dropped in airily before whispering, "Now listen, sweetie."

Rebecca pressed the phone closer.

"I stayed at Mum and Dad's last night and, to be honest, I can't wait to get away. Mum's doing my head in already, but I have managed to talk her into loaning me her car. You know, the red Alfa Romeo? So the plan is I am going to do the rounds of all the old gang, and I'll see you over at Jennifer's later tonight."

"Oh right," Rebecca replied flatly. She certainly had her day planned out, and it didn't include helping her settle in with the kids.

"Now, don't worry about doing dinner for me, sweets, because I don't know what time I'll get there but if there happens to be a spare plate—"

She was infuriating, Rebecca thought, cutting her short. "Yes, yes. Look, I've got to go."

"Melissa, I take it?" Pamela asked, turning away from the sink to look at her daughter as she shoved her phone back in her bag.

"Uh-huh." A thought struck her. "What time are Auntie Sue and Uncle Bob getting here?" Her mother's brother was bearable—but only just. As for his wife Sue, she was a nightmare, and Rebecca planned on being long gone before they arrived to house-sit.

"Sue said they were leaving around ten-ish, and it's about a three-hour drive from Waimate, so they should be here around one thirty, or two at the latest. Are you going to wait and say hello before you head off? They'd love to see you."

"Er, no. I think I should make tracks soon, Mum, and get the children settled in." Rebecca didn't meet her mother's eye, but she heard her sigh.

"It's such a shame, the bad timing. I don't know—you finally come home... You're only here for two weeks, and your father and I have to head away just as you arrive..."

"Listen, Mum—you and Dad always said you were going to do a cruise around the islands when he retired. You have been planning this holiday for years. Besides, we've got two whole days together when you get back before I have to fly out. Go—you deserve it, okay? I will be fine, the children will be fine, and you probably won't give us a second thought once you board that boat."

"Cruise liner, darling. You couldn't call the *Pacific Princess* a 'boat'. As for not giving you girls a second thought, you'll realise one day when you're a mother what a ridiculous thing that is to say." She gave a pained sigh. "I still don't know why your sister feels the need to take a holiday without the children, right now of all times."

"What do you mean by 'right now of all times'? That's the whole point of my being here—so she and Mark can go on holiday."

"I know that, but Jack's been acting up lately and with your, ahem, dare I say it?"

"Go on, Mum, be a devil."

"Don't be sarcastic; it doesn't suit you. What I was going to say was that you've hardly had a lot of experience on the parenting front. It's not what I'd consider the best timing for your sister and Mark to head away."

"Thanks for the vote of confidence, Mum."

Walking away to prevent her mother from seeing the big eye-roll that followed, she made her way out to the driveway. Pamela followed her to where Dick was unloading Jennifer's bags from the boot of her shiny four-wheel drive beast. Of course, Rebecca couldn't resist voicing her opinion as to the reasoning behind anyone needing a five-seater vehicle to cart two children around in being beyond her. Pamela leapt to her eldest daughter's defence, saying that everybody got round in big Land Cruisers these days. Everybody except her mum and dad, Rebecca thought ruefully, glancing over at their reliable little Honda. As a cool wind blew in, the bystanders watched in amusement while it wrestled with the strands of hair her father had obviously combed over his bald spot.

"What's with Dad's hairdo, Mum?"

"You know full well he's sensitive about his hair loss."

Indeed she did, Rebecca thought, smirking. The subject was taboo. All it took was a glance in the direction of his dome and he'd go all red in the face and start spluttering, "What? What are you looking at?" Speaking of which, Dad was starting to go red now as he tried repeatedly to slam the boot shut.

"Maybe the timing isn't the best, Mum, but Jen and Mark do need a break. It can't be easy for them," she said through gritted teeth. "They're both so busy with their careers and the children that it will do them good to spend some quality time together, just the two of them."

Her mother raised a sceptical eyebrow. "I suppose I should be grateful that despite all your squabbling, you girls at least stick up for each other." She managed a small smile. "Do you remember that rake of a lad your sister used to date? The one who spent more time doing his hair than she did? What was his name?"

"Peter and it was the 1980s, Mum. Men had big hair back then, even Dad."

"Don't compare your father to Peter the Poofter!"

"Mum! That is so un-PC!"

Pamela giggled girlishly. "It was your father's pet name for him. Oh and by the way, I know your sister used to sneak out to meet him."

Rebecca was gobsmacked. Sneaking out to meet her boyfriend was the only truly rebellious thing Jennifer had ever done throughout her teenage years, and their mother had known about it all along. She recalled how she had tiptoed into her big sister's room and found her with one leg hanging over the windowsill and the other one on its way out behind it. "I'm in love," Jennifer had declared passionately in explanation before handing her five dollars hush money.

"So how did you find out?"

"That's ancient history now, but my point is that you covered for her then, and I know you're covering for her now."

Chapter Ten

"HANNAH JANE CARLTON, get to bed now!" Hauling herself up off the couch for the umpteenth time that evening, Rebecca frogmarched her niece back up the stairs.

"But I don't want to go to bed, Auntie Becca," the little girl stated matter-of-factly, as if this in itself should be reason enough for her to be allowed to stay up.

Rebecca's patience had just about frayed right through, and she found herself snapping, "Now you listen to me, miss—" Breaking off mid-sentence, she realised with horror that she sounded just like her mother.

Oh, crumbs! Does that mean it's true what they say about daughters eventually turning into their mothers? Mightily disturbed, she tipped her niece back into bed and pulled the bed covers up around her. "It's nearly ten o'clock, Hannah, and you are only three and a half years old, so that means it is time for sleep."

"But I wanna milk."

"No, you've already had a drink."

"Just a little milk in my cup."

Seeing her small face beginning to crumple and scared that she'd wake Jack—who was in his room next door—if she began howling, Rebecca backed down. "Just this once, okay, and then it is bedtime."

Popping Hannah's special Beatrix Potter cup in the microwave for thirty seconds and watching it twirl around, she felt like she'd just filmed a segment for one of those awful parenting shows. She was one of those parents who cripple under their toddler's tyranny, and the viewers sit at home, shaking their heads. The microwave beeped and, retrieving the cup, Rebecca traipsed back upstairs. As she passed Jack's bedroom, a tousled head appeared round the door.

"What do you want, Jack? I thought you were asleep," she asked irritably.

"I want to go to the toilet. Auntie Becca?"

"Yes?" she answered wearily.

"You look funny when you're mad, sorta like that."

Following the direction his finger was pointing in, she was treated to a view of Pinky, the family cat's, posterior as she sauntered towards the stairs, tail held high. Giggling, Jack raced into the bathroom, banging the door shut behind him. That was the second time this month she'd been told her face was reminiscent of a cat's bum, she brooded. Should she be worried?

By ten thirty, the house was quiet at last. Rebecca stretched out on her sister's taupe-coloured, Italian leather five-seater. What was it with Jennifer and five-seaters? Perhaps she had a subconscious yearning for a third child, she mused. She reached over to pour herself a healthy glass of the Sauvignon Blanc she'd found chilling in the fridge earlier. A welcome note had been attached to it.

Enjoying the wine and soothed by the warm, earthy tones Jennifer had picked out for the living room, Rebecca felt herself relax for the first time since she'd left her parents' house at lunchtime. After sobbing her heart out and having to be physically dragged from her mother, Hannah had gone to sleep in the back of the wagon. Her brother, meanwhile, hadn't given Jennifer so much as a backwards glance. He was eager, Rebecca had assumed, to get on with the adventure of having his auntie with them.

Now she was beginning to think her assessment was wrong—little Jack seemed more interested in pushing her buttons than spending quality time with her.

Jack had been unusually quiet on the drive over earlier that afternoon, allowing Rebecca to soak in the scenery. Once they'd passed by the smattering of new subdivisions on the city's periphery, they found themselves sandwiched between craggy hills to the left and flat marshland that stretched out to the sea on the distant right. In her rear-view mirror, she could make out the ragged outline of the Southern Alps decked out in their winter snowsuits despite the mild weather for this time of year. She had forgotten how breathtaking her homeland was.

Little River's blink-and-you'd-miss-it stretch of cafés and galleries heralded the end of the flat road, and they had begun a spiralling ascent.

"Bloody cyclists!" Rebecca had spluttered at a pair of lovebirds who were not only insisting on wearing head-to-toe matching Spandex but on riding double breast, too. Her little outburst prompted Jack to speech, even if was only to state the obvious: "You swore, Auntie Becca."

"Yes, I know, Jack. I'm sorry but honestly, if a truck was heading the other way, well..."

"Our blood and guts would be splattered all over the road?" Her nephew filled in the blanks nicely for her as a sign caught her eye.

"Look—we're nearly at the Hilltop! Shall we stop and have a look?" Ignoring his indifferent shrug, she indicated left as they approached the old pub.

Pulling into a bay next to a tour bus that had also just pulled in with a cargo of sleepy-looking Japanese tourists, she glanced back over her shoulder. Hannah's head was still lolling over to one side, and her mouth was slack. Satisfied that her niece was out for the count, she turned back and asked, "Coming then?" Jack unbuckled his seatbelt and clambered out of the car. She took that as a yes, and a moment later she was standing with her arms resting on his shoulders, breathing in the volcanic vista spread out before them.

I've stood here looking at this same view in summer, spring, autumn, and now winter, she reflected. Each season served up its distinct flavour. In spring, the hills framing the basin were lush and green with leaves beginning to sprout from the grapevines that snaked their way over the countryside. Summertime made the vines heavy and ripe for the picking while the hills were bleached the colour of wheat. The water filling the basin from which they rose would reflect plump white clouds resting in the blue South Island sky. Come autumn, the tones intensified with the vines turning port red and the earth a sharply contrasting green. The water would lose its aquamarine sparkle to become deep and mysterious like a Scottish loch. Today, the branches of the grapevines were knotty and tired, and the hills muddy, but there was a wildness to it all that took her breath away.

Listening to the excited jabbering of the Japanese tourists who were now wide awake, she felt absurdly proud, as though she had had some input into the landscape laid out before them. Then, Jack broke the spell by wriggling away from her to join in the jostling crowd intent on peeping through the telescopes.

REBECCA CHEERED AS they rounded the last bend and drove into the village of Akaroa. Slowing the car to a crawl past the big old pub on her right, she caught fleeting glimpses of the still waters of the harbour. It peeked at her between the melting pot of quaint craft shops, art galleries, and al fresco cafés. The businesses had moved into the original colonial structures clustered along Rue Lavaud. Arriving at Rue Balguerie, she swung left away from the hub. She'd always loved the charming mix of paint-peeling, bougainvillea-clad cottages that forged their way upwards along this road until the dense greenery of the bush took over. It was up here, partially hidden by nature, that the Carlton family lived, overseers of the undulating hills and harbour.

"We're home." She had smiled as the sign announcing Cuisine with Carlton's swung gently in the chilly afternoon breeze, inviting them in.

When Jennifer and Mark had first moved here, the steep incline that was their driveway had been a 'take your life in your hands' kind of experience. It had been filled with potholes and loose stones, but that was a distant memory. Pale terracotta stamped concrete swept away from the main road. Guests were greeted with a view of the oversized log cabin that once upon a time had housed rows of bunk beds but was now home to Cuisine with Carlton's Cooking School on their left. To their right was the huddle of rustic two-bedroom log cabins and at the end of the driveway, the restored grandeur of what Jennifer had named the 'Cook's Quarters' waited for them to register their arrival.

Seeing their car pull up outside the house, Betty had excused herself from the classroom. The aroma of coriander and coconut had snuck out behind her and carried on the late afternoon breeze to where Rebecca was unloading the children. Sniffing appreciatively, she turned and caught sight of the older woman making her way up the garden path towards her.

"Hi, Betty. Long time, no see." Rebecca waved before unlocking the front door so Jack could attend to his urgent call of nature. Turning back, she saw that Hannah had thrown herself into Betty's arms. You'd think she hadn't seen her for weeks instead of just one day, she thought, smiling at her niece's effusive greeting.

"Welcome home, dear!" Betty grinned broadly at her as she placed Hannah back down and wrapped Rebecca in a warm hug. "Let me get a look at you." Releasing her, she held her at arm's length. "Goodness me, what's your secret? You haven't changed a bit, and it's been what, two years?"

Rebecca nodded—Betty was nice enough to ignore the extra poundage acquired over the years. "It's whizzed by, I know. It's so great to see you again, Betty, and you look great."

The plump cook guffawed. "A lovely thing to say, dear, but either you or my bathroom scale is telling porkies." Betty had indeed increased a couple sizes from when Rebecca had last seen her, but who could blame her? If I did what she did all day, I'd be the size of a bus, Rebecca thought. Her stomach rumbled as she caught a whiff of coconut floating past.

"What's that smell? It's divine."

"Thai green curry. I'll bring a bowl over for your dinner if you like."

True to her word, Betty had appeared in the house half an hour later, looking like Little Red Riding Hood's granny as she peered over the top of her glasses and handed Rebecca an aromatic container. Just like Little Red Riding Hood's granny, though, appearances could be deceptive. Betty's cooking skills had seen her employed everywhere from a highland castle, to a mansion in Bel Air, to a sheik's palace in Dubai. Somehow she'd found time in between jobs to get married and raise a family. She'd come out of retirement to take the job at Carlton's, claiming that lazing on the couch with a good book wasn't all it was cracked up to be.

"Apparently she was driving her husband bonkers at home," Jennifer had whispered to Rebecca conspiratorially. "His loss is my gain; I'd be sunk without her."

While Rebecca dined on Thai, the kids had eaten beans on toast with eyes glued to the plasma television. Though Rebecca warned them that next time they'd eat at the table, she figured caving this once might get her in their good graces. Betty's eyes had crinkled with a suppressed smile as she watched Rebecca's discipline skills vanish when under pressure.

"I think you're wonderful, Rebecca, coming home to look after them like you have." Her eyes grew serious, and she lowered her voice as she added, "I don't know the ins and outs of what has been going on between Jennifer and Mark. I don't want to either, but what I do know is that children sense when things aren't right between their parents and those two have had a rough time of it lately. Especially Jack, so, if having their tea in front of the tele keeps them happy, then I'm all for it."

When evening had approached, Rebecca passed out her Irish souvenirs and rounded up the children for bed. Delighted with her new leprechaun paperweight, Betty kissed the children on the tops of their heads as she passed through the living room. Rebecca trailed behind her out to the hall following the swathe of the antique Persian runner to the front door. Switching the outside light on, she'd been planning on seeing the older woman to her car when they'd been distracted by raucous laughter. Squinting into the night, they sourced the laughter to two elderly ladies sitting, despite the cool night air, at the picnic table on the porch of the 'Russian Tea Room'.

Cabin one, as it was otherwise known, was decorated in the same glitzy, decadent style as its New York namesake. Jennifer hadn't laughed when Rebecca once suggested christening cabin two the 'Gordon Ramsay'.

"It's a famous London restaurant," Rebecca insisted, but Jennifer had refused, instead opting for The Ivy and Sydney's Rockpool, saying they gave her more scope for decoration.

"Fluffy Duck!" shrieked one of the ladies and Rebecca watched in disbelief as the old dear banged the spirit glass she was holding down hard on the solid wood table. She then proceeded to knock its contents back in one gulp.

Turning towards Betty, who was also watching the proceedings across the lawn with some interest, she asked, "Uh, who exactly is it that's staying this week?"

Betty chortled. "The Timaru branch of the Nifty Knitters. Though it would seem Lois and Ivy over there are keen to do something other than knit."

"The Nifty Knitters?"

"Yes, you heard right," Betty assured her. "I'd never heard of them either, but apparently they're a nationwide organisation. Of course, trips away are usually reserved for knitting conventions, but according to their president Maureen, there were rebellious rumblings when the annual trip to Invercargill rolled round. Maureen's granddaughter did a course with us here last year and raved about it, so Maureen suggested they do something different."

"Like Thai cookery?"

"Exactly—and Ivy and Lois have thrown themselves into the spirit of it, literally. That Mekhong's lethal stuff."

"What's Mekhong?" Rebecca asked.

"Thai whiskey. I had a couple of bottles left over from my last trip to Phuket, and I thought leaving a bottle in each of the cabins for a nightcap added an authentic touch. I had no idea they'd play drinking games with it!"

Laughing, Rebecca had cupped her hands on either side of her mouth and called out, "You go, girls," receiving a bottoms up in return.

"Don't encourage them; they'll pay for it in the morning as it is," Betty chastised as she climbed behind the wheel of her gleaming Black Ford Falcon Ute.

They say there's a bit of a rebel in all of us, Rebecca thought as the wagon roared to life. Betty was a study in casualness with her sleeves rolled up, one hand on the steering wheel, and her free arm resting on the open window, oblivious of the cold. *All she needs now is a cowboy hat and a roll-your-own in her mouth.*

Coming back to the present, Rebecca placed her wine glass down on the hand-carved coffee table that Mark and Jennifer had picked up on their Indonesian honeymoon. They'd be in Mooloolaba by now, she realised, wondering how they were getting on. What a shame that this trip was a last-ditch attempt to save their marriage instead of what it should have been—a second honeymoon. Then, stretching forward to pick up the list of instructions Jennifer had left for her, Rebecca began by reading the handwritten note at the top:

Hi Rebecca,

By now you will have arrived safely and gotten the children off to bed. If I know you, the bottle of Sauvignon I left in the fridge will have been cracked open, and you'll be lying on the couch reading this. It's a good vintage from one of our local wineries, so enjoy. I have written out in detail below how mine and the children's day usually plays out, but I don't expect you to take it as gospel. You're in charge, so take what you want from it, remembering of course that children do love their routines. I thought I'd phone in at 6:30 pm so Mark and I can say hi to them both before bed each day and hear how you're getting on. Speak to you tomorrow and thanks again.

Love, Jennifer

X

Rebecca smiled to herself. Typical Jennifer, she thought, running her eyes down the list:

1. 5:30 am – 6:30 am

Hannah gets up, wanting her milk in her special Peter Rabbit cup. Once she has this, she climbs into bed for a cuddle.

1. 6:45 am

Jack wakes up and switches TV on to watch the Disney channel until break-fast. A piece of toast tides them both over while you shower quickly.

1. 7:05 am

Proper breakfast (one Weetabix for Hannah, two for Jack, and a glass of milk for both of them).

1. 7:25 am

Help Hannah get dressed and then lay Jack's clothes out for him. You may have to threaten him with the withdrawal of television privileges if he refuses to get dressed.

1. 7:45 am

Supervise face washing, teeth brushing, and hair brushing.

1. 8:00 am

Make yourself presentable for the day; Hannah usually likes to help.

1. 8:15 am

Put a load of laundry on and clear up breakfast dishes.

1. 8:30 am

Pack their bags, ie lunches (best made the night before and kept in the refrigerator if you want the morning to run smoothly). Also, make sure you have packed a change of clothes for Hannah, and Jack's PE kit before loading them in the car.

1. 8:45 am

Arrive at school.

1. 9:00 am

Arrive at preschool.

1. 9:20 am

Arrive home.
FREE TIME!

1. 12:15 pm

Leave to get Hannah for 12:30 pm pick-up.

1. 12:45 pm

Try to get her to have a little rest.

1. 1:15 pm

Set Hannah up with an activity.

1. 2:45 pm

Leave to get Jack for 3:00 pm pick-up (remember to take Hannah with you).

1. 3:20 pm

Jack will need to do his reading homework and maths if he has any and then it's free play.

1. 5:00 pm

Dinner time (I have bagged up a selection of frozen dinners for each night we are away and suggest a serving of fresh seasonal veggies straight from the garden on the side). NB: Night-time can be a testing time but try to remember that you are the adult.

1. 6:00 pm

Tidy up time.

1. 6:10 pm

Bath time for Hannah and Jack will have a five-minute shower after his sister's bath.

1. 6:45 pm

Storytime.

1. 7:00 pm

Hannah's bedtime.

1. 7:30 pm

Jack's bedtime.
PS: I limit the children's television consumption to one hour a day.

PPS: Overleaf, I have included some healthy ideas for the lunchboxes.

"Holy crap," muttered Rebecca as she flicked the note over to see that her sister had indeed been full of bright ideas when she'd penned it. How like Jennifer to run her home like a boot camp and treat her like a complete imbecile, she thought while reaching for her wine glass. *A good vintage, eh?* Rebecca's tastebuds agreed that it was before she rolled off the couch with a big sigh. She couldn't sit here relaxing, not when there were lunches to make.

Standing back, admiring her handiwork—two lunchboxes filled to the brim with heart foundation approved foods—Rebecca heard a car door slam. A moment later, Melissa was air-kissing both her cheeks and pushing her way up the hall and into the lounge, leaving her bags in the doorway.

Rebecca sighed and picked them up, staggering into the lounge to find Melissa had already commandeered the couch and the wine. "Oh, I need this—cheers." Melissa raised her glass. "How are my adopted niece and nephew, Becs?"

"Good. They're asleep, *finally*. Jen's left me a list of what she normally does in a day. Have a look at it." Rebecca gestured to where it lay on the coffee table.

"I'm surprised she didn't have it laminated," Melissa said, reaching over to pick it up.

"It's horrific," Rebecca shook her head, "and she's not expecting me to do any of the Cuisine with Carlton's stuff. I have no idea how Jen does what she does on a daily basis."

Melissa tossed the note back down on the table. "Well, I was right."

"About what?" Rebecca was puzzled.

"Your sister was indeed Wonder Woman in a past life. Either that or she's a chronic anal retentive."

Ignoring the comment, Rebecca frowned. "I don't know how I'm going to do it all."

Rebecca glanced across at Melissa, who refused to meet her eye. "You know I love Jack and Hannah as much as if they were my own, but I'm crap with kids."

"Oh, pass the wine over here, you great big prima donna," Rebecca retorted, pouring out two generous glasses.

Chapter Eleven

AT APPROXIMATELY 5:40 the next morning, Rebecca was bitterly regretting her decision to open that third bottle of wine. The words, "I wanna milk, Auntie Becca... a big one in my rabbit cup," were being shrieked into her left ear. When instantaneous action was not forthcoming, it was shrieked again. Hearing her niece take a great big breath with the obvious intention of raising the volume, she capitulated and crawled from the bed.

"Alright, alright, Hannah," Rebecca croaked, fumbling around in the dark for her dressing gown and slippers. "I've got the message." Feeling as though she had a percussionist taking centre stage inside her head, she staggered downstairs into the kitchen to fill Hannah's cup.

A few minutes later, she climbed gratefully back into bed; it was as Jennifer had predicted. Once Hannah's little hands were wrapped around her warm milk, she cuddled into her. Rebecca almost forgot that she had a disgusting wine headache until a little voice from the depths of the duvet giggled, "You stink."

The sound of Jack stampeding down the stairs into the lounge an hour later was followed closely by a violent din. Lying in bed with one ear cocked, Rebecca presumed he'd switched the Disney channel on which, bugger it, meant that it was time for her to get up. First things first, she thought, squinting painfully and taking the stairs with trepidation. Her headache had moved to its usual position over her left eyebrow. It was a bit like being on an aeroplane that was going down, she surmised, rummaging for a box of Panadol as she waited for the jug to boil. *The parent's oxygen mask must go on first before one could effectively take care of the kids.* As Rebecca's oxygen supply of coffee and paracetamol eventually wound their way through her bloodstream, she began to feel like perhaps she had a chance of survival.

"HANNAH, PUT YOUR CLOTHES on now!" Her naked niece dove behind the couch and screeched with excitement. *Deep breaths, Rebecca. Calm; that's it—calm. Try to remember who is the adult and who is the child.* "Hannah, get out here right now. I mean it!"

"I pity the poor bloke who winds up marrying you, Rebecca. You're a shrew." Melissa wandered into the room yawning and rubbing her temples; she looked decidedly rumpled. "Could you keep it down? I feel a bit delicate this morning."

"Get stuffed," Rebecca snapped back. "Make yourself useful and tell Jack to hurry up and get dressed. His clothes are on his bed."

If she didn't get this child dressed asap and move on to number six, she was going to have turban hair all day.

"You look like crap, Rebecca. You can't drop the kids off looking like that. What will all the single fathers think?" Melissa had positioned herself in front of the door, a human barricade.

Attempting to shove her aside, Rebecca muttered, "Get out of my way. I don't have time for this."

But she wouldn't budge, wagging a finger in her friend's face. "When you're single, you have to make time. I mean, what is with the hair?"

Rebecca's hand flew up to try to smooth down her poor fringe, the victim of being wrapped in a towel for too long. "While you were busy applying a full face, I was running around, sorting the children."

"Don't blame me. Honestly, you need to take some personal responsibility. Set your alarm earlier or something."

Thinking of her 5:40 am start, Rebecca didn't trust herself to reply, and with superhuman strength, she pushed Melissa out of the way and dragged the children outside to the waiting wagon.

"BEN!" JACK WAVED OVER at another late straggler, wrestling himself away from Rebecca, who was trying to do what she assumed all good substitute mothers did: kiss their on-loan offspring goodbye. The curly-haired boy Jack was calling to was legging it in through the open gates of the primary school. She watched from the side of the Land Cruiser as he stopped and waited while Jack caught up to him.

"Hi." A male voice from behind her made her jump. "Sorry, I didn't mean to give you a fright." The voice's rather gorgeous source held his hand out, and she shook it lightly. Warm, dry, and strong, she thought as he released his grip and introduced himself. "I'm Ben's dad, David, and I guess you're Rebecca, right?"

Momentarily flummoxed as to who this God was with whom she'd never slept but who knew her on a first-name basis, she managed to reply, "Uh, yeah, that's right." *Good on you, Rebecca. Impress him with your scintillating small talk.*

He gestured towards his son and Jack, who were halfway across the netball court and laughed at her perplexed expression. "Don't worry, I'm not psychic. Those two are great buddies except for when they're up against each other on the motocross circuit!" He shoved his hands deep into the pockets of his sexy, slouch-fit blue jeans. "That's how I came to hear you were coming to look after Jack and Hannah for a couple of weeks."

As he paused to watch the two boys run up the concrete ramp leading to the one-storey, wooden rectangle housing their classroom, she seized the chance to check him out properly. She wouldn't have to stand on her tiptoes to kiss him, nor would she have to leave her high heels at home. And even though he was veering towards the lean side of forty, there was no sign as yet of a middle-aged paunch. Yes, she decided, completing a quick head-to-toe inventory of broad shoulders, toned torso, and strong thighs, he worked out. His mid-brown, slightly too long hair was not peppered with grey, nor did it show any evidence of being tampered with. Thank goodness, because men with highlights were a non-starter.

She was already in love with the etching of laughter lines spanning a set of greenish-grey eyes that complemented his smooth, olive complexion. The smattering of almost black chest hair peeking cheekily out at her from the top of his V-neck sweater added to the mix. As her eyes roamed languorously back towards David's face, they collided with his. Rebecca felt herself flush while a little smile played at the corner of his mouth as though he knew what she had been doing.

For a few agonising moments, neither of them spoke until David decided to break the standoff. "Mark and Jennifer are a great couple." Grateful for the distraction but not having learned her lesson, she watched hungrily as his lips continued to move. "I don't know how they do it all. You know, running Cuisine with Carlton's, Mark's architectural practice, and raising two great kids. If anyone deserves a break, they do. It's Aussie they've headed to, isn't it?"

He obviously didn't know the finer points of their marital situation, she deduced, as her mouth automatically formed the sentence. "Uh-huh, Mooloolaba on the Sunshine Coast." Once more, she hoped she hadn't intimidated him with her sparkling repertoire.

David showed no signs of intimidation, though; more grim determination to elicit a two-sided conversation. "So, I hear you've been in Dublin working?"

"Yeah."

Spurred on by a response, he said, "It was pretty good of you to leave the Irish summer behind for this." He indicated towards the gunmetal sky. "How long is it they've gone for?"

"Two weeks and, believe me, it's no biggie leaving the Irish summer behind."

"I guess it's not so bad. Not when you consider we're supposed to be having the mildest July on record for ten years."

"Yeah, if only I'd known that, I could have left my thermals back in Ireland where they belong!" Her giggle threatened to turn into a snort. *Where had that come from?* Now she'd given the sexiest man she'd laid eyes on in a long time a mental picture of herself in polypropylene. It didn't seem to put him off, though.

"So I take it the rumours are true about it raining all the time over there then?"

"Four seasons in one day," she affirmed, wondering how much longer they could stretch this meteorology discussion.

Thankfully, David changed the subject. "Ireland's on my wish list of places to visit one day."

"Oh, you should go," Rebecca breathed excitedly. "Dublin's such a fun city, but you want to bring a babysitter." He laughed, and she watched the way the lines round his eyes scrunched up, giving him a lived-in sort of look.

"Are you available for a two-week stint in 2008 then?"

It was her turn to laugh, and she was pleased that it came out sounding like a ladylike titter and not the nervous guffaw she'd let rip earlier. "No way! If this morning is an indicator of what I'm in for over the next two weeks, then my child-minding career will be over the minute Jen and Mark set foot back onto New Zealand soil."

"That's a shame. I guess the trip will just have to wait until my daddy duties are redundant then. Am I to take it that you don't have kids of your own?"

She suddenly noticed the raspberry jam handprint emblazoned on the arm of her polo fleece with embarrassment. *He must think she was a right mess.* "Uh-huh."

Following her gaze, he smirked. "Ben prefers peanut butter. It's a pity they don't come with a survival manual, don't you think?"

"Oh, mine did," she chirruped, filling him in on her sister's lengthy list.

"If you need a break, Jack's welcome at my place anytime. It's easier to have two than one, believe it or not."

"I'll take your word for it, and thanks for the offer," Rebecca said, knowing she'd be taking him up on it, whether she needed a break or not.

The next thing she knew, David produced a worn, brown leather wallet from his back pocket and flicked it open. "I've got a card in here somewhere... here you go." He handed her his small white business card. *Handcrafted Furniture from Akaroa* was centred on the top of it in bold black italics while beneath it in lighter type were the words *by David Seagar.* Scanning the bottom of the card greedily, Rebecca wished she had a photographic memory; much safer to commit his contact details to memory than to rely on a flimsy piece of cardboard.

"So you make furniture?" *That wasn't stating the obvious or anything. Surely she'd sweep him off his feet with her conversational skills now.* She hoped he hadn't noticed the battle she was having trying to wedge the card into the pocket of her jeans. *Bugger the bloody slim fit.* That would teach her for buying jeans designed for women with no hips or buttocks, criteria she didn't meet. By now, she thought ruefully, he'd probably accepted her strange behaviour as being the norm.

"Yeah, when Ben's mum and I split, Ben and I moved here," he gestured expansively, "to paradise and I did what I should have done years ago and opened my workshop. That's how Ben and Jack first met." Seeing her quizzical look, he carried on, "Jennifer commissioned me to make the dining table for Cuisine with Carlton's."

"Oh, the huge kauri one?" Rebecca replied, swiftly absorbing the fact that David was a *single* carpenter. Granted, he had a bit of baggage, but who didn't?

"Yeah, it was an amazing piece of wood to work with."

Rebecca shivered. You can work on me anytime, big boy, she thought, visualising his hands lovingly moulding an imaginary lump of wood.

"Speaking of workshops, I should get back to mine. It was great talking to you, Rebecca, and I meant what I said about two being easier than one." He gave her one last lazy smile before fishing his keys out and striding off towards the only other vehicle left in the car park, a mud-splattered Land Rover. Rebecca stood where he'd left her, entranced by the rhythmic motion of his high, rounded rear when an ominous click sounded from inside the wagon.

Spinning around, she was confronted by a grinning Hannah, who, in Houdini-like effortlessness, had freed herself from her car seat restraints. She had flicked the internal locking switch and was now sitting behind the Land Cruiser's steering wheel, proclaiming, "I'm driving the bus!" As Hannah jerked the wheel from left to right, the expression on her face was so maniacal that Rebecca couldn't help but laugh.

"Good for you, Hannah!" she applauded before attempting to retrieve the keys from her pocket. It wasn't the simple task it should have been, as she could only push one finger into the tight denim at a time. Finally, she squeezed her middle finger in and, waggling it around, realised with a plummeting sensation in her stomach that there were no keys in there. *Shit!* She quickly patted down her left pocket. *No, nothing in there either. Bugger!* Putting her hand up to the car window and peering in, she spied them swinging happily to and fro in the ignition.

Okay, Rebecca, don't panic—deep breaths. "Hannah, sweetheart, push that button there and unlock the car for Auntie Becca."

"No. I told you, I'm driving the bus!" She poked her tongue out and broke into song. "*The wheels on the bus go round and round.*"

Shit, shit, shit! What was she supposed to do now? Reason with a three-year-old? There was nothing else to do but begin negotiations.

"Come on, Hannah, sweetheart, there's a good girl."

"No! *The horn on the bus goes beep, beep, beep.*" Hannah was now flicking the headlights on and off, having a high old time.

"Need a hand?" David asked, bemused, as he pulled up alongside her.

"I've left the bloody keys in the car."

Leaving his engine idling, he opened the door of his Land Rover and jumped down. "Number one rule when your vehicle's parked up with children inside it: never leave the keys in it."

"I know, I know, and I can't believe I was so stupid. I didn't think she could get out of her car seat," Rebecca wailed. "And besides, I was right here the whole time."

Gently elbowing her aside, it was David's turn to peer in the window. He spoke in a firm voice. "Hannah, it's time to stop messing around now. Open the door please."

Rebecca watched in disbelief as her niece did as she was told. "Who are you?" she murmured, awestruck. "The toddler whisperer?"

He flashed her a sexy smile as he hopped back up behind the wheel and the thought crossed her mind that if he had been wearing a trilby hat, he would have tipped it at her.

"I'm a man of many talents," he said enigmatically and then he was gone.

"I bet you are, Mr Seagar. I just bet you are."

Glancing in the rear-view mirror as she crawled out of the car park, Rebecca let rip with a "FUCK!" She followed it up with an apology. "Shit, sorry, Hannah, I didn't mean to swear." She'd forgotten she hadn't put any make-up on before she'd left the house. Oh, why did she have to meet David Seagar today of all days? There was no way he'd fancy her in her current nude-faced state and with turban hair to boot. It wasn't fair.

"HI THERE. I'M REBECCA Loughton, Hannah's aunt. Jennifer would have told you I'll be taking care of Hannah for the next fortnight?" Rebecca shouted her introduction over the din of preschoolers charging around the colourful playroom. There were a dozen or so bright paintings hanging up to dry on a piece of washing line stretched across the middle of the large, airy room. Children in plastic aprons were sitting industriously at activity tables dotted across the vinyl-covered floor. She spied a sign proclaiming 'Quiet Zone' over in the far left-hand corner where a small couch with foam stuffing sprouting from its seat was placed next to an overflowing bookshelf. French doors, closed against the morning chill, led out to a covered outdoor play area and up against the wall was a rack of dress-up clothes.

I'd have been straight into those, she thought with a pang for her childhood as the teacher rose from one of the little tables where she'd been supervising cutting and gluing. She was apparently opting for the safety net of a career in childcare since her looks obviously weren't going to get her a free ride through life, Rebecca deduced. *Playaways—early education through play* was emblazoned across a pink sweatshirt worn over black slacks and flats.

"I'm Anna, the manager of Playaways. And yes, Mrs Carlton has informed us that you'll be Hannah's primary caregiver while she and Mr Carlton are away."

Ooh-ah, primary caregiver. Rebecca liked the sound of her new job description, and she and Hannah followed as she was shown where to leave Hannah's bag and lunchbox. She hoped Anna would be impressed with the latter's contents.

Clapping her hands authoritatively, Anna called, "Linda, Abbey—this is Rebecca Loughton, Hannah's aunt, and she's going to be doing Hannah's pick-up and drop-off over the next fortnight." Two other identically kitted-out teachers with wailing toddlers hanging off them looked over and grinned. She didn't envy them their jobs. Anna bent down, holding her hand out to Hannah, who was clinging tremulously to Rebecca's leg.

"Come along now, Hannah. Auntie Rebecca can't stay here all morning, can she?"

She beat a hasty retreat as the little girl looked up at her scary preschool teacher and replied earnestly, "Fuck, shit."

Chapter Twelve

"WHAT A MORNING! YOU would not believe it." Rebecca trudged through into the lounge, dumping the car keys into the little pot sitting on the fireplace mantel. These days, the fireplace was purely ornamental as gas and a heat pump had long since replaced the open fire. Melissa brushed past her impatiently, her arms laden with magazines. Stepping into the toasty warmth of the sunroom, she sighed happily. Rebecca followed her, leaning against the timber framing as she arranged herself on the window seat. She epitomised country living in her casual but hellishly expensive olive-green merino. No doubt, Rebecca thought a touch cynically, she'd carefully picked it for the contrast it afforded against her spray tan and camel cords.

The sunroom was an alcove off the lounge with a large bay window overlooking the front garden and classroom. It was Rebecca's favourite room. The neutral Spanish white, that Jennifer had chosen for the walls throughout the house, flowed to give the room an airy feel while rosy pink stripes in the floor-to-ceiling drapes and window seat cushion added warmth. It was in total contrast to the earthen minimalist style of the living room. In summer, the roses in the garden outside grew tall and fragrant, framing the bay window so that you felt like you were looking out at a painting. Today, their withered branches tapped at the window as if begging to be allowed inside, where it was warm. It was an oddly relaxing sound.

Jennifer had opted to leave the original floorboards bare, sanding the solid rimu boards back and polishing them until they shone with their former glory. Her finishing touch had been the plush pink Oriental carpet, which kept the chill off bare feet.

"Be a love and make me a coffee," Melissa ordered while settling down to flip through one of her magazines. Not up for an argument, Rebecca moseyed off to make a brew and, depositing two mugs on the windowsill a few minutes later, she hoped they wouldn't leave a mark.

"Scrunch up." Pushing Melissa's feet out of the way, she plonked herself down on the edge of the seat while her friend grunted with annoyance at being disturbed. Ignoring her, Rebecca launched into the David Seagar saga. She'd just gotten to her favourite bit where he'd told Hannah to unlock the doors when she slopped her coffee with fright. Melissa was stabbing frenziedly at a picture of Paris Hilton.

"Look there!" she screeched. "She does have cellulite; I knew it!"

Shaking her head, Rebecca watched Melissa scrutinise the photo, her face illuminated with bitchy delight. How silly of her to assume that her having possibly met the man of her dreams was newsworthy compared to the staggering revelation by some vindictive photographer that Paris had the teeniest amount of orange peel on her thighs.

Rebecca got up to check for any coffee spray and, finding none, she headed to the lounge, noting that the morning's devastation had not been tidied away in her absence. Oh well, she'd deal with it later. Taking an absentminded sip of her coffee, she realised it was officially her free time now. *What to do, what to do? Emails—yes, that was it.* She'd catch up on some goss of her own.

With its proximity to the front door, what had been the study when Mark and Jennifer took possession of the house now acted as the 'Cook's Quarters'. It was a reception area for guests to register upon arrival. The little room caught the afternoon sun, which was an ideal arrangement as this was when most of the guests arrived. At this time of the morning, though, a definite chill pervaded it and Rebecca shivered, looking around for the heat pump's remote, wishing for good old-fashioned central heating. The remote wasn't hard to find; her sister was a big believer in putting things back where they came from. True to form, she'd stored it neatly away in the top drawer of her oversized oak desk. With its gleaming array of mod cons arranged neatly on top, the desk dominated the room. Opposite and flush with the wall was a cream chaise longue for guests to sit on while their booking was processed. Watercolours from local artists dotted the walls.

A moment later, as the heat pump and computer sprang to life, Rebecca spied three messages winking out at her from her inbox. Without thinking, she moved the mouse to click on the message from Ciaran first.

To: Rebecca Loughton

Subject: One More Sleep Til Galway

Dear Rebecca,

I am sorry I didn't get to say bon voyage to you properly. As you discovered, before I came out to introduce myself to Kate, I was working on a very important quiz. Thanks for answering number 20; it had been twisting me up all week. Before I knew it, I was running late. I am sure you'll be relieved to know that the client bought my excuse. I tried to phone you later that night, but no one answered at your apartment. To prove you have forgiven me for not wining and dining you, can you please bring me back a Kiwi bird key ring or something equally cheesy?

From my personal experience of long-haul flights, I can only hope yours wasn't too horrific and that despite the jet lag you are managing to be a responsible aunt. On the home front, I'm impressed by Kate, as she's very keen. She came to the office on Saturday morning and this afternoon to help me get things straight before I head away in the morning. Don't you worry your head about work (as if) because she's more than able to keep on top of things.

There's one area where she's not up to speed though, and this is through no fault of her own. Given that she is about ten years younger than you, she's only got a vague familiarity with the 1980s. She can't help me with number 33: "What band did David Coverdale sing with before forming glam rock band Whitesnake?"

I will be taking my laptop with me to Galway so your swift reply to my email would be appreciated.

Love, Ciaran

Rebecca leaned back in the chair. She stared at the computer screen, her irritation at reading of Kate's 'keenness' and ability to 'keep on top of things' passing as two words loomed out at her: *Love, Ciaran*. Not quite the norm when it came to signing off one's emails to one's PA. Mind you, e-mailing your PA with non-urgent information while she was on holiday wasn't the norm either, even if they did have an amicable working relationship. Mind you, if she wanted to get into it, sleeping with her boss—while clichéd—wasn't exactly an everyday occurrence either. Still, at least, unlike her brother-in-law, Ciaran wasn't married.

She flashed back to that morning when she'd woken up in his bed and sitting up in fright had found herself staring down at her boss. He'd been snoring his head off but even with his mouth hanging open, he'd looked gorgeously vulnerable. Instead of lying back down and snuggling into him, though, like any *normal* woman would have, she'd panicked. She was frightened as to what his reaction to her being there in the cold light of morning would be and so, she'd gotten quietly dressed and let herself out before he stirred.

Sighing, she put the memory back where it belonged: in her box of mistakes. What did it matter? Ciaran had never once alluded to what had happened between them and now here he was about to head off on holiday with the Queen of Lycra, Pariah. *Cow!*

And as for *Love, Ciaran,* well, she had to face facts. The man had tried it on with over half the female employees of Fitzpatrick and Co; she was already just another notch on his bedpost. It was time to let that night go and move on. She would not think about the rapport he had with Jordy and the way he made the little boy's face light up. Nor would she dwell on the time he had couriered a hamper stocked with a box of cold tablets, a packet of tissues, some lemons, and a pot of honey to her apartment. She had been home with a stinking head cold at the time. *Stop it, Rebecca!* Dragging her gaze away from the screen, she glanced down at her watch. *What would the time be in Ireland now?* Mentally calculating the eleven-hour time difference, she concluded it must be about 11:30 pm on Sunday night. Ciaran would be tucked up in bed by now and wouldn't get her email until he checked his messages in Galway. She hit the Reply button because she couldn't help herself.

To: Ciaran Cahill

Subject: One More Sleep Til Galway

Dear Ciaran,

Thanks for your concern regarding my flight. May I just say that flying economy is a truly horrific experience at the best of times but throw in an obese travelling companion with flatulence issues and, well, you get the picture. I survived the ordeal, and it was great to see the family, albeit briefly. My parents have swanned off on their cruise, and my sister and her husband are currently working through things on the Sunshine Coast. So, that leaves me with Hannah and Jack. They have survived one evening and one morning in my care. And I have survived one evening and one morning of running after them. Why did I ever think I was capable of being responsible? My biological clock is no longer ticking.

My friend Melissa, who was also supposed to be going to Galway, surprised me by announcing that she was coming home with me instead. My apologies on Melissa's behalf for letting you down at the last minute, but apparently she felt I needed a hand holding (not enough to travel in economy with me, though). Remember I told you that she was Tamara Lewis's personal assistant? Well, Tamara pulled some of her pop star strings and got Melissa upgraded to first class. I don't know how much help she is going to be over the next fortnight, either, because she has been sitting in the sunroom reading magazines all morning, and I fear she has taken root there.

So there, you have it, my news to date. I am pleased the office of Ciaran Cahill will not grind to a halt in both our absences, thanks to the capable Kate. I'm not sure I appreciate being reminded that I was around for Madonna's debut, though.

Love Rebecca

PS: Your apology for not seeing me off in the style I deserve is duly noted and to prove I don't hold a grudge, here's the answer to number 33. David Coverdale was Deep Purple's front man. He had such fabulous hair and 'Here I Go Again' by Whitesnake is a musical gem.

She hit Send before she could chicken out and change *love* to *yours faithfully* or *yours sincerely* and, refusing to dwell on him any longer, opened the next email. It was from Nicola. Her wedding plans were a welcome distraction. She happily banged out her newsy reply before catching up with Emma, who was obviously not the letter writing type, judging by her short message that read:

Back in Brisvegas. It hasn't changed. Still can't believe you and spotty James. Ha, Ha ha. Grrrowl!

Rebecca took great delight in sending her friend an equally informative reply of 'Sod off'. Her eyes dropped back down to her watch again. *Hmm, she still had three-quarters of an hour left before she needed to collect Hannah. Maybe she should wander down to the cooking school and say hi.*

Strolling along the garden path, she paused to admire the view. She had to admit that her sister had waved a magic wand over this property. Thick trees formed a line at the base of the section. Glimpses of blue were visible through their foliage and on a sunny day, the water would be a vivid blue dotted with white sails. Today, however, the sea mimicked the murky sky.

The property was two-tiered on a sloping section with the house and garden sitting on the top tier and the cabins and cooking school neatly laid out below. She could still hear Jennifer's self-important voice as she'd told her, "I am going to offer boutique accommodation," referring to the newly renovated cabins. What did boutique mean? she had wondered, not wanting to give her ignorance away and deciding that it was probably just a more exotic word for expensive. She'd been right; fancy rooms paid off. Once Jennifer had gotten the web page up and running, the school took off internationally as well as nationally and these days it was permanently booked out months in advance.

The garden leading down to the second tier was like something out of a magazine, even in winter, thanks to Colin the gardener, who, in Rebecca's opinion, strongly resembled a garden gnome. Over to her left was the herb garden, the school's lifeblood, and Rebecca wandered over to it, bending down to pick a sprig of what she was fairly sure was rosemary. It was confirmed as she held it up to her nose and inhaled.

It smelt gorgeous, conjuring up images of a succulent roasting lamb. She was just as passionate about food as her sister was; it was just that Jen had gotten the *actual* cooking gene while she, who could just about boil an egg, had been gifted the eating gene. It wasn't very fair, she mused, letting the rosemary fall from her fingers. Her gaze swung to the far corner of the section where, virtually hidden by a flowerless profusion of camellia shrubs, nestled the vegetable patch.

It was Jen's pride and joy because it enabled her always to use the freshest seasonal vegetables in the classroom. It was out of bounds for Colin, as Jennifer insisted on tending it herself, saying the hands-on approach helped her come up with new ideas for Cuisine with Carlton's menu.

The cottage garden over to her right was bare this time of year, but come the summer it would be a riotous bed of colours all vying for attention. Behind her, the gnarled limbs of the rose garden stood sentry.

The 'Cook's Quarters', as the house was known, was almost Cape Cod in style. Painted white with a pretty blue trim, it still had all the original lace fretwork in place. The wide veranda, running down the right-hand side of the house, afforded a magnificent view out over the surrounding hills. It was impressive, she thought, squinting up at the stately pile, remembering how daunting the initial renovation job had been for Jen and Mark.

They'd wanted the house to retain its original charm that, over the years, had gotten lost under layers of peeling exterior paint and an interior harking back to the 1960s. She smiled, remembering how it had been all hands on deck as the whole family pitched in for weekends of wallpaper stripping, the highlight of which had been the ceremonial ripping up of those heinous worn, floral carpets. What a thrill it had been, rolling them back to find that the original timber boards underneath were in excellent condition.

That was the last time she could remember them all having fun together. It had been fun, too, camping out in the cabins. They had shared dinners in the makeshift kitchen Jen had set up in the old dormitory building while they were waiting for the new kitchen to be installed up in the house. Rebecca had even found herself warming to her swine of a brother-in-law as she watched the way he supported her sister in her new venture. It had been so good to see Jen come alive again, and she had been genuinely caught up in the excitement of what her sister was creating. In turn, Jennifer had been grateful for her younger sister's enthusiasm. For the first time in years, they forged a tenuous bond, but since then she'd gone away, and now it seemed like they were back to being strangers.

Coming out of her reverie, Rebecca noticed that the roses had been pruned back for the winter, but she could see tiny buds beginning to form on their knotted limbs due to the mild weather. As she carried on down the path, she inhaled, imagining she could smell their perfume on the breeze. Caught up in the moment, she found herself singing, "I've been to paradise, but I've never been to me."

"What's that tune you're humming, dear? I recognise it. Was it on a Flake chocolate bar advert?" A sprightly woman in her mid to late seventies startled her by appearing on the classroom steps. Thankfully, Rebecca was spared having to confess she was singing a song by a one-hit wonder called Charlene. The woman waved the lighter she had clenched in her hand and announced, "I'm just off for a sneaky smoke, but you're just in time for morning tea. Go on in."

"Oh, goody." Rebecca sniffed appreciatively. "It smells delicious; what is it?"

"Rhubarb and apple cake with caramel sauce."

"Yum! That doesn't sound much like a Thai dish, though."

The woman's chortle turned into a wheeze, but she managed to gasp out, "No, it isn't; we were feeling a bit rebellious this morning after last night's green curry. When you get to our age, dear, spicy foods go right through you, if you get my drift."

Rebecca got her drift and, not wanting to be put off her helping of cake, she let Smoky the Bear tiptoe down the path. She watched with a smile as she ducked furtively behind an old oak tree.

Chapter Thirteen

"EVERYBODY!" BETTY CLAPPED her hands together, her grey apron emblazoned in black with the words 'Carlton's Cuisine' secured tightly around her waist. She was standing at the narrow end of what looked like an upside-down T-shaped room. Despite being a functional room with its four built-in wall ovens down one side and commercial-sized sink, dishwasher, and espresso coffee machine down the other, Jennifer had still managed to create a country cottage ambience.

Leaving the walls in their natural timber state, she'd strung polished, copper-bottom pots, along with bunches of dried herbs and strings of garlic bulbs, from the heavy beams supporting the pitched ceiling. Lined up and down the centre of the room in four neat rows were the gas hobs and state-of-the-art kitchen workbenches. Each housed a complete set of cooking utensils in the cupboard space below. Perched on tall wooden stools around these benches were members of the Timaru Branch of the Nifty Knitters, a veritable sea of tight perms. At the very back of the room was a wide alcove. It was home to the handmade twelve-seater kauri dining table that David had been commissioned to make. Rebecca gave an involuntary tremble at the thought of his hands lovingly shaping what had once been a hard lump of raw wood.

The table was currently laid out in anticipation of morning tea, and the espresso machine was doing overtime as two old dears elbowed each other.

"It's my turn, Gwen; you did it yesterday."

"Yes, but everyone said what a good job I made of it."

"Excuse me!" Betty clapped her hands again and, apart from the hissing of the coffee machine, a sudden hush settled over the room. "Thank you, ladies. I'd like to introduce you to Rebecca Loughton, our hostess Jennifer Carlton's sister. As you know, Jennifer was called away, and Rebecca here has come all the way from Dublin to hold the fort."

"Hello, Rebecca," the ladies dutifully chorused.

A rotund woman with a chest you could rest a plate on somehow managed to ease herself off her stool. Rebecca couldn't help but wonder how she'd gotten up there in the first place. "I'm Maureen, the president of the Nifty Knitters Timaru Branch," she boomed.

Rebecca smiled. "Hi, Maureen." Then, directing her gaze to the room, added, "I hope you are all enjoying your stay at Cuisine with Carlton's." Enough of the pleasantries already, she thought, her eyes alighting on the main event. Cut the cake and pour that caramel!

"We are indeed enjoying ourselves, aren't we, girls?"

There was a mass of bobbing curls as the 'girls' chanted in unison, "Yes, Maureen."

Oh great leader, Rebecca mentally added, thinking back to the debacle outside cabin one last night, some of you are enjoying yourselves more than others.

"Righty-ho. Make yourselves comfortable, ladies. Rebecca, we're going to sample our wares over coffee now! You're more than welcome to join us." Betty winked at her and indicated the spare stool next to Maureen.

"Come on, dear. There's room for a little one." Maureen patted the stool, and Rebecca reluctantly squished in beside her.

"This is amazing. If I pop down here every morning, I'll have gone up a dress size by the end of the week," she stated a moment later, dunking her forkful of cake into the artfully poured sauce with gusto.

"MS LOUGHTON, YOU WERE supposed to pick Hannah up twenty minutes ago." Anna's malevolent expression clearly indicated that she didn't think Rebecca was up to the job of primary caregiver. "We have a teacher-to-pupil ratio, and it is strictly adhered to and by being late, you jeopardise the welfare of all the children here." She gestured around the roomful of little cherubs who, as if on cue, all gazed accusingly over at Rebecca.

Talk about laying it on thick, she thought guiltily.

"I'm so sorry, Anna. We had an emergency at Cuisine with Carlton's. The, um..." She flung about wildly for an excuse. *Ah yes, Lois!* "One of the students didn't extinguish her cigarette properly and, well, I had a small bush fire to contend with before I could get here. It was a blessing I spotted the smoke, or the whole school could have gone up."

She hoped she hadn't overdone it with that last bit, but Anna was looking slightly mollified as she replied, "Yes, well, I always maintain smoking is bad for one's health."

By the time, Rebecca had finished with, "I won't be late again, I can assure you," the preschool teacher was almost smiling as she handed Hannah over.

"NO REST, NO REST, NO rest!" There was an ominous thud. An even louder crash followed. It was 1:00 pm. Hannah had been in her room for fifteen minutes and was not resting.

"What is going on?" hissed Melissa from the bottom of the stairs up to where Rebecca was standing outside her niece's bedroom door, anxiously biting her nails.

"Jen said Hannah might like a little rest when she gets home from preschool," she offered lamely.

Melissa raised two disbelieving eyebrows. "Does it sound like she's having a little rest to you?"

"Er, no."

Both girls jumped as a particularly loud thump resonated from the room. "Oh, I can't stand it, I'm letting her out!"

Rebecca marvelled at the devastation a three-and-a-half-year-old could wreak. In the space of ten minutes, Hannah's pretty pastel green room looked like a tornado had ripped through it. The heavy children's blackout curtain festooned with yellow daisies was lying at an odd angle, having been half tugged off its track. And with the superhuman strength of a preschooler in a tantrum, she'd gone on to yank the yellow drawers of her tallboy out, the contents of which now lay strewn around the room. The bottom shelf of her bookcase stood empty while the bright picture books it normally housed had been tossed into the melee of clothes.

The star of the show herself had donned a sparkly tiara and was hiding amidst the sea of pink tulle that was her fairy outfit. Clutching her magic wand, she pointed it at Rebecca and screamed, "You naughty!" before collapsing in a sobbing heap. Rebecca instantly felt like the big bad fairy and, racked with guilt, she began doing what it was she did best: grovelling. "I'm sorry, Hannah. Mean old Auntie Becca won't put you to bed tomorrow; I promise." Sensing an opportunity, her niece hiccupped and upped the volume. Tiptoeing through the debris and crouching down to rub the little girl's trembling back, she asked, "Would you like me to snuggle buggle you on the couch with a choccie milk and a Wiggles DVD?"

Hannah didn't hang around. She tossed the fairy dress aside and thundered off down the stairs to throw herself onto the couch in anticipation of her promised movie and milk deal. Feeling decidedly manipulated, Rebecca half-heartedly opened a tin of tuna for her and Melissa's lunch. Hannah appeared to have put the trauma of being asked to have some quiet time well and truly behind her as she slurped happily on her chocolate milk and gazed adoringly at Captain Feathersword.

Melissa, meanwhile, had reclaimed her position in the sunroom and was keeping one ear cocked for the lunch bell. She was born in the wrong bloody century, Rebecca fumed as she gave the can opener one last violent twist. She would have been in her element in the days of *Upstairs Downstairs*. Slapping two tuna sandwiches together, she carried them through to the dining room before announcing, "Lunch is served, milady," throwing a little curtsey in for good measure.

Ten minutes later, Melissa was waggling an 'I told you so' finger across the table. "I knew you should have made more of an effort this morning." Rebecca had filled her in on the David Seagar saga once more and was fast beginning to wish she hadn't.

"Honestly, Becs, when you're past your prime, you can't afford to walk out that front door looking anything but your best."

Here we go. Rebecca cringed as she held her hand out for Melissa's empty plate. *I wonder which self-help book she's going to quote this time.*

"Work with what God gave you, girl!"

Good grief, that was bad even by Melissa's standards. "Not everybody views life through such superficial rose-tinted glasses. Did it not cross your mind that perhaps David saw past my fringe curl to my inner beauty?"

Melissa gave a derisive snort. "Inner beauty?"

Rebecca nodded, feeling a tad timid in her argument now.

"Oh, my friend, you are so naïve! Don't you know the whole concept of inner beauty is a ruse devised by an ugly girl clutching at straws? Now get up those stairs and put some bloody lipstick on!"

"HI AGAIN." DAVID LEANED nonchalantly against the door of his Land Rover. It was a look that suited him, and Rebecca had to fight the urge not to hustle him into the back seat for a spot of ravaging. A time and place, she admonished herself, and then found herself standing a little straighter as she caught his admiring glance. She was pleased now that she'd passed Melissa's front door inspection. Her advice of 'don't act desperate but make sure he knows you're interested' had trailed annoyingly behind her as she'd gotten into the car.

"Where's Hannah?" He raised a quizzical eyebrow in the direction of the empty booster seat in the back of the car.

Oh, don't tempt me, she thought, writhing back-seat of the car images flickering before her. "I left her with Melissa. That's my friend who came over with me. She's staying up at the house too."

He nodded as the three o'clock bell sounded and, like a burst dam, a hodgepodge of children flooded out of the classrooms.

"Dad, can Jack come over to our house to play?" Ben ran through the gates, Jack following closely on his heels. Jack looked up at Rebecca beseechingly, and David smiled.

"Looks like you're outnumbered. Why don't you both come over? I'll even put the kettle on and make you a coffee, if you can stomach instant? My way of welcoming you to Akaroa."

YES!!! Rebecca was mentally performing a victory dance when she remembered Hannah. David read her mind. "Your friend, Melissa, is it? She wouldn't mind watching Hannah for an hour, would she?"

Rebecca *had* been practically waiting on Melissa hand and foot; it was the least she could do for her. "I'll just make a quick call." She smiled sweetly at David as she pulled out her phone.

"THERE YOU GO, WHITE and one."

"Thanks." Rebecca took the mug and placed it on the wooden countertop in the kitchen of David's 'work in progress' cottage on Langlois Lane. She'd just been treated to the grand tour. It was a labour of love, he'd told her, turning this house into his and Ben's home. Oh yes, she decided, watching as he placed a large plateful of chocolate chip biscuits between them before arranging himself on the stool opposite hers. Even with its crumbling lathe and plaster walls, she could see herself being a happy little homemaker here.

There was an almighty commotion as, having sniffed out the biscuits, Ben and Jack careened in through the French doors that opened out from the kitchen into the garden and began helping themselves. If he tells me they're homemade, I'm definitely going to marry him, she thought, helping herself to one before they all disappeared. "Mm, these are lovely; you didn't make them, did you?" She crossed a finger behind her back, but he smirked.

"I wish! I bought them from the bakery. I'm afraid my culinary skills stretch to basic survival, and I only got to that point after your sister kindly gave me a few pointers."

Rebecca laughed, hoping he hadn't noticed the crumbs that had flown involuntarily out of her mouth. "You wouldn't think Jen and I were related if you saw me in the kitchen. I'm a beans and toast sort of a girl." *Where had that come from?*

Jack, treating them to the sight of a masticated chocolate chip biscuit, suddenly piped up with, "We had beans last night, didn't we, Auntie Becca? I know a real good song about beans too."

Rebecca squirmed in her seat; she didn't like the sound of this. Perhaps it was time to change the subject. "My goodness, that's a big slide, boys." Having outgrown the rusty old swing and slide set she was gesticulating to down at the bottom of the garden, neither boy looked the slightest bit interested. When Ben announced he knew the song too, she knew it was inevitable.

"Baked beans are good for your heart! Baked beans will make you fart!" She muttered, "I like spaghetti too."

Snatching the last two biscuits off the plate, the two boys ran back outside.

"What is it with boys? Don't they walk anywhere?" Rebecca asked. David grinned, treating her to a flash of white, evenly spaced teeth that any Hollywood actor would have been proud to put their name to.

"Nope and listen..." She cocked her head to one side. "I can't hear anything except the two of them shrieking."

"Exactly." He tapped the side of his nose. "A word from the wise—it's when you can't hear them that you've got to worry."

"Oh right, thanks for that. I need all the help I can get."

"That bad, huh?"

She nodded gloomily into her coffee cup before owning up to Hannah's eloquent little speech at preschool that morning. He threw his head back and roared with laughter, but Rebecca chewed anxiously on her bottom lip.

"Apparently I jeopardised the student-to-teacher ratio by being late as well. I am officially a crap primary caregiver. Jennifer will go mad when she finds out."

David tried to look serious but spoiled it by winking at her. "I won't tell her if you don't."

The next half hour flew by as David skillfully moved the topic of conversation away from her lack of practical parenting skills to that of life in Dublin. She was glad to find that her earlier awkwardness around him had disappeared. He seemed genuinely entertained by her Irish name pronunciation anecdotes, asking, "So Padraig is in fact pronounced Porag, to be sure, to be sure?"

"Pretty much, yeah." It was her turn to laugh. "You sound like Tom Cruise did in that horrid little flick he did back in the good old days with Nicole."

"They didn't have the luck o' the Irish with dem, tats for sure."

"Stop it!" Then, catching a glimpse of the time, she hopped reluctantly down from her stool, feeling her shyness return as she thanked him for the coffee.

"No worries. Tanks for ta Irish lesson."

She tapped the side of her nose. "A word from the wise, David. If you were to wander around Dublin telling everyone 'you've the luck o' the Irish with you to be sure, to be sure,' you'd probably get a fat lip."

"What?" he asked in mock surprise. "You mean they don't actually talk like that?" And there it was—that sexy smile charming her socks off.

"WHEN YOU SAID POP IN for a coffee, I thought you meant for half an hour, not two and a half bloody hours. It's nearly five thirty!" Melissa's normally sleek brown pageboy was standing on end, and chubby chocolate fingerprints decorated her olive-green jumper. Jack had angrily stomped up to his bedroom after Rebecca nearly had to drag him kicking and screaming to come home. And behind her, Hannah was standing on the couch, chanting "my dinnertime" like a demented pixie.

"So let me have it—did you indulge in a spot of afternoon delight or what?"

"With two seven-year-old chaperones? I don't think so."

Melissa pointed to her jersey in disgust. "Well, whatever you did, it better have been worth it. I won't be responsible for my actions if chocolate doesn't come out in the wash."

Rebecca filled her in on the afternoon's events, spending extra time ogling over David's charming smile while she heated up the macaroni and cheese she'd left defrosting on the bench earlier.

Inspecting a French-polished fingernail for signs of chipping, Melissa casually inquired, "You didn't happen to notice any other dishy daddies outside the school, did you?"

Rebecca shook her head, but Melissa was undeterred. "Don't know why I bothered asking because you've had blinkers on from the moment you saw David. I'll come with you in the morning and check them out myself."

"You will not! I am not having you standing outside a primary school trying to pick up some poor child's dad."

"Why not? You did."

Rebecca ignored her. "You are not coming, Melissa, and that's the end of it."

Melissa's mouth set in a determined line as she followed her to the lounge.

"Hannah, stop jumping on the couch, please! Tea's ready now. Will you take her to wash her hands?" Rebecca pleaded.

"Only if you let me come to the school tomorrow morning."

"Look, just because you spent the afternoon looking after a preschooler doesn't entitle you to behave like one."

"Pretty please. I'll be your best friend."

Rolling her eyes heavenward, Rebecca knew when she was beaten. "Oh, go on then, but if you get arrested for loitering with intent, you're on your own."

That same evening, at six thirty on the dot, the telephone rang.

"That'll be Mummy and Daddy." Rebecca smiled at her deceptively angelic niece sitting with a picture book open on her lap, fresh from her bath in pink flannelette pyjamas. Rebecca stretched over to answer the phone. "Hi, Jen."

Her sister's puzzled voice echoed down the line. "How did you know it was me?"

"The itinerary you left me kind of gave it away."

"Oh yes, right." Jennifer had the grace to sound sheepish as she asked if Rebecca found it useful. As much as it galled Rebecca to admit it, she did.

"Good. I didn't want you to feel like I don't think you're capable or anything but kids do need their routines. So how are they?"

"The children? Oh, they're fine."

"You're managing okay then?" Jennifer sounded relieved.

"Of course. They're a breeze to look after." Across the room, Melissa snorted. Rebecca scowled back at her and quickly changed tack. "How are things at your end?"

Jennifer's curt "good" suggested that Mark was in the room, so the probing ended there. Leaving Hannah to lisp her day's activities to first her mother and then her father, Rebecca went in search of Jack.

A strip of light peeked out from under the bathroom door, so she knocked lightly. "Jack? Your mum and dad are on the phone."

"I'm busy."

"Come on, Jack, they want to say hi to you." From behind the closed door, there was silence. "Jack?"

Suddenly the door flew open and, resplendent in motocross pyjamas, Jack stomped past her into his bedroom. "I don't want to talk to them!" he retorted, shutting the door in her surprised face with a finality more befitting that of a teenager. She ran her fingers through her hair exasperatedly. Rather than waste time with unsuccessful negotiations, she'd have to go and tell Jen he didn't want to talk to them.

"Er, Jen?"

"I thought you were putting Jack on?"

"Um, the thing is—"

Jennifer interrupted, "Oh before I forget, Hannah's just been telling me what she learned today."

"Oh yes?" Rebecca licked her lips, feeling extremely nervous as to what was coming next. *Oh please God, don't let her have sworn at her mother.*

"Yes, it's very interesting. In fact, it was news to me too. I mean, were you aware that Paris Hilton's got cellulite?"

Rebecca's laugh was one of giddy relief. "Yes, I did hear a rumour, courtesy of Melissa."

"Ah, right—Melissa. I should have guessed. So, can I talk to Jack now? I'm missing the kids. It's a funny thing, having children, because there are times you'd give anything to get away from them for a bit but then when you do, you feel like part of you is missing."

She sounded quite jovial now, and it seemed a shame to put a damper on her mood, but Rebecca couldn't stall any longer.

"I'm sorry, Jen, but he doesn't want to come to the phone."

"Pardon?"

"He's in a bit of a sulk in his room." The worst bit over, she found herself ploughing on. "To be honest with you, I think he's picked up on the fact that things aren't right between you and Mark. He feels like he's been abandoned. Maybe you guys should have tried to work things out a little closer to home."

Jennifer was quiet for a moment, and when she spoke, her voice had lost its jokey ring. "I'd appreciate it if you left the psychology bit to the professionals, Rebecca. It's a bit rich coming from you."

"I'm sorry, but I'm only telling you what I—"

"Well, one day when you are in a long-term relationship, you might be qualified to comment. Until then, Mark and I are aware of the effect our problems are having on the kids, which is the whole point of our being here now, giving our marriage one last shot. If it's too much of a problem for you, I'll get on a plane and come home."

"No! And I know, look, I'm sorry. I didn't mean to upset you, but I'm out of my depth with Jack. I don't know what I'm supposed to say to him."

"Just tell him his mum and dad love him and miss him very much and that we'll phone again tomorrow night."

The rest of the conversation was stilted, and it was with relief that Rebecca finally replaced the handset.

"That went well," Melissa commented from her prone position on the couch.

"Honestly." Rebecca rolled her eyes, wishing Jennifer didn't have the ability to wind her up so easily. "It's not my fault her husband did the dirty, but she still manages to make me feel guilty, even though it's me who's helping her out."

Melissa just shrugged. "Sisterly love, eh? I'm glad I'm an only child."

"Come on, miss. Time for bed." Rebecca hauled Hannah up and marched her protesting little body up the stairs. Surprisingly, after a few feeble attempts at escape, Hannah settled down, a huddled mound under her duvet, thumb in mouth. Tiptoeing out of the room, Rebecca took a deep breath. Time to deal with Jack. Bloody Jennifer could explain to Tarquin why her trip back home had turned her prematurely grey when she got back from her farcical love-in, she bitched silently. When she reached Jack's bedroom door, she knocked softly and waited for admittance.

He was sitting up in bed with his bedside light shining down on an open magazine.

"What you reading?" she asked, perching at the end of his bed. He flicked the magazine shut and then held it up for her to see. The vaguely familiar title, *Motocross Action*, was emblazoned across the cover, along with daredevil shots of the sport's latest stars. She shuddered at the thought of Jack one day attempting to launch himself into space, gripping onto a dirt bike while doing a double somersault.

"You bought it for me."

That's right, she'd bought the subscription against her better judgement, after much wheedling on his part. She wasn't sure if it was such an ideal choice of bedtime reading, but he was obviously enjoying it.

"Mum and Dad were a bit sad they didn't get to talk to you."

Jack picked his magazine up again. Seeing the conversation was to be one-sided, Rebecca sighed. "Mum told me to tell you that they both love you very much and that they'll phone again tomorrow night." Standing up, she leaned over to kiss him on the forehead. "Five minutes then turn your light out, okay?"

He nodded without looking up.

Chapter Fourteen

"ALRIGHT, ALRIGHT, KEEP your knickers on," Rebecca muttered in response to the insistent rapping at the front door. She had no idea how long whoever it was had been out there because she hadn't heard the knocking over the whining of the vacuum cleaner. Opening the door, she blinked into the sunshine that was just beginning to break through the remains of the morning mist and rapidly blinked again, not quite believing her own eyes.

"I nearly died of hyperthermia. What kept you so bloody long?"

There, tapping her foot imperiously, was the camel-coated vision that was her sister.

Rebecca stared at Jennifer, slack-jawed. "What are you doing here?"

"Well, hello to you too, sis. I do live here, you know."

"You know what I mean. Where's Mark?" Rebecca looked over her sister's shoulder to where her brother-in-law's car was parked, expecting to see him unloading the boot. There was no sign of him, and she swung her gaze back to her sister. *What was going on?*

"He stayed on in Mooloolaba because he couldn't see the point in us both missing out on a five-star holiday that's bought and paid for. Now stop standing there with your mouth hanging open like a simpleton and let me in. I was sunbathing in twenty-three degrees heat yesterday, you know."

Rebecca stepped out of the way and her sister picked up her suitcase and swished past her with a proprietary air. Shutting the door behind her, she scuttled up the hall, nearly shunting into Jennifer as she stopped to shrug out of her coat. She watched as she tossed it onto the coat stand and then, shaking her hair free from her roll neck, asked, "The children are at school and preschool, I take it?"

"Of course. Um, Jen—what's happened? Why are you back so early?"

"Jack obviously wasn't coping with Mark and me both being away. So I caught a late flight back last night and stayed in a motel in Christchurch." She shot her sister an accusatory look concerning her son's ongoing refusal to come to the telephone, picking up her case once more and dragging it up the stairs. "Alright if I put you in with Melissa?" she called over her shoulder.

"I could have handled Jack. We've made it this far; he would have been fine. You didn't need to come back because of him," Rebecca called after her, but Jennifer either didn't hear or didn't want to hear her. Rebecca had a feeling it was the latter.

"Where is your sidekick then?" Jennifer asked, flicking the kettle on ten minutes later. She grabbed two mugs, adding, "I'll have a cup of tea with you then I'll pop down and tell Betty I am home. I can greet the new guests before I go and pick Hannah up."

Rebecca bit her lip. Her sister had been home half an hour and already she'd taken charge, leaving her feeling surplus to requirements. "If by sidekick you mean Melissa, she has gone into town for the day to meet some friends for lunch and contrary to what you seem to think, we are not joined at the hip." She took a deep breath and told herself to play nice. "I'll come with you to get Hannah, if you want?"

Jennifer waved her hand dismissively before picking up the squealing jug. "No, there's no need. Why don't you read a book and relax or something?"

Her sister was such a bossy boots. "Jen, I didn't fly over ten thousand miles just to sit and read a book for the week. I was supposed to be here helping out, remember?" Rebecca saw Jennifer's shoulders stiffen, and she sloshed boiling water onto the bench as she put the kettle back down with more force than was necessary.

"I'm sorry about the way things have worked out, Rebecca. I didn't know Jack would react the way he has to Mark and me being away." Her voice was low and controlled as she turned around. "But I am home now, so you and I just need to make the best of it, okay?"

"That's not what I was—" Oh what was the bloody use? Rebecca thought, scraping the chair back and standing up. Jennifer just didn't get it. All she wanted was to feel useful, not like a houseguest. "Look, don't worry about the tea. I'll leave you to it. I'm going to go and check my emails." She hovered in the doorway. "If that's alright with you?"

Jennifer didn't bother replying to the sarcastic request and as she watched her sister turn and march out of the room, she sat down heavily. Leaning her elbows on the table, she pressed her palms into her eyes in a bid to stop the tears that were threatening. "I will not cry," she muttered to the empty kitchen, wondering why it was she seemed to be at cross purposes with everybody who mattered in her life. She'd even had words with her mum about heading to Mooloolaba in the first place but then Pamela hadn't known the circumstances surrounding the trip.

She pressed harder until her eyes hurt. Sometimes it all just seemed so hard, so damned hard, she thought, and she was just so damned tired. Sleep had gone out the window in the last month since it had all come to a head with Mark. As she released the pressure and dropped her hands onto the table in front of her, she studied her nails for a moment. There was a great big chink in her otherwise perfect coral nail polish. It was almost symbolic, she thought ruefully, knowing that she didn't have the energy to pop down and see Betty or the new guests. Besides, she was going to have to head upstairs and clean up the panda rings her mascara had no doubt left behind before she went and got Hannah. She couldn't let anybody see the crack in her armour, the chink in her polish. Jennifer sighed shakily. All her life, people had viewed her as strong, and she had long since learned not to let her vulnerability show.

Needy wasn't a role she was allowed to play, or at least not for long. In their family, that space had been firmly reserved for Rebecca. If she were honest with herself, too, she'd always enjoyed being viewed as the more capable sister. The parts they each played in the family dynamic had always been clearly defined. She'd carried that capable big sister role through into her adult life, adapting it slightly when it came to being a wife and then a mother. Look at what an almighty mess she'd made of that initially, too, she thought, flashing back to the mire she'd sunk into after Jack had been born. That was why she'd come back from Mooloolaba early—she wasn't going to let him down again. *To hell with Mark.* The tears threatened again, and she blinked them away furiously as she pushed the chair back and stood up.

She wasn't going to go there, not today—not when it was all she could do just to muster up the strength to get through the afternoon. Heading up the stairs to repair the damage before she went to collect Hannah, she told herself now was not the time to think about what an awful mess she'd made of her marriage.

REBECCA FLOUNCED OFF to the computer room, picking her phone up on the way. *Bloody Jennifer*. She couldn't believe she was back already. Not when she'd just begun to settle into a good routine with Hannah and Jack, not to mention meeting David at the school gates both morning and afternoon. The last few days had gone well, and she had found herself enjoying the responsibility of it all. The children had given her a sense of purpose and yes, okay, she got that Jennifer was worried about Jack. She was his mother; it was only natural. But she should have taken her word for it when she said he was doing fine, and concentrated on working on her marriage instead of jumping on the first plane home. That was the problem, though—always had been. Jennifer didn't take her word when it came to anything. She still treated her like that podgy kid sister she'd once been and not as an equal.

Opening the door to the office, she flopped down in the chair and checked her phone. A text had arrived from Derbhilla and glad of the distraction from her current train of thought, she opened it.

It took her a moment to scroll through and decode it because her friend, who was obviously three sheets to the wind, had sent her message in separate texts. Eventually, she pieced it all together. Despite the fact that Derbhilla and the gang had left the first day of the races—the Big Bash—poorer, they'd had a blast, which wasn't to say that Rebecca hadn't been missed. (She smiled at that.) Pariah had placed all her bets on Ciaran but so far hadn't got him past the starting post. She frowned at that, gripping the phone tightly as if the little piece of technology were to blame for the information. "Bloody Pariah," she'd snarled, imagining her pulling her dumb blonde act. *"Who do you think I should place a bet on, Ciaran?"* She'd probably stuck her boobs as well as her racebook under his nose.

Not adhering to that old saying of don't shoot the messenger, she gave the phone a look of disgust before tapping out a quick reply. She informed her friend of her sister's unexpected homecoming and then she turned her attention to the computer. There was another email from Ciaran:

To: Rebecca Loughton

Subject: Flatulence when flying

Dear Rebecca,

It is a subject close to my heart. Last time I was on a long haul from Dublin to Boston, I got stuck in the window seat next to a middle-aged couple from Sligo—Nora and Ted. They took me under their wing—you know, the way older couples do when you're a young person travelling on your own. After four hours of listening to Nora and Ted's life stories, Nora finally dozed off, and Ted put his headphones on and shut his eyes. The plane was in semi-darkness and most of the passengers were either sleeping or trying to when Ted bolted upright and, completely forgetting he had headphones on, yelled out, "Did you fart, Nora?" The poor woman was mortified, and I felt sorry for her until the smell drifted over my way and then it was a case of nowhere to run, baby. I still recoil at the thought of it now.

Do you think perhaps we should set up a flatulence travel blog? I wonder if they fart in first class? You could always ask your friend Melissa. Galway is a blast. Though I will probably be working right up to retirement age the way things went yesterday. Still, it could all change in an instant and tomorrow is Ladies Day, traditionally a lucky day for me.

Now I need to ask you for a little favour. The answer to number 46: "What glam American metal band sang about a rose?"

Love, Ciaran.

So she replied:

To: Ciaran

Subject: Flatulence when flying.

Dear Ciaran

I think a travel blog is a great idea, and I am almost looking forward to the flight home now so I can get some more material to post on it. My mood had improved since my last email because, despite Hannah's tantrums and Jack's sulking, they are both still alive. I thought to myself that I must be doing something right, but then my sister showed up an hour ago. She caught an early flight home from Australia and in her usual style has already managed to make me feel like I'm ten years old again.

Overbearing big sisters aside, I have met a nice man through Jack, though. His best friend Ben's dad, to be precise. Children do have their uses. Though Melissa is taking things a bit too far by insisting on tagging along for the school run in an attempt to pull herself a solo dad. As for me and David, well, it's early days. But you know me, Ciaran: I can work fast when I have to.

Good luck with Ladies Day, though knowing you as I do, I doubt very much you'll need it. As for your query regarding number 46, that's easy because it still brings a tear to my eye: Poison—'Every Rose Has Its Thorn'.

Love, Rebecca

Put that in your pipe and smoke it, Ciaran Cahill, she thought, reading over her references to David before punching Send.

"SHE'S IN BED," REBECCA hissed in reply to Melissa's question as to where her sister was, having phoned her earlier in the day to warn her Jennifer was back.

"What do you mean, she's in bed?" Melissa hissed back over the tops of Jack and Hannah's heads, each bent earnestly over their respective dinners. The poor things were starving. Rebecca had been late in serving up, deciding to wait for Jennifer to come down and join them before she did so—only she'd never appeared.

Putting her fingers to her lips and shooting a meaningful look at her niece and nephew, Rebecca beckoned for Melissa to follow her through to the lounge, away from flapping ears. "Slow down, you two! Nobody's going to take it off you!" she tossed over her shoulder before shutting the door behind her. Both children ignored her and carried on shovelling and chewing like half-starved orphans.

Once the door was shut, she reiterated, "It was weird. Jen went and picked Hannah up. She wet her pants, she was so excited to see her, but Jack wasn't impressed at all or if he was, the look on his face when he got home from school didn't give it away. Honestly, I thought it was teenagers who were supposed to cop an attitude, not seven-year-olds." She shook her head at the thought of her sulky nephew. "She hardly spent any time with either of them before she disappeared off upstairs. I don't think she's even been down to tell Betty she's back yet. I went up to see her about coming down for dinner, but she won't get up. She says she's too tired."

"But it's only a three-and-a-half hour flight from Brisbane. It's not as though she'd have jet lag."

"I know that."

"And she told you she came back because of Jack?"

"That's what she said."

Melissa waved her hand dismissively. "Rubbish—I bet things weren't going well with Mark, so she decided to come home. Jack was a convenient excuse to use until she decides to face up to the fact her marriage is a dead duck in the water." Her brown hair bobbed self-righteously as she added, "Lying around in bed isn't going to help make things better, though."

"Oh, I don't know—maybe all the stress of what's been happening with Mark has taken its toll. Stress can do funny things to you, you know." Rebecca had once heard someone say this, and it had sounded very wise.

"Mm, she probably just needs a good night's sleep, that's all." Melissa had a very short attention span when it came to listening to other people's woes. "She'll be back to normal tomorrow. You'll see. I'm off to have a lovely long soak in the bath followed by bed. Jennifer's not the only one who needs a good night's sleep. What a day!" She stretched theatrically, dropping her arms back down to her sides as a thought occurred to her. "Hey, have you got any of that yummy Body Shop stuff with you?"

Rebecca shook her head and bit her lip to stop herself from saying that yes, it must be hard work swanning around town, wining and dining with friends.

"Oh well, never mind. I'll have a sticky beak in the cabinet and see what I can find instead. See you in the morning, sweetie."

With that, she skipped off up the stairs in a very spritely manner for one so tired, leaving Rebecca to wonder for the zillionth time why it was they were still friends. She knew the answer to that little conundrum. It was because she was scared of being on her own, that was why, and having Melissa around was better than having no one at all. She was distracted from pursuing this train of thought further by an indignant voice yelling, "Auntie Becca, Hannah just threw a carrot at me."

Throwing food around was Hannah's way of saying she was full and with a sigh, Rebecca went back to the kitchen—it looked like she was in charge again. For tonight at least. Melissa was probably right; Jen would be fine by the morning.

But she wasn't.

Chapter Fifteen

REBECCA HAD TAKEN AN age to get to sleep; her mind had gone into overdrive playing over her sister's unexpected arrival home, not to mention her email to Ciaran. She'd forgotten all about Melissa's annoying little snoring habit too, and she was just thinking about smothering her with a pillow when she must have dropped off into a deep, deep slumber. She was in the midst of a most peculiar dream. It involved David, only he was David with Ciaran's face. The Haglund Ride (an all-terrain Arctic vehicle she had once taken her niece and nephew for a terrifyingly bouncy ride on at Christchurch's Antarctic Centre) was in there too. David's voice was growing high-pitched and annoyingly insistent. She popped an eye open to find Hannah's face looming.

"Wake up, Auntie Becca—wake up! I wanna MILK!"

"Sort the rug rat out. Some of us are trying to sleep," Melissa mumbled, turning over onto her side, so she was facing the wall.

Humph, Rebecca thought, opening the other eye and rubbing at them both; the hour that the girl had taken herself off to bed last night, she should have been up and at it hours ago. "Go and wake your mummy up, Hannah," she groaned. Jennifer was home now, so it was only fair she resume her early morning duties; they were her children, after all.

"I have, but she's not waking up."

Something in the way this innocuous statement was delivered triggered fear deep in Rebecca's belly. It penetrated her groggy brain as random thoughts about her sister's strange behaviour yesterday jostled, stirring her into wakefulness. Sitting up and swinging her legs over the bed, she didn't even bother with her dressing gown and slippers as she stampeded down the hall in the direction of the master bedroom.

Pushing open the door, she peered into the darkness afforded by the heavy drapes. They were so tightly pulled that not so much as a crack of light could peep through. The musty smell of a heavy slumber assailed her nostrils, and she made her way towards the bed, where she could just make out the huddled form of her sister. Her pace slowed as she drew closer to the bed because she was suddenly filled with trepidation as to what she might discover. Rebecca was dimly aware of hollering coming from down the hall, but she remained focused on Jennifer. Her peripheral vision registered a bottle of pills on the bedside table. Reaching down to gently shake her sister awake, she sent up a silent prayer for her to be alright.

"Jen? It's me, Becca. Time to get up—wakey, wakey," she whispered.

The lump under the bedcovers didn't move.

"Please, Jen, come on. It's time to wake up!" Her voice took on a note of urgency, but there was still no response. "Jen, please wake up. WAKE UP!" She bellowed the latter in desperation and gave her sister a good whack.

"Ouch—what the?" Jennifer rolled over and squinted at her. "Rebecca, what did you do that for? Fuck off!"

Rebecca took a step back. *She was alive and well then.* "You're okay! Thank goodness," she breathed, unable to stop herself from stating the obvious.

"Of course I'm okay." Jennifer hauled herself up to a sitting position. Her blonde curls were mussed. She'd have fun getting a hairbrush through that, Rebecca thought. She watched with a sense of relief as Jennifer fiddled around, plumping up a pillow to stick behind her back before asking, "What's going on?"

Rebecca's bottom lip trembled, and the tears that followed were an instinctive release. "I—I thought you'd done something stupid. The way you were yesterday and Hannah said you wouldn't wake up; then when I saw the pills, I just thought—"

"Oh my God, Rebecca, you seriously thought I'd taken an overdose?"

Rebecca nodded and swiped at the tears. It did sound rather silly now that Jennifer was sitting up looking reasonably perky for somebody with a beehive for a hairdo who'd found herself being woken up by a screaming madwoman.

Jennifer's voice softened. Becca was in a state; she owed her an explanation. "I took a tablet last night to help me sleep, you silly old thing. With everything that's been going on lately, I just haven't been sleeping properly, and I decided I needed an unbroken night because things never look so bleak after a good night's sleep. At least that's what Mum always says. It's nice to know you care, though."

"Of course I bloody well care." Rebecca wiped at her nose as a particularly ear-splitting shriek rebounded down the hallway.

Jennifer's eyes narrowed. "What on earth is that ruckus?"

"I'm guessing Hannah is trying to get Melissa up. She was desperate for her morning milk fix. From my experience, though, the only thing that will move Melissa is to whisper in her ear that Brad Pitt is on his way over and that she hasn't got her make-up on. That usually shifts her quick smart."

Jennifer snorted at the mental picture and then her face sobered. "Becs, why do you bother with her?"

"What do you mean?"

"I mean she is a self-centred madam who treats you like her PA instead of her friend. She always has done."

"That's not true." The words tripped automatically off her tongue. "She does have some good qualities." Rebecca was on the defence.

"Oh yeah?"

"Yeah, loads of them."

Jennifer raised an eyebrow expectantly. "Like?"

"Um, well, she's, she's—oh crap, I can't think of any."

They collapsed into giggles. "You're a good tonic, Becs," Jennifer said, wiping her eyes that were still puffy from sleeping so heavily. She glanced over at the bedside clock. "Bloody hell! Look at the time—the kids will be late!" Throwing back the bedcovers, she announced, "I'm already in Jack's bad books, and this is so not going to help. He hates being late for school."

Rebecca held her hand up. "Stop! Calm down, Jen." She pushed her sister back on the bed. "Look, since I am so obviously full of sisterly love this morning, I will do the school run and let you have a lie in, okay?"

"Are you sure?"

"Of course I'm sure. I came home to help out, and that's what I want to do. So please don't go playing the martyr, okay?"

"Yes, boss." Jen gave her a mock salute and then frowned as she tucked her hair behind her ears. "You won't get any argument from me because I couldn't face anyone this morning. Especially not the mummy mafia at the school gates. I tell you what, Becs, there are some fabulous pluses about living in a small community, but there are some bloody great minuses too."

The disconcerted look on her normally self-assured sister's face prompt-ed Rebecca to ask, "Jen, are you okay? I mean really okay?"

Her sister chewed her bottom lip for a moment, and her eyes grew suspi-ciously bright. "No, I'm not."

Rebecca squirmed. "That was a stupid question, sorry." And it had been but there was just something about the look in Jennifer's eyes that worried her. "Of course you're not okay—how could you be with all this crap going on with Mark. Do you want to talk about it?"

Her sister gave a funny little half smile and shrugged. "I don't know."

"It might help."

"We'll see. But you had better be getting a move on if you're going to get that son of mine to school before the bell goes." Jennifer laid her head back on the pillows and sighed as she heard Rebecca begin rounding up the troops. There was so much she wished she could say to Becs, but she just couldn't bring herself to confide in her. Her little sister was far too naïve to ever understand. There was nobody she could tell, she thought, wishing that she were the type of woman who had close girlfriends. Then maybe she wouldn't feel so alone now but she had never been a woman's woman. She'd been too driven and too focused on her career to spend time nurtur-ing friendships. Her closest confidante was Betty, but she couldn't bring her-self to open up to her either, even though she knew Betty would never sit in judgement of her. The problem was, though, she judged herself. A cloud of fatigue began to descend, and she closed her eyes, telling herself it was just for a moment.

JACK SLAMMED THE CAR door shut and, as his auntie headed down the driveway, whined, "We're late. I told you we would be late. It's all Mum's stupid fault."

Rebecca glanced up into the mirror and spied her nephew with his bottom lip protruding.

His annoyance at his mother was palpable, and she frowned. *Surely it wasn't normal for a kid his age to be filled with this much angst?* "Don't talk about your mum like that, Jack," she admonished, deciding the time had come to deploy a distraction technique. "I'll bet you fifty cents that we'll make it to school before the second bell goes." She held up a silver coin that was sitting in the ashtray and waved it temptingly.

It did the trick and the bottom lip receded to its rightful place. "Make it a dollar."

Rebecca lost the bet and, shoving the gold coin in his pocket, Jack ran in to join the handful of other late stragglers, one of whom happened to be Ben. She cast her eyes around the car park, hoping to spot David, but he'd already seen her and was making his way over.

"Hi there."

His hair was still wet from his shower, and he smelt like a pine forest after it had rained, Rebecca thought, smiling up at him. "Hi, how's it going?"

"You were cutting it fine too." He inclined his head towards Jack and Ben, who having reached their classroom, were disappearing inside the door.

"Ah yes, but *I* had a good excuse. Did you?"

"Um, does forgetting to set the alarm count as a good excuse?"

"Nope, sorry, that one doesn't cut the mustard."

His eyes crinkled. "So come on, fess up—why were you late?"

"Jennifer's back, that's why. We got chatting and lost track of the time. I don't suppose that cuts the mustard either."

His eyebrows shot up. "I thought she wasn't due home for at least another week or so?"

"She wasn't but apparently she was worried about Jack because he's been acting a bit weird with her and Mark. So she came home early."

"Mark came home too, I take it?"

"No, he stayed on. He didn't see the point in them both missing out on the holiday since they'd already paid for it."

"Oh, right." He looked thoughtful as he processed this information.

He was probably wondering how the hell Mark could carry on sunning himself in Mooloolaba when his son was obviously having difficulties. She didn't blame him if he was because she couldn't believe what a selfish arse her brother-in-law was either.

"So where does Jennifer being home leave you?" His expression was one of concern, and Rebecca hoped it was because he was worried it might mean she'd cut her trip short. Well, he needn't worry.

"I'm going to stay on because I have a feeling Jen's going to need me around." She didn't know how much David knew about her sister's marital situation but was saved from any awkward questions by the blaring of the horn.

"Honestly, that child! I thought she'd be over the terrible twos at three and a half."

David laughed. "I think she's telling you she's ready to go and didn't you know it's the terrible twos, the diabolical threes, horrific fours... do you want me to go on?"

"No thank you. I get the picture." She jumped as the horn blared again. "Right, well, I have obviously got to go." She hesitated, hoping for—well, she wasn't sure what she was hoping for but whatever it was, it wasn't forthcoming.

"Hey, tell Jennifer I said hello, won't you?" David said before turning to walk back to where his vehicle was parked.

Rebecca was disappointed. "Sure. See you."

He waved, and she hotfooted it over to the car to berate Hannah, who having spotted the look on her aunt's face, was frantically clambering back over the car seat and into her booster.

MELISSA HAD TAKEN UP her usual pew in the sunroom when Rebecca arrived home and, spying her friend, she inclined her head towards the kitchen. "The queen of cooking is up as of five minutes ago. I must say, she's not looking her usual blonde and beautiful self, though. I thought it best I stay out of her way until she's had a cup of coffee; otherwise, I would have done the dishes."

Yeah, right, Rebecca thought as Melissa bent her head back over her magazine, signalling the conversation was closed. She rolled her eyes and pushed on through to the kitchen.

"Hi."

"Hey." Jennifer looked up, and in the light of day Rebecca could see there were dark rings under her eyes and her face looked wan despite the hours spent in bed.

"Jen, you don't look too flash. You're not coming down with something, are you?"

"No. I'm just tired, that's all."

Rebecca didn't want to ask how she could still be tired after all that sleep, so she busied herself making a drink. "Have you been to see Betty yet?"

"No, not yet." Her sigh seemed to emanate from the depths of her soul. "Oh, Becs, everything just seems like such a monumental effort and I haven't got the energy."

Rebecca turned around to where her sister was sitting, her laced fingers propping up her chin. Her hair was falling on either side of her face, forming a bedraggled frame. "What do you mean?" She was completely unprepared for the floodgates that suddenly opened as Jennifer broke into noisy sobs.

At that same moment, Melissa popped her head round the door, cup in hand. "Any chance of a coffee?" Spying Jennifer, she backed out of the kitchen. "Er, maybe I'll leave you two to it and head into town for a proper frothy coffee."

"Good idea," Rebecca stated firmly, going over to her sister and wrapping her arm around her quaking shoulders.

"I feel like my life's spiralling out of control." Jennifer sniffed, taking a tissue from the box Rebecca was proffering.

Rebecca sat opposite her, watching as she gave her nose a good blow. The last time she had seen her like this was after Jack was born.

"You do like to be in control of things, Jen." Seeing her sister's shoulders stiffen, she hastily added, "I don't mean that critically; it's just part of what makes you who you are. What I'm saying, though, is that it must make things hard for you sometimes because life does have a tendency to veer off course. Take it from someone who knows."

Jennifer managed a small smile at that, and Rebecca, emboldened, found herself asking something she had often pondered. "Was that the problem when Jack was born, and you had that bout of the baby blues? You felt like you had no control?" She cast her mind back to those early days when her sister had struggled to adjust to sharing her life with a baby.

Jennifer shook her head forcefully. "No. You and everyone else only saw what you wanted to see. It was never just the baby blues, you know, a few tears a couple of days after he was born while my hormones settled down. I was diagnosed with postnatal depression."

This was news to Rebecca and her eyes widened. "Oh my gosh; do you mean like Brooke Shields?" She'd read an article about how she'd suffered after the birth of a daughter she'd been trying to conceive for years. It had made for sad reading.

At that, Jennifer gave a little laugh. "Yeah, kind of; it manifests itself differently for different people, though. Promise me you won't repeat this conversation to Tom Cruise, okay?"

Rebecca reddened, vaguely remembering having also read or heard that the movie star had gotten in bother over his insensitive remarks where postnatal depression was concerned; her knowledge of this subject was somewhat limited. "I just assumed you found having Jack hard going at the start, like most new mums. All my friends who have had kids go on about what a major lifestyle adjustment it is."

This time her sister's laugh held no mirth. "If you can call 'hard going' being unable to summon up any feelings at all for this tiny thing you've just given birth to and feeling like you no longer exist as a separate entity. Like you're drowning on a daily basis in this neverending quagmire of sleep deprivation, leaking from every orifice, and overwhelmed with nappies and baby sick. And feeling that when you gave birth, you fell into this deep and dark hole. A hole so deep and dark that no matter how hard you tried, you couldn't see any light filtering in at the top of it. Then, yeah, I got through it."

"I thought I was the one prone to dramatics."

Jennifer raised a rueful smile. "You are, and I am not dramatic. That's what it was like."

Rebecca couldn't get a handle on what she was hearing. "I knew things weren't great, which was why I didn't jump up and down with excitement when you bought this place, but I had no idea it was that bad!"

"If it makes you feel better, I thought your lack of enthusiasm when we bought it was because you were jealous. It seems like we both misread each other. Perhaps we should have tried communicating a bit better." The smile that played at the corner of her mouth was sad because you couldn't go back. If you could, she would have handled things differently. "As for not knowing how I was feeling back then, well, nobody knew except Mark. I was good at keeping the fact I wasn't coping hidden. I didn't want anybody to know." She shrugged. "I thought you and Mum and Dad would think I was going mad if I told you what was going on because to be honest, that's what I thought was happening."

"Mark knew, though?"

"Yeah. I tried to explain the things that were going through my mind in the early days after we brought Jack home."

"Why didn't he do anything then?" Rebecca interrupted indignantly, grateful to be able to lay the blame at somebody else's door.

"His wife suffering from postnatal depression didn't fit the picture Mark had painted of family life. He withdrew into work and just left me to get on with it. To be fair, he didn't understand it. Perhaps if he'd been some support, I might have found the strength to get some help sooner instead of feeling like such a freak of nature." Bitterness crept into her voice as she carried on. "I'd go along to these coffee mornings, Becs, where all the mums would sit around scoffing biscuits, talking about breastfeeding and how hard having a new baby was. I could tell that despite their moaning they were all besotted with their children. Then there was me, just going through the motions."

Rebecca's heart broke for her sister. For the first time since they'd been kids, she saw a vulnerability in Jennifer that she thought she had long since grown out of. There had been no one she felt she could turn to; no one who would understand. Even their mum probably wouldn't accept the idea that her daughter was incapable of loving her baby. Jen had thought that she was a total failure at motherhood and marriage, and had been blaming herself. After all, it had all been her choice. Like everything else in her life. It was all her own doing. She'd made the decision to get married and to have a baby, but her body somehow couldn't accept it.

"When I had the idea for Cuisine with Carlton's," Jennifer broke into Rebecca's contemplations, "it was like somebody had switched a light on in my brain. If I hadn't of set the business up, I would never have met Betty. And it was Betty who was my salvation in the end."

"Betty?"

"Yes, Betty. She'd been through it herself with her first baby. She picked up that things weren't what they should be between me and Jack and you've no idea how good it felt to talk to someone who understood. Someone who didn't see me as this unnatural monster. She gave me absolution by telling me I was sick, and I'll always love her for that. She frogmarched me off to the doctors."

The two sisters smiled at each other, Jennifer remembering Betty bossily taking her under her wing and Rebecca fully able to picture the scene. "It took a while. But with the right medication and time, eventually things began to get better."

"And how do you feel about Jack now?" Rebecca ventured this with trepidation, unsure what the answer would be.

Jennifer examined the transparent look of terror on her sister's face. "It's okay," she answered reassuringly. "Like I said, things got better. Now I feel how any mother feels about her child. I love him so much I'd lay down my life for him. Jack and Hannah are my world."

"But not Mark?"

"No, not Mark. Not anymore. We've tried our hardest, Becs, but the affair was only a symptom of a long illness because after Jack, we never really got things back on track."

"Is that why you had Hannah?"

"If I say yes, it sounds terrible—like Hannah was a Band-Aid baby or something."

"Was she?"

"I'd be lying if I didn't admit to a little bit of that in my reasoning, but mainly my motivation for getting pregnant again was purely selfish. I wanted to experience motherhood the way other women experience it."

"You must have been petrified of it happening again," Rebecca whispered tenderly.

"Yes and no. I knew that this time round I'd recognise the signs and get some help or at least I thought I would. With Jack, I had a blissful pregnancy, unaware of what I was in for, but with Hannah, I was uptight for the whole nine months. I needn't have been, though; everything was fine."

"But it's not fine now."

"No, it's not. I feel like I am on this bullet train that is approaching the end of the line and can't stop. I am so damned scared of what comes next, Becs." Her breath was ragged, and Rebecca got up and wrapped her in a tight hug. For the first time in her life where their relationship was concerned, she was the one in charge.

Chapter Sixteen

LATER THAT NIGHT WITH the children tucked up in bed and Jennifer fast asleep, Rebecca explained to Betty what was going on with Jennifer while Melissa sat riveted to some inane reality TV show.

"I think she just needs plenty of TLC while she gets her head around everything that has happened and is going to happen. Starting with lots of rest because she's been running on empty for too long."

Betty nodded sagely. "Yes, she has. I knew things weren't good between her and Mark, and I've been worried about her, but you know your sister. She's always determined to soldier on by herself, and she wouldn't let me in to help her."

Yes, Rebecca thought, that was the Jennifer she knew and loved but even she had her breaking point and she had reached it.

"I'll pop up and see how she's getting on tomorrow. She's not to worry about the cooking school. I have it all under control. I'll tell her she needs to loosen the reins and let me get on with it while she gets herself sorted." Betty looked thoughtful, adding, "You know, Rebecca, love, it's a godsend you being here for her too."

Rebecca sat a bit taller hearing that but then was distracted by a phone announcing the arrival of a text message. All three women reached for their handbags and began rifling through them, but it was Rebecca who held hers aloft triumphantly before scrolling down her messages.

"Who is it from?" Melissa asked sulkily, tossing her red leather Balenciaga bag over the side of the couch as though it were worth no more than a plastic supermarket bag. A mute Rebecca squeaked a reply as her face went white upon reading the message. Melissa didn't need to be a brain surgeon to figure out that whatever had just been conveyed to her friend wasn't good.

Unsure of what to do, Rebecca only knew that she needed a moment on her own, preferably with a large glass of something alcoholic. "Excuse me for a minute, Betty. I don't feel too good." Her legs carried her through to the kitchen on automatic pilot, and then, flinging open the fridge, she poured the remains of a bottle of wine into a glass. Gulping its contents down, she banged the empty glass down on the bench, half expecting its stem to shatter.

"Are you alright, Becs?" Melissa appeared in the doorway, her expression anxious. Leaning back against the kitchen bench, Rebecca wrapped her arms protectively around herself and took a deep breath.

"Those texts were from Derbhilla. She said she didn't want to be the one to have to tell me but that she felt that it was better coming from her."

"What, for goodness' sake?" Melissa urged.

She licked her suddenly dry lips. "It would appear that my boss struck it lucky on Ladies Day."

"Ciaran? Who with?"

"None other than the Queen of Lycra."

"No!"

"Yes."

"But you more or less told me you weren't interested in him anymore, so why the drama?"

Melissa's question was loaded, and Rebecca felt a surge of anger at her that she was taking such a hard line. "Because it was with that cow and because, oh, I don't bloody know." She ran out of the kitchen, through the lounge, and took the stairs two at a time.

A bewildered Betty watched her go, her matronly features creased in concern. "I don't know," she muttered to the empty room as she shook her head. "These young girls and their dramas. I'm glad I'm past all that."

REBECCA PRETENDED SHE was asleep when Melissa came up to bed; she didn't want to talk. All she wanted to do was lick her wounds privately because it stung that Ciaran had slept with a woman who yearned to be Rachel Hunter but resembled Mariah Carey on a *very* bad hair day. And why did it hurt so much? It wasn't that she fancied Ciaran. No, she had been there and done that—or rather, done him—so no, that couldn't be it. After all, she had David to ogle over now. Still, it was only natural to have a teensy bit of affection for someone with whom one worked so closely. She shivered at the memory of that one night they had shared together. It had been so very good. Even if Ciaran felt the same way, she knew he would never act on it, not with his PA. The fact he hadn't even bothered to phone her afterward to ask why she had sneaked out the way she had the morning after proved that. He had simply shown up at work on the following Monday and acted as though it was business as usual. The simple truth of the matter was that he relied on her professionally. Far too much so to ruin their working relationship with a romp. Besides, if he could sleep with the likes of Pariah, then it showed what kind of girl he wanted—certainly not Rebecca. White stilettos and a big hair kind of a gal she was not! Nope; she had to let it go and focus her energies on David.

Staring up into the darkness, she realised her return ticket had her scheduled to fly out a week from today. By then she'd have been away for nearly two weeks. It had seemed like a lifetime in purgatory initially when she'd booked the ticket. The thing was, though, she wasn't so sure that she wanted to fly out anymore and not just because Jennifer so obviously needed her around. What was there for her to go back to now?

Her brows knitted together in a Botox-inducing frown; she wasn't sure if she could face working for Ciaran anymore. The flirty banter that had made her job fun would be meaningless now that she knew there was no chance of it ever spilling over into something deeper. Forcing her eyes shut, she tried to banish the images of that night, but they kept coming, and she found herself back at Ciaran's apartment.

Their first kiss had been soft, searching almost. It had grown in its intensity as Ciaran, gaining in confidence, had unwrapped his strong arms from around her and begun to explore. Those long, shapely fingers she'd admired so often as they scribbled out memos, or typed emails, were at last reaching out—touching, stroking—and it had been exquisite. She shivered, giving herself over to the memory as she smiled into the darkness at what came next: two bodies entwined as one—hot despite the chill.

THE SATURDAY MORNING cartoons were in full swing, occupying the children, when Rebecca mooched through to join Melissa, who was sitting in the sunroom enjoying the unexpected winter bonus of sunshine.

Melissa looked at her friend hopefully. "Do you fancy a spot of people-watching? There're all sorts of new cafés that have opened in the village since I was last here, and it might take your mind off you-know-who."

"Mm, sounds good." She had woken up determined to be cheery and not to think about Ciaran. One depressed sister in the Loughton family was enough, and she had already promised Jen she would take the children off her hands for the day. "We should make the most of the weather. There's that lit-tle park down by the water; maybe we could grab a couple of takeaway lattes while the kids have a play?"

Melissa frowned. That wasn't quite what she'd had in mind. Instead, she'd been picturing herself crossing her legs seductively outside a Parisian-style café while men stumbled over themselves at the vision, sipping her milky lat-te made with trim milk, of course. Sitting on the damp grass watching squeal-ing prepubescents at play was not her idea of fun. Still, she liked to think she was a good sport and so, getting up from her seat, she went in search of her jacket. The weather was far too nice to be in a bad mood. Lattes to go would have to do.

They managed to drag the children away from the television and out the front door to herd them into the Land Cruiser. Indicating left onto Rue Lavaud and cruising slowly down the main road, they were amazed by the number of people out and about. "Where have they all come from? Bloody day trippers," Rebecca muttered like a local as, with no parks in sight, she in-dicated right onto Rue Jolie. "We'll try for a park up here. We should have walked. Serves us right for being so lazy."

"I don't do walking, Becs; you know that. What's the point in spending ages getting ready just to get all hot and sweaty before you get to wherever it is you're going? There's one, there!"

With the children clapping in the back seat and Melissa making mutter-ings about the f****** Brady Bunch, Rebecca executed a perfect parallel park.

"Where'd you learn how to do that?" Melissa was impressed.

"Dad—it was a male pride thing. He reckoned if God couldn't see fit to give him a son, then it was up to him to make sure his daughters knew how to parallel park like men."

"I'll be telling your dad he's a sexist old fart next time I see him."

"I wouldn't bother; I've been telling him that for years. Come on, kids. Let's go."

They wandered towards the Saturday morning hub at a companionable snail's pace, thanks to Hannah, who refused to go in her stroller, opting for the independence of toddling instead. Her brother kept himself two steps ahead.

"It is gorgeous here," Melissa said as, turning onto Rue Lavaud, they were met with the stunning vista of French Bay's blue water sparkling in the sunshine. Up ahead, the boulevard was teeming with people, a vibrant mix of backpackers, tour groups, families, and locals. They joined the throng and had only been ambling along for a few minutes when Melissa nudged Rebecca sharply. The third woman they'd seen on their short trip thus far, passed by them dressed in nautical stripes, white slacks, and tennis shoes. She had what seemed to be a requisite yapping poodle attached to a long lead.

"Spooky. Do you think they're clones?" she whispered, and Rebecca giggled. "Shoot me if you ever catch me contemplating blue and white stripes."

As they passed the first of many eateries, the cry went up: "Can I have an ice cream, Auntie Becca?" Jack's face was hopeful, and his sister began chanting, "Icecweam, icecweam."

"It's a bit cold for ice cream, isn't it?" Even before the words had finished flowing from her mouth, she knew they sounded ridiculous. When, as a child, had she ever thought it was too cold for ice cream? The children obviously thought the same as they chorused "No!" like a polished double act.

"Oh, I suppose so then. What flavour do you want?"

Bad move because UN-style deliberations followed over ice cream flavours until she told them that if they didn't make their minds up in the next ten seconds she'd make them up for them. It worked.

"Melissa, what do you want?" Rebecca asked, pushing open a nearby coffee shop's door.

"A trim latte, please," she answered, sitting down outside the café with the children to wait.

"Such a good night; man, I need a sausage roll."

Melissa looked up as a group of pretty, young girls looking worse for wear, staggered past her with the hems of their jeans scuffing the pavement. Those were the days, she thought, feeling a flare of nostalgia, when I could put away a pie and a sausage roll without it going straight to my hips. Her train of thought was interrupted by a high-pitched whine coming from a little boy who looked to be a year or two older than Jack.

"Dad, I wanna see the dolphins *now*. You said we could." He was one of those funny-looking kids with an adult face. Come to think of it, there was something about that face.

She looked closer as the boy tugged at his father, who was doing his best to ignore him. Behind them, a haggard woman with over-bleached hair pushed a buggy containing a wailing baby. Happy families, she thought smugly, shifting her sights to her two charges who were on their best behaviour as they awaited their ice cream. The father's gaze flicked over her with the practiced habit of a man who checks every woman out. He obviously liked what he saw, she thought huffily—a right Merv the Perv. There was something about him as well, though. "Oh my God!" She inhaled deeply, flapping her hand as though it were an imaginary fan. "Jeremy Thompson. I don't believe it!"

As she pushed open the café door, Rebecca registered three things as Hannah's single scoop, orange choc-chip simultaneously slid from her grasp to land with a splat at her feet:

1. Melissa was talking to a man.

2. The man just happened to be her first love.

3. At the sight of her ice cream lying forlornly on the asphalt, Hannah had begun to scream.

"SO WHAT HAPPENED THEN?" Jennifer asked, referring to Rebecca's first sighting of Jeremy Thompson. The girls had arrived back from town, children in tow, to find Jennifer curled up on the couch once more. At least she'd run a brush through her hair, Rebecca thought, perching on the end of the couch as she began filling her in on the morning's events.

"Not a lot really. Jeremy said hi and asked me how I've been. I said fine and asked him what he was doing in Akaroa, and he said they were just over for the night. Then his wife, who looked totally fed up with her lot, gave him a shove so he introduced her. Vanessa or Veronica, something like that. I can't remember what his kids were called." She waved her hand disinterestedly and then smiled. "He asked if Hannah and Jack were mine and looked pissed off when I told him Melissa and I were footloose and fancy-free, living it up in Dublin."

"Good one." Jennifer managed to raise a smile at this one-upmanship.

"After that, we all just eyeballed each other until Hannah's screaming got too much. I said it was good to see him but that I'd better go and get another ice cream before she committed harikari."

"Remember when you met him, Becs?" Melissa forged her way into Rebecca's past.

"How could I forget? He broke my heart."

"I never heard that story. Tell me what happened," Jennifer urged, sitting up, glad to have her mind taken off her problems for a short while.

Rebecca slid down onto the couch and, leaning back into the leather cushions next to her sister, began relaying her tale. "Well, we were fourteen—you'd left home by then."

"Only just. I moved into that awful flat with Tessa, the waitress from Sophia's, and her friend who was at polytech doing something or other." Jennifer shivered at the memory of the cold and damp weatherboard house that had given her her first taste of freedom.

"That's right—that place was a hovel. Okay, so it was our first school disco, and it was a huge event on our teenage social calendars, wasn't it, Melissa?"

Melissa's silent nod reiterated this fact.

"We'd spent weeks planning our outfits." Rebecca smiled, flashing back to a bygone era of big hair and blusher as she described the black tube-skirts with white shirts and black ties they'd settled on. "I dressed my outfit up with black fishnets and flat ballerina-style shoes."

"And I put a big side bow in my hair, Madonna-style," Melissa interrupted, laughing out loud at the memory.

"Ah, the eighties—I remember them well." Jennifer looked nostalgic. "I loved Culture Club and Cyndi Lauper." She began humming *Girls Just Wanna Have Fun*. Rebecca couldn't help but wonder at the irony in her sister's choice of song and Jennifer, for her part, was aware her sister was looking at her with a perplexed expression. She stopped humming and, tucking the hair that had fallen across her face behind her ears, mumbled, "Sorry—carry on with your story."

"We were nervous, weren't we?" There was another silent nod of agreement from Melissa, and Rebecca's eyes took on a dreamy quality as she got caught up in her story once more. "It was as if we knew it was going to be a special night before we even got there. Remember how we stood in your mum and dad's room doing those Tai Chi moves you got out of a *Cosmopolitan* magazine to calm our nerves?"

Melissa grinned. "That's right, and then just before we got in the car, we stood with our arms around each other in front of Mum's full-length mirror and shouted, 'Looking good! Feeling great!'"

"Affirmations," Rebecca explained, "and a fat lot of good they did."

Stepping back in time and into the darkened school hall, Rebecca could almost taste the atmosphere that had been electric with music and hormones. "The DJ was our geology teacher, Mr Duncan, or Spunky Dunky as we used to call him." Melissa grinned at the analogy. "I can still hear Spunky Dunky announcing in a proper DJ voice that he was going to play the current number one hit throughout the nation—Madonna's *Material Girl*. Of course we all went mad with excitement; Madonna was just the ultimate in cool, you understand, and as I stood up to do my robot moves, Jeremy Thompson appeared in front of me."

She paused for a minute, heightening the drama. "Oh, Jen," she gushed, "you should have seen him; he was gorgeous. He had a look of John Taylor—remember him from Duran Duran?—about him."

"I was always a Simon Le Bon girl myself, but I wish I had seen him." Jennifer looked sad at the realisation that she had probably been oblivious of a lot of the monumental events in her sister's life over the years. She had been far too caught up in what was going on in her own. For a moment, Rebecca held her gaze, trying to work out the underlying meaning behind Jennifer's words before carrying on.

"He had the softest brown hair with a bleach-blond fringe that flopped down, on purpose, over one eye and he was wearing these hip, baggy, bop pants with a pink shirt." She sighed wistfully. "We made a striking couple on the dance floor."

"They did," Melissa affirmed emphatically.

"I'm not arguing." Jennifer held her hand up in self-defence.

"We danced the night away, only stopping when we were asked to clear the floor and let the fourth-form bop group do their moonwalk display. The night just flew, and I couldn't believe it when Spunky Dunky announced the last song. It still sends a shiver down my spine when I hear it—New Order's *Blue Monday*. I've got goosebumps just thinking about what happened next—look." She pulled up her sleeve and held out her arm to prove it.

"What happened?" Jen was on the edge of the couch, and even Melissa, who knew the story of old, was sitting forward in anticipation.

"He took my black lace fingerless gloved hand in his and kissed me, ever so softly."

"Tongues?" Melissa always asked this, even though she knew the answer. "No."

"Good," said Jennifer, unable to stomach the idea of her then fourteen-year-old sister French kissing a randy teenage boy.

"Tell her what he said to you, Becs," Melissa urged, almost in a trance by now.

"He pulled away from me gently, looked into my eyes, and said, 'You're beautiful. How come I've never noticed you before?' I smiled up at him. I mean, what was I supposed to say to that? Then he made all my high school fantasies come true by asking me if I would go round with him."

Melissa wrapped her arms around herself, caught up in the moment. "What did you say?"

Rebecca played the game. "Yes, of course! I floated home that night. Not literally; Dad picked us up—eleven o'clock curfew and all that."

"Hey, don't complain—you had it easy. I'd already carved the way for you," Jennifer interjected. She thought back to the explosive rows she'd had with Pamela and Dick in her teenage bids for more freedom.

"I suppose you did. I never thought about it before. Thanks, sis."

Jennifer raised a weary smile. "You're welcome."

"The next day, for the first time in my secondary school career, I couldn't wait to get to school."

"Everyone was talking about her." Melissa leaned towards Jennifer conspiratorially.

"To this day, I don't know what happened." She shrugged. "Who knows—maybe he got a hard time from his friends because he dumped me—just like that, over by the cricket field."

"The bastard! No wonder you've always had self-esteem issues!" Jennifer was aghast. "I don't know about John Taylor—he'd have looked like that Shane whatsit from the Pogues by the time I got through with him. That's if I'd known anything about it. Why didn't you talk to me about it?"

Rebecca didn't get a chance to explain that she'd felt too embarrassed to admit to her older and popular sister that she had been given the heave-ho.

Melissa, quick as flash, butted in. "Well, you didn't know anything about it but she had me, Jennifer. To be honest, she'd never have gotten through it, either, if she hadn't." Leaning over, she patted Rebecca proprietarily on her shoulder.

"I wouldn't go that far." Rebecca shrugged her off, feeling a bit annoyed that both her sister and best friend seemed to view her as incapable of fighting her own battles. "As I recall, you were in a snit with me for weeks afterwards because you fancied Jeremy's best mate. Simon Freeman, remember? You reckoned there was no way he'd go near you after I got dumped so publicly. Do you know, Jen, I had to buy two tickets to the Police. Want to know what she said to me when I gave Melissa her ticket?"

Jennifer nodded, even though she was well able to imagine.

"She said, and I quote, 'Alright, I'll let you off the hook, but Sting's mine.'"

"Melissa! That's awful."

"Yeah, yeah, whatever."

"Oh well, Rebecca," Jennifer said, "it sounds like he's tied to a right old ball and chain these days."

"Yeah." She sighed. "And I'm still single twenty years later."

"Twenty-one years, actually."

"Melissa!" the two sisters chorused, their eyes meeting in mutual solidarity for the first time in a long time, and Melissa had the grace to disappear upstairs.

Chapter Seventeen

"SO HOW ARE YOU FEELING?" Rebecca asked, poking her head round the living room door later that afternoon to check up on her sister. She was still curled up on the couch, a throw rug pulled over her legs like an old lady in a rest home. It shocked Rebecca seeing Jennifer, who never sat still for longer than it took to knock a latte back, like this.

"Not desperate like I was but not quite up to the Boston Marathon yet either."

Rebecca smiled. At least she still had her sense of humour; surely that was a good sign?

"What about you though? How are you feeling? Melissa told me about your boss and the receptionist."

Trust Melissa to blab her private business, she thought, pursing her lips. "What did she tell you?"

"Everything, but it's not Melissa's fault. I made her fess up as to what was going on when I heard you stomping about last night."

"Sorry. It must be a bit close to home."

Jennifer waved her hand dismissively. "We're not talking about Mark."

"No, you're right—we're not—and Ciaran's a complete shit, but then we weren't a couple. So I don't suppose I have any right to be so angry about his choice in women. I just thought..." Rebecca shook her head. "Oh, I don't know what I thought."

"That perhaps something might happen between the two of you?"

Rebecca decided she needed to tell someone. "That's the thing, Jen. It already did, but afterwards we both acted like it never happened. I didn't know how to go back and let him know I was interested after that. I suppose I was frightened of getting knocked back." She shrugged. "There's always been this feeling, though, that what was between us was unfinished except now he's gone and made sure it's bloody well finished."

"If you ask me, it sounds like you've had a wake-up call and that you are better off without him. Don't waste your energy thinking about him," Jennifer said in that no-nonsense manner of hers. "Maybe what you should consider, though, is how you are going to feel going back to work for him now after what happened." She looked hard at her sister. They were both going to make some big decisions in the very near future.

Rebecca shifted uncomfortably because going back to Ireland was something she'd been trying not to think about. Deciding not to go down that track, she put on her happy face. "I know, and you are probably right about my having had a wake-up call. Men, aye?" Realising what she'd said, her hand flew to her mouth. "Sorry, Jen! I wasn't thinking. What a stupid thing to say. I'm such an idiot."

Jennifer raised a weary smile. "No, no, you're not and believe me, I know exactly where you're coming from."

Leaning over, Rebecca patted her sister's hand. "You'll get there, sis. You know, when things look at their grimmest, I always try to imagine my life in a year's time when the problems of today are all resolved and seem trivial in relation to the here and now."

"Is that what you are doing now—imagining yourself in a year's time?"

"Kind of."

"And what do you see?"

She frowned. "That's the thing—I just don't know."

Not wanting her sister to delve any further, Rebecca changed the subject. "Do you feel up to a walk around the garden? Some fresh air might do you good." *Crumbs, now she even sounded like she was visiting her nan at the retirement home.*

"No thanks. I'm saving my energy for when the kids get home and don't think that I don't know what you are doing, Rebecca."

"What am I doing?" She was genuinely bewildered.

"Changing the subject. That's what you always do when you don't want to face up to something. The thing is, sis, if you run away from your problems, they will catch up with you eventually and when they do, they'll bite you hard in the bum."

Rebecca unconsciously clenched her bum cheeks. "Charming." She knew Jen was right, but she just wasn't ready to go there yet. Her thoughts were still too jumbled. "I have another week to clear my head and think things through."

"Promise me you will think about where you're headed, though, Becs—properly."

"I promise." Then, deciding it was Jen's turn to be put on the spot, she asked, "So have you heard from Mark?"

"He phoned my mobile this morning to say hi to Jack and Hannah." She frowned. "Jack was quite chirpy on the phone to his father; it's obviously just me he has the problem with."

"He'll get over it, whatever it is. You just get yourself better before you think about tackling him. While we are on the subject of the kids, I'll go outside and check on what they're up to. You rest up."

"Becs?"

"Yeah?" Rebecca turned in the doorway.

"Thank you."

"For what?"

"Being here."

"It's no biggie. That's what family is for."

The children, thanks to the weather, were entertaining themselves quite nicely for once—Hannah in the sandpit and Jack playing with his remote control Moto-X out the back. Leaving them both to it, she went back inside to make herself a cup of tea just as Melissa—with her seemingly psychic ability to know when a cuppa was being made—appeared.

"I forgot to mention it before." She flopped into a chair. "Betty's hanging out with Jennifer tonight and she suggested that seeing as it's Saturday and with us being two single girls, we should head out on the town. Are you up for it?"

"I'm up for it," Rebecca decided, knowing the change of scenery would do her good and help take her mind off things where a certain boss of hers, who obviously couldn't keep it in his pants, was concerned. Melissa didn't hear her; she was too busy mentally dressing herself for the occasion.

A few hours later, Rebecca was perched on a bar stool, sucking on the straw of what was left of her bourbon and lemonade. The pub was quintessentially Kiwi, she thought, casting her gaze over the stained, navy carpet flanked by tall, lean-to tables designed for drinking. It was fairly obvious it hadn't had a magic makeover fairy wave her wand over it in the past thirty years. The two friends were propped up at opposite ends of one of these tables and, leaning across it to make herself heard, Rebecca told Melissa, "Betty's got the magic touch with the kids. Did you see how they just took themselves off to bed when she told them to?"

"Yeah, well, someone has to—Jennifer's not exactly much help, is she? You wouldn't even think they were her children the way she had everybody else running around after them."

"She's not in a good space, Melissa; you know that. Leave her alone."

Melissa pulled a face and began scanning the room while Rebecca climbed down from the stool and went in search of more drinks.

Up at the bar, Rebecca shouted out her order, "Two double bourbon and lemonades—could you make that diet, please? Thanks."

"I'll get these," a masculine voice informed the bartender while simultaneously handing over a fifty-dollar note. She swung round to see who her mysterious benefactor was and there, with his palm outstretched in readiness for his change, was the one and only Jeremy Thompson.

"Oh no, there's no need; it's fine." She snatched the fifty back out of the startled bartender's hand and thrust it at Jeremy. He put both his hands up as though to ward her off.

"No, no, please, Rebecca. I'd like to get them. Okay?"

Against her better judgement, she nodded. She watched as he handed the note back to the bartender, who quickly stuffed it in the till, throwing a quick wink Rebecca's way as he counted the change back to Jeremy. Wrapping her hands around the drinks, she muttered an insincere thanks, determined not to look into those deep brown eyes of his.

As she took a step to walk away, she felt his hand on her arm gently stop her. Her gut reaction was to shake him off, but common sense told her that would be a waste of good bourbon. So instead, she found herself asking tightly, "Where's your wife, Veronica, is it?"

His hand shot back down to his side as though scalded. "It's Vanessa and she's back at the motel unit with the kids."

That confirms it then; he's still an asshole, Rebecca decided. Taking his family away for the weekend and then leaving them to it while he blows the household budget buying other women drinks. "That's a shame. Well, um, thanks again, Jeremy. It was good to see you again, but I'd better get back to Melissa."

She hotfooted it back to their table, not caring anymore that she was slopping the drinks in her haste. If Jeremy bloody Thompson thought standing a round of drinks gave him an automatic invitation to join them, he had another think coming.

"What an asshole!" Melissa agreed as Rebecca finished telling her about her little rendezvous up at the bar. "Still, good on you I say, Becs, for cadging a free round. Cheers."

Rebecca refused to clink her glass, protesting, "But I didn't. He insisted on paying. Probably his way of trying to ease his conscience. If he even has a conscience after what he did."

Two rounds later, they'd forgotten all about Jeremy Thompson as the lights dimmed and the motley band, calling themselves Cruise Control, sprang into life with a Doors cover.

"Oh, I love this song!" Melissa exclaimed, hopping off her stool and proving her point by doing a little shimmy. "Come on, Becs!" She clapped her hands, singing along to the old hit, *Roadhouse Blues*.

Rebecca joined in singing along. Clutching their drinks, they jostled their way onto the dance floor. Tossing their handbags on top of one another, they began dancing their way around them to *Sweet Caroline*. It was followed by a scary version of Pink Floyd's *Wish You Were Here*, at the end of which Rebecca held up her hand and gasped, "Enough, enough! I need water, and these bloody shoes are killing me. I'm going to sit the next couple out."

Leaving Melissa, who had hooked on to a leering admirer, to it, she picked her way through the crowd to the bar and ordered water. The bartender winked at her again and this time she managed a small smile as, taking the glass from him, she cast her eyes around for an empty table. Making a beeline for one over by the back exit, she plonked herself down at it gratefully. Raising her legs one at a time, she rotated her ankles in semicircles in an attempt to get the circulation going in her ridiculously high heel-clad feet again. If the stupid things didn't make her legs look so much longer, she'd have whipped them off and tossed them out that exit behind her.

"No gain without pain," she muttered.

"Pardon me?" Startled, her left leg fell back to the ground with a hefty thud as she looked up into a pair of familiar brown eyes.

"Um, nothing. I was talking to myself."

She quickly adjusted herself into a more ladylike position. Jeremy looked on with a Cheshire cat grin. "I saw you on the dance floor; you looked like you were having a good time, but then you always were right into dancing, weren't you?"

"Ballet, yes, and what can I say? *Girls just wanna have fun,*" she replied, echoing one of her sister's all-time favourite songs.

He laughed at that, a bit too loudly, and she realised he was nervous. Ha! It had taken nigh on twenty years, but the shoe was finally on the other foot, so to speak. Without waiting for an invitation, he parked himself in the chair opposite hers and placed his pint glass down on the table.

"It's been a long time, hasn't it?"

"Yeah, it has."

"Those were the days, aye, Rebecca? High school." His eyes glazed over nostalgically, but Rebecca's nimble skip down memory lane only conjured up lots of pimples and angst. Seeing his faraway expression, she fancied he was wondering what might have been between them. Unbeknown to her, he was reliving the moment he'd kicked the rugby ball cleanly into touch, winning the game and thus gaining himself high school hero status.

"So," he drawled, having dragged himself back to the present, "you said you live in Ireland now. What is it you do there?" He held up his hand. "No, hang on—let me guess." He looked pensive for a moment as he rubbed his chin before slapping his knee and declaring, "I know—you're a dancer in Riverdance!" He quite liked the mental picture of Rebecca in a short green dress that statement conjured up.

"I did ballet, not Irish dancing, and I'm a legal secretary, actually. I work for a partner in a Dublin firm. Ciaran—he's a hot shot lawyer."

Jeremy frowned. "I always thought you'd go on to be a dancer. That's all you talked about at the disco that night. What happened there?"

"I wasn't good enough," she said flatly.

Sensing this topic was not going to win him any brownie points, he decided to move on. "I'm an electrician. I finished up sixth form and did an apprenticeship. I always planned on doing the big overseas adventure but I never quite made it. I met Vanessa and got married instead."

"No regrets though," Rebecca stated firmly for him.

He didn't reply, asking instead, "So you're still single?"

"Yes, I haven't been in one place long enough to meet Mr Right," she tinkled lightly, mentally adding, and I don't do married men.

"Must be great to be able to go where you want, when you want. No chance of that with children."

"It is." No way was she going to admit that it could also be bloody lonely.

"You're looking great."

His gaze was unnerving. "Um, thanks."

He raised his glass and took a deep slug from it before reaching across and touching her hand lightly. "I'm sorry about what happened. You know, back when we were at school."

Rebecca was grateful to the dark for hiding her flush. "Don't give it a second thought; I haven't. It was just dumb teenage stuff." She wondered if her nose had just grown.

Jeremy kept his eyes downcast and, as he toyed with the soggy beermat in front of him, she felt herself soften. Maybe he wasn't such a wanker after all?

He raised his eyes to zap her with his soulful expression. It was the one that usually worked a treat with the thirty-something, single babes grateful for the attention, any attention. He whispered huskily, "Look, I'm not one to beat around the bush. I think we both know that there's unfinished business between us. So, how about it? We can't go back to mine obviously, so why don't we go back to your place and pick up where we left off all those years ago?"

Rebecca, who'd just taken a sip of her water, felt it go down the wrong pipe as she swallowed in shock. Jeremy was lucky it didn't come right back out in a spray all over his arrogant smirk. Once she'd finished coughing, and the water had stopped running out of her nose, she wiped her tears away and took a good, hard look at Jeremy Thompson. He wasn't that hunky fifth former who'd broken her heart anymore. The only vaguely recognisable feature from those days was his eyes. She dragged her own away from his and registered the onset of belly overhang and a hairline that had receded enough to leave a shiny forehead in its wake. Oh yes, his glory days were long gone. She could see the stark white band where his wedding ring should be. He was gripping his pint glass tightly in anticipation, and she felt a moment's sadness for the loss of the adolescent he'd once been. Then, glaring at him, she pushed her chair back and stood up, knocking his pint glass accidentally on purpose into his lap.

"Whoops, how clumsy of me. Still, that should cool the old boy down." Stalking off like a proud lioness after a kill, Rebecca left Jeremy and his sodden crotch back in the past where they belonged.

She felt so empowered! Wow, she should stand up for herself more often because revenge was oh so sweet. The ghosts of school disco past were finally laid to rest. Rebecca realised what a lucky escape she'd had and from that moment forth, she knew that the song *Blue Monday* would never give her goosebumps again.

Mentally congratulating herself, she took a sip of the drink she'd just purchased. That small victory for womankind had called for another shot of bourbon. Her eyes flicked around the room until she spotted another familiar figure. Her stomach somersaulted when the vision turned around—David Seagar. There he was, larger than life, standing on the fringe of the dance floor. He hadn't seen her yet, so she allowed herself a moment to stare at him with unadulterated lust plastered all over her face. He was wearing a white shirt over dark denim jeans, and she just knew that he'd smell good. Taking a swig of Dutch courage, she threaded her way across the room.

"Hi, David," she simpered, popping up by his side a moment later. He turned towards her in surprise.

"Oh, Rebecca, hi. Fancy meeting you here." At least he didn't say, "Do you come here often?" His slow once-over indicated that he must have liked what he saw, because as his eyes meandered back up to her face, he smiled at her approvingly. "You look lovely."

"Thanks." She was glad the lighting was so dim so he couldn't see her blush at the compliment.

"So who gave you a leave pass then?"

"Betty and Jennifer are having a girls' night in. Betty reckoned it was a criminal offence for two single girls to sit at home on a Saturday night." She half expected him to snort at the way she'd loosely bandied the word girl about. It was, after all, a bit of a stretch where she and Melissa were concerned, but he didn't.

"She'd be right too. I use a local lass, Katrina. It's a bit of pocket money for her, but she came recommended—by Jennifer, now that I think about it. How's she doing?"

"Um, good," Rebecca lied and slurped on her straw.

"Who are you here with?" David asked, and she pointed to the dance floor where Posh was breaking out the Spice moves. "She looks like she's enjoying herself."

Melissa caught his grin and winked at Rebecca, receiving a scowl in return.

"So, what have you got planned tomorrow?" David asked.

Oblivious of his question, Rebecca sniffed again; he smelt delicious. Sort of fresh with those undertones of pine she had smelt the other day, yet musky too. Then, she caught sight of his expectant expression and flushed again as she realised he'd asked her a question.

"Oh sorry!" she blustered. "I didn't catch what you said over the music."

Looking bemused because the band had just announced they were going on a break, he asked her again what she was doing tomorrow. Recapping the plans she and Melissa had made with Betty to score a free lunch courtesy of the Thai buffet being put on by the Nifty Knitters earlier that evening, something sprang to mind. Hang on just a sec; through her bourbon-addled brain, she could feel a bright idea forming.

"Why don't you come to the buffet too?" Oh yes, that was a good idea; she warmed to her theme. "Jack would love to see Ben and if the food I have been getting whiffs of from the cooking school is anything to go by, it should be a real treat." She decided not to mention that she was sick to the back teeth of the smell of coconut and lemon grass but hey, a free lunch was a free lunch.

"Sounds great, if you're sure there's enough to go round..." His voice trailed off.

"There'll be far too much food and the more, the merrier; Betty won't mind nor will Jennifer."

"Jennifer will be there?"

"Um." She hesitated. "I think so, unless something else crops up."

"Right, well, I'm sold."

Melissa had drunk herself more or less sober by the time the band called it quits. She was ready to go home and spying Rebecca and David deep in conversation, she decided it was time to break up their cosy little conversation. She made a big show of tapping her watch as she approached. "Rebecca, it's quarter to twelve—you know you turn into a pumpkin at midnight."

"I told my babysitter I'd be back before midnight too. How are you ladies planning on getting home?" David interjected.

"Walking." Melissa's reply was curt and intended for Rebecca. "It will do her some good to get a spot of exercise."

Ouch! Melissa had whipped out the boxing gloves, but a good match involved two competitors, Rebecca thought, aiming her punch. "I thought you said you didn't do walking."

Melissa was saved from having to think of a comeback by David.

"I'd offer to drive you home, but I'll be walking myself." He pointed at his glass with a shrug.

Rebecca, whose sense of responsibility was sitting at the bottom of her empty glass, could have just as happily stopped out all night. Especially when she was pretty sure that around about now Ciaran would just be waking up. No doubt, with a monumental hangover and Pariah standing at the ready with a glass of water and two paracetamol. I bet her bloody dressing gown's made of Lycra too, she fumed. But knowing better than to put up too much of a fight when Melissa was in a mood, she reluctantly said goodnight to David, firming up their lunch arrangements for the next day as she did so. Humph, she thought a moment later, fishing around in her handbag for the ticket that would retrieve their coats. Now she knew exactly how Cinderella had felt when she had to leave the ball just as it was hotting up. Shooting a nasty look in Melissa's direction, she decided her so-called best friend fitted the bill of one of the ugly stepsisters to perfection.

Chapter Eighteen

"I SPEND HALF MY LIFE looking for things in this bloody bag," Rebecca muttered, her hand fumbling around inside it as she tried to find the front door key. She was sure she'd zipped it into the inside pocket so as to avoid this little debacle. Standing under the sensor light, she held her bag open. Peering inside it, Melissa's jiggling from foot to foot grew more frantic.

"Just hurry up or I'm going to wet myself," she hissed, but her voice was muted by the sound of a car whining up the hill they had not long staggered up themselves.

Sound always carries at night, Rebecca thought, paying it no heed as she at last located the errant key that somehow had jumped inside her make-up bag. The drone of the engine grew louder, and both women turned around. They found themselves pinned by its headlights. Looking like a stunned possum, Melissa momentarily forgot she needed the loo. "Who the bloody hell would that be at this time of night?"

The word Taxi was illuminated upon its roof, and the engine idled for a moment while whoever was inside paid their fare. "It's probably Mark," Rebecca deduced, peering into the dark. "He must have decided to come home early." But as the passenger door opened and a figure unfolded itself, she saw that it was too tall to be Mark. She could only make out a shadowy outline in the misty, thick night air, but she already knew instinctively that it belonged to the last person in the world she'd expected to see.

"Ciaran?" she eventually whispered, gaining confidence as the apparition in front of her didn't vanish in a wisp of smoke as expected. "What the hell are you doing here?"

His bravado slipped as the taxi drove away. The reality of having just sat on a plane for thirty-odd hours to show up uninvited at his secretary's sister's house on the other side of the world suddenly hit him.

"I, uh, I wanted to experience long-haul flight flatulence for myself. You know, Becs, give the blog authenticity."

"You're weird, Ciaran, and despite my misgivings about leaving my best friend alone in the dark with a mad Irishman, I'm off. I need to wee."

"Thanks for sharing. Good to see you too," Ciaran replied as Melissa glowered at him before snatching the key off Rebecca. Opening the door, she wiggled inside with knock-knees. "Shout if you need me, Becs." Then, eye-balling Ciaran one last time, she shut the door and left them to it.

Ciaran took a step towards Rebecca and when he spoke, his voice was low and husky on the night air.

"The blog's not the only reason I'm here, of course. I, uh, I needed to ask you something in person."

Rebecca looked back at him blankly, still in shock.

"It's the last one, you see. Question eighty, and it's been driving me mad." His face crinkled with the endearing lines she knew so well as he emphasised his point. "I can't eat or sleep and I knew you were the only one who could give me the right answer."

The music quiz—he was on about the music quiz? Maybe Melissa was right, and Ciaran was mad.

He took a deep breath and went on. "It's a song by Foreigner, all about love." His dark eyes glittered as she registered his choice of song.

Her heart somersaulted, and her stomach contracted as she whispered the answer: "*I Want to Know What Love Is* by Foreigner. A true blue classic."

Ciaran reached out then and wrapped her small cold hand in his big warm one as he began crooning the lyrics softly.

A tide of emotions dumped themselves on her as suddenly the spectre of Mariah Carey popped up between them, screeching 'We belong together' as she simultaneously flicked Rebecca off and looked beseechingly at Ciaran. Rebecca shook the image away and wrenched her hand free. Her steps faltered backwards as her eyes flashed. "Why the blazes did you sleep with Pari-ah then?" she demanded.

For a moment, Ciaran was speechless, but as he looked at Rebecca's face, pale and angry in the dim light, he rubbed ferociously at his stubble. Things weren't panning out how he'd planned. Realising he had a bit of explaining to do, he decided he'd rather do that indoors. "Can we head inside to talk?"

He rubbed his hands together. "Jaysus! I thought New Zealand was a Pacific nation, not part of the feckin Antarctic."

"I guess so." He was right, she thought, shivering; it was cold. And against her better judgement, she opened the front door. "Come on then." As he followed her into the living room, whistling through his teeth as he took in his surrounds, she tossed over her shoulder, "I can tell you straight off, though, you've had a wasted trip. There's nothing you can say that's going to make the fact you slept with that tart alright, but I suppose I can't send you packing without a hot drink. You are my boss, after all."

She heard him mutter, "Ouch." At that last remark and as she flicked on the kitchen light, her eyes began to prickle with hot unshed tears.

He came up behind her and, resting his hands on her shoulders, soothed, "Ah, come on now; I've come a long way. Promise me you'll at least listen?"

Rebecca turned and shrugged his hands off, staring up at him for a moment. He was standing far too close to her for her own good, and she began backing away before conceding, "Alright, I'll listen." Unable to tear her eyes away from the dark stubble decorating his jawline, she felt an erotic thrill as she imagined what that stubble would feel like rubbing against her. As she collided with the table, Pariah popped her head over Ciaran's shoulder once more. *Damn it! Why was he making her feel like this?* To be tearful one minute, and then spitting tacks the next. And in between those two mood swings, having hot flushes and sexual fantasies. *Was this what menopause was like?* Scowling, Rebecca lowered her gaze and stomped over to the bench. Flicking the kettle on and opening the cupboard to retrieve two mugs, she took advantage of those few seconds to compose herself before asking, "So where are you staying?"

"At a B and B near the water called Sea Breezes. Not a very original name, I know, and it's run by a mad old biddy, Mrs Doody, but it's cheap enough."

She poured the boiling water over the milk, wishing there was some of that Mekhong filth still lying around. Damn it, she could do with a shot of something serious, but she settled for making them both hot chocolate instead. Ciaran had pulled out a chair and sat down at the table. His hands were clasped and rested lightly in his lap while his legs were splayed out in front of him. "I now know what a sardine feels like."

Rebecca threw a glance over her shoulder. "I take it you didn't fly first class then?"

"Nope. Couldn't put this trip down as a business expense and I wasn't very popular upping and leaving the way I did either." He looked like a little lad who had had his hand smacked as he thought back to Fitzpatrick, the senior partner's, reaction to his sudden departure. "I'll have you know I endured hours of having my legs wrapped around my ears to see you."

Rebecca avoided his eye because she knew if she caught it, she'd smile, and he'd win. At that moment, the door swung open to reveal Jennifer, and Ciaran immediately straightened up and sat to attention.

She stood in the entrance, blinking reactively to the light. A blonde Egyptian mummy-like vision wrapped in her chin to toe terry-cloth bathrobe, she was trying to shake off the fog of sleep and work out why there was a strange man sitting at her kitchen table in the wee hours of the morning.

"I heard voices." She spoke up at last.

"Sorry, Jen. I didn't mean to wake you." Rebecca placed the two mugs down on the table.

She ignored her sister and stared at Ciaran. "Who are you?" She thought, massaging her temples, Rebecca should know better than to drag strays home from the pub. Especially when it wasn't *her* home and the children were asleep upstairs. If Jack were to wander in and find him after what had happened—well, it didn't bear thinking about.

Ciaran got up with a noisy scrape of his chair and held his hand out. "I'm Ciaran, Ciaran Cahill. You must be Rebecca's sister Jennifer?"

Jennifer blinked again. "You're Rebecca's boss Ciaran, from Ireland? Good grief—did you fly the Concorde to get here?"

"Uh, yeah, that would be me and no, it wasn't the Concorde. I wish it had been. I managed to get a seat via a last-minute cancellation with Air New Zealand. I'd like to apologise for showing up at this time of night, too, but my bog standard plane didn't get in until late this evening, and I needed to talk to your sister here."

"What about?" Jennifer was wide awake now, and she didn't like this scenario—not at all and especially not with her sister's soft-touch tendencies. She glared at him for a moment. He was attractive. She could see why Rebecca carried a torch for him, but he was also, from what she could gather, a womaniser and someone her baby sister did not need in her life.

"Um, Jennifer, we were just about to get to that, so if you wouldn't mind..." Rebecca shifted her gaze to the door, hoping her sister would take the hint and leave them alone.

She shuffled from slipper to slipper for a minute, deciding what she should do. Rebecca was a grown woman, so she couldn't very well tell her she was not to let this lothario lounging at her kitchen table sweettalk her. She could, however, tell him in a roundabout way to bugger off. "Right, well, I hope you have somewhere to stay, Mr Cahill, because it is very late, and I have young children who will be up and about very early."

"Of course. I was just telling Rebecca I'm booked into—"

"Good." Jennifer cut him off. "Rebecca, make sure you lock up behind him. I'm going back to bed." Turning on her slipper-clad feet, she marched out of the kitchen.

"Well, I won her over. Was she a Rottweiler in another life perchance?"

Rebecca wasn't going to make this easy for him and so she sat staring silently down into the contents of her mug until she sensed him shift in his seat. Good, she thought; her silence was making him uncomfortable. He might be the boss back in Ireland, but he wasn't in charge here.

Running a hand through his short, dark hair, Ciaran sighed; he might as well get straight to the point because he certainly wasn't going to win her round on good looks and charm alone.

"Rebecca, I haven't got any excuse for sleeping with Tania, apart from the fact that I was blind drunk." Still not a flicker. "I was practically comatose, for Christ's sake!" he added dramatically, to which Rebecca raised an eyebrow.

"Well, something was obviously working."

"It was on automatic pilot; I had no control over my bodily functions, and that is the absolute truth."

She tossed him a disparaging look. All of a sudden, the long flight coupled with the spur-of-the-moment decision to jump on the first plane he could and throw caution to the wind caught up with him. "I wish I hadn't listened to your bloody pal now."

"What do you mean—what pal?"

"Derbhilla. Who else do you think convinced me that I wouldn't be wasting my time by flying out here? I should never have listened to her. It was only a few weeks back that you were putting it about with that little git James, for chrissake."

Rebecca choked into her hot chocolate. "I was not putting it about, thank you very much. I snogged him when I was blind—"

"Let me finish that sentence for you, shall I? Drunk. Touché. And it is not as though we have been in a committed relationship to date, is it?"

Rebecca couldn't think of a comeback. He was right, and he wasn't finished yet either. "Why did you cold shoulder me after we slept together and then proceed to spend a year teasing me? Or does a spot of flirtation warrant a relationship in your book?"

"I left that morning because I freaked out. And you were the one who acted like it was business as usual afterwards and if it doesn't, what are you doing here then?"

"Oh, don't be so bloody childish!"

Rebecca banged her fist down hard on the table. How dare he say she was childish! He was the one with the mentality of a randy sixteen-year-old, and that was another thing. "Besides, you've always been far too busy shagging for Ireland to notice me. What did you expect me to do? Put my hand up and say, 'Oh, pick me, pick me—I'm a keeper'?"

As she sat panting from her outburst, Ciaran snorted, and she half expected steam to come out his nostrils. She'd backed him into a corner, and he was frantically trying to find a way to win this argument. For goodness' sake, man, you're the lawyer, he told himself angrily; you argue for a living. But for once in his life, Ciaran Cahill couldn't think of a single thing to say.

They sat in stony silence until at last Rebecca sighed and rubbed her eyes, leaning back in her chair. What a day; it was all too much, she thought as a great weariness settled over her like an enveloping eiderdown. "Why are you here, Ciaran?" She raised her wide hazel eyes to his. "I mean, what did you expect to happen when you got here?"

He eyed her back as he pondered her question, and Rebecca found herself swallowing hard and turning away; his expression was far too intense.

"Why am I here?" He shrugged, tapping the side of his mug thoughtfully before answering a moment later. "I'm here because I knew you wouldn't forgive me for sleeping with Tania. I knew I had to do something drastic and totally mad. So I decided to get on a plane to try to explain why I did it and to tell you how I feel about you." His expression was almost childlike as he went on, "And I'm here because I'm terrified you might decide not to come back to Ireland." Before she could stop it, Rebecca's hand snaked forward and rested on his; he felt a flicker of hope and played his blinder. "But most of all, I'm here because I think I love you."

She snatched her hand back as though she had been scalded and rubbed her temples. Her brain hurt. Why, when she already had so many thoughts as to where she was headed racing around her head, did Ciaran have to pop up and put a great big bloody spanner in the works? She exhaled slowly, knowing that she simply couldn't deal with this tonight. She might be acting, as Jen would say, true to form in delaying an inevitable conversation but at this moment in time, she simply didn't care. "Ciaran, I know this sounds like a total cliché, but I really need you to back off and give me some space."

"But—"

"No, listen!" She held her hand up to silence him because she was not going to let him out-talk her. "I know you've come a long way to say your piece, but it's not fair. You can't just show up out of the blue and land all this on me and expect me to collapse into your arms. I need some time to think."

"Is it your man, the solo dad?"

"No." But even as the word snapped from her mouth, she wondered, was it David? Was he the reason she was holding back? Or was it something more? Whatever the answer, she wasn't going to analyse it now. "Look, it's late and you heard Jen—the kids are up with the birds."

"Okay, okay. I can take a hint."

As she walked him outside, Ciaran took her hand and squeezed it for a moment before letting it drop. "I'm booked into the B and B for a few days. I won't pester you. I'll respect your wishes and give you time to think. When you're ready, you come and see me, okay?"

Rebecca looked straight ahead at the black nothingness; she knew if she turned to face him, she'd cave. "Okay."

"Good night then. I'll be walking home now, all alone in the dark." He took a reluctant step away from her.

"You're a big boy; you'll be fine."

He took another step and then turned round. "I don't suppose there's any chance of a quick shag to see me through the next few days?"

"Bugger off!" She saw the whiteness of his teeth as he flashed that naughty grin of his.

"Can't blame a man for trying." And then the darkness swallowed him up.

Chapter Nineteen

"SO WHAT THE BLOODY hell was that all about last night?" Melissa demanded. Her head was throbbing, and she was ruing that last drink she had knocked back before they left the pub. Rebecca was sitting on the floor, playing Snap with Hannah and looking ridiculously perky for someone who had been up half the night having a deep and meaningful and goodness knows what else with her nutcase of an employer. Stretching out on the couch, Melissa rested the back of her hand on her forehead like some old-time movie star as she waited to hear what her friend had to say for herself.

"Hannah, why don't you bake Melissa and me something yummy?" Rebecca pointed to her niece's toy oven. "We'll play another game in a minute." Her niece dutifully began banging pots on her cooktop before announcing she needed the toilet. As she took herself off up the stairs, Rebecca relayed her conversation with Ciaran to Melissa. "I still can't believe he's here. It seems so surreal that he's come all this way." She frowned. "He's thrown me, showing up the way he has, and I don't know how I feel about him being here at the moment."

"So you didn't sleep with him last night."

"No. I sent him packing but that's not to say I didn't want to, but then the thought of him with that... that..."

"Slapper."

"Yes, that's the word I was looking for, thanks—well, it just leaves me cold." She shuddered. "I told him I need some time to think, and he's agreed to give me a few days' space. Besides, David's coming for lunch today and I want to see what happens there. I don't want to burn my bridges with him just because Ciaran's decided he might be ready for a relationship."

"Okay, so let me get this straight," Melissa, whose head was getting worse, replied sardonically. "What you are telling me is that you've left Ciaran, whom you've always maintained you didn't fancy, dangling because you think David fancies you. Although on what you base that I have no idea."

Taken unawares by this surprise attack, Rebecca opted not to stoop to Melissa's petty level. She was obviously jealous and so with lips tight and chin up, she ignored her. It was a good question, though. Did David like her? Or was she a rebound from his recent divorce—a mere distraction? Then again, there was nothing wrong with taking it slow. But how slow was too slow? Look at her and Ciaran, for goodness' sake—all that wasted time and now it felt too late.

Noting her best friend's pained expression, Melissa's guilt urged an immediate apology. "Sorry. I'm sorry. That was bitchy, but I'm dying here. Could you get me some painkillers? Pretty please."

"If it means you'll stop being a super cow."

"Agreed."

Rebecca flounced off to the kitchen, bringing back a glass of water and tablets a moment later. Suddenly Melissa remembered her friend's disappearing act at the pub the night before. "So where did you get to last night when you left me on the dance floor? You were gone for ages. You weren't hooking up with David, were you?" Her eyes narrowed; she didn't like it when Rebecca held out on her.

Rebecca smirked. "If only—get those pills down you and I'll tell you all about it."

Hangover forgotten, Melissa cracked up laughing at the picture she mentally painted of Jeremy Thompson with his ardour somewhat dampened, when a shout resounded from upstairs.

"That will be Hannah wanting help on the loo. I better go and check if she's okay."

"Rather you than me. Where's her mother? Surely that's her job?" Melissa shuddered as Rebecca bounded upstairs.

"Jen was away early. She left a note to say she had a meeting with suppliers in Christchurch. I don't mind looking after the kids. It was what I was supposed to be here for," she called cheerily down the stairs, pleased her sister was up and about. Not just because it was a good sign health-wise but because it would stave off the twenty questions, she'd no doubt fire at her as to what Ciaran was doing here last night.

A moment later, though, she had to agree with Melissa as she handed her niece a wad of toilet paper and sent up a silent thank you for small mercies, like not having a hangover herself. Leaving Hannah to stand on her hippopotamus stool to wash her hands, she decided to check on Jack. She found him orchestrating a head-on crash between his Porsche and Audi slot cars as they raced along the figure-eight track set up in the corner of his room.

"How's it going? Ben will be round soon."

"Yeah." His voice was flat as the two cars smacked into each other. Rebecca ducked to avoid the Audi that came flying off the track as a result of the collision. Then, kneeling down next to him, she laid her hand on his shoulder but he flinched, mumbling, "Ben doesn't have a mum, you know. He told me that she went away."

Oh, shit, where was Doctor Phil when you needed him? How was she supposed to handle this one? It was one for Jennifer but then he didn't seem to want much to do with his mother at the moment. "I know, sweetheart," she said quietly. "Sometimes that happens. It is very sad but," and she tried to inject some brightness into her voice, "Ben's got a dad who loves him lots, and you do too."

When this didn't elicit a response, she clapped her hands together. "Hmm... now let me see. Your dad will be back in..." She counted on her fingers to demonstrate. "One, two, three, four, five, six sleeps. Mum's only gone into town for the day; she'll be home later this afternoon."

Jack frowned. "I'm not a baby anymore, Auntie Becca." Stretching over, he snatched up his toy Porsche and began turning it over to check for damage. "Ben told me he thought his mum was coming back, but she didn't."

"Jack, honey, your dad will be back, I promise." Yes, she could promise he would be back but she couldn't promise he would be back under the same roof as his children, she thought, putting her arm around him again and this time he let her.

Hearing voices from the living room below, she stood up and glanced at her watch. David and Ben were early. She gave her nephew a final pat on the shoulder. "Come on, love. Let's head downstairs."

Fifteen minutes later, they all piled up the stairs into the classroom. "Where's Jennifer? I thought she'd be here," David said, his gaze scanning the room as Jack and Ben began doing a circuit around the benches. Hannah trotted off behind them, trying to keep up.

"Oh, she had to go into town to pick up supplies," Rebecca answered, watching the Nifty Knitters, who were in full swing, bustling around. It was probably a good thing Jen had taken herself off for the day. There was no way she'd cope with this crowd. Betty, akin to a Girl Guide leader doing sema-phore signals as she directed them here, there, and everywhere, spotted the small group gathered at the entrance, wiping her brow before calling out, "Come in! Phew, what a morning, but we got there in the end, didn't we, ladies?"

"Yes!" the ladies all chimed.

Betty smiled at their enthusiasm. She beckoned her guests down to the dining room, and Rebecca attempted more introductions. The Nifty Knit-ters were like bees to honey with the arrival of a big strapping man in their midst. Rebecca and Melissa were shamelessly elbowed out of the semicircle. Reluctantly, they stepped back, and the frightened face of David Seagar re-emerged.

The scene that ensued reminded Rebecca of when she and Melissa had done the forty-hour famine as teenagers. They'd had the best of intentions, filling up their sponsorship books and sucking on their barley sugars every four hours. Then Melissa had broken down. Unable to take the pressure, she'd phoned Rebecca and told her she was holding a Toffee Pop biscuit in her hand.

"Don't do it—don't do it!" Rebecca had cried, but Melissa ignored her, making all sorts of orgasmic noises as she chomped into it in an attempt to corrupt her friend into doing the same. She'd been strong, though, and made it down to the school hall for the one-minute countdown. She could still see the table, legs bowed under the weight of shared party plates, as she waited impatiently alongside her fellow dribbling, pubescent participants. *Five, four, three, two, one!!!!* They'd stampeded over, and pounced on that table like pigs let loose at a trough.

Yes indeed, quite similar to today's little luncheon, she thought, watching the scuffle between two old dears for a seat next to David. She'd been tempt-ed to join in herself, but the one with the blue rinse was stronger than she looked. Rebecca pulled Ben, Jack, and Hannah protectively to her side, and once the fracas died down, she dragged out seats for them on either side of her.

When everybody was at last seated, Betty stood to attention at the head of the table and tapped her glass with a spoon as she asked everyone to raise their glasses. "Before we begin, I would like to take a moment to welcome our guests today, though most of you have already extended a warm welcome." Her tongue-in-cheek comment was met with a smattering of girlish tittering. "And secondly, I would like to thank the Nifty Knitters, for being such wonderful pupils. I hope you have all had as much fun learning the art of Thai cookery as I have had in teaching it. Cheers." She raised her glass, and her short speech was met with a frenzied clapping. "Well, everybody," she shouted over the din, "the proof is in the pudding, or so they say. Dig in!"

Rebecca's eyes stood out on stalks as she looked at the colourful array of food laid out in front of her. Crisped fish with chili-tamarind sauce and savoury fried shrimp cakes were the kids' favourites as they talked with their mouths full, sending bits of mulched shrimp flying. She stole a surreptitious glance at David. He had a forkful of something interesting poised halfway to his mouth and was nodding his head intently. It was as though old Blue Rinse, who he was sitting next to, was the most fascinating woman he had ever met. He suddenly looked over at Rebecca and, meeting her gaze, winked. He was something special, she thought. She'd be a fool to write him off just because Ciaran had brought himself over here on a whim. She sucked up a noodle and hoped he hadn't noticed it flick up to hit her on the nose.

Good wine, good food, and good conversation—the last bit was debatable—later, Rebecca reached across Jack and touched Betty lightly on her arm. "Thanks for last night and today, Betty. I hope you didn't mind us springing the couple of extra guests on you?"

"Not at all." She winked knowingly in David's direction. "I thought you might have tried a bit harder, though."

"Sorry?"

"Put it this way, dear: if I were thirty years younger, I would have made damn sure I was sitting next to him."

Rebecca grinned sheepishly. "Age before beauty and all that."

"Looks more like Beauty and the Beast to me." They both looked over to where poor David was being monopolised by Blue Rinse and chuckled. Betty turned her attention back towards Rebecca. "What's that on the end of your nose, dear?" She leaned in for a closer look.

"Snot probably," Jack chimed in.

"Don't be disgusting; it's a bit of sauce," Rebecca snapped, wiping it away quickly before glancing down the table to make sure nobody had overheard her charming nephew. Five minutes later, the children were playing a sort of game of Hide 'n' Seek. Hannah was yet to twig that the boys weren't going to find her, having taken themselves off outside.

Melissa and Lois had been put in charge of coffee, and Rebecca glanced over to the hissing, sputtering machine in time to see Melissa batting bossy Lois's hand away from the various knobs and switches. She smiled, catching David's eye as she did so; he was grinning too, and she felt a warm tingly sensation that had nothing at all to do with the coffee. She swatted away the mental picture of Ciaran holed up alone in his B&B and focused her attention on Betty. She was giving another short speech before handing out the certificates that stated that each of the members of the Timaru Nifty Knitters had completed their Cuisine with Carlton's course. There was much self-congratulating and pats on the back before everybody reluctantly got to their feet to begin the daunting task of clearing up.

"I'll rinse; you can stack, dear," Blue Rinse instructed David. Canny old bird, Rebecca thought half-admiringly, half-enviously; she just wanted a chance to view David's backside as he bent over to stack the dishwasher. Hauling Hannah out from her hidey hole, she lifted her onto a stool by the sink she'd filled with bubbly water. Throwing in a few non-breakables for her to wash, she decided she'd be having a word with Jack later. Leaving his little sister to sit in a cupboard for half an hour just wasn't right.

Once the classroom was restored to order, the Nifty Knitters reluctantly said their goodbyes to David, scurrying up to the cabins to attend to the last of their packing before their coach's imminent arrival. David announced he had to make tracks. "Thanks for a great afternoon, Betty. Best food I've ever had."

The group of five wandered outside, and he cupped his hands to either side of his mouth and shouted in the general direction of the back garden where the boys had last been spotted. "Ben, mate, we're leaving!" After a few seconds, a tousled head appeared from around the side of the house, and

David signalled that it was time to go. As he waited for his son, he shoved a hand into his pocket to produce his keys before turning towards Rebecca. "I enjoyed today; thanks for inviting us along."

She smiled shyly. "So did I."

There was a split-second's silence before he blurted, "Have you ever swum with the dolphins?"

For a moment, she was thrown. "Um, no... can't say that I have. Why?"

"Do you fancy it?"

Oh yes, indeedy I fancy it, she thought, nodding and eyeing his muscular framework at the same time. *Thank goodness she could multi-task.*

"It's just that I bumped into my mate Steve after you left the pub last night. He runs Spitfire Tours. Do you know the one?" The name rang a vague bell; she'd probably seen one of their boats in the harbour. "He owes me a favour and this time of year it's not a problem to squeeze a couple of extra passengers on." He looked at her expectantly.

"Won't it be a bit cold?" She shivered at the thought.

"Nah, not once you've got the scuba gear on. It's something else, I promise. Akaroa's the only place in the world you can swim with the Hectors." Seeing her nonplussed expression, he explained, "They're the world's rarest and smallest dolphin; I can't even describe what it's like being in the water with them."

Orgasmic, she thought optimistically before giving his Jacques Cousteau impersonation a ten out of ten. Oh, what the hell; she could live without the experience of swimming next to frisky fish, but swimming next to David, well... "Sounds awesome; I'd love to."

"Great! I'll jack it up for one morning this week and let you know. How does that grab you?"

I wish you were grabbing me. "Great."

After David climbed behind the wheel and turned the ignition, he popped his head out the open window. He shouted over the noise of the engine, "Hey, Rebecca, I meant to ask you earlier, how's Jennifer doing? I was hoping to catch up with her today."

She was surprised at his question. Maybe he was better friends with Jen than she'd realised. "She's okay. I'll tell her you were asking after her." Spying another vehicle coming up the drive, she added, "Hang on—she's here now if you want to say hi."

"Nah. I'll catch her another time," he said. "Just tell her I was asking after her." He disappeared down the drive, waving out as his Jeep passed Jennifer. Her sister didn't return the wave, and Rebecca registered her sister's obvious annoyance with surprise. Mind you, in her current state of mind, she probably wasn't in the mood to catch up with anyone.

The grinding of gears distracted her—a coach was labouring up the driveway's steep incline. This place was busier than Grand Central Station, she thought, watching the Nifty Knitters elbow one another out of the way as they jostled to climb aboard their waiting coach. The driver, who was throwing suitcases into the luggage hatch, paused to shoot a petrified glance in Betty's direction. She was attempting to herd the ladies aboard in an orderly manner and, catching his expression, grinned and mouthed, "You'll be fine." The driver was not a bingo player, and so he had never seen so many plump elderly women all at once. At last the door hissed shut, and the engine chugged into life. The coach slowly moved off, and a sea of grey, blue, and purple perms bobbed up and down as they fought over the window seats.

As it rounded the bend, they heard a rousing rendition of *She'll Be Coming Round the Mountain* being struck up. Melissa, Betty, and Rebecca collapsed against one another in a fit of the giggles.

Chapter Twenty

"SO WHAT HAD JENNIFER'S knickers in such a knot tonight? The last time I saw her that pissed was when you stole her new Revlon blusher." Melissa reached over for her mug, and then, gazing petulantly at its chocolaty contents, asked, "Um, where are the marshmallows?"

Rebecca ignored the request for marshmallows and shook the image of Ciaran dining alone in a café away. Blowing over the top of her drink, she took a tentative sip before replying, "I only *borrowed* her stupid blusher—she totally overreacted then, and she totally overreacted today too." She shrugged. "She had a face on her like she had been sucking on a lemon as soon as she got back from town, and it turns out it was because David had been here." Rebecca frowned; she'd had it with pussyfooting around her sister, not after the way she'd spoken to her this afternoon.

"What was *he* doing here?" Jennifer had demanded as soon as Rebecca had walked back inside the house. The smile she had on her face in anticipation of sharing the success of the luncheon with her sister vanished upon finding her pacing the lounge. She had flashed back to the way their father used to look when he was waiting up for her if she'd broken curfew.

"Are you talking about David Seagar?"

"Yes, David Seagar. Though I am having trouble keeping up with all the men you seem to have coming and going." Her voice was clipped.

"Ciaran showing up was not my doing and as for David, I invited him and Ben for lunch. Is there a problem?"

Jennifer stopped pacing and squared up to Rebecca angrily. "Yes, there is a problem. I don't like the man and I don't want him on the property—how do you even know him?"

Rebecca told her how they'd met doing the school run. "I don't get it. He implied you were friends." She frowned, unable to comprehend the vitriol coming from her sister in waves. "What's he done to make you dislike him so much?"

Jennifer made a sort of strangled noise. "Never mind; just trust me on this. We are not and never have been friends. I commissioned him to make a table for the cooking school, and that is the extent of our relationship. It's our boys who have a friendship."

"I still don't understand what the problem is."

"I just don't want you hanging around him, that's all."

"Oh, for goodness' sake, Jen, don't be ridiculous. Listen to yourself—you sound just like Dad used to. And I am not *hanging* around him, as you so eloquently put it."

"Yes, well, maybe Dad knew what he was talking about after all," she muttered.

"So was it to do with the table? Did he overcharge you or something?"

"Or something—like I said, it doesn't matter. I just don't want you seeing David again. He is not a man you can trust."

"Oh, for goodness' sake. *And the Oscar goes to...*"

"Don't take the mickey, Rebecca. I am serious."

"I can see that. I just don't get it, that's all, and you can't tell me who I can and can't see."

"Don't be childish."

That was the second time in the space of twenty-four hours she had been called childish and had to vigorously deny it. "I'm not! I happen to like the man and as a grown woman, I will decide whom I choose to see, thank you very much."

Jennifer snapped then, her eyes flinty. "For goodness' sake, Rebecca, you are worse than a Mills and Boon heroine. You always gravitate towards the bad boys and what was with the big boss man's impromptu appearance last night?"

"He's flown out to try to make amends and to tell me that he thinks he loves me, and I do not always go for the bad boys."

"Oh yes, you do. That Ciaran is a womaniser. He's proved that to you, yet all he has to do is make an idiotic grand gesture, and you go all weak at the knees. Melissa told me he can't keep it in his pants, for chrissakes!"

"Well then, you should be pleased I have met David because he might be the one to help me get over Ciaran." Rebecca's voice was raised now too.

"Oh grow up, Rebecca! Bouncing from one male root bag to another is not going to make you happy."

Ah-ha, Rebecca thought, cringing at her sister's crass terminology; now she was getting somewhere. "So David is a bit of a lad about town, so what? I'm not exactly virginal myself, you know. Why do you always condescend to me?"

Jennifer looked more like a coiled snake ready to spring as she hissed, "Because you always make stupid choices, that's why. I haven't got the energy this time to pick up the broken pieces. Not if you go down that track with David—or Ciaran, for that matter." She shook her head. "Is it any wonder I treat you like a child? You've always played the baby."

Rebecca shook her head and opened her mouth to issue a rebuttal, but Jennifer wasn't going to let her get a word in.

"You drift along, never sticking at anything or seeing anything through, expecting me or Mum and Dad to pick you up and dust you down each time you stuff-up. But for some reason, *I'm* always supposed to have my life in perfect working order."

For a moment, it seemed as if Jennifer had stepped back in time to her teenage years. It was how she used to be, raging in frustration at her parents. Only now, it was Rebecca on the receiving end. Tears trickled down both their cheeks. "You have no idea how damned hard it is having to get it right all the time." The fight went out of her then, and she flopped down on the couch.

Rebecca wondered how an innocent visit from David Seagar had ended up like this.

Jennifer's head was in her hands, and Rebecca's back was to the stairs, so neither woman noticed Jack. He was rubbing his eyes ferociously as he spied down on his mum and her sister from between the balustrade at the top of the stairs.

Taking an audible ragged breath, Jennifer looked up; she hated feeling like this. Running her fingers through her hair, she looked at Rebecca's face and knew she had overstepped the mark. She couldn't afford to alienate her, not when she needed her so much. "Look, Becs, I'm sorry. You didn't deserve to be attacked like that. What you decide to do about that boss of yours is your decision, but I do stand by what I said about David—stay away from him."

Rebecca bit back a terse reply and decided to accept the white flag. What Jen had said couldn't be unsaid, though, and the worst thing of all was that deep down she knew that the stuff her sister had said about her was all true.

"Bloody hell, I wonder what her problem is?" Melissa pondered, bringing Rebecca back to her Milo. "That was a bit OTT, even for Jennifer." She tapped the side of her mug thoughtfully. "Perhaps it's something to do with David's ex-wife?"

Rebecca shrugged, and her mouth set in a stubborn line. "Maybe. I don't care because whatever it is, it's her problem, not mine." She wasn't just annoyed at her sister's abhorrence of David or what she'd said about Ciaran. It was the fact she had made her think about the very thing that had been teasing the periphery of her brain for the last few days. What the hell was she doing with her life?

"What about Ciaran?" Melissa leered over at her. "I bet you're tempted to whip down to that B and B for a good old rodgering?"

"Nope. I would rather sit here and watch *Coronation Street*," she lied.

Upstairs, huddled under her duvet, Jennifer hugged the pillow that Mark's head had once upon a time lain on to herself. She felt the weight that always bore down on her when she thought of her husband settle on her chest. She thought back to a movie she had adored when she was a little girl, *Bedknobs and Broomsticks*. She craned her neck to look at the headboard and wished she could rub the bedknob and magic herself and the children away somewhere. Anywhere but here.

She had enough to worry about without throwing Rebecca into the mix. She was worried for her because she knew that the one thing she had forgotten to point out during her personality assassination that afternoon was how her little sister always did exactly the opposite of whatever she was told. She'd driven their mum to distraction with her contrary Mary ways as a child. Always digging her heels in and going in the opposite direction. She squeezed her eyes shut and willed the nothingness of sleep. She'd said her piece where David was concerned but at the end of the day, she knew that nothing she had to say would matter except the one thing she could never say.

The next morning, deciding to act like yesterday's fight had never happened, Jennifer forced herself to put on a cheerful face. Taking a deep breath as though she were about to go on stage, she'd sailed down the stairs and plastered a smile firmly on her dial before clapping her hands together and announcing with the enthusiasm of a kid's camp leader, "Come on, we've got places to go and things to do, guys. It's time to get dressed."

Famous last words. Bedlam ensued as Hannah couldn't find her pink boots. "The ones with da zips on dem," she lisped before insisting with the single-mindedness of a preschooler that no other footwear would do. Recognising the steely look on her daughter's face, Jennifer began to search, eventually locating the errant boots behind a plant pot on the veranda. Then it was Jack's turn to perform. He began by refusing to get dressed and wouldn't be bribed into doing so, choosing instead to lie on the couch, watching the TV.

His deliberate obtuseness irked his mother. She was having none of it, and her patience was wearing thin. She stormed over and switched the television off. Jack just smirked, though, and flicked it back on using the remote. Jennifer's blood boiled, and a wrestling match ensued as she leapt on the couch and tried to confiscate it, to no avail. Then, standing up in desperation, she screeched, "Right, that's it! Enough is enough," before planting her frame in front of the television to obscure his vision. Eventually, the little boy decided he was sick of looking at his dressing gown-clad mother and swung into action.

"Bloody hell," Jennifer swore softly, all her nerve endings jangling. "I'm never going to get them to school."

Rebecca, who had been up and dressed since the dawn chorus began outside the bedroom window, now stood in the doorway, chewing on a piece of toast. She was relishing the sight of her unflappable sister so flustered and would have offered to drop the kids off herself but after yesterday, Jennifer could bloody well ask her if she wanted help.

Asking for help was something that didn't come easily to Jennifer, especially as doing the school run was how Rebecca had met David in the first place. Her brow furrowed as she debated the odds of getting up the stairs, throwing on her clothes and getting out the door in the space of two minutes. It was all too much, and she knew it wasn't going to happen; she didn't have a choice. "Uh, Becs, seeing as you're dressed, do you think you could do me a favour and drop the kids off for me?"

"Sure," Rebecca answered, scooping up the car keys, revelling in being the cool, calm, and collected member of the family for a change. "Come on, guys. We are out of here."

As she crawled into the car park, it was like the sun had suddenly come out from behind the nasty black cloud that had been hovering since her fight with Jennifer. There, standing by the school gates with Ben nowhere in sight, was David. That could mean only one thing. A tight ball of nervous excitement formed in the pit of her stomach as she realised something: he was waiting to see her. Jennifer and her overprotective ranting could just bog off, she thought, pleased she'd taken that extra five minutes to get ready. Risking a quick check in the mirror, she decided she was not looking too bad, not too bad at all. *Ha! Eat your heart out, Ciaran.*

"Watch out, Auntie Becca!" Jack shrilled over her shoulder as she nearly rear-ended a Mr Bean-style Mini. "That's my teacher, Mr Reynolds's, car."

Flustered now, she hissed, "The silly man shouldn't have such a small car; I could hardly see it." A moment later, she parked without mishap and switched the engine off. Having learnt her lesson the other day, she went round to Hannah's side first and, freeing her niece from her restraints, swung her up onto one hip. Jack had already opened his door and, slamming it shut, slung his backpack over one shoulder.

"See ya," he called, and then he was off and running across the asphalt without so much as a backwards glance.

"That was close." David indicated towards the Mini with a smile. Rebecca blushed.

"It was Jack's fault; he distracted me by undoing his seatbelt. It's one of my rules, you know, that seatbelts are to stay on until the car is turned off." *Good save.* However, he looked more amused than impressed by her sense of responsibility.

"I hung around to see if you fancied meeting me for a coffee in the village after you drop Hannah off. I thought we could have a chat about the swimming with the dolphins?"

She'd dance the bloody tango naked with a dolphin if it meant spending time looking at him. "I'd love to. Where did you have in mind?"

"Do you know Cleo's, down by the water?" She nodded, pleased with his choice of café, which she knew to be very quiet and intimate.

"Okay then, I'll see you there soon."

As he walked away, she admired the way his rear fit ever so snugly into his jeans. Returning his wave as he drove off, she secured Hannah back into her car seat, asking, "Did you hear that, Hannah? Your Auntie Becca's got a hot date. Oh yes! A bit of the old morning delight is coming my way."

Hannah giggled, and she found herself getting on a bit of a roll seeing as she had an audience. "Hey, hey, hey, it's rumpy-pumpy time," she growled in her best *Fat Albert* voice before winking over her shoulder at her niece and then, being careful to avoid Mr Reynold's Mini, she reversed out of the car park.

Five minutes later, she was clapping her hands as she frogmarched Hannah into preschool. "Chop, chop, now; we haven't got all morning," she bossed, opening the door to the playroom.

"Morning, Hannah." Anna greeted the little girl as chipper as a children's television presenter, saving her grumpy cow impersonation for Rebecca.

She could almost empathise with the poor woman, Rebecca thought magnanimously. She obviously wasn't getting any. Producing Hannah's Hi-5 lunchbox, she placed it on the trolley beside the kitchen alongside all the others. Unlike moi, if I play my cards right, she thought. She blew a kiss across the room to where Hannah was now sitting at a play table, sinking her hands into a mound of wet clay.

"See you, sweetheart. Either Mummy or I'll be back at half past twelve to pick you up. Have a great morning."

"Half past twelve *sharp,* if you don't mind, Ms Loughton," Anna shot back with a condescending smile from the other side of the room. Rebecca ignored her; nothing was going to take the shine off her morning. Giving a final wave in Hannah's direction, she pulled open the door.

Her niece's voice rang out proudly as she did so, "My Auntie Becca's gonna have some rumpy-pumpy dis mornin."

Chapter Twenty-One

BY THE TIME REBECCA had pulled into a convenient park right outside Cleo's, the violent flush that had spread up her neck and worked its way up her entire face was beginning to settle down. Stepping out of the car and locking it, she glanced furtively round in case Ciaran was out for a morning stroll along the waterfront and then wondered what exactly it was she was feeling guilty about. Nevertheless, she was relieved to find the coast clear and so took a moment to peer at her reflection in the car window. She was pleased with what she saw. She'd teamed a soft pink angora jumper with her jeans. Its boat neck was flattering and with her hair falling over the top of her shoulders, the overall effect was soft and feminine. The colour suited her, giving her skin a warm glow. Or was that just the remnants of the flush? Whatever it was, she couldn't be worrying about it now, not when she had a hot date waiting for her over on the other side of that wall.

Tucking her hair behind her ears and licking her lips, she tottered into the café. Her footsteps echoed forlornly around the empty café and, upon hearing them, a tall blonde girl dressed in a white skivvy and jeans appeared from the kitchen.

"Good morning." She smiled.

One of those attractive Nordic types who didn't need any make-up, Rebecca surmised, managing a smile and cordial greeting back at her. Through the French doors, she saw a courtyard dappled in the morning sunshine. There was David, sitting at one of the wrought-iron tables, toying with a little pot full of salt, pepper, and sugar sachets.

Miss Sweden shot round from behind the counter to beat her to the French doors. "I think I'll open these right up since it's such a lovely morning." The woman sent a cacophony of seagulls up into the air as she did so.

Startled at the whining bird outburst, David looked up and then relaxed into a smile as Rebecca slid into the seat opposite him.

"Do you guys know what you're after?" the waitress asked, with pen and pad in hand.

"I'll have a latte in a bowl, thanks. Rebecca?"

"Oh, right, um, a flat white with trim milk please." She'd read somewhere that not asking for trim was like shoving a teaspoon of butter into your mouth. "And do you have any caramel slice?"

Miss Sweden raised an eyebrow. "Sure do."

After scooping up the froth of her drink and devouring half of the slice—which David had declined to try—Rebecca took a moment to admire the sparkling blue water spread out in front of them.

"Lovely spot, isn't it?" David asked over the rim of his enormous bowl of milky coffee, as if reading her mind.

"It is. I always thought Akaroa was pretty, but for some reason I seem to be seeing it through fresh eyes this time round."

"That's age."

Hang on; implying she was old was not part of the expected programme. "I beg your pardon?"

"Age," he reiterated with a cheeky grin. "The older you get, the greater your appreciation of the beauty around you becomes." As his mouth formed the end of his sentence, his eyes held hers and a feeling she couldn't cope with at nine thirty in the morning ricocheted through her, despite her earlier bravado.

"You're right," she agreed, determined to stay on course. "I know when I was a kid and we'd go on holiday, the only scenic thing I was interested in was a great big ice cream."

David redirected the subject with an abruptness that startled her. "Did you pass on my regards to Jennifer?"

"Yeah, I did." She shifted uncomfortably, unsure how to word what it was she desperately wanted to know without insulting the man. "Um, to be honest, David, she gave me the impression you two don't exactly get on."

He looked up sharply. "Really? First I've heard about it. I thought we got on just fine." He appeared genuinely puzzled, peering into the depths of his bowl of milky coffee as though it held the answer to this revelation. "Like

I told you, your sister showed me a few basic survival recipes when I first moved here. Akaroa's a small community." He gave a small shrug. "Everybody knows everybody else's business. Me moving here on my own with Ben initially created a bit of speculation as to his mother's whereabouts, and I think Jennifer felt sorry for me. I don't know Mark quite so well, with him working in the city. If I've offended her in some way..."

Rebecca backtracked, her curiosity as to exactly what had transpired between David and his wife freshly aroused. She wanted to hear more about David and his ex-wife, not talk about Jennifer and her ever increasing issues. "Maybe I read the situation wrong. In fact, I'm sure I did. Jen's just a bit fragile at the moment, so don't give it another thought." She held her breath, waiting to see whether he would elaborate on what exactly had transpired between him and his ex-wife. He did.

It was his wife Maree's decision to leave, arguing that she should never have gotten married so young. A clichéd excuse when a partner wants out, he told her, sparing no details as he explained how the two lovebirds met through a job David had done for her parents in Christchurch. It was the last job he ever did for them. Completely averse to the idea of their nineteen-year-old daughter dating a thirty-three-year-old, they resented their relationship from the start. Maree got pregnant and one shotgun wedding later, they started their 'happily ever after', only it wasn't so happy. Their ill-fated marriage couldn't survive Maree's relationship claustrophobia. While all her friends were out having a good time, she was stuck at home: a pregnant, married lady at the ripe old age of twenty.

Maree's affluent background demanded that the princess get what the princess wanted. She'd gone from being Mummy and Daddy's little girl to a wife and mother and she'd had no comprehension of what it was like to have to pay for groceries, household bills, and a mortgage out of one meagre income. David had no choice but to work all the hours under the sun; it was that or starve. As he rehashed the dirty details, his tone was harsh, but he either didn't notice or decided to ignore it.

"Her parents paid for Ben's day care and she went back to university to finish her degree. The day she graduated, she told me it was over between us. She'd been offered a position in some bigwig company up in Auckland that was just too good an opportunity for her to pass up. She had it all figured out; Ben was going to stay with her parents until she'd tested the waters up there. I didn't get a say in anything and, to be honest, for the first couple of months after she left, I was a wreck. I wasn't there for Ben emotionally, and that's something I'll always hate her for."

Rebecca could almost taste his bitterness.

"Of course, Maree decided she enjoyed her freedom far too much to have her son take it away from her. When I realised she didn't plan on coming back, I took her to court. She didn't fight me, but her folks did. It wasn't pleasant, and it was a tough thing to put a five-year-old through, but I am his dad," he shrugged his broad shoulders, "and here we are."

Rebecca was quiet as she mulled over the sad story she'd just been told. Then, reaching across the table, she laid her hand over his, holding it there briefly as she said, "Thank you for telling me, David."

He gave her a weak smile, but it never reached his eyes. "It's all in the past now. Kids are amazingly resilient. They seem to have their way of working things out, you know?"

If Jack's recent behaviour was anything to go by, she wasn't too sure about that, but not wanting to enter into a debate on child psychology, she nodded. "So does Ben see his mother or his grandparents?"

"Yeah. It took a while for Rex and Anne to put the bitterness of losing out on full custody to one side, but then they realised if they didn't, they'd lose him altogether. It's strained, but we're all very civil. He goes to stay with them every second weekend and Maree flies down once a month to spend a weekend with him."

Rebecca wondered at the sort of mother who could so blatantly put her needs before that of her child. It was unnatural, surely? It was David's turn to reach over and clasp her hand, giving it a gentle squeeze. "Don't judge her too harshly."

They both fell silent. David appeared lost in the past. Rebecca wasn't good at meaningful silences, and she was fighting back the urge to mention swimming with Flipper and his pals. Don't be ridiculous, she admonished herself; you'll come across as flippant. She had to bite back a nervous laugh at her unintended and not very funny pun. She began fidgeting in her seat. The silence stretched out, and she clenched and released one buttock at a time, like those exercises she'd seen in Melissa's magazine under the heading, 'Make Every Movement Count'. The picture, alongside a gravity-defying, bikini-clad bottom, had inspired Melissa, and she'd been doing one hundred of them every night since she'd come across the article. Fifty a side—that was dedication for you.

"Are you alright?" David asked, his eyes suddenly clearing.

Rebecca stopped, left cheek mid-air, and squeaked, "I'm fine, thanks."

"Have you got the time on you?"

She checked her watch and at the same time lowered her cheek back down to its normal resting position. "It's eleven o'clock."

"Bugger!" He jumped to his feet. "I've got a client coming over in five minutes. I'd better run." He pulled his chair back and, standing up, he grabbed her, pinning both arms to her sides as his lips brushed the side of her cheek.

"I'll call you." It had been something and nothing, but it left her flustered nonetheless, and she didn't trust herself to speak. Scooping her car keys off the table, she followed him out of the café.

Arriving back at the house, she'd just climbed out of the car when she heard Betty calling her name with a definite note of desperation in her tone. Alarmed, she looked across to the cook school, where she saw the older woman beckoning her over. She hurried down and only had one foot on the bottom step when Betty grabbed hold of her hand and yanked her inside. Attempting to peer round to see who the new guests were, she was surprised at just how nimble Betty was for a larger woman as she did a neat little sidestep, effectively blocking off her view.

What on earth was going on? Betty was behaving positively antsy.

"A little moral support would be good, Rebecca, dear."

"Er, okay."

Betty squeezed her hand gratefully before stepping aside to leave her totally unprepared for the sight sitting before her.

Ten Xena Warrior Princess clones in full battle regalia were seated at the workbenches. All ten grinning at Rebecca's flummoxed face.

"Well, howdy, lil lady; ya'll must be Jennifer. Gee, that's such a purdy name. Betty here told us you'd be a swingin' on by to say hi. Ma name's Mindy-Lou and I'm the president of this here Memphis branch of the Xena Fan Club." The source of the southern drawl stood up, revealing herself to be a rather short and dumpy Xena, who bore no resemblance whatsoever to Lucy Lawless.

That outfit does nothing for her and as for that wig, it's worse than Donald Trump's, Rebecca thought. She fought back the urge to giggle at the absurdness of her thoughts that, in fact, were no more absurd than the situation she currently found herself in. At last she managed to choke out that she was in fact Jennifer's sister, Rebecca. She told them she was over from Ireland on holiday. This news was met by a mass scraping of stools as short, tall, fat, skinny, and even ginger Xenas came bounding forward to shake her hand.

By the end of the introductions, Rebecca's hand felt bruised. Xena would have been proud of her fan club's warriorlike grips. As the Xenas slowly filtered back to their seats, she risked a glance at Betty.

The poor woman looked dazed as she whispered, "Don't blame me. I had no idea your sister took the booking. Thank God Jennifer opted to leave the meet and greet to me. This would have surely pushed her over the edge."

Rebecca had to agree; however, once the initial shock began to subside, it made way for curiosity. And when the Xenas were all sitting back down on their stools, she just had to ask, "So how long have you all been Xena fans?"

Mindy-Lou didn't give anybody else a chance to answer as she stood up, hand on heart. "I remember it like it was yesterday." Pausing, her piggy eyes surveyed the room to make sure she had a captive audience. "Season One, 1995. From the moment Xena changed her evil ways and rescued sweet lil Gabrielle, I was hooked." A collective sigh of remembrance went around the room. Rebecca and Betty must have looked a bit baffled because Mindy-Lou explained, "Gabrielle was just the cutest lil blonde thing you ever did see. She went on to be Xena's bard, and you know what? It has been implied that the two of them were more than just friends, if you catch my drift."

The Xenas tut-tutted, but Mindy-Lou held her hand up for silence. "So that you know, we don't buy into that whole scenario."

"You tell 'em, sister!" Ginger Xena bawled across the room.

And Mindy-Lou did. "No siree, we at the Memphis branch of the Xena Fan Club believe that to be no more than an ugly rumour started by a small man. Small in every aspect, if ya catch my drift." Her ribald wink left no room to miss it. "Who could not believe that a woman could be strong, beautiful, and prefer the company of other women without any shenanigans going on? We do, don't we, girls?"

"Sure do, Mindy-Lou!" Foot stamping and whistling followed.

Rebecca glanced round the room, looking for Jerry Springer.

Once the furore died down, Mindy-Lou carried on. "Ma marriage broke down on account of me bein' a strong, independent woman and him being a no-good sumbitch. I felt an instant kinship with Xena the first time I saw her on TV, and I thought to myself, now what would she do in my shoes? And the answer came to me clear as day. She'd kick his cheatin' ass all the way to Kentucky and go looking for Gabrielle lickety-split, that's what. So that's what I did." Mindy-Lou puffed out with pride at this point, in danger of spilling out of her chest plate as she spread her flabby arms wide to encompass her fellow Xenas. "And here they all are, ma Gabrielles, ma warrior sisters!"

Rebecca waited for her to add that they could make a cash donation by telephoning the following 0800 number, but instead she heard mutterings of dissent amongst the ranks.

"Mindy-Lou knows full well we're all Xenas, so how comes she's always trying to make out we're all her lil Gabrielles?" That came from Bonnie-May, whose wig had unfortunately slipped to one side to reveal a zebra-like do of bleached blonde and black roots.

"If she's not careful, we'll have one of them there coups and get us a new president," came from Candy-Sue.

"Well, that's just great, Mindy-Lou," Betty jumped in. "Thank you for sharing your story with us all, but now it's high time we got on with the business at hand, isn't it, ladies?" The Xenas looked towards Betty expectantly. "Cooking, of course!" This elicited a fresh round of yee-haws and wahoos, as well as a few whistles. Rebecca couldn't help but admire Betty's style, especially when she managed to silence them all by producing, a moment later, the biggest fish anyone in the room had ever seen.

Its mammoth, scaly body had been laid to rest on a silver platter, and Betty's knees were in danger of buckling as she staggered under the weight of it. "This morning, ladies..." It was Betty's turn to make sure she had a captive audience. Gee, she was getting into the swing of things now, Rebecca thought, looking on with admiration. "I have the pleasure of introducing you to the gourmet delights of Akaroa salmon!"

As the room exploded, Rebecca could have sworn the salmon turned one glassy eye on the ringleader, Mindy-Lou. However, she also saw an opportunity to escape, and no one heard her polite goodbye over the cacophonous din.

Rebecca's breath was coming in ragged bursts as she cleared the path and leapt up onto the front porch. Pulling the bundle of keys from her pocket, she cursed as they slipped from her grasp and dropped in a jangling pile to the ground. Snatching them back up, it took her a moment to sift through them for the right key, and it was a blessed relief when, on her second try, the key turned. Pushing the front door open, she risked a nervous glance over her shoulder, half expecting to see a tribe of Amazons charging towards her. The coast was clear. Stepping into the hall, she shut the door behind her with a slightly hysterical giggle.

I don't know about Amazons; more like fried chicken-munching maniacs, she thought, collapsing onto the couch. *What a morning!* Unzipping her boots and kicking them off, she decided to check her phone. There was a text from Derbhilla, asking what had happened with Ciaran. That's right, she mused; Derbhilla was the one who had urged him to get on a plane and come here. Rebecca sighed; she wanted to muster up annoyance at her friend for interfering, but she knew she'd done it with the best of intentions.

Closing her eyes, she wondered what Ciaran was doing right at that moment. He was probably sipping on a latte at one of the waterfront cafés. Oh yes, he would be reading the paper and enjoying the view, she mused. No way would she give in to the overwhelming urge that suddenly assailed her to hotfoot it down to the B&B. Instead, she quickly tapped out a one-word reply to Derbhilla's question: Nothing.

Chapter Twenty-Two

"BECS, I AM SORRY ABOUT all that stuff I said about you yesterday. It wasn't fair, and I don't want to fall out with you." Jennifer came out of the office and Rebecca noticed she was looking a lot more put together than she had first thing that morning. She also noticed the apology didn't extend to what she had said about David or Ciaran, but she didn't want a fight on her hands either.

Jennifer looked hard at her sister. Her face was red and blotchy, and she had little bits of hair stuck to her forehead. "Have you been running?"

"Only from the cooking school."

"Part of your new keep fit routine, is it?"

"Ha ha. You haven't met the new guests yet. If you had, you'd understand."

"They're American, aren't they?"

"More like alien," Rebecca muttered.

"Pardon?"

"Yes, they are American but they are also travelling under the umbrella of the Xena Warrior Princess Fan Club and have to be seen to be believed."

"Seriously? I'll have to head down and take a peek." Jennifer frowned. "The booking was made under the name of Mindy-Lou from Memphis; she didn't say anything about being part of a fan club."

"Well, like I said, seeing is believing and don't say I didn't warn you because that group of gals you've got staying down there make Trekkies look normal. Oh and Jen?"

"Mm?"

"Can I have a hug?" Her encounter with David that morning was making her feel magnanimous. "Because if you do go down there, it might be the last time I see you alive."

Jennifer laughed and held out her arms. "They can't be that bad."

"Oh ye of little faith," Rebecca said, hugging her sister back and inhaling her familiar essence. She smelt of expensive salon shampoo and Chanel No. 5. It suited her because just like the write-up on her favourite perfume, Jen was complex. Despite her sometimes cool and always impeccable exterior, when you got beneath that, Rebecca realised, she was beginning to discover there was a likeable warmth.

For her part, Jennifer breathed in a light, refreshing scent that reminded her of the sea. It was frothy and fun but with a hidden depth and it was Rebecca, she thought, smiling and getting a mouthful of hair in return. They were opposites in so many ways but at the core of their differences was the knowledge that when push came to shove, the other would always be there. Friends might come and go—scratch that thought because Melissa was a bloody limpet—but she and Rebecca were sisters and right now she was glad hers was here.

"I meant what I said before. I really was out of line with some of the stuff I said to you yesterday," Jennifer said, breaking away from the embrace.

"No, not all of it, you weren't." Rebecca shook her head. "What you said about me was true and you got me thinking. In fact, you might have done me a favour." She wasn't ready to disclose the plans that were forming around the edges of her brain just yet and neither sister was prepared to broach the subject of David Seagar again.

"You're late back. Did you meet up with Ciaran?" Jennifer inquired, carefully keeping her tone light.

"Uh, no. I ran a couple of errands." She hoped her face didn't give the falsehood away. "Ciaran's agreed to give me a bit of space for a few days while I wrap my head around the fact he is here and what he wants me to do about it."

He went up a notch in Jennifer's estimation; at least he wasn't hounding her into making a decision.

"Oh, look—it's twelve twenty. Time to face the music," Rebecca said, her eyes straying to her watch before Jennifer had a chance to grill her as to what she was going to do about him.

Jennifer looked at her quizzically. "Do you mean to go and pick up Hannah? Because I'll get her."

"No, let me go, please. I'm only here for another few days, and nobody ever greets you with as much enthusiasm as a preschooler. Why don't you go down and check out the Warrior Princesses and we'll see you back here shortly? That's if they don't decide to make you their high priestess or something."

IT WAS WORSE THAN WHEN she'd been late the other day, and Rebecca wished she had let Jennifer pick her daughter up. This time there were three pairs of eyes boring into her back as she hurriedly shoved Hannah's empty lunchbox into her backpack. Deciding the best way to deal with the situation was simply to brazen it out, she took a deep breath and swung round with a cheery smile plastered firmly in place. "Has Hannah had a good morning?"

There was a flurry of action as, embarrassed at having been caught gawping, Linda began giving the broom what-for. She swept up the remains of what appeared to be lunch while Abbey put some elbow grease into wiping the tables down. Only Anna didn't seem flustered, smiling superciliously from where she was supervising a huddle of children engaged in a spot of painting—ever the professional—and Rebecca found herself half admiring the woman's style as Anna informed her, "Oh yes, Hannah's done a lot of messy play today. She especially enjoyed the clay and playdough, didn't she, Linda?"

Linda nearly dropped the broom, startled at having a question directed at her. She managed to point over to a table covered with bits of green and pink dough before stuttering out, "Ye-ye-yes, she's been very creative."

"And yourself, Rebecca? Did you have a good morning?" Anna was almost salivating as she played the situation for all it was worth.

"Me? I had a wonderful morning, thanks. I went and did a workout after I dropped Hannah off here; the best one I've had in years. Got myself into positions I had no idea the old bod was capable of." Then, giving a tinkly laugh, she went on. "I'll be walking like a cowboy for at least a month!" Ha! That would sort them out, she thought and unwrapped her niece from her leg before she took her firmly by the hand to lead her out of the classroom.

She left all three women agog as she casually tossed a "see you tomorrow" over her shoulder.

Before the day care escapees made it to the car, Hannah was already yawning. This whole motherhood thing was beginning to grow on her, Rebecca realised. It felt nice to be in control for once, and one sleepy tot equalled a quiet afternoon for all of them.

"Do you think a little rest might do you some good when we get home?" she asked, once the child was safely secured in her car seat.

And that was when she knew she was no longer in control. Hannah's chin began to wobble slightly; a split second later, her face turned a blotchy red as she shrilled, "No! No rest."

Time for damage control. "Perhaps a choccie milk and a DVD then?"

Hannah smiled to herself as victory was once again hers. It was child's play, wrapping these adults around her little finger.

Phew! Rebecca felt relieved when the car swept past the classroom and up to the house with no sign of Cuisine with Carlton's newest arrivals lurking in the bushes. She ushered Hannah inside the house and as there was also no sign of Jennifer, she sorted her out with the promised DVD and chocolate milk.

"Sweetie, will you be alright here if Auntie Becca goes upstairs for a few minutes? I think Mummy must be down at the cook school."

Hannah nodded without moving her eyes away from the big screen in front of her.

"Good girl. I won't be long; just shout out if you need me." She skipped up the stairs and down the hall to her room. It was now or never.

Flicking the light switch on, she pulled the heavy, cream-brocade curtains closed before getting down on her hands and knees to drag her suitcase out from under the bed. Unzipping it, she began rifling through, flinging the top layer of clothes to one side. She knew exactly where they were because she'd deliberately stashed them at the very bottom of her case. She'd packed them purely as a token gesture, with no intention whatsoever of wearing them. It was winter, after all, though if things with the children had gotten dire, she might have bribed them with a trip to Hanmer Hot Springs, but now, needs must. *Ah-ha, there they were, rolled up neatly and still bearing the price tag.* Tossing them onto the bed, she stood up to look at them, pleased with what she saw.

The chocolate-brown contrasted nicely with the aquamarine trim, she decided, holding the bikini top up to her chest. *Oh yes, I'll fill that out nicely.* Letting it fall to the ground, she tentatively picked up the bottoms before holding them up against her nether regions.

Right—she rubbed her hands together—*let's get down to business, starting with that mirror.* The straight up-and-down angle of the full-length mirror that Jennifer obviously preferred was okay if you were one of the fortunate few weighing in under sixty kilograms. For the masses who didn't, however, it was terribly unflattering. What a pity Jen didn't own one of those skinny mirrors like they had in the jeans shops. She smiled fondly, thinking of those floor-to-ceiling mirrors that would see you stepping out of the dressing room with a sense of foreboding, only to find a svelte size ten staring back at you. The undoubtedly skinny eighteen-year-old shop assistant would then hang up the phone on her girlfriend and come flying out from behind the counter. She would gush at how terrific the jeans looked on you while you turned this way and that, totally in love with the vision before you. So what if nine times out of ten she'd gotten home with a pair of jeans that would never see the light of day because the size ten had been a short-lived but nonetheless very happy optical illusion?

With her tongue protruding from the corner of her mouth, Rebecca struggled to ease her sister's rather heavy antique mirror into a more flattering position. At last, she was satisfied that it was as good as it was going to get. Pulling her jumper over her head and stepping out of her jeans, she flung her knickers and bra off, squeezed her eyes shut, and refused to look until she'd put the bikini on.

With a deep breath, she opened her eyes, did a pirouette and threw her arms wide. "Ta-da!" Then raising her arms high, she bent them into twin arcs that met above her head as she simultaneously angled her feet outwards, heel to heel and bent down into a deep plié. Catching sight of the two centimetres growth on either side of her bikini reflected back at her in the mirror, she decided that perhaps that wasn't such a good look, but hey, it was easily remedied. She'd be wearing a wetsuit for the best part of the day, so did it matter? She tried to picture what she'd look like in head-to-toe black rubber. "A fucking seal, that's what." She scowled into the mirror.

"A what?" Melissa asked from the doorway as in one fell swoop, her eyes swept over the drawn curtains and her semi-naked best friend. Flustered, Rebecca snatched up her jumper in a futile attempt to cover herself.

"I never heard you come in. I thought you were going to spend the day in town?"

"Obviously," Melissa said with an arched eyebrow. "I changed my mind."

"How come?" Rebecca asked, trying to distract her while she stretched her leg across to where her jeans lay and attempted to drag them over to the bed with her foot.

Melissa took a step into the room, shrugging. "Wasn't in the mood. But never mind that..." Melissa waved her hand impatiently. "What on earth are you up to?"

Rebecca sighed, knowing she'd been well and truly busted. "I was checking out my togs, if you must know, for the swimming with the dolphins thing."

"Stand up then and give us a twirl."

"I don't want to."

"Oh, for heaven's sake. We're all sisters here, aren't we?"

"I suppose so."

"Well, come on then!"

Reluctantly she stood up, instantly wishing she hadn't as her friend's mouth dropped open. "Good grief, girl! The frigging dolphins will think they've gone back to the Ice Age and a woolly mammoth's after them!"

"Thanks for that, Melissa. I was just brimming over with confidence as it was, without a remark like that," Rebecca snapped back, tracking her friend's distracted gaze and then realising with horror what it was she had spotted. They both dove at the same time, but it was Melissa who stood up, triumphantly holding them aloft between her thumb and forefingers in a pincerlike grip.

"And what exactly do you call these?"

Rebecca blushed, snatching her favourite up-to-the-waist knickers out of her friend's grip. "Comfortable, that's what I call them."

"You," Melissa wagged a bony finger at her, "are in need of some serious help, my girl. How do you ever expect to hook a man, let alone actually keep him, if you get around in knickers like those? If you'd flashed these little beauties at Ciaran the other night, he'd have hopped straight back on the plane, and you wouldn't have this little ménage á trois dilemma of yours."

Rebecca shrugged rebelliously; she'd made up her mind not to let the thought of Ciaran ruin the anticipation of her date with David, but Melissa wasn't done yet.

"And what is with the middle-aged, Eastern European woman bikini line? Don't give me that blank look either—you know what I'm talking about."

Surely, Rebecca thought with horror, she wasn't being compared to the woman they'd seen prancing along the beach in Croatia a year or so back. She'd had a growth on either side virtually down to her knees.

She bowed her head and took a good, long look down under. Then, with desperation written all over her face, she pleaded her case. "It's winter! I didn't think it would matter if I just left it."

Sensing she may have gone a bit too far, Melissa decided it was time to add a bit of a softener.

"Look, babes, the togs are hot." Then again, not too much of a softener because that simply wasn't her style, and Rebecca would know she was lying. "What's hanging out the side of them, unfortunately, is not."

"I'll sort it out," Rebecca said defensively. "What are you staring at?"

"Shush, I'm thinking." Giving her friend the head-to-toe once-over, Melissa suddenly sprang into life, barking out a plan of attack. "Right, here's what we'll do. I'll book you in for a wax and a spray tan." She pinched Rebecca's thigh.

"Ow! What did you do that for?"

"That's nothing compared to a wax job, babe. You're going to have to get tough if you want to get beautiful. A de-fuzz and a bit of colour will improve things drastically. I'll go and make an appointment right now."

In her element, she flounced importantly out of the room and Rebecca seized the opportunity to begin getting dressed. She'd just gotten one leg in her knickers when Melissa's head bobbed back round the door. "Don't you even think about putting those passion killers back on, Rebecca Loughton!

For goodness' sake, woman, they're a crime against all of womankind. Have you no self-respect?" When no reply was forthcoming, she answered for her, "Obviously not because self-respect, my friend, starts with a pair of sexy knickers."

Suitably chastened, Rebecca bent down to have a quick rummage for another pair in her case. "Will these do?" She held up a pale blue thong and got the nod of approval. *Bugger it*, she groaned inwardly. She'd only worn the bloody thing once before, and she'd spent the whole day ducking around corners, trying to dislodge it. Melissa's work, however, was temporarily done. Rebecca was about to slide back into her jeans when a thought occurred to her: she'd no doubt be seeing David again when she went to pick Ben up.

She pulled the curtain open and peeked outside. It was quite a mild afternoon in the middle of winter; why not wow him with a skirt? Prove to him that she owned one. On the flip side, would he think it funny that she was all dressed up just to pick up Jack? Mind you, she could always say she had an appointment in town. The frown disappeared to be replaced by a little smile; after all, if Melissa came through with her salon booking, she wouldn't be lying really.

Yes, she'd made her mind up. It was a golden opportunity to dress to impress. If she teamed her favourite grey A-line skirt with that fitted black cardigan she'd bought from River Island at the start of winter, she'd look hot to trot. Her knee-high boots would finish the look off nicely, and David would be none the wiser that she was off for a much-needed appointment to get her legs, and other unmentionables, waxed.

Now, where had she put the skirt?

Chapter Twenty-Three

AS SHE CAME DOWN THE stairs, she heard Melissa's voice carrying from the kitchen. "I wouldn't ask if it wasn't a total emergency, but she's in a bad way. Yes, yes, that's right; like I said, it's halfway down her thighs. I know—it's terrible. I couldn't believe someone could let themselves go like that. Can you? Four o'clock? She'll be there. Thanks so much, Marina. You're a lifesaver. Bye."

Hanging up the phone, she had the grace to look startled as Rebecca, who'd crept silently into the kitchen, planted herself in front of her, hands on hips. "What are you looking so aggressive for?"

"Why don't you take an ad out while you're at it, Melissa?"

"I had to make it sound bad for her to fit you in straight away; honestly, Rebecca, a little thanks now and again would go a long way. What are you all dressed up for?"

"Yes, Rebecca, what's the occasion?" Jennifer was poised in the doorway, Hannah perched on her hip, sucking her thumb with her head resting on her mother's shoulder. It was then Rebecca noticed the keys dangling from her spare hand.

"No occasion," she lied, "I just felt like putting a skirt on, that's all."

Jennifer raised a knowing eyebrow, and Melissa wisely kept out of the exchange.

"If you say so. Oh, and I see what you mean about the new guests. They're certainly a unique bunch, but Betty seems to have them firmly under control. I'm off to get Jack now." She gave a rueful smile. "Maybe he'll talk to me if it's just the two of us. Would you mind watching Hannah for me?" Not waiting for a reply, she passed her sleepy daughter over to her sister.

Rebecca heaved her niece onto her hip. *What to do—what to do?* Her plans were ruined, but she couldn't very well make a song and dance about

193

it. Not after what Jen had said about David; besides, she had a strong suspicion that having a chat with her son was not her only reason for picking him up. She deposited Hannah into a startled Melissa's arms and scurried outside after her, hoping for a last-minute brainwave just as Betty appeared on the cook school's steps.

She waved out. "Yoo-hoo! Jennifer, can you spare a moment? I could do with a hand with the salmon."

Jennifer scowled; she couldn't very well say no and turning, she reluctantly handed the keys over to Rebecca.

Five minutes later, Rebecca pulled into the school car park. David waved as she climbed out of the Land Cruiser and, waving back, she spied Jack dragging his school bag along the asphalt behind him. Ben, who must have been first out of his class, was already by his dad's side. Once he saw her heading over towards them, he began pulling at his dad impatiently. "Come on, Dad; you know I've got karate."

"I won't be more than a sec."

As Ben climbed into their waiting SUV, Rebecca called out to him, "No Jack? You two are normally joined at the hip." Mustn't have heard me, she thought with a shrug as, never even glancing up in her direction, Ben pulled his door shut.

"He's got karate this afternoon; can't get there quick enough," David explained.

"Oh, right. I've heard that it's great for teaching kids self-discipline," she replied, trying to sound knowledgeable but he just laughed.

"Yeah, and how to kick some ass. What about you? Where are you off to, all dressed up? Not karate by the looks of it."

Unconsciously she straightened, pleased he'd noticed her efforts. "No, not karate, though learning a bit of self-discipline wouldn't do Jack any harm..." She trailed off then, realising she hadn't answered his question. She replied mysteriously, "I've an appointment in town."

Thankfully, David wasn't the nosy sort. "We never got round to making a date with the dolphins, did we?"

As she opened her mouth to reply, Jack was suddenly upon them. His fingers pulled at hers, trying to pry the keys from her grip.

"Give me the keys," he demanded.

"Hello to you, too, Jack; good day, was it?" When he successfully snatched the keys out of her hand, he took off at a trot. "What about saying hi to Mr Seagar?" she called after him, but he was already halfway across the car park. Embarrassed, she turned back to David. "See what I mean about needing to learn a bit of self-discipline? A few manners wouldn't go astray either."

His smile was understanding, and his eyes flicked to the back of his vehicle, where his son was moodily kicking at the back of the driver's seat. "A day out will do us both good."

"Sorry?"

"Swimming with the dolphins. I was saying we never got round to making a time to go. I'd like to get to know you a little better." Pausing for a moment, a dimple appeared on his left cheek as the corner of his mouth lifted in a smile. "So tell me, when am I going to hear about your history, Ms Loughton?"

She tittered nervously. "Oh, nothing to tell. I'm an open book." She could tell he knew that wasn't entirely true by the way his eyes—which looked decidedly grey today against his light-blue work shirt—bore into hers.

A sudden loud honking made them both jump. "I don't believe it," Rebecca muttered through clenched teeth. Jack had plonked himself in the front seat of the Land Cruiser and was cheerfully hitting the horn. "Has nobody ever taught that kid that patience is a virtue!"

David laughed. "I love the way you do that."

"What, screech like a banshee?"

"No, speak in clichés all the time. It is charming."

As the horn parped again, she turned away and stomped across the car park before he could see her blush.

A moment later, David pulled up alongside them as she slammed the back door shut on Jack's protests. Leaning out the window, he said, "I got hold of my mate, Steve, after I saw you this morning. He's running a tour on Friday morning. The boat leaves the jetty at ten o'clock."

She pasted what she hoped was an excited grin on her face. "Great! I'm looking forward to it."

"Yeah, me too." He gestured over his shoulder with his thumb. "Gotta run or the karate kid here will be late for his lesson."

Rebecca glanced over at Ben and was surprised to see him looking steadfastly ahead; her gaze flickered over to the back seat of her wagon to Jack. He, too, was seemingly absorbed in studying the fabric of the seat in front of him. *That was weird; maybe they'd had a fight?* She made a mental note to ask Jack about it on the way home. Peering in closer, she saw that the little sod hadn't done his seatbelt up either. Sighing, she opened the door; with the mood Jack was in, she'd be better to do it herself.

As she leaned across to make sure her sulking nephew was clicked in, a blast of warm air ripped through the car park. How bizarre; a nor'wester in the middle of winter, Rebecca thought as she experienced an aerated sensation. Remembering she'd left her tights off in anticipation of her waxing appointment, she instinctively straightened up to pull her skirt down, when a sharp thud resounded as she smacked her head on the car roof.

"Shit!" she yelped, simultaneously clutching her skirt and her head when she spotted David's Jeep. It was sitting, indicator blinking, waiting to turn out onto the road.

"Didn't see a thing!" he shouted, leaning out the window. "Blue's your colour, by the way." With a wink and a smirk, he turned right and disappeared off down the road.

She didn't know about blue being her colour—more like flaming red! Kicking Jack's door shut, she got behind the wheel and revved the engine like an ageing boy racer. For once in his short little life, Jack had the sense not to speak to her on the hairy ride home.

An irritatingly peppy little tune she recognised from Hannah's Hi-5 DVD welcomed them when they got home; it was a sound that did not befit her current mood. Striding into the lounge a moment later, it became apparent that Melissa had relaxed her no dancing with preschoolers policy and that Hannah had gotten her second wind. Pushing past them into the kitchen, she fished out a couple of biscuits and poured a glass of milk. Not that Jack deserved afternoon tea, she thought darkly, blaming him for the car park debacle.

Seeing his auntie's grim expression, Jack silently reached up to the bench. He decided not to ask if there was any chance of chocolate biscuits instead of those horrible plain ones she'd just put on his plate, before running upstairs with his stash.

"This is great exercise, Rebecca. My pedometer says I've already burnt off two hundred seventy calories." Melissa held out her wrist to show her the evidence. She couldn't resist adding, "You want to try it sometime."

Refusing to be riled any further that afternoon, Rebecca instead asked for directions to the salon Melissa had booked for her. In short, breathy bursts, she puffed out the straightforward instructions.

As Rebecca headed out the door, Melissa was far too busy doing a particularly high leg kick—while Hannah looked on in wonderment—to notice her friend's departure. So, banging the door shut behind her, Rebecca left them all to it.

On Rue Lavaud, Rebecca found the hairdressing salon by the café where they'd bumped into Jeremy Thompson the other day. Pulling into a parking spot in one tidy manoeuvre, she locked the door behind her and gazed at the building where she was about to be beautified.

With slightly flaking paint, what once had been a home was now a business, though, the building had seen better days. Somehow it carried the image off, still managing to retain its colonial charm. A folk art-styled sign proclaiming the shop's name *Hair for You* was swinging in the dastardly nor'wester, emitting little squeaks as it rocked back and forth on rusty hinges. Rebecca hoped it wasn't a sign of things to come as she pushed open the salon door.

A bell jangled somewhere out the back, and her eyes flitted around, registering that there were no other customers or, for that matter, stylists in the salon. A dual set of washbasins at the far end of the room sat poised for action, as did the two black swivel chairs facing the wall mirrors. She noted, glancing over at herself, that they could do with a bit of a spit and polish. Behind the deserted front counter, an oversized poster of a model with a cherry-red bob and matching pout, peering out from behind a peek-a-boo fringe, had been Blu-tacked onto the wall. Probably to hide the fact the place desperately needed a paint job. No wonder business wasn't exactly what you'd call brisk.

A rustling noise from the back of the shop distracted her. *So there was someone else here then.* Looking towards its source, she spied a woman emerging from behind the beaded curtain separating the shop from what she assumed were private quarters. Looking at the woman, the word 'resplendent' sprang to mind. A resplendent vision in tie-dye. Never mind that the pale two-toned lavender pinafore clashed something terrible with the halo of red frizz sitting on top of the woman's head; that she had a presence, there could be no doubt. A waft of smoke followed behind her, snaking its way out from whatever lay behind the curtain. As it drifted in Rebecca's direction, her nostrils flared suspiciously. *Oh yes, whatever was smouldering in the ashtray out the back there would give old Rollo the airport beagle something to get his rocks off over.*

Suddenly, she became aware that she was staring. With a forced blink and smile, she at last managed to speak. "Hi. I was looking for Beauty for You. I've got an appointment at four o'clock."

"Are you Rebecca?" The woman's voice was low and husky, and as her heavily made-up eyes swept over her, they paused momentarily on her nether regions, causing Rebecca to flush as she answered, "Yes." It had been unnecessary for Melissa to be so over-the-top on the telephone because the woman wasn't run off her feet. She did, however, look sympathetic to her cause.

"Well, it's nice to put a name to the face, Rebecca. Melissa told me all about you and," she tapped the side of her nose, "shall we just say, *your little problem.*" She took a step closer, and Rebecca inadvertently stepped backwards, nearly stumbling over a broom.

She didn't appear to notice, grinning widely and reminding Rebecca of Ronald McDonald. "I'm Marina. As you can see, I run a bit of a double act, doing hair down here," she laughed and pointed up at the ceiling, "and as you know, hair up there or down there, as the case may be."

Ha ha, bloody ha. Rebecca cringed; this was far worse than she had imagined, and they hadn't even got to the waxing bit.

A feeling of trepidation stole over her as Marina turned on a fleshy, veined ankle and walked heavily back towards where she'd come from. Holding the beaded curtain to one side, she whispered a bit too theatrically for Rebecca's liking, "Follow me."

So this was what it must have felt like to enter Doctor Who's Tardis. Half expecting to find a group of hippies lying around on old mattresses as they passed a bong around and discussed the meaning of life, she was surprised to find instead a small but tidy kitchen. An ashtray sat smouldering on the bench and Marina, following her gaze, winked at her. "It's purely for medicinal purposes. Stress." She waved her hand. "You know what it's like. Today's busy world and all that."

Rebecca, who was beginning to feel very stressed herself, nodded her head sympathetically and followed Marina up the squeaking, narrow staircase that was hidden away at the back of the alcove like an afterthought. Beauty for You operated out of two tiny rooms. As Marina disappeared off into one, she called out, "Have a seat, love; I'll be with you in a jiffy."

Rebecca looked around the nook and found herself standing alone. At least it was sunny. An old-fashioned sash window permitted entrance to the late afternoon sun in slivers of light. Beneath the window was an overstuffed armchair. Foam was beginning to ooze out from one of its faded floral arms, and next to it a pile of magazines spilled out from their cane rack. The overall effect was unexpectedly inviting.

Near the door through which Marina had disappeared was a U-shaped white counter. The clinical look of the stainless-steel wall unit standing to attention behind it looked oddly out of sorts with the rest of the room. On closer inspection, Rebecca saw that the unit's shelves housed row upon row of expensive-looking, shiny white boxes. Picking one up randomly, she turned it over in her palm to read about the miracle properties it no doubt contained within, but realising that the writing was all in French, she gave up.

The price sticker, however, was in English and Rebecca gleaned comfort from it. Surely Marina's setup here couldn't be that Mickey Mouse if she sold pricey French things? Plonking herself down in the armchair, she picked up a *Woman's Weekly* featuring Princess Diana and her latest scandal. It was practically vintage. It was strange to see a headline enticing you to read all about the princess when you knew what lay in store. She was pondering Diana's unhappy ending when the door opened, and Marina beckoned for her to come through. Closing the magazine reluctantly, Rebecca hauled herself up out of the depths of the chair.

Although she would have thought it near impossible, the other room's proportions were even smaller than its counterpart. White and windowless, she couldn't help but think of a cell. Hang on, though, she thought; no windows was probably a good thing, seeing as she was getting her bikini line done. The fewer spectators at that event, the better. In the centre of the room and adding to the whole *Bad Girls/Prisoner* feel of it was a narrow bed with a white cotton sheet draped over it. A neatly folded white towel was placed at the bottom of the bed like an upside-down pillow and squeezed between the wall and the bed was a trolley housing all sorts of gooey-looking pots. It all looked quite professional, she concluded, beginning to feel marginally more confident about what was about to transpire.

"Ready, love?"

"As I'll ever be." There was a stinging sensation as the hot wax hit Rebecca's tender skin, and then, "AAAAAGH!"

"No kids then?" Marina stated rather than asked.

Twenty minutes later, Rebecca stole a glance downwards. "Um, Marina, I don't usually go that wide."

Marina looked at her blankly, a blob of wax landing on the top of Rebecca's thigh as she paused.

"What do you mean you don't normally go that wide? You're booked in for a Brazilian, love."

"Sorry, a what?"

"A Brazilian. You know, it's the latest craze; does wonders for the libido—both his and hers."

She winked and Rebecca blathered, "I know what a Brazilian is. I just never planned on having one."

"That's not what your friend Melissa said when she made the appointment."

She couldn't argue with that. *Bloody Melissa!* She'd kill her, and no court in the land would uphold a conviction after hearing what had driven her to it.

Marina was looking a bit worried now. "Do you want me to carry on? Might look a bit funny if we don't."

Rebecca gazed dolefully at the remains of what had never been her crowning glory and mulled over her limited choices. She could attempt a combover like her dad, or worse, look like something out of the film *The Last of the Mohicans*.

She nodded, giving Marina the silent go-ahead, and then shut her eyes until at last, her ordeal was over.

"There you go, love; it's all done. That wasn't so bad, was it?"

Stupid, stupid question, you stupid woman, Rebecca thought, not bothering to answer it. Opening one eye, she leaned up on her elbows and peered down, instantly recoiling in shock.

"Hope you haven't got a hot one planned tonight, love!" Marina chuckled, and then seeing her panicked expression soothed, "Look, don't worry, love. The spots will have gone down by tomorrow and then he won't be able to keep his hands off you. Might pay to leave the spray tan for today, though."

Rebecca, not only virtually pubic hairless, was also rendered speechless by Marina and her not-so-comforting words of wisdom. Sensing now might be a good time to leave the room, Marina left Rebecca to get dressed.

Sitting up, she eased her legs over the side of the bed gingerly. It took her an age to slide into her clothes, but at last fully dressed, she ambled into reception like a cowboy heading for a showdown. Marina was standing behind the counter with her hand already hovering mid-air in anticipation of ringing up the bill.

"REBECCA!"

Oh crap, she thought, turning around and seeing Ciaran jog towards her, looking casually rumpled in his faded jeans and hoodie as she closed the salon door behind her. She didn't want to see anyone and especially not him. It wasn't just because seeing him in the early evening light on Rue Lavaud instead of their normal Dublin office setting was bizarre. It was also because it was paramount that she get home and dab calamine lotion where the sun didn't shine.

"Hey, fancy meeting you here." He reached her and kept stride as she headed for her car.

"Yes, fancy." Considering the population of Akaroa was roughly 630, it wasn't exactly a staggering coincidence—just a badly timed one.

"Are you okay, Rebecca? You are walking kind of funny."

She paused and softened, seeing the genuine concern on his face. "Um, yeah, not used to these heels, that's all." A little white lie but she could hardly tell him the truth.

"Oh right, well, you look lovely." He gave her the once-over, and she winced, thinking, if only he knew.

"Thanks." They looked at each other and for a moment Rebecca was aware of nothing but the gentle lapping of the nearby water and the nearness of Ciaran. She forced herself to break away from his gaze, annoyed with the way her stomach automatically somersaulted every time she laid eyes on him.

"Where have you been?" he asked, glancing over at the salon.

"Er, just to get a little trim." She fluffed up her hair. This time it was a definite half-truth. She was relieved to see that they'd reached her car, and she fished around in her bag for the keys. "What have you been up to?"

"A bit of exploring. It's a beautiful place, although I'd much rather you were showing me the sights."

If only he knew the sight she could show him! "I, uh..." She shifted from foot to foot. This was awkward and at seeing him, she couldn't help but feel guilt about her impending day out with David. It was like she was two-timing him but then she reminded herself that she didn't owe him anything. "I'll, uh, I'll be in touch." She just wanted to get away because she was not going to be swayed by the hurt and puzzled look in those brown eyes of his.

Chapter Twenty-Four

"MELISSA! I WANT A WORD." Rebecca kicked the front door shut behind her. Barging her way into the living room, she found Jack curled up in the armchair. A bowl of what she presumed to be dinner was balanced on his lap, and he was watching the TV. Though goodness knows how he was managing to do so, as Hannah and Melissa were absorbed in what looked to be some boisterous game. Hannah was sitting on the couch, shouting out animal names while Melissa cantered around the room, braying, "No! Try again."

Rebecca's expression was not one of amusement as she asked, "What on earth are you doing?" Her hand flew up for silence. "No, on second thoughts, don't answer that because I don't want to know. Outside—now."

Melissa stopped cantering. "Anything you've got to say to me you can say in front of Jack and Hannah. Right, kids?" Hannah, her new BFF, nodded while Jack didn't even bother looking up from the TV. "Besides, me and Hannah are busy. We're playing animal charades. I made it up, and it is such a cool game! Do you want to join in? We've already had pigs, cows, and what was the other one, Hannah?"

"Sheep!"

"And who's winning?"

"You are, Lissa!"

Rebecca's face contorted. "Hardly surprising when your competitor's aged three and a half, which is precisely why I cannot say what I need to say in front of her." She clicked her fingers and pointed to the back porch. "Outside NOW!"

Recognising her friend's expression as one not to be trifled with, Melissa did as she was told. "I'll be back in a minute, Hannah. Why don't you pretend you're a hen while I'm gone?"

She obligingly hopped off the couch and began flapping her arms, simultaneously making an awful screeching noise.

Rebecca stood in the kitchen with the back door wide open, waiting.

"Bit cold now the sun's gone in to go outside, isn't it?" Melissa shivered as she hovered nervously around the kitchen entrance. "Can't we just sit down somewhere nice and warm and talk about whatever it is that has upset you like rational adults?"

"I would dearly love to sit down, Melissa. Believe you me, I really, really would. Thanks to you and your little beautician's appointment, I probably won't be able to sit down for the rest of the week. So, considering what I have been through this afternoon, a moment of your time outside is not much to ask."

"I suppose not when you put it like that." Grabbing the navy-blue windbreaker hanging off a hook on the other side of the door, Melissa quickly slid into it. Then, taking as wide a berth around her angry friend as she could manage, she stepped out into the encroaching darkness of the porch, instantly regretting not having put a pair of shoes on her feet. As Rebecca pulled the door closed behind her, a sensor light suddenly kicked in, and both girls found themselves bathed in a strong white light.

It was Melissa—who was busily hopping from foot to foot to keep warm—who managed to say her piece first. "I betcha it looks fab though, babes, and you know how the saying goes: *no pain, no gain*." She grinned smugly and Rebecca saw red.

"I wouldn't go that far! A denuded chicken would be a better description!"

Taking a step back, Melissa held up her hand. "No need to shout; I'm right here." Then, thinking of a point to win her case, she added enthusiastically, "Just think! Tucking those little strays back in will be a thing of the past. I did you a favour, if you think about it like that."

"With a friend like you, who needs enemies?" Rebecca felt her stomach begin to roil at the sight of Melissa's smug face. The words she'd wanted to say to this so-called friend of hers so many times over the years finally erupted forth. "Do you know what, Melissa? I have had enough. I came home to look after my sister and her family, and you don't need to be here, so why don't you head on inside and pack your bags. All you've done while you've been here is sit on your bum and make snide remarks. In fact, that's all you ever do, and I have just come to the realisation that I no longer need you bringing me down."

Wow! She put her hand on her pounding heart and steadied her breath while Melissa's face turned chalky. Rebecca was not good at confrontation, but she had to say she felt liberated—she felt amazing! Melissa had indeed done her a favour because it might have taken something as silly as a botched bikini line but she had, after twenty-something years of a very one-sided friendship, finally said her piece.

"Becs, you don't mean it. I truly had your best interests at heart. I figured you needed a break or at the very least a bonk with David because it might wake you up where Ciaran is concerned—and I just wanted to give you the best chance possible."

"Bring out the violins, why don't you? You forget that I know you only too well. You never have anyone else's best interests at heart. So go on, Melissa. I mean it—pack your bags."

"Yee-hah! You go, girl!" whooped a voice from the darkness, followed by several claps and a solitary, "Wahoo!"

Melissa stalked over to the wooden railing and peering out into the early evening gloom, snapped, "Who's there?"

"Mindy-Lou to you, sugar." She whistled between her teeth. "Darn tootin'! I reckon you jest got told where to get off, possum-pie," bounced up at her.

Rebecca lingered outside, breathing in the night air after Melissa—having shot her with her best deeply wounded look to no avail—retreated inside to do as she'd been told. Rebecca's expression had brooked no argument, and it wasn't long before she heard a car door slam and the engine rev. She exhaled slowly, emitting a fine white mist into the night air as she watched Melissa's headlights sweep down the driveway and out of her life, albeit for the time being.

Who knew, she thought, turning and returning to the warmth inside; she might soften her stance in a day or two but only if Melissa took on board what she'd said. She had a feeling she'd be hearing from her before the week was out, grovelling, because Rebecca suddenly knew with clarity that Melissa needed her more than she needed her. The balance had shifted, and it felt good.

"Melissa's gone. She said you were real mad with her." Jack's eyes never moved from the television. "What's a denuded chicken?"

She flushed. "Jack, you should not eavesdrop on other people's conversations. It's bad manners."

"I wasn't eavesdropping; you were shouting."

He had her there.

"Yes, well, sorry about that."

"So what is it?" He obviously wasn't going to let this one go.

"It's a chicken that's had all its feathers plucked."

Seeing his face turn pale green, she demanded, "Now what?"

"I feel sick." He glanced uneasily over at his empty dinner bowl.

"What did you have for tea?"

"Chicken."

"What an afternoon! I thought I'd never get away. They're not a bad bunch of gals down there, though, not once you see past all the warrior get-up." Jennifer appeared in the living room. "Hello, sweetie-pie. Have you had your dinner?" Hannah had run over to her mother as though it had been months and not a matter of hours since she'd last seen her.

"Lissa made it cos Auntie Becca had her hair taken out, but then she got mad, and Lissa's gone now," Hannah lisped as her mother, who wasn't listening, smiled and swung her up, planting a big kiss on her cheek. She turned her attention to her son. "Hi, Jack, love. Did you have a good day?"

"Yeah." He didn't move his gaze from the television.

"Look at me, please, son, when I'm talking to you."

He still didn't move his eyes away from the screen.

"Jack!" Jennifer admonished sharply.

He swung around to face her. "I said yeah!" Then, flinging the remote down, he stampeded off up the stairs.

"What did I do?" Jennifer asked, looking at Rebecca before plonking herself down on the couch with a weary sigh.

Rebecca shrugged. "No idea. He was behaving like a toad when I picked him up, so maybe something happened at school. I'll go up and talk to him once he's calmed down if you want?"

"That would be good. He might tell you what his problem is because I just seem to annoy him at the moment."

"Don't take it personally, sis. He's seven."

Jennifer gave her a watery smile as Hannah climbed onto her lap and snuggled in. She stroked her daughter's hair and within seconds she was fast asleep, emitting soft and snuffly snores with every other breath. "You know, Mark being away is hitting him harder than he's letting on. Thank goodness he's back in a couple of days. I suppose that's when the real fun will begin, though." She looked uncertain. "There are counsellors who can help kids cope with marital splits. I think Mark and I are going to need all the help we can get where the kids are concerned. I'll have to look up some names tomorrow."

"That's a good idea. If in doubt, take it to a professional, I always say."

"Where do you get these little sayings from?"

"Dunno—they just pop into my head."

"You're mad, you know that? So come on then—what was the to-do I heard before all about?"

"You heard me?"

"I'd say they heard you down in Little River. Now come on, spill."

Rebecca filled her in on how she had finally found her chutzpah where Melissa was concerned, and Jennifer clapped her hands delightedly.

"Well done, you. She's had that coming for a long time! It's going to be awkward when you go back to Ireland, though, isn't it, what with you sharing an apartment?"

"I have a feeling Melissa will come crawling well before it's time to fly back, but Jen, I wanted to talk to you about that." She hesitated for a moment because if she said the words out loud, there would be no going back. "I, uh, I don't think I am going to go back." There, she had said it, and now that she'd given voice to the idea that had begun to take seed over the past week, it suddenly sprouted. "I—and please don't laugh—I want to open a dance school."

Jennifer felt some of the fog that she had been wandering around in for the past couple of months dissipate as excitement penetrated it. Sitting forward, her face was the most animated Rebecca had seen it since she'd come home. "Why would I laugh? I think that is a fantastic idea. Mum, Dad, and I always hoped you'd go back to your dancing one day. You had so much talent and then you just pulled the pin on it. I never got why you did that."

"I didn't pull the pin, Jen. I failed my grade nine exam, which meant I was never going to make it as a professional ballerina, and that was my dream. It was such a slap in the face. How would you have felt if you realised you would never get further than working in the kitchen at Sophia's?"

Jennifer nodded slowly as understanding dawned. What she had seen at the time was a moody sixteen-year-old who refused to get back up and fight her corner at the first serious knockback that came her way. She had always viewed her sister as a bit of a dilly dreamer who had gotten a rude shock at a taste of rejection in the real world. Perhaps out of the two of them, though, it was her who was the realist after all. Rebecca was facing up to her future whereas she was in denial, unwilling to take responsibility for her part in the great stuff-up that was her marriage. Thankfully her sister saved her from falling into the abyss that this train of thought always led her to.

"I think teaching might be something that would give me the best of both worlds. I can pass on my passion to others but without all that pressure. I was never cut out to take that side of it. I like my food far too much for one thing and this way I could have my cake and eat it too!" She grinned and Jennifer had to smile back at her analogy. "I've looked into it and the Royal Academy of Dance runs a two-year distance course, which means I could sit for my Certificate of Ballet Teaching and work at the same time."

"So when did you come up with all of this?"

"The idea's been niggling at the back of my mind for a long time, but it always seemed way too hard." Rebecca shrugged. "It was easy to do nothing about it while I was in Dublin. I think maybe that being home has made me stop and take stock of a lot of things."

"Like Ciaran, perhaps?" Jennifer raised an eyebrow. She'd seen the sappy look on her sister's face when she'd faced him across the kitchen the other night.

"Yes. No. I don't know. What I do know is that if I don't sign up for this course now, then I will always regret it."

"So what are you going to tell him?"

"The truth, I guess—that I would like nothing more than to take the easy option and hotfoot it back to Dublin with him and everything I know over there. But I've been running away from what I want to do all these years because I was scared I'd fail. What I've just realised, though, is that if I don't even try, then I am a failure."

Jennifer absorbed what her sister had said for a moment before struggling to her feet with Hannah a dead weight in her arms. "Come on, oh great wise one, let's get the kids off to bed so we can crack open a bottle of vino and talk about it. Honestly, though, Becs," she flashed a genuine grin at her sister, "this dance school idea is the best news I have heard in a long time."

Rebecca, buoyed by her sister's enthusiasm, rose too and then winced as she swaggered towards the stairs.

"Jack," she called out softly, tapping on his door before opening it. He was sitting cross-legged on his bed and by the looks of the toy car that was in bits beside him, playing mechanics. "It's time for bed, mate," she said, easing herself down next to him.

He didn't move.

"Is everything okay?" There was no answer. "Jack?" When he finally replied, his chin was so far down in his chest that she had to strain to hear him properly.

"I had a fight with Ben." With everything that had since happened, she'd forgotten about the way the pair of them had been behaving when she picked him up from school.

"What about?" When no reply was forthcoming, she put her arm around his shoulders, surprised at how tense they were. "Sweetheart, I promise you that you'll feel much better if you talk about it." As his small face looked up at hers and she saw how upset he was, Rebecca had a sinking feeling. It was going to be another one of those awkward, auntie moments where she was most likely going to have to wing it.

"Ben said my mum and dad don't like each other anymore, just like his mum and dad." He swiped angrily at his nose, which was beginning to run. "And he said that Hannah will get to stay with Mum cos she's a girl and that I'll have to go and live with Dad in Christchurch."

It just wasn't fair, she raged silently. Jennifer and Mark's splitting was going to hit this little boy so very hard. What was she supposed to say? She couldn't lie to him and say that Mum and Dad were the best of friends. All she could do was plaster over things until Jennifer and Mark decided to tell him the news. She cuddled him in next to her and, in as stern a voice as she could muster, said, "Now listen to me, Jack Carlton. That is just not going to happen. I have already explained to you that Ben's situation is different from yours. You're going to have to be the bigger boy and ignore it if he says anything like that again, okay?" There was an imperceptible nod. "You don't want to fall out with him because he's your best friend and everybody needs their best friend, don't they?" Melissa's face sprang to mind, and she gave her a good mental kick up the backside. This time he nodded like he meant it. "So, tomorrow you go to school and tell Ben that you're sorry for whatever you said. And if he says anything else about your mum and dad, you're just to say that you don't want to talk about it with him. Ask him how he's getting on with his karate lessons instead, okay?"

Rebecca was relieved to see the worried frown between his dark brows vanish as he raised a small smile. Perhaps this hands-on auntie thing wasn't so hard after all. Who knew? Maybe she was, at long last, growing up because she felt very learned as she kissed him on his forehead. "Come on, into bed. It's time to snuggle down."

She met Jennifer outside in the hallway. "You need to talk to him." She relayed what he had conveyed to her in a whisper and put her hand on her sister's arm as her face crumpled.

"But I don't know what to say to him."

"Wing it—I did," she told her firmly before spinning her around and giving her a shove in the small of her back. "Now get in there and reassure him that he is not about to get shipped off to Christchurch to live with his father."

As she tiptoed back downstairs, she made a mental note to mention to David what Ben had been saying. It sounded as though the little boy wasn't coping quite as well as he seemed to think.

Jennifer came back downstairs a short while later in her pyjamas.

"How did you get on?" Rebecca had been waiting, twisting her hair around her index finger anxiously.

Wrapping her dressing gown around herself as though giving herself a cuddle, Jennifer shook her head. "I don't know, Becs. He's so angry at me. He blames me for everything that's going on."

"But that's so wrong." Rebecca was indignant. Mark was the one who had the affair, and he isn't even here helping to deal with the fallout.

Jennifer shrugged. "Maybe, but I can't very well start slagging off his father to him, can I?"

"No, I guess not." It sucked having to be a grown-up sometimes.

"At least I got to say my piece to him, though. He knows I love him and that he's not going anywhere. I reassured him his dad will be home in a few days too."

"Did you tell him that you and Mark are separating?"

Jennifer looked startled. "I think deep down he already knows but no, I didn't. Mark and I haven't even talked about the logistics of it ourselves yet. It's ironic, I suppose. There we were thinking a holiday might get us back on track when what we needed all along was the distance between us to face up to the reality of going our separate ways." She shook her head, and her loose hair swished softly over her shoulders. "It still feels surreal hearing you say that we are separating like that, though."

"Sorry."

She shrugged. "There's nothing for *you* to be sorry about. It's the truth, and we are both going to have to deal with it. Mark and I need to sit down and nut out how we are going to make it work for the kids. When we have it clear with each other as to how we are going to do things, we'll talk to Jack and Hannah." She shuddered at the thought of that little conversation. "I need a drink." She disappeared into the kitchen with Rebecca trailing behind her.

From the depths of the fridge, Jennifer produced a bottle of locally produced wine and poured out two large glasses, holding one out to Rebecca.

"Thanks." She took a sip; it was gorgeous. "Yum."

"Yeah, it's not bad for a Chardonnay. Here's to you coming home and to opening your very own dance school." She raised her glass.

Rebecca felt a frisson of excitement at hearing the words her *very own dance school*—it truly was possible. Sure, it would take two years to get her teaching certificate but hey, she had whiled away so many more years tip-tapping on a computer doing others' bidding. Two years in the grand scheme of her working career was nothing. She smiled and clinked her sister's glass. "Cheers." Then, seeing Jennifer shiver, she suggested they head through to the warmth of the living room. Jennifer acquiesced, and they wandered through to curl up companionably at opposite ends of the couch. "What's a good name for a dance school?"

"Ballet with Becs has a good ring to it."

Rebecca cringed. "For someone with supposed business savvy, I hope you are joking. No, it would have to be something professional sounding, like, um, oh, I don't know—what about Loughton's School of Dance?"

"I'll grant you that does sound a tad more prestigious. So what will you do while you train for your teacher's certificate?"

Rebecca shrugged. "I suppose I'll have to get a legal secretary job in Christchurch to pay the bills in the interim. It's only two years; it will fly by."

Jennifer looked thoughtful for a moment. "What about staying on here and helping me out as my nanny cum Girl Friday while you study? You said the course was distance learning."

"It is but are you serious? We'd probably wind up killing each other."

"Becs, I am beginning to think we would rub along nicely, and the kids love having you around. It makes sense because the cook school's getting busier every week, which means I am getting more and more tied up with the paperwork side of things when I would much rather be hands-on."

"My gosh, girl, are you actually admitting you can't do everything?"

"I am, yes. So what do you reckon?"

"I reckon you'd have to promise not to be bossy."

Jennifer laughed. "I can't make promises I know I won't keep."

"Well, it would make the transition home much easier for me and I have had thirty-odd years of you bossing me about so… I think it is a bloody fantastic idea. Thanks, sis." Rebecca leaned over and gave her sister a hug.

They lapsed into satisfied silence after that, each lost in their thoughts, before Jennifer, leaning forward to pick up a magazine lying on the coffee table, asked, "Whose is this?" She held up the cover. *Cosmopolitan*.

"It's Melissa's, of course. I don't know how she can read it month after month. It's been going for about a hundred years, and it's always the same: a thousand ways to reach orgasm or how to find your G-spot, blah, blah, blah, boring," Rebecca stated.

Jennifer peered over the top of the magazine before flicking through it. "Actually, sis, it's not boring at all once you know where your G-spot is."

Rebecca waved her hand. "Ugh, too much information."

"Can I take it from those comments then that you're not interested in John the twenty-six–year-old firefighter from Essex?"

"Who?"

"This month's totally nude centrefold."

Rebecca leaped forward and snatched the magazine out of her sister's hands, knocking her wine over in the process.

"Jeez, sis—down, girl!"

"I have a lot of pent-up frustration." Rebecca had a quick glance at John's impressive vital statistics before running to the kitchen for a cloth.

"I'm going to head up to bed," Jennifer stated, tossing the magazine aside and leaving Rebecca to mop up the wine. "Too much excitement in one evening for me."

Chapter Twenty-Five

REBECCA PULLED UP OUTSIDE Sea Breezes B&B at nine the following morning. It was a cool, overcast day, and it suited her sombre mood down to the ground. She got out of the car and peered up at the two-storey house Ciaran had chosen to take up temporary residence in. It looked at least a hundred years old and judging by the peeling white paintwork, it had indeed been victim to the sea's salt breeze. Opening the little wrought-iron gate, she wished the sick feeling that had settled in the pit of her stomach from the moment she had opened her eyes that morning would go away. She didn't want to do what she was about to do, but Ciaran didn't deserve to be left dangling, as Melissa had worded it. Wandering up the path to the front door, she licked her lips nervously before pulling the string back and forth vigorously as she rang the old-fashioned bell.

Footsteps echoed down the hallway inside, and a woman's thin voice warbled, "I'm not deaf, thank you very much." The owner of the voice was an elderly woman with long silvery hair pulled back into a loose bun. She had blackcurrant eyes that narrowed beadily as she opened the door and checked her bell was still intact before turning her gaze to Rebecca. "Yes?"

"Um, hello, er, sorry about the bell. I wanted to see a guest you have staying, Ciaran. Ciaran Cahill."

"Rebecca, hi!" He appeared behind the silver-haired harridan. "Mrs Doody, this is Rebecca Loughton."

Mrs Doody nodded acknowledgment but didn't budge to let her pass. This young lass had floozy stamped all over her and so long as she had breath in her body, there would be no shenanigans in her establishment.

"I called because I need to have a word, Ciaran." She was tempted to add 'in private' but truth be told, she was scared Mrs Doody would cast a spell on her if she did. She bore an uncanny resemblance to the witch in a Margaret Mahy book she'd read to Hannah the other night.

"Right, well, I'll grab my jacket and we'll go for a walk, shall we?"

THEY FOUND A BENCH on the waterfront and, huddling down into their respective jackets, they watched the grey water lap hungrily at the rocks in silence. Ciaran didn't want Rebecca to speak because he had already surmised that he wasn't going to like what she had to say. He couldn't stop her, though, and despite her dry mouth, Rebecca forced herself to try to swallow before spitting out what it was she had come to say. He sat silently, staring straight ahead while she explained the plans she had hatched with Jennifer the night before.

"You know I have feelings for you or you wouldn't have come here in the first place. I'm not going to label them or try to explain them to you, though, because they're just not enough." She softened her tone, trying to take the sting from her words. "If I don't stay and see this teaching course through, then I will never be all I can be. In the long run, that would mean it wouldn't work between us because I'd be short-changing us both." It was like talking to a brick wall, she thought, taking in his ramrod posture as his gaze never wavered from the misty horizon. "I have to do this, Ciaran. It's time for me to come home. Jennifer needs me, the kids need me, and I want to be here for them." Her voice trailed off; as she finished and saw his face was still set in stone, she changed tack. "Believe me, I am so, so sorry you had to come all this way for me to tell you that I am not coming back."

He let his breath out slowly. "Yeah, so am I."

The quiet stretched out between them, broken only by a scream from a seagull as it swooped, searching for food.

"I had no idea you were a dancer," Ciaran eventually said. "I didn't think knowing all the moves to 'The Time Warp' counted."

Rebecca couldn't bring herself to smile. "It doesn't and I haven't been, not for a long time. It's always been in me, though, and I think I always knew I'd find my way back to it one day."

"Would it have been different if I hadn't... you know... with Tania?"

"No, because this isn't about you; it's about me." Rebecca stared at the hundreds of mussels glued to the rocks, impressed by their staying power as the waves fought to knock them free.

"Well, I don't suppose there's much more to say." He got up, and Rebecca wanted to reach out and say—what exactly? She'd said what she needed to, and now she had to sit and watch as he walked out of her life for good. She swallowed the lump that had risen in her throat, hoping she hadn't just made the biggest mistake of her life.

She sat on that bench for a long time after Ciaran's hunched form had disappeared from view, trying to find solace in the rhythmic shushing of the waves. Eventually, the damp salty air began to penetrate her bones and standing up, she walked briskly back down the boardwalk to her car. She'd made her choice; there was no going back, she thought, climbing behind the wheel, determined not to look up at Sea Breezes for fear of finding Ciaran looking back at her.

BETTY WAS IN THE GARDEN with an armful of herbs as Rebecca pulled up outside the Cook's Quarters. It was a relief to see a solid and reliable, friendly face because she knew heading into the house would be useless. There was no way she would be able to settle at anything, apart from maybe a spot of vigorous vacuuming. What she needed was a good distraction like Betty and besides, she had been feeling guilty about not having been down to the cook school sooner to see how she was managing with her new charges. Slamming the car door, she wandered up to greet her and was met with an enthusiastic kiss on the cheek. Linking her arm companionably through the older woman's, they strolled back down the path towards the classroom.

"How've you been getting on with your, er, guests then?"

"Well, they're certainly enthusiastic. I'll give them that. It's kind of catching, which is nice. It's been awhile since I've gotten so fired up about our local produce."

Rebecca nodded, even though she found the image of the warrior princesses drooling over a lamb loin that presented itself quite disturbing.

Betty caught her expression. "You know, once you get past their armour-plating, they're actually quite a lot of fun."

Rebecca squeezed her arm. "Sorry. I'll take your word for it. I'm pleased it's going well because when I walked in the other morning and saw them all, to be honest, I thought you were in for a right week of it."

Betty chuckled. "Yes, they did take a bit of getting used to. I think this lot is going to seem like pussycats compared to next week's guests, though."

"Really?" Rebecca was intrigued. Who could be worse than the Memphis Branch of the Xena Warrior Princess Fan Club?

"The Daniel O'Donnell Fan Club, all the way from every rural province in Ireland. Apparently he's touring at the moment, so they've teed up three days here after his Christchurch concert."

Rebecca didn't get a chance to digest this news because a voice suddenly called out, "Well, hey there, lil lady! Long time no see."

She held her hand up in greeting. "Hi, Bonnie-May. Betty's just been telling me how much she's enjoying having you all."

The princess-wannabe looked pleased and with her armour chinking, skipped down the steps to fling her chunky arms around Betty.

"We think Betty here is jest the sweetest thung too."

"You won't if you don't get any lunch today. Did you manage to finish the marinade and get the lamb in the oven while I've been gone?"

"Sho did, sugar-pie."

From inside the classroom, they heard a shout: "Bonnie-May, what in tarnation are you up to out there?"

Her face reddened. "That Mindy-Lou! One of these days, I swear, dogonit." She caught herself before she finished the thought. "I best be doing what she says and get myself back inside because we're in the middle of acting out episode three." She looked at them gravely. "That's the one where poor Gabrielle is kidnapped to become the bride of Morpheus and Xena has to rescue her."

The two women nodded knowledgeably at Bonnie-May's retreating back and as the door closed behind her, Betty whispered conspiratorially, "Like I said, they do take a bit of getting used to."

Rebecca grinned by way of reply. *Oh, to be so open-minded.*

Making her way up the stairs, Betty turned and asked, "So what are you going to do with yourself today, young lady?"

Rebecca shrugged. She didn't want to explain what had transpired with Ciaran, so she couldn't very well say she planned on spending her day moping. "My day's not going to be anywhere near as exciting as yours by the sound of it. I thought I'd get stuck into a spot of hoovering." She shook her head. "The mess kids can make with a bowl of Weetabix and a piece of toast has to be seen to be believed."

Betty smiled and patted Rebecca's arm. "That's children for you. You're a good girl, Rebecca."

"Thanks, Betty. Oh, before I forget, could you tell Jen I'll pick up Hannah and head to the supermarket on our way back to pick up the bits and bobs on her shopping list?" She wanted to keep busy.

"I'll pass it on. Jennifer will wonder how she ever managed without you around. Now though, I'd better go on inside and rescue her." She frowned. "I hope I don't get drafted in again. Yesterday I had to pretend to be the evil Callisto or someone or other."

Rebecca was still laughing, albeit rather hysterically, as she plugged the vacuum cleaner in ten minutes later. She put her back into it and had the downstairs finished in no time. Unplugging the machine, she stretched, feeling like she'd just done a full body workout. She was just standing back to survey her handiwork when she heard a pounding on the door.

Trotting over to answer it, she spied a courier van haring down the driveway, having left a package on the doorstep. Bending down to retrieve it, she glanced at the addressee and was surprised to see her name. *Who would be sending her parcels here?* Carrying it through into the kitchen, she rummaged in the drawer for a pair of scissors and snipped it open before thrusting her hand into the bag to see what it contained. Whatever it was, it was soft and silky, she thought, pulling it out and gazing at a gorgeous emerald-green bra. A further rummage produced the matching set of knickers and a card. The knickers had been the giveaway clue as to who her mysterious benefactor was and Rebecca opened the card without bothering to read the verse about friendship on the front.

I'm so sorry, Becs.

I miss you and I will stop being an obnoxious and lazy cow, I promise. Please ring me.

Lots of love,

Melissa.

She'd chosen the underwear well, Rebecca thought, running her finger over the lace topping the bra's cups. The colour was her too. The set was French, and it would have cost her a fortune. She would phone Melissa but not just yet.

Shoving the underwear back in the bag, she glanced at her watch and tossed up between running upstairs to get changed or knocking back a well-earned coffee before going to pick Hannah up. Opting for the coffee, Rebecca sat down with it at the dining room table, her eyes gazing out through the French doors to the haze of hills in the distance. Looking but not seeing.

Blinking rapidly as a thought occurred to her, she wondered what she would do if David were to make a move on Friday? Did she even fancy him or was he just a good-looking, convenient distraction from Ciaran? Whatever he was, she'd already decided not to tell Jen what she was up to. Not after her reaction the last time she had seen him. All the telltale signs that David was interested in her were there, though. Who knew? If she didn't give things a chance and go out with him, she could be missing her shot at something special. Especially now that she and Ciaran had reached the final chapter.

The problem was that if Jennifer found out, she could be jeopardising her fledgling relationship with her sister over no more than a what-if. Sighing deeply, she tried to remember that catchphrase of Melissa's. What was it again? Oh yeah, that was it: *analysis is paralysis.*

With 'analysis is paralysis—go with the flow' as her affirmation for that afternoon, Rebecca picked Hannah up. Anna looked quite dejected as she appraised her tracksuit bottoms and worn jumper. Surely that wasn't the attire of a nymphomaniac? Rebecca hadn't been fazed, though, because she was just going with the flow. Twenty minutes later, halfway down the confectionary aisle of Super Value, 'go with the flow' flew right out the sliding doors.

Hannah, seated at the helm of the trolley, was unable to comprehend the simple fact that she couldn't just take anything she fancied off the supermarket shelves. So, the little girl bided her time while Rebecca, holding a shiny purple and gold package in her hot little hand, had been in deep contemplation of a bar of Turkish Delight for dessert that night. Hmm, should she, or shouldn't she? Go on, live a little! Chocolate always makes things better, a devilish little voice inside her head had urged. So, she decided to ignore the sugar content and focus instead on the conscience-salving words: *60% less fat than a standard bar of chocolate.* That was good enough for her. With her mind made up, she'd turned to drop it into the trolley only to be confronted with her niece, safety belt flung aside, standing up on the narrow seat.

Teetering precariously, she was frantically attempting to wrestle a packet of jelly dinosaurs off their hook. It all happened quickly after that. Picking the screaming Hannah—together with the egg-sized lump that protruded from her head—off the floor, Rebecca abandoned the shopping. Her new affirmation as she bundled the little girl straight into the back of the car being, "Bloody, bloody hell!"

A pitstop at the pharmacy on the way home revealed that Hannah would live, and a course of chocolate milk and a DVD was prescribed.

Jennifer deposited Jack back at the house shortly after three o'clock before asking Rebecca if she would be okay to watch them while she carried on down at the cooking school. "They're a full-on group of girls. I think Betty needs all the help she can get."

Feeling that some serious brownnosing was required after the supermarket trolley incident, Rebecca had smiled and replied with a breezy, "Sure, no problem."

It wasn't long before she was regretting being so obliging, as Jack wasn't exactly sunshine and light. Ben, she managed to wheedle out of him, had been away all day, hence his mood and before she knew it, she had World War III on her hands. Hannah, playing the injured soldier to the hilt, refused to forfeit even one minute of the Wiggles. A compromise was reached only after intense negotiations (ie, screaming like a banshee at the pair of them to cut it out before telling Jack he could go and watch the TV up in her room). Watching as he trooped up the stairs with a handful of hastily-grabbed biscuits, she rolled her eyes. It meant sharing her bed with a thousand biscuit crumbs tonight, but hey, greater sacrifices had been made in the name of peace.

The ceasefire remained in place until dinnertime, when both of them turned their noses up at the vegetarian lasagne their mother had lovingly prepared. She'd left it out on the bench to be reheated. Unable to face any more fighting, Rebecca snatched the two dinners up off the table and threw them in the bin. Jack and Hannah watched in amazed delight as she tossed a pizza in the oven instead. If you can't beat 'em, join 'em, she decided twenty minutes later, opening her mouth wide to chomp into a generous triangle of meat lover's supreme.

Despite feeling like she'd overdone it in the cheese department, the next couple of hours passed almost without a hiccup. She had gotten the children into bed and had just settled in to watch *Coronation Street*. Even though the episodes were nearly a year behind what they'd been watching in Ireland, there was something comforting about watching the reruns. Finding *Corrie* on the tele was a bit like spotting McDonald's golden arches in a foreign country, Rebecca concluded—you instantly felt at home. As the actors' familiar voices washed over her, she relaxed into the sofa. She was determined to immerse herself in their problems and forget the look on Ciaran's face when she'd told him she wasn't going back to Dublin with him.

Chapter Twenty-Six

THE NEXT MORNING, SHE awoke to find blue skies had swept away the gloom of the previous day, bringing a little sunshine to perk up her mood. For the first five minutes at least. Today, she promised herself, she wasn't going to think about how utterly defeated Ciaran had looked yesterday.

Nope, today was David's day, and she owed it to him to push Ciaran Cahill into the past, where he belonged. As she slid neatly into the last car parking space along the stretch of waterfront by the main jetty, Rebecca allowed herself a congratulatory moment. It had been touch and go, but the boat was still there and she'd made it, and with good hair. No thanks to her niece and nephew, who had been their usual unaccommodating selves as she'd revved them up to get ready earlier that morning.

Knowing she was brooding over Ciaran, Jennifer must have decided it was safe to let her do the school run again. Rebecca did feel guilty not telling her what she was up to today with David, but then Jennifer had made it more than obvious that where she was concerned, the subject of David was closed.

In a panic, she'd pushed Jack and Hannah out the front door, feeling like a camp leader as she chanted, "Come on! Come on! Hup two, three, four. Let's move it on out, kids! Left, right, left, right!" Jack had moaned at her not to push him, to which she'd replied (and not unreasonably, she thought), "I am not pushing you, Jack. I am steering you in the right direction," before bellowing, "NOW GET A MOVE ON!"

That had spurred the pair on, but it was too late for her hair. Their tardiness left her with another terminal case of fringe frizz. Not that it had mattered, because David and Ben were nowhere to be seen outside the school. That's right, she thought, recalling Jack's mood at his friend being away yesterday too. She hoped the little boy wasn't home sick. Surely David would have cancelled if that were the case? Crossing her fingers, she fervently hoped his plan was to meet her down at the wharf. Either way she'd find out soon enough what was up, hopefully.

Despite the uncertainty as to whether or not David would show, Rebecca was relieved to make the round trip back to the house with a whole five minutes to spare. Her sister, thankfully, was busy down at the cooking school, and she raced inside and up the stairs to begin damage control with her hair straighteners. "I don't know why I'm bothering, considering I'm going to look like a drowned rat in a couple of hours," she muttered to herself, though she did know why she was bothering: she wanted to leave him with a good *first* impression.

With her hair done in record time, Rebecca stood up, arms outstretched, and did a twirl in front of the mirror. Her faded jeans and black wool poloneck set off her shoulder-length sheet of dark blonde hair; yes, she had the 'casual but smart' look down pat.

Pulling her bikini bottoms, which she'd worn under her clothes to save time, out from where they were already riding up her left cheek, she took the stairs two at a time. There was a skip in her step as she closed the front door and made her way to her car.

GRABBING HER DAY PACK off the back seat, she locked the wagon and turned to squint into the morning sun. The sleek white catamaran bobbed gently on the waves, and she could make out a cluster of people milling around on its deck. Two figures stood at the end of the jetty, but with the sun in her eyes, she couldn't tell if one of them was David. Inhaling the crisp sea air, she assured herself, "He'll be here and remember that you, Rebecca Loughton, are a cool, calm, and confident woman." As she began striding purposefully down the jetty, one of the figures she'd spotted raced towards her. As it drew nearer, she was assailed by a vision of sleek muscles rippling under rubbery confines.

She momentarily forgot that she was a cool, calm, and confident woman as she realised that David had indeed shown up. She was in no way prepared for the sight of him in his wetsuit. Thankfully he didn't appear to notice her almost menopausal flush.

"Rebecca, hi! I didn't think you were coming. I'm sorry I haven't been in touch for a few days, but I'll explain what's been happening later." His eyes flicked down the jetty to where the other figure was waiting. "We'd better get a move on; Steve's been holding the boat for us."

"Sorry. I know I'm cutting it pretty fine, but the kids were a nightmare. I'm sure you know how it is." She wasn't sure he did know how it was because she was pretty sure David would never be late for anything at the hands of a bad hair day.

He didn't agree with her theory, though, replying, "Yeah, tell me about it." He took her elbow and steered her briskly past the changing sheds that were stacked in a neat multi-coloured row beside the check-in building. "You're not going to have time to get changed now. Okay to do it on the boat?"

So long as there was a bathroom of some description, she thought, nodding. David bounded up the metal gangway, hauling her on board behind him to where a stocky man decked out in a thick grey polo fleece and black knee-length shorts was waiting to rope it off. "Here she is," David announced. "Rebecca, meet my mate Steve."

She held out her hand in greeting, blathering out an apology for being late and instantly liking the way Steve's eyes crinkled at the corners as he smiled down at her. "Steve handles the show." Was it her imagination or had David's voice just dropped an octave?

"No worries. Welcome aboard. You're Jennifer's sister, right?"

"Yeah, that's me."

"Top lady she is." Before she had a chance to puzzle over the brief look that passed between him and David at the mention of her sister's name, Steve rushed on. "Ever been swimming with the dolphins before?"

"No, but I'm looking forward to it."

Steve was too busy gazing up at the clear sky to notice her putting her hand up to her nose and having a surreptitious feel to make sure it hadn't grown.

"It's a beaut day for it and we've only got eight of you swimming today, so that means more time in the water." Seeing her perplexed frown, he explained, "Only ten in the water at a time."

"Oh," Rebecca said and his grin broadened.

"You'll love it, Rebecca. It's better than sex, aye, mate?" He winked at David.

"Speak for yourself, mate." They had guffawed blokishly before Steve slapped him on the back.

"Spot you later, mate; it's time I got this baby humming."

Rebecca found herself wondering what it was about men and outdoor pursuits that unleashed some primeval urge to drop the word "mate" into every single sentence.

"Come on, I'll introduce you to a couple I met earlier." David led her into the little group she'd spotted from the car park milling about on the boat's deck. "Rebecca, this is Giovanni and his wife Monica; they're over from Switzerland."

"Hi." Blinking as she was very nearly blinded by the contrasting whiteness of their teeth against their deeply tanned skins, she managed to bare her off-white pearlers in return.

How come Europeans always looked so bloody fit and healthy, she grouched silently before asking the obvious for the sake of politeness, "So are you touring around New Zealand?"

"Yes," Giovanni answered in clipped English. "We have visited the North Island for one month, and it is very nice, but we love the South Island, don't we, Monica?"

She nodded enthusiastically. "Especially the Luge in Queenstown but, swimming with the dolphins is our dream. We are very excited."

The fibs began tripping off Rebecca's tongue once more: "Yes, it's going to be a pretty special experience. Better than sex, so I'm told." *Where had that come from?* David reddened as Monica's eyes flitted down towards his nether regions, and then back over to hers with an expression of sympathy. *Well done, Rebecca*, she admonished herself. *You're off to great start.*

As the boat spun its way out to sea, the enthusiastic patter of Tina, their friendly guide for the day, filled the cabin as she explained the procedures they were all to follow. David leaned in close, whispering in her ear, "Ben and I have been away for a few days staying in Christchurch with Maree and her parents."

"Oh," was all Rebecca could come up with in reply to this revelation; she hadn't expected that.

"The family counsellor said that it was pointless, just me and Ben coming in to see her." He shrugged by way of explanation. "We all needed to be there."

"How was it?" she probed.

"Oh, I don't know; who knows what goes on in a kid's mind? The way they interpret things is usually completely different than the way we do. He's been told that Maree and I splitting up had nothing to do with him time and time again. I still think that deep down he'll always feel he played a part just by being born." He ran his fingers through his hair. "The only new thing to come out of the session was that Maree is going to consider relocating back to Christchurch. She's a few years older now so who knows, maybe she feels she can cope with shared parenting at long last." His face twisted. "Of course, she's always got her parents there to pick up the pieces if she can't, and it'll be me who will have to deal with Ben's fallout if that happens."

Rebecca winced at the bitterness that crept into his voice. It was so sad that two people who had created such a lovely little boy like Ben could have so much animosity between them. She squeezed her eyes shut; she desperately hoped that that wouldn't be the outcome for Jennifer and Mark. Jack and Hannah didn't deserve to grow up with that kind of chasm between their parents. Even though she knew the answer, she found herself asking, "So how do you feel about that?"

He looked at her directly. "That's just it, Rebecca; it's not about me or how I feel. I have to think about Ben and what he needs, and I think he needs his mum."

She knew it sounded trite, but she couldn't think of anything else to say. So in a small voice, she said, "Maybe Maree has grown up."

"I hope you're right, I do."

She was grateful for the distraction when Tina, multi-tasking in her dive gear with the tea trolley, stopped in front of them. She was holding up a jug of boiling water and pointing to the little packets scattered in a container. "Tea or coffee?"

"Coffee," Rebecca said and David asked for the same. As she trundled off, Rebecca took a cautious sip through the take-out lid, mulling over what David had just told her when she noticed two hardy passengers still on deck. On closer inspection, she saw that it was Monica and Giovanni. They looked like a pair of playful seals in their wetsuits as, seemingly oblivious of the cold, they jostled with each other for the best view.

"Did you want to head out too?" David asked, tracking her gaze outside.

Turning her head back to face him, her answer was emphatic. "Oh, no thanks! I'm getting cold just watching them."

He smiled at her. "Yeah, we'll be out there soon enough."

The warmth in her smile faded as the realisation of missed opportunity hit her, and she cursed her stupidity for not having been brave enough to face the elements. It would have been the perfect chance to feign hypothermia and snuggle into that big, broad chest of his.

Catching a flurry of peripheral movement, she swung her head back and watched in alarm as outside Giovanni began gesticulating wildly. His arms were forming great semaphore circles as he battled desperately to stay on board; Monica, beside him, stood like a statue. *Oh, crumbs!* Rebecca gasped audibly, her hand automatically reaching out for David's as she waited for him to fall in. Suddenly Monica snapped to and leapt into action with an impressive lunge forward, managing to clutch hold of his arm, steadying him to his feet. A collective sigh of relief went through the cabin as the two passengers staggered around in a happy frenzy of black rubber.

The drama wasn't over just yet, though. The sound of Darth Vader-like breathing caused the microphone into which Tina had been happily explaining about the breeding habits of the Hector a moment earlier to crackle. Stomping through the cabin, she let in a blast of freezing air as she flung open the door. "What did you think you were—?" Her voice was cut off as the door hissed shut behind her. The body language—lots of expressive motioning towards the rails and inflatable life rafts combined with a ferocious scowl—gave the rest of them the general gist of things. *This was great*, Rebecca thought, smugly enjoying the show. She was pleased that for once it wasn't her in the starring role. Then she realised her hand was still in David's.

It was abruptly released as Giovanni and Monica re-entered the cabin. Despite their heads being bowed, Rebecca could see they were both pale beneath their tans. Behind them, Tina brought up the rear, locking the cabin door behind her, lest they try to make a bid for freedom. David got to his feet as the trio made their way back to their seats, and she was surprised to see that his face was frowning with genuine consternation. He was a nice guy.

"Are you guys okay? You gave us all a real fright," he asked.

"Yes, yes." Giovanni waved his hand dismissively, embarrassed now by the scene he'd caused. "I'm sorry for all the fuss, but it is her fault." As he pointed at Monica, she swung around and poked him in the chest. She said something in her native tongue that, despite the language barrier, Rebecca hazarded to be something along the lines of "get stuffed, you stupid man."

"She told me she saw a shark," he further explained to David, and the rest of the cabin, who were all earwigging, gasped.

Neighbour turned to neighbour, asking, "Shark? Did you know anything about sharks?" Rebecca's ears were burning. Not once had David dropped the word shark into the same sentence as a dolphin. *Bloody great*, she seethed. So much for throw a leg over; she'd be lucky if she had any at all at the end of the day! Tina quelled the building mutiny by assuring them all that no sharks had ever been spotted in the fifteen years that the dolphin tours had been operating.

Monica, however, wasn't convinced, spending the rest of the ride entertaining everyone with her impersonation of a shark while Giovanni hummed the tune from *Jaws*. Who would have guessed they were a couple of comedians? Of course, if Monica were to drop the writhing on the floor from her act, she might find that audience interest would soon dwindle.

Rebecca felt sorry for Tina. Poor thing was doing her best to provide them with a lively commentary of their surroundings from her vantage point hunched over a microphone at the front of the cabin, but no one was paying the slightest attention. Rebecca tuned in briefly, but it was a no-brainer—dolphins or David?

Peering out from under her eyelashes in what she hoped was a covert manner, she put Ciaran firmly to the back of her mind as she began a study of his thighs. *Hmm, very taut.* She licked her lips and allowed her eyes to begin their languorous journey upwards.

"Hi, it's Rebecca, isn't it?" Tina's voice startled her. Sure the other girl would have noticed where her grubby little mind had been headed, Rebecca blushed, managing to stutter out a "y-yes." Tina's smile gave nothing away as she heaved the wetsuit she'd dragged through the cabin onto Rebecca's lap.

"This is for you. We'll be stopping in about five minutes so you might want to slip into it now."

"Er, right, thanks; wouldn't want to miss a moment with those Hectors!" She bared her teeth at Tina, and her enthusiasm was rewarded by an approving smile from David.

Buggery-balls and bollocks, how was she supposed to change into an enormous piece of rubber discreetly? She was not prepared for this scenario. A hot panic swept through her as she cast her eyes frantically around the constricted cabin. Her eyes settled on the haloed toilet sign, and she felt the panic abate as her pulse rate slowed to an acceptable rate of beats per minute.

"I'll just duck in there; won't be a mo." Gesturing towards the toilets, she got to her feet, trying not to stagger under the weight of the wetsuit. *Bloody Monica's probably only weighed a quarter of what hers did*, she thought while stalking past the Swiss woman's skinny body as it convulsed from yet another shark attack. Perhaps it would be fatal this time, she hoped, locking the toilet door behind her.

The toilet was not of generous proportions and Rebecca prayed that the boat wouldn't strike any mini-tsunamis, or things could get ugly as she stripped down to her togs. As her elbow connected with the solid timber wall, she let rip with a loud expletive, rubbing the tender spot for a moment before attempting to jiggle into the wetsuit. The sharp knock on the door saw her bang her elbow again in fright. "Ow! Shit, shit, shit!"

"Everything alright in there, Rebecca?" It was Tina; obviously soundproofing wasn't a feature on catamarans.

"Fine, thanks, Tina."

As her footsteps moved away, the corners of Rebecca's mouth twitched. She was reminded of that awful inevitability on a long-haul flight and found herself mentally typing an entry onto her and Ciaran's flatulence travel blog:

Long Haul Loo Etiquette

On any long-haul flight, you can guarantee that at some point you will find yourself waiting for the little red occupancy sign on the toilet door to turn green. After what always seems an age of hopping from one foot to the other, the door is at last wrestled open to reveal the person who has been holed up in there for the last ten minutes. He/she steps out giving you an apologetic smile and your eyes meet in a silent exchange of: "Sorry, but I just had to go." "Hey, don't sweat it; these long-haul flights wreak havoc on your system." "I know, but thanks for being so understanding." "No problem." "Oh, before you go in there, a word of

advice." "Yes?" "Hold your breath." "Will do. Thanks." "I'm off then; we'll never
see one another again once we land." "Too right. Bye then." You take a last gasp
of the regurgitated air being pumped through the cabin and disappear into the
cubicle to begin your balancing act.

Yes, Ciaran would find that hilarious, she thought, grinning; he loved toilet humour. *Stop thinking about him; it's over. You are here with David!* she
admonished herself. *Long, lean, and lovely David, for whom you'd better get a*
wriggle on, my girl. Taking a deep, steadying breath, she jumped up and down
one more time. It did the trick and at last she was in, all zipped up and ready
for action.

Well almost; her face felt red and sweaty from exertion and a quick check
in the mirror proved that this was indeed the case. She needed a moment
to calm herself, but unwilling to attempt deep breathing exercises within the
confines of a glorified port-a-loo, she opted instead to whisper her mantra of
"cool, calm, and confident." Wasn't there a deodorant ad that had used that
as their jingle? Yes, that's right; she remembered it now. It had featured some
gorgeous young thing skipping down the street as a shipload of sailors raced
after her. Rebecca was pretty sure she needn't worry about the same thing
happening to her because she was unsure whether she could walk, let alone
skip in her snug scuba gear. With the onset of claustrophobia, she reiterated
to herself that while she may be unable to inhale or exhale for fear of busting
a seam, she was, nevertheless cool, calm, and confident.

Unlocking the door and peering out, she was pleased to see that Giovanni and Monica were still milking their near-death experience for all it was
worth, so nobody would notice her shuffling gait. No one would have either
if it weren't for Tina. She had asked in what would have been a sympathetic
manner had she not still been leaning into the microphone, "Would you like
me to dig you out a larger size, Rebecca?"

All eyes swivelled towards her.

"Nobody told me we were whale watching too." Giovanni guffawed
while the rest of the cabin tittered, and Rebecca felt a suffusion of heat make
its way up her neck and over her face. She felt a hand on her elbow. It was
Tina, her eyes round with concern as her petite frame bobbed around anxiously in embarrassment. "I'm sorry about the microphone; it was so stupid

of me." She lowered her voice until it was barely audible. "Would you like me to get you the next size up?"

"No thank you, Tina; you guessed right with the ten," Rebecca hissed, wishing the tour guide would take her tiny frame and bog off. With a supreme effort on her part, Rebecca managed to lighten her tone and add, "Besides, water makes you weightless, doesn't it?"

Tina looked even more anxious, unsure whether she was supposed to laugh or not. "Yes, but you don't look..."

Giving her a glare that would have silenced a classroom full of hormonal teenagers, Rebecca scraped together her last remnants of dignity and went to sit down, ever so carefully, by David.

"Alright?" He grinned.

She tried to inject an enthusiasm into her voice that she did not feel. "Yeah great, thanks."

David's grin melted into a look of concern. "Are you sure you're okay?"

At that moment, however, a shriek went up, and David was distracted by his fellow passengers stampeding like wildebeest over one another to peer out the catamaran's windows: the first group of Hectors and thankfully nothing else had been spotted.

Chapter Twenty-Seven

AS THOUGH AWARE OF their audience, two dainty Hectors appeared on the left-hand side of the boat, providing an escort, much to the delighted laughter of everyone on board. Even Rebecca managed to put aside her misery and allow herself to be captivated.

"You know, I see this nearly every day and I never get sick of it," Tina confided, kneeling on the cushioned seat next to Rebecca's to watch the unfolding show.

"I don't blame you; they're beautiful."

"Magical is the only way to describe it. They're such special creatures."

Rebecca surveyed Tina out of the corner of her eye, seeing the girl's passion for her work written all over her pretty features. She turned her blue eyes on Rebecca and dropped her voice to a whisper. "I'm sorry about opening my big mouth before. I just didn't think." Smoothing her blonde hair back and twisting it into a ponytail, Tina secured it with the band she had around her wrist before winking at Rebecca conspiratorially. "Besides, men much prefer a woman with a bit of meat on her bones. I mean, who'd want that low-fat Subway roll over there?" She shot daggers in Monica's direction, and Rebecca found herself laughing out loud. The wetsuit incident was well and truly behind them.

A moment later, as Steve turned the catamaran's engine off, there was an anticipatory hush among the passengers. The only sound was that of the water lapping all around them as the boat rocked vigorously back and forth. *Men weren't the only species who preferred a bit of meat on their prey's bones,* Rebecca thought, darting a nervous glance at the expanse of dark-blue water surrounding the boat from every angle. The silence was broken when Tina, smiling broadly, opened the door to the deck and the noisy exodus to meet the dolphins began. Rebecca dawdled, figuring if there were any great whites lurking around out there it was only fair they should get Monica and Giovanni first since they'd shoved their way to the front of the queue.

Steve's voice boomed from behind her. "All set, guys?"

David swung around at the sound of his friend's voice. "You going in, mate?"

Here we go again. Rebecca rolled her eyes and shuffled forward to watch as Giovanni jumped in with a loud plop.

"Nah, Tina's in the water today, mate; I drew the short straw for lifeguard duty." Both men were silent as Monica's shapely form wiggled and jiggled as she psyched herself up to join her partner. Their conversation resumed once Monica had disappeared over the side of the boat, and David pointed to the ten or so black rounded dorsal fins circling the boat curiously. "Good turnout, mate."

"Yeah, the pod's out in force today; you guys timed it well."

David placed his hand on the small of Rebecca's back to steer her forward, and she nearly ruptured a seam at the electric shock that bolted through her. *So much for rubber acting as earth*, she thought. Her excitement was quelled, though, by the stocky Welsh girl in front of her. She jumped in, leaving the way clear for her. Rebecca stood watching for a moment, hypnotised by the Welsh girl's flippers. They were flapping wildly as she doggy paddled her way over to the nearest fin.

"Rebecca, are you ready?" Tina was standing to one side of the ladder that dropped down into the water, holding a scuba mask out. Rebecca didn't move to take it. Tina leaned in close, out of David's earshot. "If I thought there was the slightest chance of a shark being in there, I wouldn't be going in myself, now would I? You'll be fine," she whispered, and Rebecca flashed her a grateful smile. She took the proffered mask and pulled it down. Then, swinging her leg out behind her to feel for the first rung, she chanted silently, "Ready, steady, on the count of three, go!"

As her body spiralled down under the cold, dark water, she took back every curse she had uttered about her wetsuit. Instead, she felt immensely grateful for the warmth its snugness afforded. Her head bobbed up out of the water. Now slightly disorientated, she treaded water as she swivelled around, looking for the boat. Ah, there it was, and what perfect timing. She was treated to a quick glimpse of David's taut rear view just before it was submerged. She spied Tina waving over at her mouthing, "Way to go, girl!"

Rebecca gave her a thumbs-up before kicking confidently away from the boat towards the Hector she'd already nicknamed Horatio.

So this was true love then, she thought a moment later as they danced around each other in the water. Horatio appeared to look her straight in the eye. Deciding he liked her, he butted her with his snout, looking for all the world as though he were smiling at her. Her hand stretched out tentatively to touch him, and he floated patiently beside her, allowing her to stroke his sleek grey body before flicking his tail up and racing a short distance away from her. Realising he wanted to play, she swam towards him. He circled the same spot until she'd nearly caught up to him. He then doubled back the way he'd come, as though he didn't want to lead her too far from the safety of the boat. Their game of cat-and-mouse carried on for a few more minutes until he disappeared beneath the water. Before she had a chance to miss him, he leaped out of the sea a short distance away from her, startling her into swallowing a mouthful of salty water. She didn't mind, though, because the acrobatic display he proceeded to put on for her benefit was one worthy of the Cirque du Soleil.

A conscious feeling of calm descended over her for the first time in forever as she watched Horatio perform. It was a sensation like nothing else she'd ever felt before, marred only slightly by the twinge of guilt she felt remembering all the Flipper jokes she'd made. Horatio nuzzled her, and all the background noise seemed to fade away, leaving the two of them alone to bond in their special way. Just then, something tugged at her leg, and she went under with her arms flailing.

Horatio swam off as David popped out of the water next to her, laughing and taking up where Monica had left off by humming the tune from *Jaws*. For the first time since she'd laid eyes on David Seagar, Rebecca felt annoyance with him and wished he'd piss off over to where Giovanni and Monica were frolicking. His childish antics had ruined what had been a precious moment.

She didn't stay in the water much longer after that, unwilling to take second best after her awesome one-on-one experience with Horatio. While the rest of the group admired the main pod, it paled in comparison. Clambering back on board the boat, she waved at Steve, who was cheering Monica on.

She was doing, what looked to Rebecca, very much like a constipated otter impersonation but was more likely supposed to be a dolphin. Steve grinned. "She's great, isn't she?"

"Yeah, terrific," Rebecca lied. Horatio would find Monica's behaviour positively insulting. Then, leaving a trail of water behind her, she went to warm up inside the cabin.

From her cosy, cushioned vantage point inside, she saw David emerge by the side of the boat some fifteen minutes later. Watching him take his time climbing back on board, she smirked and found herself silently mouthing, "Bond, James Bond." Just like the undercover agent, he did rather fancy himself. The way he shook his head vigorously showered a spray of droplets over Steve, who reflexively dodged them. How come she'd only just noticed that particular trait?

"Sorry, mate." David grinned in a way that said he wasn't sorry at all. "That was totally awesome, mate. You can book me in with Ben next time."

"No worries, mate; I've always got room for the little fella. How is he?"

David answered with a vague wave of his hand. "You know what kids are like."

Steve offered a knowing wide-eyed nod. "Sure do, mate. Jess is five going on fifteen."

David smiled, and then glanced back over his shoulder at the water. "I couldn't see Rebecca out there."

"That's because she came back on board awhile ago; cold, I think." Steve gestured towards the cabin, but the late morning shadows hid her from sight. Steve shrugged. "Maybe she's on the loo." Then, mumbling something about Jennifer, he shot a furtive look back at the cabin.

As words shot back and forth, the conversation that played out between the two men was obviously heated. David's pissed-off expression and stance gave that much away, but Rebecca's strained ears failed to discern anything specific.

"What did you think? Out of this world, isn't it?" David asked her a few minutes later as he stepped into the warmth of the cabin, looking unruffled by whatever had just transpired outside.

"Yeah, it was." Her reply was curt, but he didn't appear to notice as he pulled a towel out from his holdall and began rubbing his hair dry with gusto. Sitting there watching him, Rebecca found herself fluctuating between annoyance over his stupid shenanigans in the water and curiosity as to why he and Steve should be discussing her sister in such an obviously intense manner.

Curiosity won out. "What were you and Steve talking about outside just now?"

David paused before answering smoothly, "I was telling him how much Ben would love to do this. Hey, we should tee it up with Jack, too. What do you think?"

Rebecca wasn't going to be deterred. "It's just that I thought I heard you mention Jennifer."

He turned away to shove the damp towel back in his holdall and, not meeting her eyes, his voice was adamant.

"Nope. You must have water in your ears; Jennifer's name didn't come up at all."

This time it was Rebecca who couldn't meet his gaze as she sat there wondering why on earth he'd just lied to her.

An uncomfortable silence stretched out between them. She was relieved when Monica and Giovanni made their noisy entrance, both eager to outdo each other with their adventures. Rebecca sat for a moment, letting their broken English banter wash over her. There was a nauseous, gnawing sensation in the base of her stomach. *This bloody wetsuit*, she swore to herself; *it was so tight it was making her feel sick.* Now was as good a time as any to get changed out of it, so she snatched up her backpack. David barely looked up from his lively exchange with Monica over the mating habits of the Hector as she excused herself and made her way across the cabin.

Locking the toilet door behind her, she flipped the toilet's lid down and sat on it, willing the sick sensation away. She knew full well it was nothing to do with the snug fit of the wetsuit, though casting a rueful glance down at her tummy, she decided that it was indeed tight. She couldn't even pass the feeling off as seasickness seeing as the boat was hardly moving. Something was wrong, though, and if David's blatant lying before was anything to go by, she wasn't likely to find out what it was in a hurry either.

As she sat there racking her brain for answers, other incidences where she'd thought David's behaviour with regards to her sister was odd flitted to mind. For someone who was a casual friend, he'd shown an awful lot of interest in Jennifer, she realised. A thought came to her unbidden and, finding it an unpleasant one, she tried to push it away, but it was the only thing that made any sense of the situation. Perhaps he fancied her? *Oh, crumbs—was that it? Was she just a ruse to make her sister jealous?* It wouldn't be the first time that had happened. Maybe he'd made his feelings clear to Jen, and she'd known that's what he was up to when he'd asked her out. It would explain why Jen had been so anti-him every time she had brought his name up.

A couple of bites on her thumbnail later, Rebecca decided that had to be it. Don't judge a book by its cover? Rebecca was suddenly very sure that David Seagar was not quite the open book he appeared to be. She hadn't been able to, or perhaps hadn't wanted to, get past his handsome outer covering to discover the real story within, whatever that may be.

So what was she going to do about it? She gloomily rested her elbows on her knees and cupped her chin in her hand because even as she asked herself the question, she knew the answer. Nothing, that's what. She'd sit the rest of the boat ride out, thank him for a lovely day, and then she'd get in her car and drive away. David Seagar could carry on his campaign to win Jennifer's affections without her unwitting help.

Rebecca forced herself to stand up, catching sight of herself in the mirror as she did so. There were slight smudges under her eyes from her so-called waterproof mascara; licking her little finger, she tried unsuccessfully to rub them away. Producing a brush from her bag, she dragged it through her bedraggled locks. She could hear Tarquin's voice: "Only being caught up in a tsunami would be a good enough excuse for the state of that do, chéri." It made her smile, almost.

Thank goodness she brought her makeup with her! Her hands automatically pulled her trusty floral purse out of her bag and wrestled with the zipper that always managed to jam due to the amount of damage control products she had stuffed inside it. Next time she was in a chemist shop, she'd definitely treat herself to a new one. Her lipstick was halfway to her mouth when the thought struck her: for whose benefit was she doing this? Right at this moment in time she didn't think it was for David, Ciaran would be long gone, and Horatio had already buggered off into the deep blue yonder.

The feeling when she managed to peel the black rubber suit away from her goosy flesh was one that should be bottled and sold. She had never been so grateful to de-clothe in all her life. Standing naked in the tiny cubical, she was unwilling to feel constricted again by any form of clothing until, realising she was bloody freezing, she clambered quickly back into her jeans and jersey.

The cabin had filled up in her absence, and the windows were steaming up due to the damp bodies and warm breath as everybody gabbled excitedly amongst themselves. Tina spotted Rebecca emerging, and she grinned over from her pew behind the microphone, tapping it before she spoke to make sure it was switched off this time. "For someone who wasn't overly keen on diving in, I see you made a special friend out there."

Rebecca's smile was sheepish. "Yeah, I did. His name was Horatio. We clicked right away, but he wasn't in it for the long haul. The story of my life, unfortunately."

Tina giggled before replying. "Oh well, it could have been worse." Rebecca looked at her curiously. "You could have met a shark." She missed the girl's wink, for her eyes had flicked across to where David was sitting, still in animated conversation with Giovanni and Monica.

"I'm starting to wonder if that's exactly what I have met, Tina," she answered cryptically before moving quietly back to her seat.

Tina completed the head count amidst some jesting about making sure nobody was left behind. Satisfied everybody was back on board, she popped her head in to tell Steve and a minute later the catamaran's engine roared back to life.

"Did you catch *Open Water*?" David asked; it was the first time he'd spoken to her since she'd sat back down.

"No, I missed that one. What was it about?" She didn't care, but anything was better than sitting in stony silence.

"It was pretty unnerving considering it was based on a true story. This American couple is on a beach holiday, and they decide to take a dive trip out to sea, only the boat leaves them behind."

"Sounds cheerful; what happened to them?"

"Sharks," he finished flatly, and Rebecca gave an involuntary shiver. Unfortunately, Monica overheard their conversation and at the mention of the S word, she was off again.

Once Monica's sideshow was over, David made a few feeble attempts at instigating conversation, but whatever it was he wasn't telling her was sitting like a roadblock between them. She couldn't be bothered with the pretence.

Without the nervous anticipation that she'd felt as the boat had sped out to sea that morning, the cruise back to the jetty seemed to take forever. Sensing his attentions weren't being warmly received, David turned his attention to his new friends, Giovanni and Monica, while Rebecca gazed at the endless expanse of blue outside. After an age, the jetty finally came into view. As the boat chugged into position, David—his earlier cockiness gone—asked, "Did you want to go for a drink? Ben's staying in Christchurch with his mum for a couple of days and Giovanni and Monica are keen to head over to the pub for a quiet one."

The Swiss duo nodded at her and, grinning somewhat inanely, made her mind up for her. "Um, no thanks. It's been a great day, but I've got to get back. For the kids. I, uh, told Jennifer I'd pick them up..." Her voice trailed off at the look he was giving her. It was obvious that this time she was the one lying.

A kerfuffle ensued as everybody gathered up their belongings and shuffled towards the door. Once they slowly began trickling off the boat, Rebecca sought Tina out and gave her a hug goodbye, thanking her for helping her overcome her nerves. Tina's smile was warm as she returned the hug.

"You're welcome. It's seeing people like you put their fears to one side and go for it that makes my job worthwhile."

"Thanks again; it was totally amazing, even if Horatio proved himself to be a bit fickle in his affections." She managed a small laugh before turning to join the disembarking line.

"Rebecca!" Tina called after her.

"Yeah?" She swung back around expectantly.

"Good luck with the fishing. I know where you're coming from. It's so easy to mistake a shark for a dolphin." They exchanged knowing glances as David, bringing up the rear, looked at them both strangely, deciding wisely not to ask for an explanation.

Steve had taken up his position by the exit and was shaking hands and exchanging farewells with his passengers. Rebecca's turn rolled around, and she shook his hand somewhat less effusively than she had earlier that morning, thanking him for a wonderful day. It was a half-truth, she convinced herself while stepping down onto the jetty. Meeting Horatio had been wonderful, and she wasn't going to let whatever David's problem with her sister was eclipse that.

The string of people made their way to the end of the queue that had formed outside the changing rooms stacked along the pier. David shuffled awkwardly from foot to foot, waiting for Rebecca to make her excuses and leave. She was pleased she'd gotten dressed on the boat, as it meant she could beat a hasty retreat instead of having to hang around, waiting for a spare changing room. Clearing her throat, she opened her mouth to say *adios amigos, don't call me I'll call you*, or something along those lines when the words dried upon her tongue. Striding purposefully down the jetty, her designer combat jacket fluttering open in the breeze, was Jennifer.

Chapter Twenty-Eight

"REBECCA." JENNIFER nodded stiffly in her startled sister's direction before turning malevolent blue eyes on David. "How could you? I hope you are pleased with yourself."

Rebecca's eyes darted between the two of them, and she felt her face grow hot, as though her sister had physically slapped her. It was staring her in the face, plain as day. Bile rose in her throat. *Oh, how could she have been so stupid?* Then, as if Jennifer had thrown a bucket of icy water over her, Rebecca began to shiver uncontrollably.

Two hours later, she sat huddled in the front seat of the car with the heater blasting, trying to rid herself of the chill that had permeated all the way through to her bones. Unable to look at her sister and David for fear of retching, she had fled. Driving away in a screech of burning rubber, all she had wanted to do was put as much distance between the three of them in the shortest span of time as she possibly could.

She'd eventually wound up here, wherever here was. Raising her head from its resting place on the steering wheel, she was almost surprised to find herself parked up on the verge of a shingle road, the twinkling lights over to her right belonging to the township of Little River. Taking a steadying breath, she held her hands out in front of her; the shaking had stopped. She threw a glance up at the darkening sky, knowing she'd have to go back sometime; besides, she was never going to get warm sitting here. With a sigh that reached all the way down to her frozen toes, Rebecca turned the key in the ignition and reversed slowly back up to the main road. She wasn't ready to confront her sister yet, but there was someone she desperately needed to see.

PULLING UP OUTSIDE Sea Breezes B&B, she got out of the car, hoping he was there and not propping up the bar in the pub or worse, waiting to catch a flight back to Dublin. She raised her hand to knock, not being game to ring the bell this time but the door swung open before her knuckles even made contact with the wood.

"Rebecca? I saw you pull up so I thought I'd save you the Mrs Doody interrogation." Ciaran registered her puffy eyes and running nose. "Hey, are you alright?"

She didn't answer, collapsing into the solid warmth of his arms.

"Come on." He led her through to the empty guest lounge just off the hallway. She sat down in the dated velveteen armchair he led her to and as he crouched down in front of her to listen, she poured out her sorry tale.

"I had no idea; Jennifer pulled the wool well and truly over my eyes." She broke away and rubbed furiously at her temples. "I am so stupid."

"You're not the stupid one, Rebecca," he soothed. "What are you going to do?"

"I'll have to go back and face her. She damned well owes me an explanation for all the lies she's been spinning." Rebecca delved into her bag and found a packet of tissues. Giving her nose a good blow, she turned to Ciaran with red-rimmed eyes. "Do you know the worst bit?"

"Tell me."

"This time here with Jennifer has been so great." She hiccupped and apologised, but Ciaran waved her apology away.

"Carry on."

"I felt like I'd finally got to know my sister and I found myself liking her."

Ciaran smiled gently at her and encouraged, she carried on. "You see, I've always held this ridiculous image of Jen in my head of her being some superwoman, but I discovered she's fallible just like the rest of us. You know, she's pretty funny when she wants to be, too, and for the first time in oh, I don't know how long, I enjoyed being around her." Pausing, Rebecca wiped at her eyes, smearing the mascara that had already run down her cheeks in twin rivulets across her cheeks. "I thought that I had misjudged her all these years, but now I find out that I was right all along. She is a self-serving, sanctimonious cow."

Ciaran reached out and hugged her to him. "Hey, come on. You need to hear what she has to say before you write her off like that. She is your sister, no matter what she's done. Do you want me to come with you?"

Rebecca managed a feeble smile. "No. I need to do this by myself. I'll come back later, alright?" Their eyes locked with the unspoken agreement that they would talk then.

Pulling up the drive to Cuisine with Carlton's some thirty minutes later, she barely noticed the brightly lit classroom in the late afternoon gloom because her eyes were fixed on the house in front of her. There were no cars on the drive. *Perhaps they were all out?* she thought, wrenching the handbrake up, only too happy to grasp at the glimmer of hope that she might be able to delay the inevitable confrontation a little bit longer. Inside, the house was cold and as quiet as it was dark.

"I'm in here, Rebecca," her sister's voice called out into the darkness from the direction of the lounge, causing her to stumble in fright. Swearing loudly, she fumbled for the light switch. She wanted to be able to see Jennifer's face when she tried to explain away her affair with David Seagar.

Looking dishevelled by her usual standard, with tendrils of hair having escaped her ponytail, Rebecca noticed Jennifer had changed into an oversized cardigan and track pants. *Might as well get comfortable*, she thought bitterly. Jennifer had moulded herself into the armchair; there was nobody here worth impressing, after all. *He* was probably down at the pub having a right laugh at her expense with Switzerland's answer to Ken and Barbie. Sitting down heavily on the far end of the couch, Rebecca asked flatly, "Where is everybody?"

Jennifer's stomach contracted; she'd never seen Rebecca look like this before. Her softly rounded features had hardened, and the unforgiving glint in her hazel eyes could have kept a hungry tiger at bay. When she opened her mouth to reply, her voice came out in a choked gasp, and Rebecca had to lean forward to hear her.

"Melissa showed up, wanting to see you, so I asked her if she'd mind taking Hannah with her to pick up Jack." She twiddled with the oversized cuff of her cardigan. "I told her that you and I needed to talk, so she offered to take them out for an early fish 'n chip supper." Jennifer attempted a wry smile. "She is in definite brownnose mode."

Rebecca's irritated glare scolded Jennifer like a naughty child. Raising her voice a notch, Jennifer squared up to her little sister. "So you can yell and scream at me all you like, Rebecca." She held out her wrist and pointed to an oversized lump of silver serving as her watch. "My guess is you've got an hour starting from now."

The oomph went out of Rebecca then, and she felt her anger deflating, leaving her feeling curiously flat. "I don't know where to start," she said evenly, shaking her head. "I just can't wrap my head around what you've done or why you lied to me. I thought I was beginning to get to know you at last."

"You do know me and it's called having an affair. Or, for want of a nicer turn of phrase, committing adultery and I didn't tell you because I know you, and I knew you wouldn't come home if I did." Jennifer spelled out the obvious.

"I know what it's called, thank you, and you're right—I wouldn't have come home. You don't deserve help. I just can't believe that you, that he...Christ, no wonder Mark stayed on in Mooloolaba." Her hands fluttered up to her face, dragging at the skin on her cheeks as she tried to put her disgust into words. "You and David, though—you're as bad as each other as far as I'm concerned. You're both liars." As she spat this last sentence out, Jennifer straightened in her seat; she'd had enough of being on the back foot.

"Do you know I was beginning to think you'd grown up at last? But you are still so bloody naïve. Life is not neat and tidy all the time. People make mistakes, and you have no idea what my life has been like these past few years because you haven't been here."

There'd be no tea and sympathy from Rebecca, not this time. "That is so typical of you, trying to turn things around, but this is about you. You are the one who has cheated on your husband. The father of your two beautiful children. And with a man who was low enough to lead me on in what I can only assume was a pathetic bid to make you jealous." Her top lip curled up in distaste. "What makes me sick, though, is the fact that you let me think you were the injured party. All those things I said about Mark—he didn't deserve any of it, and you don't bloody well deserve him!"

Jennifer interjected with a pleading inflection to her voice as the fight went out of her. "I didn't lie about our reasons for going over to Mooloolaba. It was make or break time for us. When I got home, I was so glad you were here. You have been amazing and believe it or not, Rebecca, I need you." She huddled deeper into her cardigan. "Mark's back tomorrow, but he's decided to stay in Christchurch for the time being until we can sort things out properly."

"What about Jack and Hannah?"

"He's coming to see them straight from the airport."

"Oh, I see; I suppose there's strength to be had in numbers. A show of solidarity to tell them that Mummy and Daddy are splitting up, is it?"

At those words, Jennifer looked stricken, as it hit her all again that the very thing she had fought to stave off for so long was now a reality. She couldn't meet Rebecca's eyes, appearing instead to be fascinated with a loose stitch in her cardigan.

"I don't know. I don't know what we're going to say to them."

"I take it Mark's man enough not to want to tell them that it's all down to their mum?"

A strangled sob sounded from the armchair. There was no reply, but Rebecca wasn't ready to back down yet. "Was David worth it? Was he worth this sodding great mess?"

Jennifer was quiet for a moment before pulling a screwed-up tissue out of the pocket of her cardigan and wiping her nose. "David was a mistake. A great big, good-looking, bloody mistake who happened to look my way at a time when I was at a low ebb. The man comes with enough baggage to sink a ship and while he was busy thrashing around madly for a lifeboat, he grabbed hold of me." She paused. "What he didn't realise was that between the two of us, we could have sunk the *Titanic*."

Rebecca rolled her eyes and drawled, "Pu-lease spare me the metaphors. Okay, yes, David is somewhat weighed down by what happened with Maree, but what baggage do you have?" She didn't give her sister a chance to respond. "Hmm, let me see." She began ticking points off her fingers. "Could it be the fact that you have two fabulous children who adore you? Oh yes, that must be so hard, Jennifer." Her voice dripped with honeyed sarcasm. "Let's not forget that you live in this beautiful home and run an internationally successful business. That's something that most of us mere mortals would struggle with. Oh, and it must be really, really hard staying so effortlessly slim and gorgeous."

Jennifer opened her mouth to speak up in her defence, but she was cut off. Rebecca was on a roll, pointing out all the things that had made her feel inferior for years. "Of course, you had a husband who totally worshipped you too. That was something that obviously meant about as much to you as a piece of toilet paper because you've just flushed that relationship away, haven't you?"

"Now who's using the metaphors?"

Rebecca scowled. "My point is that I rather think it is Mark who's entitled to say he's carrying a ton of baggage, not you."

Jennifer drew herself up in her seat. "Okay, I think you've had more than your say. It's my turn now. So let me tell you a little something about what you so obviously see as my perfect life, shall I?" Imitating her sister, she began ticking the points off on her fingers. "For starters, how could I not agree that I have two beautiful children? They are the most important thing in this world to me. But, unfortunately, one of them wants nothing to do with me these days because he saw me kissing someone who wasn't his dad."

There was an audible gasp from the couch; it explained so much, Rebecca could barely gather her thoughts before Jennifer dropped the next bombshell.

"Secondly, have you ever heard the saying *home is where the heart is*? Well, my heart hasn't been in this home for quite some time, and neither has Mark's. I might have been the one who set the ball rolling, but our marriage was a ticking time bomb. I've already told you that. As for an internationally successful business, have you had your eyes shut all week? What is with the Memphis Branch of the Xena Warrior Princess Fan Club?"

A mental picture of the warrior princesses seemed to hang suspended between them, and Rebecca couldn't help herself. As she smiled, the corners of Jennifer's mouth twitched too, and the smile grew into a chuckle.

Rebecca announced she needed a drink, and the two sisters sat in a silent diffusing atmosphere with a glass of wine each until Jennifer brought them back to their previous dispute. "I forgot my last point."

Rebecca had the grace to look slightly abashed. "Would that be the one about you being effortlessly slim and gorgeous?"

"Yep. I'll have you know I am one high-maintenance babe."

"Really?"

"Truly. I have succumbed to the needle."

Rebecca inhaled sharply. "What—Botox?"

Jennifer nodded. "As well as regular facials, hair appointments, oh, and dental whitening."

"I don't believe it!"

"Without a doubt, the thought of turning forty leaves me cold and I guess I kind of rebelled against it. It's been me all along who was the walking cliché with my midlife crisis. That's the price I'm paying for my so-called beauty." She snorted. "I am terrified of getting old. As for staying effortlessly slim, believe me, sister, there is nothing effortless about it!"

Rebecca appraised her sister for the first time without her rose-tinted glasses on. "Jen?"

"Yeah?"

"I haven't been much of a sister, have I?"

Jennifer's chest rose as she inhaled. "It's not just down to you, Rebecca. We've both been kind of absorbed in our worlds for a long time. I lost sight of you too."

"You're right, I guess, but you should have told me things weren't right between you and Mark, and you could have told me about David. I would have understood."

"No, that's just it, Rebecca. You wouldn't have understood. You've had me on a pedestal for years." As Rebecca shook her head in denial, Jennifer held her hand up. "Don't deny it—you did." She gave a small shrug. "I didn't want to be the one to shatter your illusions. It was always my job to pave the way for you. Look how much more of an easy ride you got in your teens than I did with Mum and Dad. Besides, since we're being so honest I might as well admit it, I liked it. It suited me to be the older, more together sister."

A lull descended on the room. Jennifer's blue eyes were sympathetic, seeing the hurt reflected back in her sister's hazel pair. Jennifer had an idea of what was on Rebecca's mind at that moment: She had made some pretty major life decisions of late. She just hoped that finding out what she had been capable of and what David was like didn't see her shelve her plans and send her running back to Ireland with Ciaran for all the wrong reasons.

Rebecca realised that it wasn't David and her disappointment at the man he had turned out to be or even Jennifer's starring role in that realisation that had sprung to mind. It was Ciaran. He was the one she had turned to when the chips were down, and he hadn't let her down. What the hell was she going to do now?

Follow her dream and lose him or follow him and lose her dream?

Jennifer ploughed on, "I'm sorry, Becs. I know I have let you down but don't let mine or David's actions affect your decision to stay." She trembled. "I tell you what, I wanted to boot his lying backside all the way back out to sea when I saw him with you today. I'd have given anything for you not to have gotten hurt again. And I'm so sorry that I am not the shining example of getting your life right that you thought I was."

"No, that you're not!" Rebecca laughed, much to Jennifer's surprise. "But do you know what?"

"What?"

"I think I like you better this way—flawed. You're human." Rebecca leaned across and took her sister's hand, and then squeezed it tightly before adding, "You're right about David, though. I looked at him today while he was in full-blown action hero mode, and I realised he was a teeny bit full of himself."

"Just a teeny bit?" Jennifer raised an eyebrow. "The man thinks he's New Zealand's answer to Daniel Craig, for goodness' sake!"

When their raucous giggling at David's expense finally ebbed away, Rebecca owned up. "I wasn't thinking of him before either."

"No?" Jennifer felt a sinking sensation she knew what was coming.

"I was thinking about Ciaran and that old Clash song—'Should I Stay Or Should I Go...'" She stopped mid-sentence, hearing the front door slam shut, followed closely by the harassed clip-clop of high-heeled boots coming down the hall. The door burst open to reveal a wild-eyed Melissa.

"It's Jack," she gasped. "He's missing."

Chapter Twenty-Nine

REBECCA SAT ON THE couch, her mouth opening and closing like a bewildered goldfish while Jennifer leapt out of her seat, spluttering, "What do you mean, missing?"

Melissa's back came into contact with the wall as she nervously shuffled backwards, wary of Jennifer in mad-mother mode, even if it was perfectly understandable. "Jack never showed up in class this morning. Apparently Mr Reynolds, his teacher—"

Jennifer took a menacing step forward. "Yes, I know who he is, thank you very much, Melissa."

"Of course, sorry. Well, he assumed he was off sick. Apparently as Jack hadn't told him you were home, he figured that Rebecca either didn't realise it was school policy to phone in and let them know or that she'd forgotten too. He's beside himself now."

As if that helped. Jennifer couldn't give a toss if Mr Reynolds was beside himself or not; the stupid little man should have phoned to clarify Jack's whereabouts. Hang on, though. She wrung her hands together as a thought occurred to her. Swinging round, she eyed her sister accusingly. "But you dropped him at the gate and saw him into class, right?"

Rebecca squirmed in her seat. "I, um, I dropped him at the gate, but, oh, Jen, I'm so sorry. Just this one time I didn't stay and watch him go in. We were running late."

Jennifer's tone was acidic. "Let me finish that for you, shall I? You didn't want to be late for your hot date. Yeah, I've got the picture. Thanks a lot, Rebecca." She turned away in disgust, but Melissa was having none of it.

"Hey, go easy. That's hardly fair and taking it out on Rebecca isn't going to help find Jack, is it?"

Jennifer felt her anger slowly dissipate. What she said made sense and it wasn't Rebecca's fault Jack had opted out of school. If it was anybody's fault, it was hers. Getting angry was her way of coping with being frightened.

"You're right." She glanced over her shoulder to where her sister sat shivering on the couch. "It's not your fault, Becs. I'm sorry, okay?"

Rebecca nodded dully. It didn't matter that Jennifer had forgiven her for not waiting; she'd never forgive herself if Jack didn't turn up.

A cold chill swept up Jennifer's spine as, swinging round to face Melissa, she suddenly realised that Jack wasn't the only one missing. "Where the hell's Hannah?"

"Whoa." Melissa held up a calming hand. "She's fine. She's with Betty. Sorry, I should have told you that straight off. When I realised Jack had gone AWOL, I drove around everywhere I could think of that he might have gone." She shrugged. "Obviously I couldn't find him, so we came straight back here. I thought it would be best if Hannah stayed with Betty while we go out looking."

Jennifer was already stuffing her feet back into her trainers. "Come on then, let's get moving."

"Okay, but before we go, though, is there any chance he could have come back here and sneaked inside without you knowing, Jen?" Rebecca leaned down and zipped her boots up before getting to her feet.

Jen tucked her hair behind her ears, giving the appearance of a worried pixie. "Well, no, I wouldn't have thought so."

"And, of course, I checked with Betty and the warrior princesses." As Melissa's mouth formed the words warrior princesses, she gave an unconscious shudder.

"Still, it wouldn't hurt to double-check, would it? You two take upstairs, I'll do down..."

Jennifer was already taking the stairs two at a time, Melissa flying up behind her.

Two minutes later, the three of them were congregated back in the lounge, having found no sign of Jack. "Right then, let's go." Jennifer snatched the car keys off of Melissa and marched off down the hall. Melissa scurried after her and snatched the keys back.

"I'm the calmest one here; besides, my mum would kill me if the Alfa got pranged, so I'll drive. Alright?"

"Whatever, let's just get a move on."

"Do you think you should call Mark and tell him what's going on?" Rebecca asked while slamming the front door shut behind her.

"If we haven't found him in another hour, I'll ring him on his cell phone. Jack will have turned up by then," Jennifer answered with a lot more confidence than she felt. "No point in worrying him over nothing, is there?"

Rebecca didn't think Mark would see his son having been missing since nine o'clock that morning as "nothing," but they'd wasted precious time as it was without arguing the point. One more hour—then she'd ring Mark herself if it came to it.

"You went to David's?" Rebecca asked, climbing into the back seat as Melissa got behind the wheel, and Jennifer scrambled in next to her.

"That was the first place I went, but there was no one home. Do you think it would be worth swinging by there again?"

"Ben's at his grandparents in Christchurch but at least if we find David, he can call him and see if Jack said anything to him about running away," Rebecca postulated.

"You don't think he would have gone there, do you?" Jennifer said, tugging at her seatbelt.

"Ben's grandparents? I doubt it. How would he get there?"

"I don't know—bus? He's caught the bus into town with me before as a school holiday treat." Jennifer buckled herself in and then froze. "Becs, you don't think he'd hitchhike, do you?"

"No! No way, Jen. Don't even go there. He wouldn't know how, for heaven's sake. He's only seven years old; look, he won't have gone far. We'll find him, okay?"

"Okay," Jennifer repeated in a small voice. Melissa turned the key and listened to the engine start up. Betty's reassuring figure suddenly appeared, backlit by the classroom on the cooking school steps. She waved and mouthed what they all assumed was, "Don't worry, you'll find him." As the car swept down the drive and out onto the main road, Jennifer peered into the darkened back seat.

"Um, Rebecca?"

"Yeah?"

"There's something else I haven't told you."

Oh, what more could there possibly be? She'd never felt so physically and emotionally drained, and she just didn't know if she was able to handle more.

"Do you remember how I said Jack saw me kissing another man?"

Uh yeah, like she could forget that little snippet of information. To Melissa's credit, she masterfully swerved and narrowly missed a tree as Jennifer announced this.

"Jeez, eyes on the road, alright!" Rebecca gasped, clutching hold of the passenger seat in front of her.

"Sorry—blame your sister."

"It does get worse."

"It sure does," Rebecca mumbled before urging her sister on. "Come on then, spit it out, whatever it is."

"Well, he never saw it was David, thank goodness, but I think—"

"WHAT!!!" screeched Melissa, pulling the car violently over onto the grassy verge.

"It's a long and sordid story, Melissa; one that I don't want to get into right now. Rebecca will give you the rundown once we find Jack."

Melissa swivelled her head to face Rebecca. "Promise."

"Promise. Now shut up and drive."

As Melissa pulled out and drove off at a more sedate speed, Rebecca leaned forward and placed her hand on her sister's shoulder. "How do you know he never saw David?"

"It was late, and Mark was away on business."

Rebecca groaned. "Please don't tell me you did it in your marital bed—MELISSA, KEEP YOUR EYES ON THE BLOODY ROAD!"

"Sorry," Melissa muttered, ears burning as she clutched hold of the steering wheel. Multi-tasking had never been one of her strong points.

Jennifer's voice rang out indignantly, "Of course I didn't. I do have some morals, you know."

"Well, that's a relief. So what happened?"

"Like I said, it was late. David showed up at the house, knowing Mark was away. Only I wouldn't let him in. I took a couple of glasses of wine out, and we sat on the back porch talking instead. When he stood up to go, he kissed me goodnight."

"Peck or pash?" Melissa interrupted.

"Does it matter?"

"Yes, it does if I am expected to assess the seriousness of the situation."

Jennifer pressed her palm against her forehead. Rebecca could only imagine the thoughts running through it. "Pash, if you must know. When I went inside, Jack was standing in the kitchen half-asleep. He asked me who I was kissing. But it's not that so much." Realising what that had sounded like, Jennifer quickly added, "Not that that's not bad enough or anything. All Jack could have possibly seen was the back of David's head, though. In his state, he wouldn't have put two and two together. I told him he was dreaming and sent him up to bed."

"Did he believe you?" Melissa and Rebecca chimed.

Jennifer shrugged. "It sounds awful, but I was so caught up with myself that I managed to convince myself he did. The thing is I don't know how long he'd been standing there, and I am praying he didn't overhear the conversation I had been having with David prior to the kiss."

It did not bode well. Rebecca felt her skin prickle with the cold and wished she'd taken the time to throw a coat on as she was bounced around in the back seat. "We were talking about what it was like for me, you know, after Jack was born."

Oh, this was bad—very, very bad.

A white letterbox signalled that they had reached David's place. The car lights sluiced down the driveway and over a darkened house. "Doesn't look too promising, does it?" Melissa said as Jennifer opened her door.

"Be right back."

The two girls watched Jennifer run up the front steps and bang on the door. When no one answered after the fourth or fifth knock, Jennifer trotted back and jumped into her seat.

"Guess we gotta go into town," Rebecca deducted. "David told me he was going for a drink when we got off the boat." Rebecca couldn't help adding, "Probably singing karaoke with Giovanni and Monica. Keep your ears open for Split Enz's 'Shark Attack,' girls."

When they kicked the double doors of the pub open in a way that would have given Drew, Cameron, and Lucy a run for their money, they found the joint teeming. Locals and tourists alike, caught up in Friday night fever, rubbed shoulders and shouted over the jukebox. As the three women elbowed their way into the room, heads swivelled. Conversations swung from the week that had been to who, or what, the stunning brunette, gorgeous blonde, and cute honey-blonde could be searching for.

It was Melissa who spotted him. Gesturing towards an alcove by the bar, she announced, "He's over there!" She stalked over, with Jennifer and Rebecca following in her wake. David didn't see them approach the lean-to; he was too busy holding court over what could pass for a meeting of Backpacker's Anonymous. David had a five o'clock shadow prickling at his chin. His sleekly muscled dark-brown forearms peeked out from the rolled-up sleeves of his Kathmandu polo fleece, and he could have passed for a strapping Italian on an adventure holiday.

Giovanni and Monica were perched on bar stools to his left, supping from southern manhandles of Speight's beer. *Obviously going for the authentic Kiwi experience*, Rebecca thought cynically as their wholesome features split into matching grins.

"Hey, Rebecca!" Monica called, banging down her glass. "You decided to join us after all. Good, maybe you can tell Dietmar here that it is true. I did see a great white in the water today."

David was staring wide-eyed at the three women, his handle halfway to his mouth and his handsome features turning a watery red mix of terror and embarrassment. It was Jennifer who kicked things off. "Have you seen Jack, David?" Not mincing her words, she stood Amazonian, hand on hip, expecting an equally straight-to-the-point reply. She didn't get one.

David, who'd been mentally preparing himself for a full-blown verbal assault, squirmed uncomfortably under her steely gaze before finally spluttering out, "Jack? No. Why?" His words sent a fine spray of beer froth flying down the table.

"Because he's missing, asshole. Or did you and your ego think that this was just my way of grabbing your attention? You kind of did that already by trying to seduce my sister."

Giovanni and Monica's mouths were agape, revealing that they did indeed have good dental hygiene habits; neither of them had a single filling between them.

David felt himself relax slightly; Jennifer had played her card, and the claws were well and truly out. At least now he knew where he stood. "I did not try to seduce Rebecca. We met up a few times and had a laugh, that's all. She'll tell you nothing happened between us, and even if it had, it's none of your business. You had made it quite clear before you went to Australia that we were history."

"Oh, save it for someone who cares," Jennifer snapped at him.

Enough is enough, Rebecca thought angrily, stepping forward and holding her hand up to silence them both. "I am here, you know, and aren't you kind of forgetting why it is we are here, Jennifer?" Turning to eyeball David, she said, "Jack has been missing since I dropped him off outside school this morning; he never showed up in his class."

Jennifer and David looked sufficiently shame-faced. "So he's missing then?"

"Yes," Jennifer whispered as her anger gave way to fear once more. Feeling angry was the preferable emotion. She drew herself into her cardigan and refused to think of any other possibilities than finding Jack safe and sound.

David snapped to, unwrapping himself from the bar stool and pulling his cell phone out of his pocket. "Ben's staying with Maree at her parents in Christchurch. I'll phone him." His shoulders slumped slightly. "Maybe Jack said something to him about what he was planning." Then, striding over to the exit, he pushed the heavy smoke stop door open, and Jennifer followed behind him. An awkward silence settled over the lean-to as its occupants pretended to find the contents of their beer glasses fascinating. Melissa and Rebecca shifted awkwardly from foot to foot, waiting for them to return.

They did a moment later, but it was not with good news. "Ben had no idea Jack was going to take off. Apparently they had another squabble the day I took Ben to Christchurch," David explained directly to Rebecca. Out of the corner of her eye, she could see her big sister's tough girl stance was in danger of shattering. So, taking charge, she told Melissa to take Jennifer back out to the car. "I'll join you in a sec."

When they'd gone, David took Rebecca's elbow and steered her away from the wagging ears over to the exit. "Look, I know I'm not your favourite person right now but the most important thing here is finding Jack, right?" She bit her bottom lip and nodded. "How about I phone around all his and Ben's mates and any other places I can think of that he might have gone?"

"That would be a big help." She didn't look up, preferring to study the stained blue carpet. "You've got my mobile if anything turns up?"

"Yeah, of course."

Turning on her heel to leave, she felt him catch her arm. She spun around and found herself pinned under the intensity of his grey-green gaze.

"I'm sorry, Rebecca," he stammered. "You're such a lovely lady. It's just that Jennifer..." His eyes clouded over, turning them the colour of an impending storm. "She kind of made me crazy, you know?"

Rebecca stood transfixed for a brief moment, expecting to feel something, anything, but she realised there was nothing there. Drawing herself up, she returned his gaze steadily. "Don't worry, David. I just hope you can get over Jennifer as quickly as I've gotten over you."

With that, she walked away, hearing his voice drift across the crowded pub as he called, "We'll find him, Rebecca." Crossing her fingers, she prayed he was right.

The temperature felt like it had dropped two degrees in the short span of time she'd been inside the pub. Wrenching the idling car's door open, she threw herself into the back seat.

"Shut the door! You're letting all the cold air in," Melissa screeched, having commandeered her place in the driving seat again.

"Alright, alright, let me get in, for goodness' sake," Rebecca grumbled, pulling the door closed before vigorously rubbing her hands together and blowing on them at the same time. Jennifer had seemingly regained her composure by the time she twisted in her seat to address Rebecca and Melissa with a steady voice.

"We need a plan. It's no good us just driving around in the dark trying to spot Jack."

"You're right." Rebecca butted in. "How about we do a search of the park and the school? If he's not there, then I vote we go home. He might have shown up there in the meantime, and if he hasn't, then I think it's time we contacted the police and Mark."

"The police?" Jennifer looked aghast.

"It's not that I think anything sinister has happened to him, Jen; it's just that they'll have a better idea of how to go about finding him. Are we all agreed?"

Jennifer swallowed hard and nodded, as did Melissa. Rubbing at the fogged patch of windscreen obscuring her view, Melissa swung the car in a U-turn towards the park.

By day, the waterfront park was filled with the squeals of children, but by night it was eerily silent. The only sound was the rhythmic slushing of the waves sliding in and out over the stony shore below. Not a bit fazed, Jennifer strode off towards the dimly lit, rickety pier, ordering Melissa and Rebecca to cover the park. Thankfully it wasn't a large area. Rebecca linked arms with Melissa in what they both understood to be a silent agreement not to leave each other's side. The silence was shattered as they all hollered out Jack's name.

As Rebecca and Melissa's footsteps squelched into the wet grass, a slight sea breeze stirred the rusty hinges of the three swings hanging forlornly from their frame, causing both girls to jump. "This is ridiculous," Melissa complained. "At the very least, we should have a torch, not to mention a jacket. I'm freezing." She huddled in closer to Rebecca.

"Exactly, and so will Jack be if he's out here, so stop moaning."

"I'll bet you anything he's sitting at home, warming his feet by the fire. He'll wish he was missing when I get my hands on him."

"What was that?" Rebecca shushed her.

"What was what?"

"Wait—there it goes again. Listen." Both girls held their breath as a violent scuffling noise erupted over by a shadowy clump of bushes.

"You go first," Melissa directed. Rebecca took a step closer and then sprang back as the prickly outline of a hedgehog on urgent business burst forth from the bushes. "How could you mistake a hedgehog for your nephew?"

"Oh, shut up, Melissa." Rebecca didn't need night vision goggles to know that Melissa was poking her tongue out at her.

Jennifer's white face was illuminated against the black night as she appeared beside them both a few minutes later. "This is hopeless. Even if Jack were hiding out here, he might not want to be found. At least not by me."

Rebecca draped a limp arm around her sister's shoulder and steered her back towards the car. They had searched everywhere, but there was nowhere left to look.

The three women were quiet as they drove back, probably reserving their meagre energy supplies for the long night ahead of them. Rebecca jumped a moment later as her cell phone sang out, alerting her to an incoming text. Pulling it from her pocket, she quickly glanced at the caller display.

"Is it from David?" Jennifer's tone was urgent.

Rebecca frowned as she read the short message of "Are you ok?" and shoved the phone away. "No, Jen, sorry; it's from Ciaran." She'd reply once she knew Jack was alright.

"Oh." She hunched back down in her seat.

The first thing they noticed as the car lights shone over the house was that it was still smothered in darkness. "Maybe he's down in the classroom with Betty and Hannah," Rebecca said hopefully as Melissa stilled the engine.

"Betty would have phoned me on my cell if he were," Jennifer answered bleakly. They climbed despondently out of the car and at that very moment the words, "What in tarnation!" ripped across the still night.

The three women exchanged inquiring looks as another shout went up: "C'mere ya no count, good for nuthin..."

The voice trailed off, and Jennifer pointed towards the twinkling lights of the cabins. "I think it's coming from cabin one."

The sound of crashing furniture split the air. Down by the classroom, the door flew open as Betty appeared, Hannah on her hip, to see what all the noise was about. Spying the three women, she waved out and made her way laboriously up the path. "What's going on?" she puffed.

Rebecca frowned and raised her hands in surrender. "Your guess is as good as mine."

Jennifer stretched her arms out and took Hannah, who was sucking her thumb sleepily.

"Doncha try an skedaddle, boy, cos I'm gonna whup your ass when I git my hands on you!"

The women's eyes popped wide open as Mindy-Lou, in full battle regalia, staggered out onto the cabin's porch, holding something small that was squirming for all it was worth. Jennifer raised her eyes to heaven and offered thanksgiving. "Thank you, God!" Then, with Hannah hanging on for dear life, she sprinted over to save her son from a good whupping.

"Well, ya'll make no mistake, I likely to pee ma pants when I first laid eyes on whad ya'll say his name is agin?"

"Jack," the four women chorused as they clustered around the star of the moment, who was cowering under cover of his mother's cardigan. Jennifer hugged her son to her and grovelled. "I can't apologise enough for my son's behaviour, Mindy-Lou. Right now, though, I think the best thing I can do is get him and Hannah home so I can get to the bottom of what's been going on."

Mindy-Lou leaned forward and ruffled Jack's dark hair. "I surely am sorry for hollerin' at ya, Jack." She raised her head to explain herself to the others. "But I was fixin' to have me a bath when I spied ya boy here hidin' under ma bed." Her hand fluttered dramatically up to her bustier. "I was fit to be tied. A few minutes later and I woulda bin buck naked. Ya'll can't blame me for thinkin' I'd caught me a peepin' tom."

"Quite right, Mindy-Lou," Jennifer assented, stroking Jack's hair and smoothing Mindy-Lou's ruffled feathers. "And I can assure you I'll be having a stern word with Jack about what's happened here tonight."

Rebecca cast an eye over Mindy-Lou's generous proportions, straining desperately at the seams of her impressive attire. Seeing Mindy-Lou buck naked would not be a purdy sight; her nephew had gotten off lightly.

"Say no more about it, sugar," Mindy-Lou announced magnanimously. "Now I am gonna have me that bath or the water will be colder than the Mississippi itself."

Once the warrior princess disappeared back inside her cabin, Betty inched away, satisfied with the happy ending. It was a hint that the evening was coming to a close. Hannah's weight was now giving Jennifer's arms a work-out as she had dropped off to sleep, oblivious of the evening's dramatic events. The little group stood huddled together on the cabin's porch, watching as the Ute roared into life and vanished into the night.

"You go on ahead, Jen. Get Hannah to bed. We'll leave you and Jack to have a chat for a bit, won't we, Melissa?" Rebecca prompted with a reassuring smile that told her everything would be alright.

Melissa linked her arm through Rebecca's and looked at her friend hopefully. "Yes, we've got plenty to talk about ourselves."

They watched as Jennifer, hand resting firmly on Jack's shoulder, herded her brood of two back to the house.

"Come on, we'll go and sit in the classroom. I've got a spare key on my house set." Rebecca shivered. "It'll be nice and warm in there." The two set off down the path with the crunch of a crisp frost settling underfoot.

Melissa's breath puffed from her mouth in the chilly air as she spoke. "I am sorry, you know, Becs. If you think about it, though, it's not my fault that I behave the way I sometimes do. It stems from being an only child."

Rebecca had to smile as she unlocked the door; it was such a typical Melissa thing to say to pass the buck like that. The poor girl was not going to take the news that she wouldn't be going back to Ireland with her well at all.

Chapter Thirty

TO HER CREDIT, Rebecca thought, turning the key in the ignition, *Melissa had handled hearing that she would be flying back to Ireland alone reasonably well.* She had opened her mouth to speak, and Rebecca would have put money on it that her first words were going to be, "But what about me?" But then she'd shut her mouth. Rebecca watched, fascinated, as myriad expressions flitted across her old friend's face. For the first time since she'd known Melissa, she was taking a minute to think about what she was going to say instead of blurting out the first thing that came to mind.

"Well, Becs, I have to say that I am stunned. Simply stunned. I never thought I would see the day where you of all people would choose a career over a man so no, I didn't see this coming. But you know what? I remember how gutted you were when you didn't pass that last ballet exam. So, if this teaching dance thing is what you want to do, then all I can say is good on you. I wish you the best of luck, but you know that I am going to miss you heaps."

It was Rebecca's turn to be floored. Perhaps her tirade the other night had gotten through to her after all. She reached out and gave her friend a tight squeeze. "I'll miss you too."

Melissa broke away then as a thought occurred to her. "Of course, Becs, I hope it goes without saying that you'll sub me half the rent until I can get a new flatmate in. It's only fair."

Ha—now that was the Melissa she knew and loved.

Rebecca sent Ciaran a quick text to let him know she was on her way over and left Melissa making herself a hot drink and rummaging for sweet leftovers to go with it. Now, as she pulled up alongside Sea Breezes, Ciaran stepped forth, materialising from the shadows to greet her.

"You should have waited inside; it's freezing out here," she said, noticing he was rubbing his hands and hopping from foot to foot in a bid to stay warm.

"What and risk you taking fright and running away if Mrs Doody answered the door? I don't think so." He shivered despite his jacket. "Come on. I'll sneak you into my room. The old duck's got the television on so loud the All Blacks could do the haka in the hallway, and she'd be oblivious."

Rebecca smiled at his comparison and hoped he was right because her day had been dramatic enough without adding an irate Mrs Doody to the mix. Following Ciaran inside, she felt like a teenager as she skulked up the hallway behind him. She was relieved to find the television volume was indeed at a level where she didn't even have to tippy-toe.

His room, she thought with a quick glance round, was reminiscent of the seventies. The orange drapes and brown duvet cover, lack of both television and toilet indicative as to why he had got the room at such a cheap rate. *The bed was pretty comfortable, though*, she thought, sitting down and giving it the bounce test.

Ciaran looked at her quizzically. "I've got a bottle of some good stuff. Do you fancy a whiskey and Coke?"

"Yes please, that's exactly what I need after the day I've had. Make mine a strong one, ta."

He poured the drinks and apologised for the lack of ice as he sat down next to her.

Taking a large swig and then shuddering, Rebecca waited for the alcohol burn to pass before she filled him in on the random events that had transpired since she had left him to confront her sister.

As her tale came to a close with its happy ending, Ciaran shook his head in disbelief. "My gosh, girl, there's never a dull moment with you around. I'm glad you sorted things out with her, though. It sounds to me like you both need each other."

"Yeah, I think we do," Rebecca said, draining her glass.

Ciaran was quiet for a moment, swilling the dregs around in his glass, and Rebecca studied his profile. He needed to shave, she noticed, liking the swarthiness of his day-old stubble. Suddenly, he inhaled sharply, as though there was something he needed to say.

"What is it?"

"What if I were to take a year's sabbatical here?" He had been brooding on the idea since Rebecca had announced she was staying in New Zealand.

She looked at him wide-eyed. "Here? Do you mean it?"

"Yeah, why not?" His brown eyes fixed on hers. "I always planned on doing it one day, except I kind of imagined myself working in Sydney or Brisbane—you know, somewhere that was feckin hotter than Dublin. But so long as I don't have to stay with Mrs Doody, then here would be more than fine. If you agree to keep me warm, that is. What do you think?"

She gave him her answer by reaching up and pulling him down towards her. They fell back on the bed with their lips locked. As his hands began to roam and to gently stroke, she mentally buckled herself in for what she knew was going to be one hell of a roller-coaster ride.

Afterwards, exhausted and spent, Rebecca lay with her leg thrown casually over his, her hand draped over his stomach. She closed her eyes, feeling the foreign sensation of utter contentment envelope her. Ciaran kissed the top of her head, and as the familiar tune of *The Bill* drifted under the door, she fell asleep.

Stretching languorously the next morning, Rebecca woke to find herself momentarily unsure whether the events of the night before had just been a woman in her mid-thirties who was hitting her sexual stride's frustrated fantasy. Then, feeling a warm and very real thigh stir next to hers, she smiled, happily noting it wasn't the only thing that was stirring. Rolling on top for round—what would it be, three?—she caught sight of the time over Ciaran's shoulder and rolled off him again. Sitting up, she rubbed the sleep out of her eyes. Surely she'd read it wrong? No, it said ten o'clock. Damn! Mrs Doody would be up and about frying the bacon and eggs by now.

"I've got to go," she whispered, throwing the covers off. "Jen will be worried about me and I want to see how she and Jack are doing." Standing up, she shimmied into yesterday's clothes as Ciaran looked on admiringly. Sparing a second for a quick glance in the dressing table mirror, she frowned at her reflection. It was as she'd suspected. Her hair was mussed beyond redemption at the back and, leaning in for a closer inspection, she noted the telltale signs of pash-rash all over her chin. Yes, she looked like she had spent the night being ravaged.

Reading her mind, Ciaran blew her a kiss and grinned over wolfishly. "Well, hurry back, lover."

She poked her tongue out at him. "You'll have to get up, *lover*, and distract Mrs Doody for me. She'll have me for breakfast if she realises I stayed the night."

AS REBECCA APPROACHED the house, she could hear what sounded like a disco hitting its peak. Smoothing her hair before going inside, she looked down at yesterday's crumpled clothes with a sigh. She wondered whether she'd be as successful as sneaking past Jennifer to the shower as she had been in sneaking out of Sea Breezes.

Opening the front door, her eardrums were assaulted by the blaring sounds of ABBA. Curiosity got the better of her and peeking round the living room door, she spied Jennifer with her long curls swinging free, clutching one end of a skipping rope while Hannah held onto the other. Mother and daughter appeared to be lip-synching along to "SOS" while Jack, his fingers jammed in his ears, was rolling around, laughing as he watched them. She stood back unnoticed in the doorway and surveyed the unfolding scene with a smile.

It was so good to see her nephew smiling, and the mother and daughter duet brought back memories. Once upon a time, it had been her and Jennifer at opposite ends of the skipping rope. They'd usually end up thwacking each other with the handles as they fought over who got to be the blonde one, though. Jennifer, being the older sister and a blonde to boot, always won out in the end.

Quietly pulling away, Rebecca took the stairs two at a time and stood for an age under the steady stream of hot water provided by the shower. Getting out and drying off, she changed into her track pants and a sweatshirt before heading back downstairs in search of a cup of coffee, knowing that if she didn't get caffeine into her system soon, the natural high she was currently experiencing would evaporate. She would be left feeling like what she was: a woman in her mid-thirties who had been bonking for the best part of the night.

"I thought I heard you," Jennifer said, pushing open the kitchen door. "I'd love a coffee if there's one going."

Rebecca dolloped a hefty spoonful of the brown stuff in her mug and got an extra cup down for Jennifer, who came over and leaned against the kitchen bench.

"I told Jack the truth," she said simply.

"The truth, truth?" Rebecca turned and looked at her, surprised.

Jennifer's expertly made-up blue eyes flitted out the window to make sure Hannah and Jack were out of earshot. They were involved in some ribald chasing game and so she continued, "I didn't tell him exactly who it was he'd seen me kissing, if that's what you're getting at. I just explained that he was a friend of Mummy's who she's not friends with anymore."

"Huh! A pretty good friend, and does David know that you won't be seeing him again?" Rebecca asked, looking directly at her sister, expecting an honest answer.

"Yes, of course, but do you honestly think it would make things any better if Jack knew his mother had had it off with his best friend's dad?" Jennifer snapped in return.

Rebecca held up her hand. "No, sorry. Look, I take it back; that wasn't called for." The tension went out of her sister's shoulders. Picking up the two mugs, Rebecca asked, "Did you find out whether Jack overheard you telling David about your depression after he was born?"

Jennifer lowered her eyes and began twiddling her rings round and round. Rebecca wondered absently what she'd do with them now. Would she keep them? Putting them aside like her marriage until she could pass them onto Hannah when she was old enough?

"Uh-huh. It took a while to get him to open up but yeah, he did." There was a catch in her voice as she carried on. "Poor wee man thought I'd never loved him and that if it weren't for him, things between me and Mark would be fine." When she raised her eyes again, they'd filled up with tears. Rebecca put the two mugs back down on the bench and put her arms around her sister. She listened as she sobbed out, "I explained it was an illness but oh, Becs, can you believe he's been carrying that around inside him?"

Rebecca smoothed her hand over her sister's hair. "I know it's awful, but you've been in an awful place for too long now; you need to put it behind you and move forward. Focus your energy on looking after Jack and Hannah and getting them through you and Mark separating."

Jennifer broke away snuffling and pulled a tissue from the box on the windowsill. "Yeah, you're right, but it damn near broke my heart to hear him say he thought I didn't love him."

Rebecca's stomach contracted with guilt at the thought of what her poor nephew had bottled up inside him. Perhaps if she'd been around more instead of being an absentee auntie, he'd have felt able to open up to her. That was going to change, though, she thought, biting her bottom lip. "Still, he knows how much he's loved now and that's the main thing." Another thought occurred to her. "What time is Mark due in?"

"His flight landed well over an hour ago, so I'd say he'll be here in about another forty or so minutes." Jennifer glanced out the window again, resisting the urge to bang on it and shout at her children to stop trampling her herb garden. "Jack's obviously sussed that we are not happy, so I think it will almost be a relief to him to hear us clarify what's going to happen."

Rebecca threw her sister a surprised look at this remark, but she just shrugged. "My children constantly amaze me. I don't give them enough credit. I mean, Jack's only seven, but he's had a better grasp of his parents' marital situation than Mark and I ever did. He'll be as relieved as we are to say goodbye to the animosity and tension of waiting for the inevitable to happen. Of course, throwing in the Crusty Demons tickets I know Mark's managed to pick up will act as a sweetener too." Jennifer gave a wry smile before taking a sip of her coffee. She rubbed at the lipstick mark imprinted on the rim and added, "As for Hannah, well, I'm hoping she's young enough just to adapt."

Ah, the Crusty Demons—they were Jack's motocross heroes. Even as she gave a small laugh at her sister's blatant bribery, Rebecca knew it was time for her to mend some bridges of her own.

She studied Jennifer's flawless features as she sipped away on her coffee and, seeing past the polished exterior to the complicated woman beneath, the great chip she'd been carrying on her shoulder for so many years disintegrated. She finally understood that her sister *was* flawed and that she had never been perfect. Nobody was. She had unfairly created an illusion in her mind, using it as a shield to hide behind for all these years. It had been too easy for her to hold Jennifer up as an example and say how could she possibly be expected to live up to that? Clearing her throat, she hedged, "Jen?"

"Mm?" She looked at her over the rim of her mug.

"I went to see Ciaran last night."

Jennifer had already noted her sister's glowing skin and swollen lips. "Yep, I guessed as much."

"I'd already told him I wasn't going back to Ireland and explained why but after everything that happened yesterday, I needed to see him again."

"And so you shagged him?" Jennifer stated with a hint of sarcasm, pursing her lips as she waited for Rebecca to tell her he had smooth-talked her out of staying.

"Um, not quite in that order—let me finish."

"Sorry. Go on."

"He has decided to take a year's sabbatical here while I get on with my studies to see how things pan out between us."

Jennifer looked at her sister in surprise. Perhaps he wasn't the smooth-talking lothario she had him down to be after all. "Wow! That's fabulous, Becs. I'm pleased for you." She leaned forward and covered her sister's hand with her own.

"Thanks. I know." Rebecca beamed.

"And my offer?"

"I'd still like to take you up on it if that's okay. I don't want to rush things with Ciaran."

A squeal sounded like a siren from the garden and Jennifer snatched her hand away and leapt up to peer out the window. "Oh crap! Jack's just thrown a handful of compost all over Hannah and Mark will be here soon." She stormed outside to sort them out and Rebecca got to her feet, scooping up the mugs. Running the tap to rinse them, she looked out the window to where Jennifer had a firm grasp on her son's elbow with one hand while she used her spare hand to wag a finger at him. Hannah stood, wailing, with her arms wrapped around her mother's leg, a sticky brown muck-coated vision.

Out of the blue, a song sprang to Rebecca's mind. She was sure she'd seen the title on that '80s music quiz Ciaran had on his desk the day she left Fitzpatrick & Co. It seemed an age ago now, she thought, marvelling at everything that had happened. The tune slipped from her lips. What was it called? That was it: *The Future's so Bright I Gotta Wear Shades*.

Making a mental note to ask Ciaran if he knew the name of the band who sang it, she put her sunglasses on and wandered outside into the sunshine.

Staying at Eleni's
Michelle Vernal

ONE MINUTE YOU'RE TRYING to live the suburban dream and the next minute you're living the dream in... the Greek Islands.

Sometimes life doesn't go to plan. Take Annie's for instance. Her fiancé won't commit to setting a date and the zipper of her dream dress won't quite do up. Her cat's just died and her best friend, Carl, thinks getting married will be the biggest mistake of her life. Annie's had enough and when her Greek pen pal invites her to come and stay at the family guesthouse on the island of Crete, she wings her way over.

Under Crete's brilliant blue skies Annie's about to discover that sometimes you have to let go of the future you thought you had mapped out and let your life make a map all of its own.

Join Annie and her best friend Carl on this humour-filled treat to the Greek Islands.

Available on Amazon

Printed in Great Britain
by Amazon